STEEL AND SHADOWS

BOOK 1 IN THE JOHN STEEL THRILLERS SERIES

STUART FIELD

To our mother, whose strength, courage and faith is an inspiration to us all.

ONE

The men made their way silently through the wood, careful that no noise came from the weapons they carried, the body-armour they wore, their heavy boots barely making a sound as they crept through the broken shadows.

It was a bright summer's day with a light breeze that made the leaves on the trees rustle gently. Birds chased each other across a cloudless sky. In the grounds of an English mansion, a party was in progress. Friends and family laughed and joked, children ran around playing, despite the formal clothes they'd been forced to wear.

The grounds were large. There was a long lawn on which stood a marquee, ready prepared for the dinner later that evening. Next to it, wooden decking had been set down as a dance floor, with lights strung above it, criss-crossing between elegant temporary pillars. Trees completely enclosed the grounds.

Slipping discreetly between the guests, waiters hurried with trays of drinks or canapés. At the back entrance to the mansion lay a gravelled area enclosed by a balcony of stone that stretched around both sides of the house, broken only by a flight of white stone steps. Music played from two speakers that stood on either side of the rear doors. On the floor trailed a cable to a microphone stand set up beside one of the large stone vases that formed part of the balustrade. A statuesque, middle-aged woman stood, keeping an eye on her two children as they drank their lemonade from plastic beakers. The lady of the manor was still a handsome woman, with expensively cut shoulder-length brown hair and flawlessly sculpted features. A lace and silk dress hugged her slender figure. She smiled as another woman approached.

'You do know, Elizabeth, it was a bad idea to make this a secret event, don't you?'

The younger woman spoke with a trace of an American accent.

Elizabeth shrugged wryly at her daughter-in-law's comment.

'I spoke to his commanding officer asking him to make sure he comes straight here. All we can do, Helen, is hope that you are enough incentive for him to follow orders for once.' Elizabeth laughed. Helen smiled and gave her mother-in-law a surprised look.

'Jonny coming marching home, following orders, that'll be a first,' said the younger woman.

She too was tall, with soft, light brown hair and eyes the colour of a tropical lagoon. Both women were beautiful in their own different ways. It was Helen's hope that her youthful, almost coltish beauty would mature into something like her mother-in-law's. The two women turned their attention to the men standing on the gravelled area, talking. One of the pair was lofty and broad-shouldered, with thick black hair starting to grey at the temples. The second man stood a few inches shorter, wirier than the other, his blond hair neatly cut. The taller of the two had a dark beard, the shorter man was clean-shaven. Both wore tuxedos, as did all the other male guests, while the ladies wore elegant and expensive-looking cocktail dresses.

The smaller man gave the other a friendly pat on the left arm and moved away to join a party of people who were deep in conversation. The dark-haired man picked up the microphone and turned to the DJ, who was hidden behind a makeshift booth at the far end of the gravel courtyard. The man tapped the mic, sending a loud screech through the speakers, making everyone wince. He smiled like a naughty schoolboy.

'Sorry, sorry!' His British accent was playful. 'Hello, everyone. My wife and I would like to thank you all for coming here this afternoon. We are here to celebrate two things: firstly, the latest blow to a certain world-wide gun trafficking ring a few days ago, when a special unit captured a horde with a value, it is thought, of over four million pounds.' Everyone cheered and clapped.

'But also, more importantly, the safe return of our elder son from a tour of duty overseas.' He raised his glass to the crowd, but his eyes were fixed on the beautiful woman he had married. She stood poised in her silk dress; her dark hair highlighted by the handmade lace trim around the low-cut neckline. She smiled at the man, her eyes full of pride and happiness. Next to her stood their younger son Thomas, a dark-haired twelve-year-old with a rather serious expression on his face. Beside him stood their daughter, a pretty young girl of no more than ten years old but looking like a miniature mirror-image of her mother. They were even clad in the same style of dress. It was a little joke that they liked to play. Sophie smiled at her mother and squeezed her hand. Elizabeth looked down at her daughter and winked.

A waiter walked up to the man at the microphone and whispered something into his ear, causing him to smile. He turned back to the microphone.

'Ladies and gentlemen, it would appear the problem with

holding a surprise party is that one never knows when, or indeed if, the guest of honour might turn up. That seems to be the case today.' The crowd laughed. 'However, I don't think he'd mind if we got started without him, what do you say?' Again, he raised his glass.

'I couldn't agree more, your lordship,' said a voice from behind him in a soft Eastern European accent.

A towering, fair-haired man had approached, all but unseen by everyone around. His bulky, solid form was dressed all in black, and his slicked-back hair glistened in the afternoon sun.

'Who are you, and what do you want here? This is a private party,' said the earl, as the man smiled and walked up to him.

'I'm afraid, your grace, for you, the party's over,' came the reply. 'And one more thing: my employer sends his regards.' With that, the stranger turned to the crowd as if to make an announcement, seizing the microphone from the earl's grasp. He raised it up as if to address the bewildered crowd of people who had just become his hostages.

Shots rang out. The interloper turned to see a bald, military-looking man with a menacing grin on his face, he held a Glock 19 semi-automatic pistol, pointing at the earl, who had dropped to his knees. His wife and children watched in horror as scarlet blossomed from his back. He fell face forward. The bald man stepped forward and fired a final shot into the back of the earl's head, which exploded in a cloud of red and white. For a moment, everyone stood frozen. Their shock was broken by the sound of automatic gunfire from the Woodline. People were falling everywhere, cut down by random blasts. The guests ran hither and thither, desperately looking for cover, only to be cut down by stray bullets.

Elizabeth saw a group of four armed men heading for the

4

marquee, followed moments later by mixed screams and gunshots. As she watched, holes were punched through the sides of the marquee, then there was silence. She grabbed her children's hands and ran for the safety of the house. Her daughter-in-law picked up her skirts and followed, her long brown hair flowing behind her.

The bald killer smiled as he saw them and shook his head. The blond man raced up to him. He grabbed the killer by the arm and yanked him towards him.

'This was not the plan, you moron, now we have to finish this,' he snapped at the bald man. 'None of the families was supposed to be harmed. The Man wanted them all alive.' The bald man wasn't listening, so the blonde man shook him again, shouting: 'No more, am I understood?'

He was answered by a false smile as the bald man headed into the building, followed by a group of men, each holding a Kalashnikov.

TWO

A taxi pulled up to the long driveway. Inside, a soldier sat, only vaguely listening to the driver chatter on about his opinions on the state of affairs in far-off lands. His passenger, weary from the long journey, gazed out of the window upon the green fields of his home. He was still dressed in his uniform battledress, the creases on the sleeves standing up like blade edges. He had been away for a long time, and now he was content to come home. He did not want any fuss, just a quiet time with his wife and the rest of the family, but he was afraid that his father was bound to come up with some sort of homecoming event.

It all seemed quite surreal to him, being home after spending so long in a land that was barren of luxuries, or even trees and grass as he knew it, so he had to readjust his thinking. Was this all a dream? Would he suddenly wake up and find himself back in the hell he thought he had left? He slowly touched the car's window glass, hoping it would be there, and it wouldn't fade away as soon as he laid fingers on it. He smiled as the feel of the cold glass sent a tingling sensation down his spine.

He rested his warm cheek against the window and closed

his eyes. 'Oh, that feels good,' he said, and the cab driver looked at him through the rear-view mirror and shook his head. As they neared the house, loud pops could be heard. The soldier opened his eyes with a start and shot upright. 'Stop the car!' he ordered, but the cab driver paid no attention.

'Stop this car now, God damn it!' The cab came to a screeching halt.

'Why shout at me, you crazy man?' said the driver, as the soldier got out of the cab and listened. Loud cracks echoed through the trees followed by screams: something was terribly wrong.

'Get the hell out of here and call the police, tell them, get this, there have been shots fired on this estate, and they weren't sporting guns, they were military weapons, have you got that?'

The driver nodded, 'military weapons, not sporting guns.' He dropped the clutch and sped away, leaving the soldier to dart into the cover of the trees.

Making his way slowly through the woods he knew so well, towards the rear of the house, the soldier had not gone far when he saw a figure all in black, holding an automatic rifle. He took him to be a sentry, put there to ensure that nobody got away. This was not a robbery, this was an invasion, an execution. The soldier looked around and crept forward.

The guard had been standing for what seemed like hours. He had no real idea why he was here or who any of these people were. All he cared about was that he was getting paid at the end of it all.

Suddenly there was a loud crack behind him, so he ducked down and trained his weapon. He could feel his heart pounding in his chest, the adrenaline surging through his body. He blew out a lungful of air as a large rabbit hopped by. He stood up and laughed in relief and turned, then gasped as a figure stepped in front of him and punched him in the throat. The mercenary dropped to his knees, clutching his fractured hyoid. A gargling sound came from the man's collapsed airway. He fell to the ground and the sound ceased.

The soldier stripped the man of his tactical vest and checked the ammo content of the rifle and the pistol: they were both full. He smiled gravely. 'Payback time,' he muttered savagely. The radios on his vest crackled to life as the teams were giving *sit reps*.

He had to find his family and any other survivors and take out as many of these bastards as he could along the way. Moving quietly and stealthily, he crept towards the house. In front of him knelt another man. The soldier watched the man's eyes darting here and there, sensing that he was jumpy and on edge. Good. On the far side of the jumpy man stood a group of his colleagues, laughing as they shot at the feet of a couple of the guests, making them dance back and forth.

The soldier crept between the solitary sentry and the armed group and suddenly sprang up. The mercenary yelped in surprise and instinctively opened fire with his weapon, just as the soldier dived out of the way. A hail of bullets slammed into the armed men in front of him. The soldier grimly watched from his new hiding place as a fire fight developed and they gunned each other down. Grinning ironically to himself, the soldier moved forwards and grabbed a dead man's ammunition belt.

As he watched, the group of terrified guests fled for the woods and disappeared into what he hoped was safety. The soldier went back to searching the dead guard more carefully and was rewarded with a smoke grenade. He frowned as he surveyed the carnage before him. Who were these men and what did they want?

There were too many questions ringing in his head, but now was not the time to ask them. He knew he needed to reduce their numbers still further, and if he could do that without being seen, then so much the better.

After all, he reasoned, he was no good to his family dead. A large group of armed men stood at the bottom of the steps to the house, put there to make sure nobody got in or out. The soldier tossed the smoke grenade thoughtfully from hand to hand and hatched a plan. With the grenade tucked safely into a pocket, and the captured submachine gun slung round his neck, he moved carefully around the marquee to the end that was secured by guy ropes. He cut the canvas, using the knife he had taken from the first sentry, and crawled in. The large tent was empty apart for a heap of corpses in formal dress in the middle of the floor.

There was still cutlery laid out ceremoniously on the tables, as if nothing had happened, and many of the candlesticks were still decorated with pretty bows. He untied a ribbon from one of the candlesticks, then pulled the grenade from his pocket. He took one of the magazines from the pouch on his vest. Sliding out enough rounds from the clip to wrap round the green cylinder of the grenade, he began to strap them to the explosive, using the ribbon. Outside, the group of killers heard someone calling, 'Help! Help me please!' The voice was fading, and they headed back to the tent, fired up with blood lust to finish off the dying man.

Ten men entered the marquee in search of the crying man, weapons trained before them as they crept in deeper. The man in the rear walked backwards to cover their retreat. He suddenly stopped as his foot was hit by something, and he tried to shout a warning before the room was filled with smoke. The group started to cough and splutter from the fumes, half-blinded, and with arms swaying they tried to find the edge of the tent.

Then, as the container began to get hot, the rounds started to fire off. Loose bullets flew everywhere, causing the group to stop and start to return fire, not caring that they couldn't see who or what they were shooting at. More men rushed into the tent to help the squad, only to be cut down as they ran through the door.

From inside the house, the blond man came to the window and watched the madness below. 'For God's sake let's finish this before all the idiots end up killing each other,' he muttered.

An enormous behemoth of a man stepped forwards and removed the automatic grenade launcher from where it rested on his back. Taking the two grips firmly in his hands, he placed three rounds into the tent. As the projectiles hit, they exploded with tremendous force. There were several bright flashes, then the marquee was ripped apart, sending pieces of timber and fabric whirling in all directions.

Where the tent had been, there was nothing to see but massive swathes of red and black flame. Burning pieces of debris, including the odd recognisable human shard, fell from the sky in a shower of fiery rain.

The man replaced the weapon on his back, grinning as he did so. 'Boom,' he said, his tone deep and hollow. The fewer mercenaries who survived, the blond man thought, the fewer they would have to pay off at the end of it. Joining the others, they proceeded to check the rooms for survivors, searching especially for the four people who had run into the house earlier.

'The mother, the other woman, and her two children are not to be harmed in any way,' said the blond man. He stopped abruptly, forcing the men behind him to come to a sudden halt, as he turned to make direct eye contact with one of them, a young man of average height, clean-shaven, an eager look upon his boyish face. 'Is that understood?' His stare became intense, almost burning through the youth, who backed off slightly and nodded.

THREE

The soldier reckoned the gardens were now clear. He had observed several mercenaries going into the house but didn't know the strength of their numbers. Moving across the body-strewn lawn, he kept low but moved quickly.

Reaching the wall and the steps he chanced a quick look, finding there was nobody to be seen. Moving slowly up the stone steps he came across the body of a man. His father. The soldier's head dropped down in anguish. All he wanted to do was scream out, but he knew that would alert the mercenaries and make it impossible to rescue any of the others. His grief distilled into a lethal rage as he vowed to kill the murdering bastards instead.

He kissed his fingers and pressed them down on what was left of his father's forehead, then he looked up to the house, fury burning within him.

He crept through the back door into the massive dining room. Beyond that lay the long hallway and the stairs leading up to the bedrooms. The soldier edged slowly towards the double doors leading from the dining room into the hall, and slowly opened one of the doors just widely enough to peer through safely. On the other side of the door stood a guard with his back to him, presumably to stop people getting out. He wasn't expecting anyone to come in. Across from that guard, at the foot of the staircase, stood another.

The soldier noted where the men were standing in the hallway, with its large marble floor and dark wood entrance doors directly opposite. A set of stairs that traversed the left wall was decorated with paintings of men and women, landscapes and animals. Apart from the two guards in front of him, he could see no one else. He closed the door and sank into a nearby seat. He had to think and think fast. The radio that sat on his shoulder pouch squawked- grabbing it hastily, he shut it off. He'd thought of a plan.

Springing up silently, he crossed rapidly to the speaker by the garden door, and taking the headset, he placed it down by the ornate black box, then, grabbing some duct tape he had found in the DJ's tool kit, he taped up the 'send' button on the handset, then carefully taped the headset's microphone to the speaker.

He stood up and looked around. *Okay, you bastards want to party?* he thought to himself.

The mercenaries walked through the house, going from room to room, firing at anything that moved. The blond man had decided to wait in the large study he had found, whose oak walls and floor were complemented with heavy-looking antique furniture. The room appealed to him. He had given instructions for his men to proceed and bring back any survivors unharmed, but he was worried about Travis. After all, these men were not soldiers, they were hired convicts and once upon a time they had been dim enough to get caught. They were expendable. Indeed, they had already expended of a great many of them, he thought drily. Travis, however, had been a commando and was a murderer and rapist of the worst kind. He was, quite simply, an animal.

The blond man had given his sidekick an instruction to keep an eye on Travis, and well, if the ex-commando did anything wrong, he would know what to do. The leader of the mercenaries strolled around the room in awe of its splendour. He found a large wooden globe in a corner and opened it, his eyes lighting up at the sight of the fine brandies and whiskies, and he helped himself to a glass of the twenty-year-old malt. He moved casually over to a massive wooden bookshelf. Dickens, Sun Tzu, Tolstoy, all the classics were there. The smell of old leather filled his nostrils as he leant forwards and breathed in the cultured atmosphere. Picking a book, he settled down on the red leather Chesterfield and started reading, sipping the whisky as he smiled and imagined for a moment that he was now the lord of the manor.

The soldier knelt by the door with his back to the wall. Reaching up, he pulled a combat knife from a scabbard on the shoulder of the vest he had taken. The long blade glistened as the rays of the afternoon sun caught its sharpened edge. He tucked it into his belt, where he could grab it quickly, then knelt with the Glock .45 in one hand and the microphone in the other, taking a moment to check through the plan. He would turn the microphone on, throw it into the speaker, causing feedback, burst through the door, take a headshot at both men, get ready for others to come running down the staircase, take them all out, get out of the hallway and head up the stairs in all the confusion. Sounded as though it could work, in his head anyway.

He mentally counted to three then, using maximum force, tossed the microphone towards the speaker he had placed by the open bay doors. Everything turned to slow motion as the missile sailed through the air and landed with a clang that shot through the loudspeakers, and, in turn, through the earpieces of the mercenaries. The men grabbed their ears in pain as the feedback hit them with full force, incapacitating them for a few moments.

The soldier swung open the doors and fired. The two guards took a round each. It was all they needed. One to the back of the head and the other dead centre between the eyes. The soldier watched as five men rushed down the stairs to find out what was going on with the speakers. The soldier cut them down with the machine pistol, and he watched in satisfaction as each of the men slammed against the walls of the staircase, the impact of each round punching through them, leaving bloody smears.

Time to move, he thought, only stopping to pick up one dead guard's pistol to replace the one whose ammunition he had just expended. He rushed up the stairs with a pistol in one hand, and a sub-machine gun in the other. He reached the upper hallway and crouched behind a wall at the top of the stairs, waited for a second, then dashed over to the first room.

At the sound of gunshots nearby, the blond man bolted out of his seat and ripped the earpiece from its place. Racing out of the door he made for the stairwell, picking up his men as he went. He had found five men recovering from the sudden blast to the eardrums, but they were okay, well, fit enough to kill someone, anyway.

As he peered through the crack of the partially open door, the soldier made out six men heading for the stairs. He knew he could take them out, but he did not know how many more there were or where they were. No, he had to leave them and press on. Going down the long corridor, he checked room after room until he reached the end.

There was nobody else. He smiled to himself. If he hadn't found anybody, then the killers hadn't either. The soldier looked up towards the attic. He had to get up there.

The blond mercenary and the others rushed into the dining room and found the microphone next to the speaker. He switched the mic off and threw it onto the lawn. Checking around, he noticed the head-set taped to the speaker. Ripping it off, he stood up.

'The boy is here,' he stated. 'Find him. And I really want him alive. Do you understand, you idiots?' The others nodded. The blond man looked at the small microphone from the headset and smiled. He glanced up at the house and cast a look from left to right, trying to work out where his quarry might be hiding. 'Welcome home, Jonny,' he muttered.

FOUR

As a small boy, the soldier often snuck rides in the old dumb waiter system but had never thought that as an adult he would be doing the same thing. The bulk of his body, plus the extras he wore, made the journey fairly uncomfortable. Once he got to the top, he used the knife to bore a small hole through which to see the attic. The roof space was dark, the only light falling from the small windows in the roof above. It was a vast expanse, running the whole length and width of the house. Dusty boxes of long-forgotten toys stood on top of one another, and as he looked, he thought that only terror would bring someone to seek shelter here. There was little opportunity to hide.

He saw that it was clear, and, lifting the sliding door carefully, he stepped out. Dropping to one knee, he drew one of the pistols, realising that he would have to make it to the other end of the room to really satisfy himself that there was nobody taking refuge in here. Walking slowly and carefully, he inched his way down towards the end. If there really was nobody here, then the only other thing they could have done was take the dumb waiter down to the kitchen or even the basement and then escape outside from there. Moving slowly, his eye caught a shape in the distance. It was only a few feet away, but the dark made it seem like miles.

Keeping down, he waited for his eyes to adjust, then he closed his eyes and took several deep breaths. Slowly he opened them and saw that it was a woman lying there. Her face was not visible, but he knew that shape and felt there was no longer any point in anything.

The blond man went back inside the house and found that the others had regrouped in the long hallway. He walked up to the large man and nodded.

'What happened, boss?' asked the behemoth.

'We have a homecoming after all, it seems. I was told he wasn't due back for another week, but never mind, what is done is done. Right, first things first.' The tall blond man looked at the group.

'Where the fuck is Travis?' he asked. Everyone looked around and shrugged.

'God damn it. Okay, find that fucking psycho before he kills anyone important, or even worse, he gets us all killed. Now move!' The men split off, and he grabbed the huge man's arm and shook his head at him. 'No, my friend, you're staying with me.' The giant smiled and reached down to take a strangely configured combat shotgun from one of his dead colleagues. As he pulled it up, the dead man's hands still clutched the weapon, refusing to let go, and this made the leader laugh as he watched his friend struggle with a dead man. 'He was always fond of that, never left his side, even more so now it seems.' The big man looked up and shrugged.

'Leave the weapon, my friend, it seems the dead have claimed it. I don't think it's wise to annoy the dead, not here and now anyway.' The huge guy let the weapon and the body drop. He was part gypsy and had grown up on his grandma's tales of the old country, its legends and myths and curses.

Despite that, the blond man had befriended him in the service. They had both joined the French Foreign Legion many years before but had later found better employment together.

The cellar was cool and dark. The mother and her two children scurried across the floor to the wooden coal-cellar door. As Elizabeth reached up, she realised she didn't have the key on her. She looked around at the small nail embedded into the wall next to the double doors, but it held no key, and she cursed the gardener, as she knew he often forgot to put it back. A noise behind them caused the trio to find a hiding space, which wasn't difficult, as the cellar was long with many rooms branching off it. They listened intently as someone moved from room to room in search of their prey. The little girl hugged her mother. Elizabeth looked over to Thomas. She could see both fear and anger burning in his expression. She grasped his hand and squeezed it. He looked up at her and his mood seemed to lighten a little. Elizabeth glanced down and saw a spark of comfort in her daughter's eyes. A sickening voice echoed down the hallway, calling,

'Come on out, I won't hurt you.' A snigger came next, and she shuddered. Did she hear him add the word 'much'?

Elizabeth noticed some old wooden barrels leaning up against the far wall. Grabbing Sophie and Thomas she hurried quietly towards them and, lifting the lid off one of the barrels, she placed both terrified children inside it.

Sophie clung to her mother, knowing she was protecting them with her own life. 'Now,' their mother whispered to them. 'You stay in here and don't move, okay, no matter what you see or hear. You don't move until the police arrive.' She gazed through glassy eyes at her children, fearing that this would be the last time she could do so, then she kissed Sophie on her forehead and took off and passed a necklace to the child. It was a golden locket containing a picture of them all.

The long golden chain swayed as her hands shook with emotion.

Sophie grasped the necklace and held it tightly to her as she stared upwards, fearfully.

'Thomas,' she told her son. 'I need you to look after your sister, okay?'

His watery eyes stared back at her.

'But—' She kissed his forehead to stop him saying anything else. 'You have to be brave. No matter what, you stick together, promise me.'

The two children reluctantly nodded.

'I love you, both of you, and I always will, remember that,' she said and, tears rolling down her face, Elizabeth replaced the lid.

As the two children listened with eyes firmly shut, they could make out the heavy breathing of a large man. While he panted and snorted like a rhino, they huddled together in their barrel and tried to make themselves as small as possible. The snorting brute came nearer and nearer, his feet shuffling on the floor. In his imagination, Thomas conjured images of the Minotaur from the Greek myths. Then the noise of someone running alerted the beast and the children heard it turn on its heel and set off away from them in pursuit.

Sophie shook with fear, her body soaked with perspiration. Thom- as held her close, comforting himself as well as reassuring his sister.

Elizabeth managed to summon the dumb waiter back to the basement, and quickly stowed herself into it. She had to go up to the attic and find Helen. The four had separated, so Helen could distract the large, bald man into following her, giving Elizabeth time to get away with the children, hoping they would get out through the coal cellar doors. But the coal cellar doors had been locked from the out- side.

Moving towards the sound of the footsteps, the brute found himself at the dumb waiter. He banged a powerful fist on the wall as he saw the elevator moving upwards towards him, then a calculated, evil grin came onto his face and he waited.

As the soldier moved slowly towards his wife, his legs felt unfeasibly heavy. It was almost impossible to take a step. Suddenly he crashed to his knees, kicking up a cloud of dust that hung in the pools of light. His face twisted with the pain of seeing her lying there motionless. He reached out a hand to grab her, his powerful fingers clawing at the distance between them.

Forcing himself, he dragged his body towards her, tears streaming down his face. His mouth moved but no sound would come from his lips. He was only feet away now, but it seemed like miles. Again, his body smashed down upon the ancient floorboards. He did not care anymore who found him, she was the one person he had wanted to save, and he had failed. He reached forwards and touched her hair, but his outstretched fingers were unable to grasp her. His body contorted by emotion, he brought his clenched fists up to his face and blew out several deep breaths.

Closing his eyes, he reached forwards, and as his fingers touched her neck, he cried out. She was still, no pulse. Gone. The animalistic howl filled the house, and even three floors below him, the mercenaries stopped and looked at one another.

'The attic!' shouted the blond man, 'And be quick!' He was already racing up the stairs, and the others followed.

The soldier knelt on the ground, holding his wife's body close to him, his tears half blinding him. Out of the shadows ran a figure. A familiar voice cried out. His mother.

'Jonny, behind you!' she shouted at him.

A gunshot echoed through the attic. Enhanced by the confined space, it sounded more like an explosion. As he looked up, his mother was spun round by the impact, blood and flesh painting the large beams behind her.

The soldier watched helplessly as his mother tried to claw her way towards him, reaching out an arm. He saw the angry exit wound in her chest. The sound of her wheezing and struggling for breath burnt into him.

Then there were heavy footsteps, laughter, and three shots rang out. The soldier looked down, numb from shock. He slowly registered the exit wounds in his body. And then, with his gaze lowered, he saw his wife's eyes flutter open just before the next shot rang out.

He heard her scream once and then there was silence. He felt the pain of every hit his body had taken. His dimming sight locked on her, he saw Helen's eyes were open, then watched as the cold stare of emptiness filled them. As he watched, he saw the last spark of life leave her body just before the next round hit him. Before he slipped into darkness the soldier smelt the foul body odour of the large man, and the sound of the man's breathing filled his ears.

'What the fuck have you done, Travis?' yelled the blond man. 'Santini will have our fucking heads for this, you animal.'

He was maddened by what he saw.

'Come on,' he ordered, contemplating executing the man he called Travis on the spot. The blond man turned on his heel and headed for the stairs. The soldier slipped into darkness just as Travis laughed and followed his leader, his laughter growing louder as it echoed in the rafters.

FIVE

The London apartment was bathed in darkness, the only light flickering blue across the study wall from a wall-mounted flat-screen television. The news channel had switched to a flash of a plane crash in the English Channel. Images from a news helicopter showed floating debris from what was left of a private jet in the ocean, just off the south coast of England, near Margate. The plane had been heading for Berlin from the City of London Airport. The small aircraft had been ripped apart as it crashed into the cold coastal waters. The reporter stated that there appeared to have been a complete failure of power in the private plane soon after take-off.

Thomas Barryman sat and watched in a candy-red leather Chesterfield office chair. His eyes were blood-shot and brimming with unshed tears. He held an almost full glass of whisky in his right hand. The study had a nineteenth century feel to it, with sombre oil paintings and statuettes in both bronze and marble. Hundreds of old books filled the dark oak bookshelves. Two matching red leather Chesterfield armchairs faced the desk behind which Barryman sat, gazing at the scene on the television.

Barryman reached a shaking hand across the desk and picked up a silver-framed photograph. Lovingly, he moved his fingers over the faces of his family on the picture, his fingers touching each of them, as if to say goodbye. He took a mouthful from the glass, then carefully placed the frame face-down on the stretched green leather of the desk. Thomas Barryman was in his mid-fifties and had aged well enough, but too many corporate dinners had taken their toll on his waist-line. He was still a fairly good-looking man, and despite his girth, the years had been kind. He opened his desk drawer and pulled out a beige-coloured file. With slow, deliberate movements, he thrust it down into the leather briefcase which stood open on the floor to the right of his desk. Drawing out his mobile phone from the breast pocket of his jacket, Barryman peered nervously at the device before typing in the details of a meeting, his fumbling fingers stumbling and stab-bing at the touch-screen keys. He had asked to meet an old friend, someone he could trust. Thomas had information on a deadly organisation. One he had been tracking for a while. One that thrived on profiteering, and chaos. Barryman and a few others had tried to stop them and failed. But now, he was out of time. He needed someone to take over the fight, and he knew the perfect man for the job: the son of the man who had started the hunt in the first place.

The meeting was to be held in Hyde Park at four in the morning, which meant he had to travel from his apartment in Whitechapel, firstly to walk to Mile End Station where he would use the Central Line to take him to Marble Arch. It was well out of his way, but he thought that the park would be a perfect place to meet the other man. He considered driving, but he was aware he'd already had too much to drink. A cab might be an option, but he couldn't risk the cabby being one of them.

When he arrived at the rendezvous, he flicked back the sleeve of his coat to check the time; it was now three-fifty. He blew on his hands to warm them, rubbing his chubby fingers together to encourage the blood flow. It was one of those crisp spring nights with a clear sky and a slight chill in the air. The full moon seemed huge, its brightness flooding the park's open spaces.

Behind him, the constant London traffic cruised past at a steady pace, and a police siren howled in the distance. Across Park Lane, the bright showroom lights looked warm and inviting, a contrast to the dark shadowy park, as if the two scenes inhabited different worlds. Making his way past the black iron fence into the park, Barryman squinted around, finding that he was alone.

An age seemed to have passed since he had arrived at Speakers' Corner. He looked at his watch again, but, despite the moonlight, it was too dark to see. Stamping his feet lightly to keep out the cold, he made his way over to the concrete path. He gazed out towards the dark shapes of the trees that lowered against the sky, creating an eerie atmosphere.

Glancing over to the wooden refreshments hut, he saw a figure in the distance. Judging by the person's build, it seemed like his contact, but the gap between them and lack of lighting made it impossible to see any more details. Barryman approached cautiously, feeling the hairs on the back of his neck starting to rise as he noticed that the man wasn't moving. The figure stood motionless, as if waiting for Barry- man to approach.

As he drew near, the stranger spoke.

'Mr Barryman, my employer was sorry to hear you missed your flight.'

Barryman stopped.

He suddenly realised that this was not his friend, but someone he didn't know, someone tall and dressed in black with a long coat. Fear kicked in, firing adrenaline into his system. He knew at that moment that this was an assassin sent by the organisation.

Barryman turned on his heels and ran. He ran faster than he'd ever run in his life, but he sensed that the distance between them was diminishing with each second. His lungs were on fire, a mixture of a sedentary life and the cold air. He could hear the sound of running feet behind him, coming ever closer.

There was a warning cry from behind him, but it was too late, as five silenced shots blended with the sounds of the night. The bullets ripped through him and everything slowed down in Barryman's mind. He did not feel pain when the first bullet hit him, it felt just like a punch in the back. When the second bullet hit him in the right shoulder, he felt it ripping through nerve, flesh, and bone.

The noise of his screams was drowned out by passing police sirens, hastening to some other crime, far off.

The assassin fired again, and this round hit Barryman in his left leg, dropping him to the ground. Barryman lay, his cheek against the path, watching the dark blood creeping across the tarmac.

As the assassin raised his pistol to aim, he did not notice a dark figure appear out of the shadows. This newcomer's approach was fast and silent. The assassin fired one last shot into Barryman's chest as the figure pounced on him, grasping him in a neck-lock. The gunman fought back but to no avail. The newcomer looked across at his fallen friend, and fury caused him to tighten his grip, and savagely twist the gunman's head. A sound like a branch breaking filled his ears as the neck snapped and, with angry contempt, he threw the corpse to the ground.

In the darkness of the night, Barryman lay dying. Gasping, he tried to suck air into his bullet-riddled lungs, but he only succeeded in spewing his blood onto Hyde Park's soft grass.

The assassin's killer sprinted towards where his old friend lay. As he approached, Barryman looked up and recognised the face of the man crouching over him and smiled the best he could. Barryman felt his friend grasp his outstretched hand, and he held it tightly as if he was fighting to hold on to life itself, if only for a brief moment.

'Steel, you're late,' Barryman muttered, not letting the pain get in the way of his sense of humour. Then he coughed up blood. The man he called Steel knelt beside his friend with sad eyes. 'New York, go to New York,' Barryman gasped. He coughed and attempted to raise his other hand to show the other man something. 'In the folder, in my case, there's a photograph of someone you must find.' Barryman managed to point to the black leather briefcase on the ground next to his feet. 'Her name is on the back.' As he coughed, Thomas spat an- other gobbet of blood onto the path. 'Promise me you'll find her and finish this for all our sakes. You've got to promise me....' With these final words, Barryman's fingers loosened their grip, and his eyes lost their life.

Steel reached down with a gloved hand and closed his friend's eyes. Then he opened the briefcase, produced a torch from his pocket and examined its contents. There were maps and photographs of buildings, crime scene reports, and an electronic key, presumably for a vehicle or a door.

Also, inside was the file, with a black-and-white photo of a woman. He turned it over and saw there was only a name, scrawled in black ink. As he stood up, a thick blanket of cloud shrouded the moon. By the time the moon reappeared, Steel had gone.

SIX

A large, bright moon illuminated New York City as if it was the mid-day sun, and a blanket of stars hung in the cloudless sky of a warm August night.

Traffic flowed smoothly, and the bright radiance from stores and streetlights served as a contrast to the dark. City folk hurried on their way, and tourists stopped to take pictures to capture memories as they stared in awe of the massive structures, savouring the delicious aromas from restaurants and delis and wallowing in the sensation of being utterly and completely overwhelmed by such a great city.

From her open office window, Karen Lane could hear the sounds of sirens wailing and the blaring horns of angry taxi drivers. But she had no time to take a moment to look out at the fantastic view below her. The air in her office was thick with humidity, and so the open window allowed a fresh breeze to sneak in through the small gap she had left.

The air conditioner in her office was on the fritz, so she was forced to open the window. Regardless of being ten storeys up, the noise was distracting. The sounds of a Thursday night in the Big Apple was almost a siren's song to her. But she had work to do, a mass of paperwork to write up for the meeting tomorrow. She'd already typed page after page, stopping only to take a sip from the water glass next to her computer.

Her hands cupped her long blonde hair and combed it through her fingers so that it fell on her back. She found that this had a calming effect, it was almost better than drinking alcohol, but didn't always do the trick.

She was tall, with an hourglass figure. Even though she was approaching her forties, she still had the face of a much younger woman, with the looks of a model. Unless you looked really closely, you couldn't see any signs of aging, and nowadays you wouldn't look that closely at any woman, even if she were your lawyer, and still remain politically correct. Karen was a partner in *Bradford, Lane, and Stewart*, a law firm with one hell of a case that was going to trial in two weeks. Her father had been the original Lane, but now the only name on the letterhead was hers. Staring at the computer monitor, she blew out a lungful of air, as she knew there was still much to do in the limited time available. The office was large with a glass-topped, clutter-free desk. The twenty-millimetres-thick glass held only her bare essentials on it: the computer monitor, keyboard, telephone, and the file.

Against the left wall stood an oak cabinet, which stored various reference books and photographs of places around the world she had travelled to. Diplomas from Columbia law school, Harvard and numerous other educational establishments she had framed and hung on the right-hand wall. Below these stretched a long black leather sofa. Its soft fabric and comfortable padding were excellent for making valued clients comfortable, sometimes she even slept on it after an exceptionally late night at the office. Not tonight though, she was going straight home.

It took her a further half hour to put the document she was working on together, and pack it away into the presentation folders, ready for the meeting the next day. She raised her wrist to look at her watch. The gold-faced Rolex showed half-past two in the morning. Letting out a silent curse, she found it hard to believe that she had been working this late again. She looked momentarily at the sofa, and said to herself, 'No, you're going home.'

Powering down the computer and switching off the lights, she locked the room and stepped into a large open space that contained a nest of booths and desks on the firm's floor. She knew that everybody else was long gone, and she hoped they were tucked up in their beds hours ago, to be ready for work tomorrow. The only sign of life Karen saw was the janitor, buffing the floor next to the elevator.

'Hi, Karl,' she greeted him with the smile of relief to see another person she recognised. Karen's arms were full with her coat, handbag, files and, balanced under her chin, her thermos coffee cup.

'Hi, Miss Karen, working late again?' said the janitor almost disapprovingly. 'Young lady like you should be out having fun, not cooped up here on a Thursday night, no sir,' he added, shaking his head.

Karen was grateful for his being concerned about her, and most of all, for being considerate enough to press the call button on the elevator. The doors opened, and Karen stepped inside.

'Good night, Karl,' she said, flashing him a mile. 'Good night, Miss,' he replied, returning the smile.

The doors closed and she nudged the button for the garage with her elbow, hoping she had hit the right one. The basement button illuminated, and Karen sighed with relief. Then she felt the slight shudder, and the elevator started downwards towards the underground garage. She observed the panel displaying the numbers, watching the count-down.

Finally, the elevator reached its destination, and with a ding, the doors opened to reveal the dark grey parking lot. She stepped out, noticing the change in climate. Upstairs the air had been hot and sticky from the building's failed air con, whereas down here it was still warm but dry.

Karen headed for a group of parked vehicles at the end of the lot. She began to hum a tune she had heard earlier that day, which was repeating in her head. Karen walked past the massive round pillars that supported the roof. She began to notice shadows dancing in front of her, contrasting with brightness from the hidden wall lights. Her car was in sight, but the uneven light played tricks on her, conjuring up all kinds of imaginary apparitions at the edge of her field of vision.

Her ears pricked to the sound of the elevator, and, as she turned, Karen noticed the silhouette of a tall bulky figure stepping out of the elevator. She started to walk quicker, and her humming began to match her steps in an attempt to calm herself. Then there were pounding footsteps from behind her. Too fearful to look around, she made for her car as fast as she could.

Who was following her? What did they want? Her pace quickened so it was almost a jog, until she was a few feet from her car. Behind her, the pursuer had also broken into a run to keep up with her.

Nearly there now, she thought, her eyes set on the vehicle before her. Her baggage of coat and coffee mug were flung aside as she ran. Her heart pounded in her chest as she searched through her bag for her keys.

'Where the fuck are my keys?' she almost screamed, as she reached her car. Fear drove her into panic as her fingers scrabbled through the bag's contents. Her pursuer's footsteps became ever nearer as she dug deeper. She cursed and threw items from her purse in her frantic search for her keys.

A large shadow loomed over her.

'Please don't hurt me, please! I've got money, look,' Karen yelled. Her body curled up in complete terror while she pressed against the side of her blue BMW, awaiting the inevitable death stroke or worse.

To her relief the sound of a calm voice filled her ears. The voice was slightly out of breath from the chase, but smooth and familiar. Karen chanced a peek from under the arm that she had raised to protect her face.

'Hey, I'm sorry to frighten you, Miss Karen, but you left these in the door.' Her arm dropped down, and she stood up from her cowering pose as if nothing had happened, quickly taking the keys from his huge dark hands. She playfully smacked his right arm with her bag and giggled.

'Karl, you scared the crap out of me.' They both laughed, and he helped to retrieve her belongings. Opening the car door for her, Karl waited until she was safely inside, then closed the heavy door; she rolled down the window and smiled again at the old man.

'Good night, Miss, and I'm so sorry for scaring you,' Karl apologised. 'You have a safe journey home now.' And with that, he turned and headed back towards the elevator.

Karen blew out a deep, calming breath. Looking at herself in the rear-view mirror, she stuck out her tongue and made a 'blaahh' sound as if to make a self-examination. *God, I look like crap*, she thought. Then she let out a small, self-indulgent smile as her thoughts strayed to the hot bath and glass of red wine that were waiting for her at home. After all that had happened tonight, she deserved it. Karen started the engine, at which the radio burbled to life. Music blared from the speakers as she sped away towards the exit. As she approached the barrier to the private parking lot, she noticed a large dumpster had drifted into the road, blocking the exit.

You have got to be fucking kidding me, she responded to this latest annoyance at the end of her day.

Whipping the seatbelt out of its fastener, she got out of her car. She walked up to this new obstacle, grasped the handles of the bin, and heaved at it but it did not budge.

Looking down, she noticed that the brakes were on. That made it deliberate, she thought as she clenched her fists and looked up, swearing at the heavens.

Why me? Karen thought as she bent down to release the brakes. Suddenly she was being grabbed from behind, and a sweet-smelling rag was placed over her nose and mouth. She struggled against her assailant, kicking and clawing, but it had no effect. Whatever chemical was on the rag very quickly took effect. A tear rolled down her cheek as she drifted into darkness and was gone.

SEVEN

J ohn and Sue Mitchell strolled down the wide street, laughing and joking like a pair of teenagers. After leaving the restaurant, they had gone to the bar where they had first met. The hours had drifted into the early morning as they wandered happily back home.

The couple had just celebrated six years of blissful marriage, and it was the first time in years they could be alone together without work or the kids to interrupt them. Even though it was now a Monday morning, they thought *what the hell*. Having palmed off the kids onto Sue's mother the night before, they had the whole day to themselves. No, the night they were about to share would be about them, and nobody else. They walked for a couple of blocks, before John suddenly grabbed Sue by the arm and pulled her into the nearest alleyway. Pushing her against the hard brick, he kissed her passionately as his hands moved all over her, caressing her slender body underneath the black satin dress. She responded to this lustful moment by kissing and biting his ears and neck. As the two locked in a passionate embrace, an almost animalistic lust for one another came over them, and they forgot where they were and who might hear or see, too caught up in the moment to care.

They moved down the alley, away from prying eyes. John pulled Sue over to a bricked-up window in an old wall and pulled up her dress. As he lifted her onto the window ledge, her screams of passion suddenly became shrieks of terror. Backing away quickly, John thought he had done something wrong. His gaze followed hers, and he joined in with her wail of horror.

A couple of well-built college students, perhaps just off a basketball court, had seen the couple dive quickly into the alleyway. The screams from the woman made them come rushing over. They assumed that the woman was in distress; perhaps the man had decided he wanted more than just dinner. To their surprise, the couple weren't moving, just howling. The man's trousers were still around his ankles, and the woman's dress was still up round her midriff, but both the man and woman were cowering like babies. A lanky black kid ran up to John and Sue, unaware of what was behind them.

'Hey guys, you two OK?' he asked, confused at first by their fear. 'Hey, what's up? You look like you all seen a ghost or something,' joked the giant skinny white kid following him. The tall black kid looked carefully at the pair, who still hadn't registered their presence. Slowly, the kid followed the couple's terrified gaze. He saw something in the darkness. He closed his eyes for a second to adjust to the lack of light, then slowly opened them. He wished he hadn't.

'Oh, shit man, that's fucked up!' The kids froze for a moment, then stumbled back to the entrance of the alleyway, where the rest of their friends stood in wait.

'Hey man, call the cops,' ordered the tall black kid to one of the others, who whipped out his phone and dialled.

'Hello, police department, what's your emergency?' asked a female on the other end of the line. The skinny blond kid grabbed the phone. 'There's a dead body in an alleyway,' he informed her, then burbled the address and gave what information he could.

'Please stay at your location; we will send a unit to your location as quickly as possible.'

The kid hung up, passed the phone back, and promptly threw up.

Detective Samantha McCall woke to the sound of her alarm. The high-pitched bleeping was irritating enough to do the job of getting her up even after a short sleep, and she leant over and checked the time on the digital display. It read 05:00, and giving a quiet moan of disapproval, she slapped the off button then collapsed back to her sleeping position.

Just a couple of minutes, she thought to herself, but changed her mind and rolled out of bed. Leaving the sanctuary of the bedroom, she made for the kitchen, where she reached for the coffee machine and clicked the button to bring it back from its slumber. From there she headed to the bathroom. She prepared to shower, the steam from the hot water filling the air, misting over the mirrors and a small window in the six-foot-square room. She stepped into the torrent of water and just let the cascade run over her for a while.

Switching off the taps, stopping the warm flow, she stepped out of the shower unit and wrapped a towel around her lean, lightly tanned body. McCall used her dry hand to wipe the fog from the mirror that hung above the white porcelain sink, then examined her reflection. Staring for a moment, she smiled and returned to the kitchen. She liked what she saw.

Coffee in hand, she headed back to the bedroom, slipped on some jeans and a t-shirt and got ready for the day ahead. Grabbing a bowl of cereal and the freshly filled coffee mug, she drifted into the sitting room.

As she approached the couch that was housed in a cut-out

section of the floor, McCall stepped onto the cushions and sat down cross-legged, grabbing the remote for the TV, and clicked the ON button. With a burst of light and sound, the set came to life and showed a blandly good-looking man telling New York all about the weather they could expect for the day. *Great, another hot one*, she thought, and then switched channels, looking for something less depressing than a news station.

McCall finished her breakfast and switched off the TV set before heading for an antique desk at the back of the room. Opening the left-hand drawer, she took out her 9mm Glock 17 service pistol and slipped it into the rear holster that nestled in the small of her back, then picked up her police badge. She gave it a quick brush with her hand then clipped it next to the handcuff pouch above her right-hand trouser pocket and gave it a friendly tap.

As she reached the front door, the police officer grabbed her short leather jacket and slipped it on. She checked her keys were in the pocket and left for the station.

Once she had reached her desk at the precinct, McCall began typing up the mundane paperwork that invariably followed the closing of a case. Unlike some, though, she did not mind, figuring it gave her some time to reflect on the crime. Also, she found that going over what had occurred during the investigation of a particular case often taught her useful lessons she could draw on in the future.

Her fingers danced over the keyboard like a pro. If a stranger had seen her at that moment, they might have quickly mistaken her for a secretary or typist, not a homicide detective.

She needed more coffee. Standing up, she reached for the stained coffee mug with the faded police badge symbol on the side and walked towards the coffee room that was next to the captain's office.

The break room was small, with a couple of chairs and a square table next to the far wall and a counter below a double window, which housed four coffee peculators and several unclaimed mugs for visitors. In addition to offering refreshments, it was also an excellent place to go to unwind, or to discuss a case with a colleague without disturbing anyone else. McCall picked up one of the steaming hot containers and poured herself a mug of the dark liquid, the potent aroma of over- cooked cheap coffee filling her nostrils. Fetching the milk from the small refrigerator, she sniffed to see if it was still drinkable: it didn't smell bad, so she topped up her brew. As McCall looked out of the other door, she surveyed the bullpen before her. She saw a bustling array of cops talking on phones or chatting to each other about yesterday's game, and she smiled. *God, how I love this life,* she thought to herself.

Taking a sip of the coffee, she turned her gaze to the desk in front of her, and the two detectives beckoned her over. Joshua Tooms was a huge black man, well over six feet four, and built like a line-backer. Sitting beside him was Antony Marinelli, a shorter, dapper man of Italian extraction, who was huddled over a desk, writing down an address.

'Yeah, I got it,' he said. 'We will be there as soon as we can.' He finished scribbling and put the phone down.

'We got one on the East Side,' he said, waving the bit of paper in his hand. 'The medical examiner is already there. You want to join us, Sam?' The two men grabbed their jackets and headed for the elevator at the far end of the room. 'I'll meet you guys downstairs,' McCall said, swigging the remains of the coffee down before she too snatched up her jacket and waited for the return of the elevator.

· · ·

The street was full of onlookers, press, and TV already prompting McCall to think to herself, *How come they get to know before we do?* Due to the blockage, she had to park some distance away from the scene, but she knew that stretching her legs would do them good. She found a space and then slipped out of the cool of the air-conditioned vehicle into the heat of the morning. Shutting the door, she combed her tawny brown hair through her fingers, letting it fall to her shoulders, and then, with a confident tap on her service pistol, she slipped on a pair of sunglasses and was prepared for action.

Walking up to the barriers, she noticed the large crowd of people shoving each other aside to get a look, and some paparazzi who were trying for the shot that would make them big money. In the corner by the walled entrance to the crime scene stood a tall, broad-shouldered, uniformed cop who, on McCall's approach, smiled, tipped his cap and lifted the tape for her. She ducked under the yellow police barrier and thanked him. Stopping for a moment before venturing down, she viewed the crowd then turned once more to the veteran cop.

'Tom, can we get these people back?' she asked. 'A long way back?' Tom chuckled, then proceeded to move the barriers into the crowd, using them like a snow plough.

'Come on, folks, the show's over, come on now, let's go.' The other uniformed officers followed suit, getting rid of the rubberneckers.

Detective Sam McCall walked up to her two colleagues, who were busy questioning witnesses. As she approached Detective Tooms, he looked up from the notebook in which he was scribbling and met her gaze. She stood for a moment, letting him finish up. He thanked the two students he'd been talking to, and as they left, McCall walked up to him.

'So, what we got?' she asked him. Tooms pointed out the couple who sat huddled together on the steps of an ambulance.

'John and Sue Mitchell, both thirty years old, just celebrated their wedding anniversary when they decided to go up the alley for a bit of wool gathering. Next thing, these student guys are hearing them screaming, and the kids called 911.' She regarded the couple, registered their fear.

'You been down there yet?' she asked Tooms. Tooms shook his head and grinned.

"Thought we'd wait for you." Tooms shrugged. *idiots* thought McCall, how can you interrogate anyone without knowing what you're interrogating them about?

She shouted at the uniformed cop by the ambulance, 'Don't let them go yet, I'll come back.' With a 'Coming?' to Tooms, she set off down the alley.

As they moved deeper into the dank and filthy alley, McCall stepped quickly out of the way of a fresh-faced uniformed officer, who almost bowled her over as he rushed past in the opposite direction. *Goddamn rookie*, she thought, watching him heading for a mass of heavy-looking dumpsters. McCall and her colleagues rounded a corner to find a tall, slender, African-American woman leaning over something; she wore blue medical overalls bearing the words Medical Examiner in yellow print. Her back was towards them, which obscured their view of the body.

'Hi, Sam,' the ME said without turning around. 'Well, we got a mean one here.'

'Hi, Tina,' McCall replied, always happy to see her friend. 'What do you mean "a mean one?"' McCall asked, as her eyes gazed past the back of the ME, and the sight before her made her want to lose her breakfast.

'Jesus, what the…!' She said, just as the other two covered their mouths and turned around.

The naked body of a young woman lay on the cold ground. It had obviously been posed, and her clothes lay neatly folded beside her. As crime scenes went, so far so good. That was, everything apart from the body itself.

'Yeah, like I say, this person is nasty… brilliant but nasty,' said the ME, instantly regretting calling him brilliant.

'Why, what do you mean?' McCall asked curiously.

'As you can see,' Tina pointed with a gloved finger towards an area where the abdomen should have been, 'the area here has been completely removed.'

There was a gaping hole, once occupied by the abdominal wall and its contents. All that remained was the upper and lower parts of the trunk and the flesh and bone structure of her back. McCall could see the kidneys on either side of the spine. The bottom section of the rib-cage, body tissue and muscle just about held it all together. 'Till I get her back to the lab I won't know any more, apart from the fact that she wasn't killed here,' the ME said.

'Lack of blood - there's none to speak of.' McCall noted. after a small pause for thought.

'Lack of' isn't the phrase.' Tina continued, 'I mean, I found no blood anywhere, it's as if she had been completely exsanguinated. But, hey, don't go shouting about vampires just yet,' she said, looking up and giving Tooms and Marinelli a *don't even think about it* gaze, just before they could comment.

Tina waved at two orderlies to come and take away the 'Jane Doe.' Two men, both in their late twenties, wheeled a gurney with a body bag on top over to the remains, then, taking great care, they placed the corpse in the bag and wheeled it back to the coroner's wagon.

The three officers waited for CSU to finish their sweep. McCall watched impatiently while the team started to take photos and collect fibres and prints.

'OK, Detective,' called a familiar voice. The grey-haired man was in his late forties but still had the style and bearing of a much younger man. 'You're clear to go in,' he said, smiling, treating her just as a grandfather might treat his grand-daughter.

'Did you find anything?' McCall was hoping that the killer

had left something, but she already had a bad feeling about this case.

'Not really. Son-of-a-bitch is smart, put her in an alley. Which means we have far too much information,' the CSU tech said, giving her an uneasy smile.

'Thanks, Jim. Oh, say hi to Denise for me, will you?' McCall responded with a gentle smile.

He waved and left, leaving the rest of the CSU to finish their information gathering.

'OK.' McCall turned to her two colleagues. 'We need to canvass the area. I want to find something that this bastard may have left. I am going to talk to the couple in the ambulance.'

John and Sue Mitchell were still shivering with fear as a result of what they had seen. Blankets covered their shoulders and they each grasped a cup of steaming coffee. As she approached them, she nodded to the paramedic who was attending to them; he immediately recognised her 'give us a minute' gesture. As he left them, she gave him a quick silent thank you. He just smiled.

She took a minute to jot down the time, date and location in her notebook, then proceeded to start the interview:

'Hi, I am Detective Sam McCall.'

'Hi, I'm John Mitchell, and this is my wife, Sue.' The woman gave a slight nod.

'I know it's difficult, but I need you to go through what happened.' McCall gave them a sympathetic smile. They both looked at each other and nodded. It was Sue who started talking: 'Well, we had just had dinner at the Italian restaurant a couple of blocks away.' Her voice was as shaky as the rest of her.

'You see, it's our anniversary and it was the first chance we've had to go out alone without the kids,' John explained, making an effort to keep his voice calm.

Sue continued after giving his hand a little squeeze. 'Well, we were just walking, enjoying the evening, when John pulls me down here to, well… to be alone.' She looked down at the ground and blushed.

'Why?' McCall enquired, then she figured it out. 'Oh OK, sure I got it.' She felt embarrassed for the woman. 'Go on, Mrs Mitchell. But I think you can leave out those details,' she added, trying not to smile. 'Well, we got down here to, well, you know, and it wasn't until we got to the end before we saw it – her.' Sue Mitchell broke down into wracking sobs that shook her, and she buried her face in her husband's shoulder. McCall realised she wasn't going to get any further sense out of the woman in the foreseeable future, so she waved to the paramedic to take the couple away. She wasn't sure she was going to get anything more that would be worthwhile from the couple anyway.

McCall walked back to the huddle of police at the entrance to the alley. She called over the other two detectives to join her.

'What we got, guys?' she asked. Tooms flipped open his notebook. 'Well, those guys over there,' he pointed with the end of his pen towards the group of students sitting on the doorstep in front of a newsstand. 'They saw the couple go down the alleyway and thought nothing of it till they heard screaming and thought the guy was doing a special on the woman, so they ran up to rescue her, and then they saw what the couple was looking at.' He closed the pad and returned it to the inner pocket of his short brown leather jacket.

'We got nothing over here, just some passers-by, didn't see anything,' Tony Marinelli said, pointing to an elderly couple standing be- side an ambulance.

McCall noticed that it was still the early hours, dawn hadn't yet broken, and the alleyway was bathed in darkness.

She motioned for her colleagues to go to the further end of the blocked alleyway, while she went back to try and mentally reconstruct how he may have got 'Jane' there. She reached the mouth of the alley and realised that all the onlookers had gone. Their interest had left when the body had been taken away.

Studying the entrance, she imagined a vehicle pulling up and stopping, then went through the movements of a person getting out and walking along the alleyway, assessing what the killer, always assuming he was on his own, may have touched or banged against. She tried to imagine the scene, and what he might have encountered. 'Why here?' she thought aloud. 'What's so special about this place?'

As McCall stared down the breadth of the dark cobbled passage, she took a deep breath and closed her eyes. As she slowly opened them, she was ready, taking her time, checking for something, *anything*.

'Sometimes things are just plain friggin' obvious,' her father used to say. McCall stopped for a second as the thought of her dad brought a small, unwelcome distraction to the moment. She shook off the memories and proceeded down the alley. There was nothing. *Damn it*, she thought. Who was this guy? Suddenly she had a feeling of not being alone. She turned to find at the alley's entrance there was a tall, dark figure, silhouetted by the bright sun behind him. All she could make out was a long jacket that flapped in the breeze of the large truck that powered past. Moving towards the figure, she drew out her badge and held it up.

'Hey, excuse me, can I talk to you?' she yelled out. 'Hey, you!'

But the figure remained motionless for a moment. Something seemed wrong about this guy, whoever he was. Suddenly something jammed up against her leg, and there was a loud screech as she kicked a ginger cat that had only been trying to be affectionate. She looked down, shocked at what she had just done, but when her focus returned to the figure, he was gone. 'Stupid animal!' she screamed, running in pursuit of the man. Reaching the mouth of the passage, she burst out, half expecting to see him running off or a car speeding away. But there was nothing; he had disappeared entirely. Who the hell was he and where did he go?

EIGHT

The midday sun was hot and stifling, the glare causing the bustling traffic to crawl across the city, while ice cream vendors worked hard to supply the demanding crowds that had gathered in the streets. Within the coolness of Grand Central Station, thousands of commuters hurried to find their platforms. As she headed for the exit, Susan Black nudged her way through the endless wash of animated people. Pushing the brass door rails of the wood-and-glass doors, Susan was immediately taken aback by the sudden change in temperature, as the startling heat slapped her in the face.

Stepping into the street, she headed for the coffee shop that sat under the Park Avenue Viaduct. She smiled to herself as she noticed a few heads turn, enjoying the appreciative glances. She was a sexy forty-year-old woman, her long blonde hair flowed attractively in the breeze, her grey business suit tailor-made to show off her slender body and accentuate the alluring curves. Men's mouths dropped open, even some women stared in admiration, and she lapped up the attention. Oh yes, she liked being appreciated. As she went into the coffee shop, one man in particular paid her attention. This raven-haired man re-adjusted his sunglasses to get a better view, then picking up his mobile phone, he pressed the speed dial button and waited.

'Yes,' the voice on the other end of the line was soft, but the tone was like nails on a chalkboard. The dark-haired man shivered at the sound of the voice in his ear. 'I have just seen something I think you will like,' he said. There was a pause.

'Can you bring it?'

The dark man smiled, 'Sure, I'll pick it up for you.' He disconnected the call, slid the phone into his jacket pocket and waited.

Susan only lived a couple of blocks away, so she took the decision to 'walk off' her long journey and the hours of sitting; it was good to be back in New York after a two-week business trip to Canada. As she waltzed down the busy streets, the sound of her wheeled suitcase rattled on the sidewalk, warning people she was coming. Susan was not far from her apartment building when a mewling sound distracted her, so she stopped at an alleyway and listened. It emanated from the depths of the dirty alley. Moving slowly closer, she strained to make out the noise.

What was that? An injured animal? She moved nearer to the noise until she realised it was the sound of a crying child.

'Hello, are you hurt?' she asked. Releasing the grip on her case, she edged in further until she found a little girl sitting in an old cardboard box, which was big enough to hold a freezer or some other sizable object. Susan knelt down just in front of the child, and smiled at her. 'Hi, are you lost, do you need help?' She didn't reply. 'Where's your mommy?'

She felt her body seize up as the taser bit into her back, and she passed out.

Tuesday morning saw Detective McCall headed to the precinct, still wondering whose body it was at the bottom of the alleyway. The day before, after examining the scene of the crime, she'd spent the rest of the time chasing missing person files and hoping Tina, the medical examiner, had come up with something. McCall hated to drive in the mornings as the traffic was its usual nightmare, but what else could she do?

Suddenly her radio crackled to life. 'Hey, McCall, if you are on the way to the precinct, don't bother, we are needed at Central Park, we are at the Bethesda Terrace.' It was Tony, and he did not sound happy.

'Why, what's up?' McCall was almost afraid to ask.

'We got another one; the son-of-a-bitch has struck again.' This time another voice spoke, it was rougher, deeper, and more authoritative: it belonged to the captain.

Bethesda Terrace was a late 1800s wonder, the two-level courtyard constructed of red and white brick, featuring a smaller forecourt on the upper level, from which two sandstone staircases descended on either side to give entry to a weathered underpass. This made the place look as if it had once belonged to a castle or a cathedral. A magnificent fountain loomed at the other end of the quaint courtyard. This was intended to be a place of dreams, a place for people to come and lose themselves in another time.

The park was awash with police, putting up crime-scene tape and barricades, the press in their droves setting up tripods and getting video cameras ready to go on air, the usual media circus and of course, the inevitable gathering of ghouls.

McCall pulled up her car as close as possible and surveyed the chaos. 'Well, so much for keeping this one under wraps,' she said to herself, getting out of her car. She gave her gun a reassuring tap and then moved forward towards the tape.

Cameras flashed, microphones were thrust in front of her face, and people were begging her for a statement, but she just shrugged them off, treating them like an unwanted infection. 'Nothing to say yet,' was her terse reply.

Passing the cordoned-off area, she moved freely, checking to make sure nothing out of the ordinary stuck out. A voice called out to her as she walked down the weathered sandstone steps and, looking around, McCall spotted the rest of the team. She headed towards the crowd of plain-clothes officers, two of whom were Tony Marinelli and Joshua Tooms. They were speaking to a very tall African-American man. This man was nearly as tall as Tooms and towered over Marinelli. He was wearing a blue suit that fitted tightly enough to advertise his massive muscular arms but not tight enough to constrict his movements.

As she approached, she nodded to Tony and Tooms, and then acknowledged her superior with a grim, "Morning, Captain.'

'McCall,' he returned the greeting. 'This is getting out of hand.'

She noticed a blue cloth covering something on the ground by the sizeable sculptured underpass, opposite the ornate fountain near where they stood. The group moved over to where they found Tina, crouched in front of a covered corpse. 'Hi, Doc,' they greeted her in chorus. Concentrating hard, she just raised a hand and waved in response to their greetings.

'So, Doc, have you got a cause of death?' the captain asked. To this, the ME turned around and sadly shook her head.

'Nope, I'm not sure how she died,' the attractive African-American ME replied, 'but I know ID is going to be a bitch.'

As she spoke, she unveiled the corpse to reveal a woman. Her naked body looked trim and athletic and, unlike the last victim, she was intact except for one small detail.

'Well, it's definitely your guy,' Tina continued. 'Blood drained from the body just like last time but as you can see, this time the head has been removed, and not just the head but also the neck all the way down to the collarbone. She's also lost her fingertips and thumbs.'

Even the usually unflinching captain had to look away from this one.

'We need to catch this bastard and fast,' he said, 'before we have a full-blown panic on our hands. Come on, let's move, people.'

'OK, Tony, you check for CCTV footage, they must have picked something up,' Sam McCall instructed. 'Tooms, can you grab some uniforms and talk to as many people as possible? Someone may have seen or heard something. Thanks, guys.' She looked around at the lay-out. The detective had to admit it was brilliantly staged: no doorways either side, and a road that ran right next to the steps. Getting witnesses would be nothing short of impossible, unless they were part of the crime.

The two men gave each other a quick knuckle-bump and left. McCall walked over to Tina, who was just finishing the location paper-work.

'Hey, you OK?' she asked the ME.

'Yes, I'm fine.' Tina paused as McCall gave her friend a meaningful look. 'Well, not really, this case is really bothering me. This perp's a real sicko.'

McCall was puzzled. During all the years they had known each other, this was the first time she had seen the ME spooked by what she had seen.

'What's up, Tina? It can't be getting to you, I've always thought you're tough as nails.'

The ME smiled at her and placed a reassuring hand on McCall's left arm.

'No, it's not getting to me, I'm just thinking, how he is doing this? Now, I've seen sick perps in our time. But when sick comes together with brilliant, then we got ourselves a problem.'

McCall gave her a quick smile.

'But we will catch this guy, don't worry.' And with that, the ME left for the morgue.

McCall waited an hour for the CSU to complete their routine crime-scene evidence collection; once they were finished, Jim Burke, the lead investigator of the team, strolled up to her, clipboard in hand.

'Hi, kiddo,' he said with a smile, in his grandfatherly manner.

'Hi, old man.' They hugged like old family friends who had not seen each other for years.

'How you holding up?' he asked, a concerned look on his face. 'I'm doing great, it's just this case is tying everyone in knots.'

He nodded in agreement. 'Yeah, this is one smart SOB,' he said, trying to be polite but failing. 'We've found nothing at either crime scene. Don't get me wrong, we found stuff, but nothing out of the ordinary. Lots of tread marks, millions of fibres, I'm just hoping the smart bastard gets too cocky and slips up – they normally do.'

'I hope so too, old man,' she said in response, unable to prevent the doubting tone in her voice.

They embraced once more, and then she was alone to walk through the crime scene and mentally run the circumstances immediately prior to the body drop.

She looked around. The best entrance point was definitely on the road by the grand steps she herself had entered by. At the top, beside the road, she ran through the events, acting them out as best she could. 'OK,' she spoke to herself. 'Stop the car, get out. I look around, make sure everything is clear.' She accompanied the thoughts with appropriate movements, using her imagination to lead her.

'OK, the coast is clear; I move down the steps, I'm nearly at my goal.'

McCall reached the bottom of the steps and turned the corner. To her surprise, she found a man crouched on the ground where the body had been.

'Hey, can I help you?' she shouted to the figure.

The man rose up and turned towards her. He was tall and wore black from head to foot. She noted that he was handsome, with a clean-shaven, chiselled jaw, his lips curved into a smile, and with his eyes masked by a pair of dark Oakley sunglasses that hugged his face. He did nothing at first, then formally placed his right hand over his chest and gave a small bow. Then he left.

She was too stunned by his brashness to follow, instead yelling: 'Hey! No! You stop right there, mister!'

But he just carried on up the steps to her right on the other side of the courtyard. She pulled herself together to pursue him, but even though his pace had not quickened, he remained well ahead of her.

'Hey, you! Get your ass back here! Police, stop or I'll shoot.' Mc-Call hollered after him, and then actually drew her pistol to make her threat real. The man carried on as though nothing was amiss. Suddenly, apparently out of nowhere, a horse and carriage darted between them, blocking her from her quarry.

'Police, move… Now!' she yelled, holding up her badge. The carriage driver quickly whipped at the steed, and they took off.

McCall looked around, but the mystery man was nowhere to be seen. *OK, now this guy is really starting to piss me off,* she thought to herself, and clenching her fists she screamed to the sky as if to blame someone up in the heavens for sending this man to torment her.

NINE

It was another warm, cloudless night and the stars in the heavens glistened like the millions of lights of the city below them. The full moon seemed to take up the sky. Its brightness illuminated the city, painting it a shade of icy blue. Cars eased their way down the busy streets, most sharing the same agenda of going home. A shadow passed down the street and slipped unnoticed into an alleyway. Silent as a whisper, the man made it to a certain point in the darkness of the passage. He knelt down and scanned the area, then swiftly rose up with the same ease as before and moved to the row of heavy garbage dumpsters. Something caught his eye and, slipping his hand between two of them, he grasped something; a dirty pair of gloves, tatty enough to have been owned by a homeless person. He examined them for a brief moment and slipped them into his jacket pocket.

From down the far end near the entrance, two beat cops with flashlights approached the white coloured outline of a figure on the ground. The pair were discussing how in a couple of years they would be detectives, busting heads and getting rid of scumbags like the fella who did this murder.

All of a sudden, they looked up to see a shadowy figure in

front of them. 'What the…!' one of them yelled. 'Hey, you ain't meant to be down here, buddy!' He reached for his pistol. Right at that moment, the moon's bright light faded as a cloud covered it, rendering the alley pitch black for a few seconds.

The cloud passed, and the alleyway was once more lit up like a winter's morning. However, the policemen stood alone. The man had disappeared.

'Frank, let's not tell anybody about this, right?' the larger of the two men said. His colleague just nodded, and they both got out of there as if they had seen the Devil himself.

The morning brought a blood red sunrise that blazed across the sky as if the heavens themselves were on fire, and a multitude of colours filled the canvas of the early morning sky. McCall rose and started her usual morning ritual; get up, make coffee and hit the shower, get dressed and have breakfast. As she sat and chewed her usual bowlful of sugary cereal, McCall scanned the TV news for what the media were giving away on this case. Luckily, they had nothing, just some babble about a serial killer. *Fine*, she thought: the less that these vultures knew the better, for the moment at least. There were too many times when the press had messed up a case because they were too eager to put out information. She finished dressing and headed for work.

The main hall of the precinct was full of people, some waiting to file reports, others to get booked. McCall passed the desk sergeant, who waved to draw her attention.

'Hey, Sam,' the large white-haired officer said, handing her a post-it note. 'The doc says she wants to see you.'

'Thanks, Sarge,' she replied, then headed for the elevator. 'Morning, Tina,' McCall greeted her friend.

Tina Franks was slightly shorter than McCall but had more of an hourglass build. Where McCall had a lean athletic look about her, Tina had the curves of an exotic cheerleader. Her father was a marine whose family had come to the States from Jamaica, and her mother had been a Brazilian law student, studying in New York; her parents had met at a mutual friend's party and the rest, they said, was history.

'Well, it's about time, girlfriend,' Tina replied, jokily.

'So, what we got?' asked McCall, eager to get some news.

'Well, the blood was drained from both Vic's so we couldn't get a tox screen, but we have other ways, don't worry, the killer's just making me earn my money,' she mumbled. 'We got nothing from this one's prints, so looks like she was a good little girl. We're waiting for her dental records.' She used her pen to point to the slab behind her.

'The other one?' McCall asked. Tina shrugged, and McCall added, ''Course, she could have just come in from abroad, and the killer knew her.'

'I wish I could tell you more, Sam, but we are backed up at the moment. Soon as I get something, you'll know all about it.'

McCall thanked her friend then left to go upstairs. *God, I need coffee,* she thought. She was soon back at her desk in the bustling chaos of the homicide department. Phones were ringing madly; there was the sound of computer keys rattling. Certainly, it was a maddening melee of noise and confusion, but to her ears it was sheer music, a Precinct Symphony.

The rest of the morning was spent going through personal records and walking around the buildings surrounding the crime scene to try to get some sort of idea of where the latest victim came from. From what they could gather, the first one had plenty of money, judging by her almost perfect appearance: with her manicured nails, flawless teeth, and stylish dyed hair, everything indicated wealth. So why had no one reported her missing? Unable to find anything from the neighbourhood, Sam returned, exhausted from the constant walking.

She sat on the edge of her desk, one arm across her waist, the other bent up at the elbow. In her hand she held a black whiteboard marker, with which she was tapping her bottom lip in thought.

The large, shiny whiteboard was filled with photos and scribbles of ideas and information on the Vic's. A thick black strip of tape ran down the centre, dividing the area into two parts, each of them allot- ted to one of the victims. McCall stared at the board intently, her eyes scanning to try to pick up something they had in common, but the harder she looked, the more she worried that she might be missing something.

Tooms joined her, while Tony Marinelli was busy on the phone. 'We checked the database for prints, came up nada, we also checked with the FBI, got nothing there either,' Tooms announced.

As Tooms spoke, Tony put the phone down and hastily scribbled something on a bit of paper before he jumped up and hurried over.

'Well, we may have a lead on the first Vic,' Tony announced, perching beside McCall on the edge of her desk.

'It appears a young lawyer in the Brookman building never showed up for a big meeting the other day, and they haven't been able to reach her.'

'Good, that may be our first proper lead. You two go there first thing in the morning as soon as the workers show up,' she answered, still studying the puzzling information board. 'OK guys, go home, get some rest, God knows we could use some,' she said, standing up and stretching.

'See you all tomorrow,' Tooms announced, as he headed for the elevator. Marinelli said his goodnights and left, flinging his jacket over his shoulder and swaggering out as if he were some kind of superstar.

She finished her paperwork, swigged back the remains of her coffee and prepared to leave. Stepping into the elevator, all she could think about was going home and sinking into a nice hot bath, while sipping a large glass of the red wine she'd bought the other day.

TEN

The parking lot was dark with just a few hints of light dotted here and there. She had parked here for years; in fact, it was the only one in walking distance of the station. The collection of cars scattered all overlooked more abandoned than parked, but it was cheap and secure so who gave a damn. In the distance she saw her car, its ancient, faded paintwork glinting under the light of the spot lamp, which gave it an almost welcoming glow. Walking towards the beloved 1966 Mustang, which originally had belonged to her father, her mind was completely occupied by the case. The darkness of the lot had never bothered her; hell, she knew she could take care of herself and she was armed, so if anyone screwed with her, she could sort it.

Stopping at the door of her car, McCall reached into her jacket pocket for the keys. Suddenly she felt the cold steel of an automatic being pressed up against the back of her neck as she was pushed forwards against the car. There was a slam as her face met the glass of the door. She heard laughter from behind her.

'Well boys, lookie what we got here, my oh my, ain't y'all a purdie little thang!' said a Southern voice behind her. She was overwhelmed by the rank smell of his sweat, and it made her want to gag.

'OK darling, y'all put your purdie little hands on the car and spread 'em.'

She heard other men in the background, giggling like school kids. She reckoned from the sound there were possibly two others there, but precisely where they were, she had no idea. McCall stood rigid, refusing to budge. She got a smack on the side of the head with his large, fatty elbow for her disobedience.

'I said, put your goddamn hands on the car and spread 'em, bitch!'

Under duress she obeyed, then she felt his hands moving slowly up her legs towards her crotch.

'Now I gotta search y'all just in case yer packin'.'

He jammed his hand between her legs and moved it back and

forth. 'Bet y'all like that, dontcha! We gonna do some more of that, ain't we,' he giggled. McCall kicked backwards and caught the man in the face. She heard him let out an agonising, 'Oomph,' then, turning quickly, McCall aiming to strike another blow, only to receive a smack to the head. She was thrown head-first against the car's roof. Despite seeing stars, she forced herself to stay standing.

'Listen, I'm a police officer,' she yelled. 'And I know you don't want to do anything stupid, so if you all leave now, we can avoid a situation. So why don't you just put down the gun and—'

A swift punch to her kidneys answered McCall's question, leaving her breathless for a moment.

'So, we got us an itty-bitty cop, do we? Well, if dat don't just sweeten the deal? Ain't never done me a cop before.'

McCall tried to lash out again; and once again he banged her head against the car.

'Well boys, we got a feisty one here, I'm gunna lurve breakin' her in,' he said, laughing.

But his was the only laughter she heard.

'Hey, where y'all fuckers got to?' He turned around to look. 'What the…?' His voice betrayed his surprise and shock.

She felt the pressure from the gun loosen, and knew it was her only chance. McCall spun round. As she moved, she round-housed the thug, catching him full in the stomach. He grunted in pain and, as his massive frame bent double from the impact, McCall followed through with a mighty upwards kick, sending a fountain of teeth and blood into the air. Before her lay three unconscious hillbillies and in the distance, a figure strolling away, his details blurring into the darkness. All she could make out was a long coat that carried in the wind like a ship's flag. He did not slow down when she shouted, 'Hey you! Mister.' But she kept her gun pointed at the unconscious hillbillies at her feet. McCall pulled out her phone and called the precinct, assistance swiftly arriving in the shape of five male uniformed officers. But all the while she was thinking, *Oh, I can't wait to explain this.*

Ruefully contemplating all the shit she would get from her colleagues at the department, she comforted herself with the fact that at least these three morons would spend the night in lockup until morning, when she fully intended to show them that it is not wise to mess with this woman.

McCall climbed into her car and drove home, the thought of that bath becoming ever more blissful. When she arrived at her apartment, she threw off her jacket and shoes, made a beeline for the bathroom and drew a bath, ensuring that the water was laced with plenty of foam. She slipped into the deeply-filled tub as she listened to the sounds of jazz wafting from her stereo system.

ELEVEN

The sun rose in a blaze of colour over a city ravaged by hordes of commuters heading off to work, streets heaving with the morning traffic, while subway stations were packed with jostling impatient people. Men and women moved in long processions. Hurrying through the grid of streets and avenues, carrying coffee cups with logos plastered on them or phones glued to their ears, as they pushed through the chaos to get to the safety of their offices or other places of work, keen to escape the mayhem of Manhattan in the morning.

Marie-Ann Talbot was a businesswoman who bought and sold real estate in the city, and had several fingers in many other pies. For her, pursuing her business interests was not so much for the money as for the thrill of it all. Having finished her 'daily shock' workout at the gym, she was eager to get to work. Coffee in hand, she waited at the side of the road for a cab, when her phone rang. She pressed the activation button on her earpiece to answer the call. 'Hello?' she said. Her voice was soft but had a slight gravelly tone to it.

She was wearing a grey sweat-suit bottoms and a white t-shirt that clung to her ample breasts, and her tall, athletic figure cast a pleasing shadow in the morning sun. Her secretary, Jenna, was on the other end of the line, and they spoke for a while about a property that had just come on the market. A yellow cab came screeching to a halt next to her, she climbed into its rear, and the lock clicked as she pulled the heavy door shut, engaging the deadbolt.

'Forty-second, please,' she instructed, and the cabbie just raised a hand to confirm he had heard her and nudged the cab into the flow of traffic. Marie-Ann continued her conversation and flicked through a magazine she had purchased earlier that morning.

'I tell you, Jenna, the place was huge, and the view was...' she broke off her conversation to call to the driver. 'Hey, buddy, where the hell you takin me?'

She looked up and saw that they were going over the Brooklyn Bridge. Fear set her heart racing.

'Hey, fella, I am not some tourist, I live here! Take me back, you asshole!' She pounded her fists on the security glass between them till they throbbed with pain. Marie-Ann grasped at the door handles and banged on the window in the hope that someone would see her plight, but no one paid any attention. After a while, she stopped. She felt so tired, so very tired.

A new fear swept over her as she realised that her tiredness was not natural, but before she could work out what had happened, she fell into blackness like no other, a sleep from which she felt as if she'd never wake.

Marie-Ann swam back into consciousness, blinking several times to help her eyes adjust, still woozy and unsure if what she was seeing was strong brightness or lack of light. She tried to sit up but, to her horror, she was unable to. What was wrong, she wondered? Where was she? She struggled but found she had been bound: her arms, legs, and her head were all tied up. Why was her head secured? From somewhere in the room Marie-Ann could hear a faint sound, something distant; no not distant, *small*. She strained to hear what it was and where it was coming from.

The noise got louder; it was music, a kind of chiming, from… maybe from a music box or watch, she concluded.

'Hello? Hello? Is anyone there?' she called out, not so much for help, for she realised that nobody was likely to hear her. Calling was a way of ascertaining if there was someone else in the room; she didn't care who it was.

The chimes seemed to be moving around her, not getting closer, just circling. She almost felt like a zoo animal being stared at. Around and around the direction of the sound seemed to be travelling, but not quickly. She listened harder and could almost hear footsteps mixed with strange breathing. The music stayed in place for a moment; it seemed to be near her head. Suddenly she felt something moving across her hair. It was not an animal, no, it was more like fingers gently brushing across the top of her scalp.

She started to shake uncontrollably and sweat began to pour across her brow as she was seized with the fear of not knowing who her captor was coupled with the terror of not knowing his intentions. Her imagination was going wild with images of what this maniac could be capable of. This was too much for her to bear.

'Please don't hurt me,' she begged. 'I'll give you whatever you want, I've got plenty of money in the bank, but please don't kill me.'

She sobbed uncontrollably, hoping that this stranger might feel some sort of compassion for her.

'You will give me whatever I want. Promise?'

That voice sent shivers down her spine. His tone was calm

and lucid, yet the pitch was a mishmash of highs and lows, like nails running down violin strings. Almost as if they had been separately recorded. But most of all she sensed the pleasure behind the eerie murmur that filled her ears. Whereas before she longed for someone to speak, she now yearned for the previous deathly silence.

'Now, now, there is no need to cry, my dear,' said the voice. His sickly sweet, oddly high-pitched voice rang in her ears. She couldn't move her head at all, so she tried imagining a face that might belong to this brute, but nothing in her worst nightmares could conjure something that obscene. Something deep inside her wanted to see his face, just to see what someone who could truss her up like that could look like. Something primal in her soul needed to look him in the eyes. A tear rolled down the side of her face, and she felt a gentle hand brush it away. As she stared up at the dimly lit ceiling, she could make out a shadow here and there, then a shape in the distance came closer. She blinked for a second or two, trying to focus better in the dim light, but as she opened them again, she was greeted by a face with wide, manic eyes, and a smile that froze her with terror.

'So, you would give me anything I want?' he repeated. His smile widened and his brow creased with a scowl. 'I like your eyes, my dear, they're so blue I have never seen anything like them.'

'Th…Tha…thank you,' she replied, somewhat shocked by the change in mood.

'No, I am afraid you misunderstand me. I really like your eyes.'

For a brief second she saw the strange instrument come into focus above her right eye, then there was blackness. Her ears filled with the sound of her own screams until she passed out, while all the time the chimes from the pocket watch played in the background, long after her screams had faded into the shadows of the room.

. . .

A gentle breeze blew through the streets of Little Italy, but it barely cooled the warm air still hanging over the city after the scorching day's sun. People sat outside at the tables and chairs that lined the sidewalks outside the many restaurants scattering the well-lit streets, the reds, greens and blues of neon signs reflected in windows and from vehicles. The night air was filled with music and laughter, and everyone seemed to be happy and enjoying the evening al fresco, bar one.

A stealthy form crept into an alleyway, carefully clinging to the shadows as it went. It came to rest at a group of stacked boxes, where it hovered, motionless, observing a large man standing in the alley, watching a TV that had been illicitly plugged into the local grid. Flickering light from the set spilled up the alley and created convenient shadows – convenient for the stranger.

Vinny Carbone was a heavy, bald man, his giant form seeming almost too large for his blue hand-stitched suit, as he danced up and down while watching the ball game and yelling at the TV.

'Come on, goddammit!' he barked in a gruff, almost gravelly voice. 'Where is Santini?' came a softly threatening voice from the figure bathed in the darkness.

'Well, well, my mystery guest is here,' Vinny answered, recovering quickly from his surprise. 'We have been expecting you- they didn't think you would show, but hey, here you are…'

The man turned halfway around just so he could lay eyes on the idiot who was disturbing him, but all he saw was shadows and a form that was shrouded in shadow. The figure held his position for a beat, then stepped into the middle of the walkway. As he did so, all light seemed to disappear from around him, as if he were a black hole.

The mysterious interloper held himself very upright, very

alert. From behind him, several large, brutish-looking thugs in jeans and wife-beater shirts appeared, brandishing weapons of all descriptions.

Vinny turned fully, ball game forgotten, not wanting to miss this confrontation. His suit was paired with a white shirt, opened wide enough to show off his bronzed barrel chest and a gold chain with a large crucifix that hung amidst the grey hair.

The light from the TV set caused flashes of illumination that danced up and down the alley but seemed somehow not to touch the stranger.

'Sort this bastard out, boys. I wanna see what he's made of.' The fat man nodded to his crew, who were coming up behind the mystery man. The shadowy character sensed a man moving up steadily behind him. The thug swung a baseball bat, bringing it downwards with such power that it splintered on the ground as the agile man sidestepped the blow. The goon let out a painful, 'Ooff,' as the mystery man spun around and elbowed him in the back of the neck, knocking him off balance and straight into a knee that came up to meet his face as his head travelled downwards.

The air was suddenly filled with an eruption of blood, bone and swearing as the man's nose exploded from the impact. Another guy rushed forward, slashing blindly at The Shadow with a large blade. Instantly the hand wielding the weapon was blocked, and his arm was dragged underneath his own armpit so that the outstretched arm was in a lock. There was a brief moment before the stranger pulled down on the arm and snapped it at the elbow. The punk screamed, and the knife fell straight into his adversary's hands.

'Stick around, I haven't finished yet,' called out the winner of that scuffle.

The newly-acquired blade whistled through the air and embedded itself into the back of Vinny's knee, the fat man screaming in agony as the steel cut through sinew and met bone. Vinny crashed to the ground with a loud thud, reeling in pain.

The Shadow turned, only to be met by two more men, one with a bat and another with a pistol.

The bat was swung at head height, but The Shadow leaned back just as the business end sailed past, so close that he felt the displaced air tickle his nose. As he came back up, he used the full force of his body to drive his forehead into the face of his attacker. There was a sickly crack, like snapping twigs, as he shattered the man's nose. The gangster stumbled, but not too far from reach, as The Shadow used him as a shield from the remaining attacker, who held the gun. The armed man bobbed and weaved, trying to get the drop on him, but The Shadow pushed the man with the newly-broken nose towards his pal, and then rushed him. There was a scraping sound as The Shadow slid across the floor, knocking his opponent to the ground and then, in the blink of an eye, he used one swift punch to the neck, laying the man out cold.

Vinny scanned the alleyway, still lit by the flickering TV images, but saw nothing. He called for his crew, but there was only silence. Crawling forward, leaving a trail of fresh blood on the dirty ground, he went to see if his boys had got the man shrouded in shadow, but all he saw were bodies lying motionless across the passage, bodies that were all familiar to him.

'Where the fuck are you, jerk off?' he screamed, his head dancing backwards and forward checking everywhere, except...

Behind him, a shadow loomed across him, long coat moving with the wind, like some phantom clawing at the breeze.

'Now, where were we?' The Shadow murmured in Vinny's ear. 'Oh yes.'

A scream filled the alley, but it was drowned out by the nearby festivities of the night. The TV flickered on, lighting up the alley, lending a backdrop to one final scream.

TWELVE

The morning tabloids were packed with tales of a psycho killer at large in the city. The police had released a statement but had supplied only enough detail to whet the press's appetite, rather than satisfy any demand.

Sam McCall read the article and chuckled to herself, wondering how long the vultures had waited before accepting that was all they were getting and being forced to supplement the crumbs of info with whole paragraphs of speculation for printing, but she was more interested in the sports page to be bothered about what was fact and what was fiction. Today was Saturday, and tomorrow she would be at her mom's for the usual family get-together. Saturdays were her 'kick back and recharge her batteries' days, and she was going to enjoy her relaxation time.

Why not, she thought? The bad guys were not going anywhere, and Josh and Tony were more than capable of handling things; but to be on the safe side, she had left instructions for someone to notify her if she was needed.

McCall plonked herself down on her brown fabric sofa and flicked on the TV, her finger rhythmically pressing the remote's button as she tried to find something decent to watch.

Not quite a breakfast feature, she thought, but then her choice was better than nothing, as an old Basil Rathbone Sherlock Holmes movie came on. She watched cross-legged, eating her milky cereal slowly, savouring the quiet of the moment.

As she sat watching, she noticed her phone dance across the table in front of her, driven by the vibration alert of an incoming call. McCall leant forward to check the caller's ID: it was the precinct.

'Yes, what's up?' she answered, trying to sound annoyed but feeling somewhat relieved. *Days off, who needs them?* she thought. There's too much to do out there.

'Get your butt back here, Detective, we got another one. The

bastard's back.'

It was the captain on the other end of the phone, and he did not seem happy. In fact, there was something different about his tone that she could not put her finger on.

It took but a moment to shower and change, and before she knew it, she was at the door of her car. The address she had been given was Pier 15. McCall knew that was going to be a nightmare of a drive, so she blue-lit all the way, finally reaching a safe parking area which was some distance from the scene, but it promised to be a beautiful sunny morning, and she figured that the walk would do her good.

McCall sat for a moment, composing herself for what they would find, before she got out and began to walk. Looking back, she saw her car's bodywork ominously stained blood red by the sunrise, as she headed for Pier 15.

The scene was chaos, with camera teams and reporters of all description pushing and shoving to get the best shot, microphones wagging like accusing fingers in the faces of anyone who might have answers to their questions.

Heading for the tape, McCall was immediately engulfed in a frenzy of press people. 'No comment,' was all they got from her as she pushed through the masses. Finally, as an officer lifted the tape, she ducked and went through, followed by a couple of shifty-looking photographers who tried to dodge the wire, only to be caught by the large, stockily-built uniformed officer.

'Get your asses back over the wire, people.' His tone was loud and aggressive, and the two men backed away, sheepishly. McCall glanced around and smiled at the performance, then carried on to the end of the pier.

On the way, she saw the crowd that had gathered in the food court peering through the sun-kissed windows, flashes from mobile phone cameras lighting up the glass that separated them from the crime scene.

'Captain,' she acknowledged him, 'Guys.'

'Hi, McCall,' the captain returned the greeting.

'What we got?' McCall asked, putting on her sunglasses.

The captain pointed to a group of CSU officers huddled around a railing at the far end of the wooden floor of the boardwalk; they seemed to be pulling on something. McCall squinted up at her captain with a searching look but received a shrug and an equally puzzled response. The four detectives moved forward warily until they reached ME Tina Franks, who was standing by with her crew and a dolly ready to transport whatever it was they were all waiting for. 'Doc,' the captain spoke softly.

'Captain,' she replied, and just nodded to the others. 'Well, I must say this is a weird one. All we were told was that there was something hanging from the balcony.' She nodded her head towards the congregation of CSU guys in front of them.

'So,' said the captain, puzzled, 'maybe it was kids messing around.' His look was slightly annoyed, as if he was afraid that their time was being wasted.

'Well, that's what I thought,' Tina agreed, 'At first. Until we saw it was bleeding.'

'Bleeding?' McCall's face twisted with disgust as she spoke.

'Yeah, two fishermen this morning tagged it by accident, and they said they saw blood in the water.'

They were interrupted by shouts from below. 'We are ready here, you ready up there?' 'Yes, OK, cutting now.'

The CSU carefully sawed through the rope holding whatever was hanging over the side, and another crew below in a patrol boat caught it. Tina hurried ahead while McCall and the others made their way to the other side where the boat was about to dock, so they could see what all the fuss was about.

As they got to the dock, they noticed a crowd of people in blue overalls with CSU lettering on the back of their uniforms. Some were taking photos documenting the scene, others just acting as a barricade against prying eyes.

McCall and the other three drew near the scene to find Tina was bending over something; around three feet long, it was wrapped in what appeared to be brown-stained bandages. The ME cut the fastenings open carefully, using a scalpel from her medical bag. As it fell open, the audience standing behind her spontaneously reeled away, holding their mouths.

The open sack contained the remains of what used to be a woman; both her arms and legs had been removed, but unlike the other bodies there were small amounts of blood visible that had found their way to the bottom of the cocoon. Taking out a small white device that looked almost like a pregnancy testing kit, Tina dabbed some of the blood on to it and waited. She searched the body and sack for any evidence that may have been left behind, but she knew there would be nothing. She was only too aware that the killer was too smart to leave anything incriminating, unless he put something there to deliberately mislead them. The CSU team recommenced collecting their photographic evidence, but would have to wait until they took the remains back to headquarters before they could look for fibres and fingerprints.

Tina examined the corpse painstakingly for physical indications, but came up empty, working from the base of the torso and slowly moving up the body until finally reaching the head. Carefully, she opened the woman's mouth, noting that everything seemed normal. Then she opened an eyelid to check for any petechiae or other unusual signs.

'Uh, guys, we have a new problem,' said Tina, sounding uncomfortable.

'Why, what's up, Doc?' asked the captain, bracing himself against the sight and cracking his regular joke. Actually, he was trying to hold onto his breakfast.

'Her eyes are gone.'

'What do you mean, gone?' replied Tooms, horrified at the thought. 'I mean gone. Missing. No longer present. Gone.' Tina stood up and waved the two orderlies to bag the body and take it downtown.

The atmosphere was tense, with the captain looking as if he were about to explode.

'OK, people, I have had enough of this dirtbag taking our city apart. We are going to find this son-of-a-bitch.' He clenched his fist and shook it at them, more as a gesture of anger and promise than a threat.

'Call in all shifts,' he announced angrily. 'We work around the clock if we have to, but I want this guy.'

The teams in front of him were New York City's finest, and if anyone could get the killer, it would be these men and women. McCall knew it and felt the surge of energy radiating from the captain in those few words, words that inspired everyone to believe that they could do the impossible.

From behind them came a voice that broke the silence, like a soft breeze on a still morning. It was gently spoken but contained an edge of steel:

'Maybe I can help.'

The group turned as one, to see a man dressed all in black. He was perched on the backrest of a bench, his shiny black boots resting on the seat, glinted in the morning sun, and the long black jacket he wore had fallen behind the backrest and was flapping in the breeze.

'Who the hell are you?' asked the captain, shocked not just by the arrogance of the suggestion that they required help, but wondering how the hell this guy had gotten past the uniforms into the crime scene, and when?

'You have got to be kidding me.' McCall's jaw hung slack at the sight of the man who had caused her so much trouble and kept eluding her. Now he was finally within her grasp but why was he coming forward? And why at this moment? But right then, the only question she had, and it was a simple one, was not 'Who are you?' or 'What are you doing here?' No. The question she wanted to ask was much less complicated. It was, 'Can I shoot him, Captain?'

THIRTEEN

Tina Franks was busy checking over what remained of the female from Pier 15. She scanned the remains meticulously, inch by inch, taking photographs of any distinguishing marks such as bruises and scars. In the background, music played softly from her MP3 that rested on top of the stereo; its blue lights broke up the sterile whiteness of the morgue.

McCall entered, her footsteps sounding loud and aggressive as they echoed off the tiled surfaces. Her expression could have frozen the very depths of hell.

'Hi, what else have we got, Tina?' asked McCall, trying not to think about the events on the pier, and the details of their ghoulish discovery.

'Well, I have got a Caucasian female with a lot of bits missing. What I'm far more interested in, is your white knight in black armour who's put in a public appearance for the first time. I gather he went off with the Cap.' Tina gave McCall a sly look that said, *more information please.*

'Oh, really,' she replied, 'and what else did you hear?' 'I heard he was British and kind of cute.'

McCall's glare stiffened. She was asking herself the same

questions she was sure Tina wanted answers to. Why was he here? Was he following her? It was strange that he always showed up just in the nick of time… but she shook off the temptation to get drawn into theorising. The mystery guy would have to wait – the case came first.

'Are there any similarities with the two other killings?' McCall was desperate for a clue. The killer was good, but in her experience, the more victims a serial killer claimed, the more comfortable they got, and the more likely it was they would eventually mess up. As a kid, she read loads of books by Agatha Christie to try to solve them before the detective. She often did, and she remembered it was always the second or third killing that gave her the clues to work out the plot, never the first.

Tina stopped what she was doing and took off her slightly scratched eye protectors. 'Well, what we have is a killer who, for some reason, drains all of his victims' blood, and removes not just body parts but *whole chunks* of body parts.' She walked between the tables on which lay the remains of the first two victims. 'What I don't get is the kind of parts that have been removed. Most of the 'trophies crew' take a finger or an ear. This is way too extreme.'

'Maybe he's fussy about what he eats.' McCall grinned, trying to lighten the mood with some gallows humour, but she couldn't shift the look of worry on the pretty ME's face.

'This guy knows how to use a scalpel,' Tina pointed out. 'So we're possibly looking for some kind of surgeon.'

McCall looked puzzled. 'What makes you say surgeon rather than just psycho?' She moved closer to the most recent corpse, unable to resist her curiosity.

Tina pointed at the right lower abdomen. 'If you look here, where he has cut the skin. You can see the incision that was made is straight and even, not jagged and ripped. No, this guy took his time, and by the look of the others I would say that this surgery was done with respect rather than out of brutality.' Tina shrugged. 'In my judgement, the person who did this, did it for a reason. It wasn't so much about the kill itself, like we see so many times. No, the parts he took *meant* something to him because of the way they were removed. And the tests have shown on our last victim, the blood wasn't even hers – it was cattle blood, which he presumably got from a butcher's. I suppose it was added maybe because he wanted the body to be found more easily. I have no idea why he is draining them.' Tina shook her head in disbelief.

McCall was at her desk when Tooms and Tony returned from interviewing the boss at the law firm where the first victim had worked. They strolled in, Tooms taking the spare chair at McCall's desk and flipping open his notepad as Tony crashed into his own seat, where he picked up his phone and started to dial.

'Please tell me you got something useful?' she asked her sweating colleagues, who had obviously been busy.

'Well, we scored,' Tooms told her. 'We got the place of work and a name, Miss Karen Lane, aged thirty-nine, and a partner in the firm. She had an apartment on the East Side, we are going to check it out once we get a warrant.'

McCall nodded, grateful that, at last, they had a lead of some sort. 'Do we know who may have seen her last?' She was hoping to establish a time frame.

'Yeah, we got a Karl Buntee, he is the janitor there, and he reckons he saw her in the parking garage at around three on Friday morning.' 'Why was she working that late at night?' McCall asked suspiciously.

'Well, it turns out they had a big meeting the following day, all to do with some high-profile case. It seems she had to get the briefs typed up in time for that.'

'OK, so we have a time frame for vic number one,' McCall said, getting up and writing the numbers on another board, this one for time frames; she drew a line from 03:00

hours until the end of the mark that covered Monday when the body was found.

'So what have we got?' McCall said, perched on her desk. 'Vic One, Karen Lane, went missing early Friday morning and was found early Monday, so on that basis, I guess we can presume he only keeps them for a few days.'

The other two joined her at the time-frame board and stared at the puzzle, hoping something would reveal itself.

'Vic Two was found in the park the following Thursday, so if he is holding to his timeline she could have been taken on the Monday. That's in theory, but until we find out who she is, it's only speculation. Same with vic number three.' McCall looked puzzled. 'What I can't get is, the others were posed but Vic Three was hung off a pier. It doesn't make sense.' She thought for a moment, and then added, 'Aw shoot, none of it makes sense. Yet.'

McCall stood and picked up her coffee mug. She needed caffeine and was hoping that a strong coffee would blow away some cobwebs. She went into the break room, followed by Tooms and Tony. The smell of brewing coffee hit them with an awakening jolt; lifting the glass jug, she poured herself a cup then offered the jug to the others, who placed their mugs on the counter next to hers for her to fill before placing the half-full jug back into the coffee machine.

'I don't get it; there is nothing we know that connects these women yet.' she began. 'We need to find out who the other two were, or this isn't going anywhere.'

The others agreed, and they sipped their hot drinks in silence for a moment before drifting thoughtfully back to their desks. As they turned the corner they saw, standing in front of the board with his back to them, the mysterious stranger whom McCall had last seen at the crime scene. His hands were clasped behind his back. Even as he studied the board, he was obviously aware he was being watched.

'Nice board,' he said, without moving. His voice was unmistakably British.

'Can I help you?' Sam McCall asked, acidly. Her voice almost growled with disapproval at the mere sight of him, let alone the idea of his staring at her information boards.

'Simple but effective,' he continued, but this time he turned slightly just to acknowledge she was there.

'But?' she prodded him to continue, almost as if she were waiting for some 'British' sarcastic remark, which never came.

'No really, I like your boards, that's all. I'm sorry if I appear to have upset your system in any way.' With that, he moved away from the displays as if he were trying to be conciliatory.

'Thanks,' she muttered, her tone somewhat hollow, unsure how she should react to him.

She grabbed her cup and headed for the break room to get a coffee, forgetting she already had one. She felt that she just had to get away. However, he trailed after her, like a lost child on his first day at school.

'Are you following me?' she growled, eyes blazing.

'Coffee,' he replied, holding up the coffee-filled jug.

'What?' Her expression went from anger to bewilderment in a second.

'I said, do you want a coffee?'

McCall stood like a deer in headlights, then remembered the full cup at her desk and snapped, 'No,' leaving him in the break room to make himself a drink. The other two detectives, somewhat bemused by this whole display, just sat back and watched this strange dance with no small pleasure and amusement.

McCall was busy typing data into the computer and had failed to notice the British guy standing beside the empty chair next to her desk; he coughed politely to attract her attention and she glanced out of the corner of her eye to see him hovering.

'What now?' Her tone was one of weariness and irritation.

'May I?' He indicated the battered looking chair. Its brown coloured fabric lay loose on the cushioning, yet it looked comfortable, somehow homely. She raised a hand as if to say 'whatever,' but continued to look at the screen in front of her.

Taking a sip of the brown liquid, his face crumpled in disgust as his taste buds were assaulted by the foulest coffee he'd tasted in years. 'What's the matter, coffee too much for you?' she said with a grin, taking a swig from her own cup, trying to ignore the vile taste in her own mouth. 'I thought a big, strong boy like you could handle something as common as coffee,' she smiled again.

Even though she was laughing at him, he couldn't resist enjoying this tiny chink in her armour.

'This is coffee? It's more like ground coal.' He stopped and then, out of the blue, he observed, 'You know, you have a nice smile, you should use it more often, it suits you.'

She stopped and looked away, embarrassed she had let her guard down.

He stared at the board until his eyes blurred and his head ached, but could not make any sense or connection. Hell, these cops did not even know who the other victims were, so any link at this point was almost impossible. He scanned the photos and the timeline associated with the first victim, but still, after the best part of an hour, nothing had come to him. He gave up, and removed his sunglasses and rubbed his eyes.

'Would you like more coffee, Detective?' he asked, returning to McCall's desk.

'No, but thanks,' she replied. 'Hey, one thing, when you use a cup you need to check the ones with marks on, they belong to people.' She had pointed it out because she had spotted that he had used a cup belonging to one of the detectives on another shift, and she knew he was very picky. 'Got it, look out for marks,' he said, going into the coffee room. Seconds later he rushed back and started examining the photos again. 'It can't be – can it?' He spoke softly, as if nobody else was present, then shot off towards the elevator.

'What's the matter, coffee get to you?' she called after him. 'No, the marks did,' he said, as the elevator door opened.

McCall stared across at Tony and Tooms, who were just as confused as she was. Tony made a crazy person gesture with his index finger, and seconds later they all jumped up and followed him, in case they'd missed something that he had picked up on.

Downtown in the morgue, Tina was in the back room checking some files. It had been a long day, and she yearned for the weekend to begin because she and some of her girl-friends were planning to go to a new club they were all excited to try. She started to dance to a little tune that she had found on her MP3 player, and the mood took her over, so she continued to boogie straight into the operating room where she saw a tall man, dressed in black, leaning over one of the bodies. The dancing urge immediately left her, and she resumed her professional demeanour.

'Hey, excuse me, can I help you?' Tina's voice was calm and steady, despite the sudden shock of seeing this unexpected stranger.

'I'm sorry, Doctor, I'm with Detective McCall upstairs, and I noticed something. It may be nothing, you see—' he was cut off in mid-sentence.

'It's OK, Tina, he appears to be with me, I'm almost sure he's on our side,' McCall explained, as she followed him into the room, trailed by Tooms and Tony.

Tina nodded towards the stranger and grinned at her friend. So this was Sam's knight in black armour, up close and personal. She grinned at her friend. McCall rolled her eyes at Tina in disapproval, but Tina made a 'no problem' signal with her fingers.

'OK, British guy, what's up?' McCall felt she had to sound as if she wasn't impressed, but deep down she hoped he'd found something, anything. 'You said something about marks, what marks?' she asked.

'There were no marks on any of the bodies, apart from those he made himself,' the ME growled, furious at the accusation she had missed something.

'What I mean is, all the areas of the body he left behind, had some sort of mark or fault,' the strange Englishman said. 'Vic One had a tattoo on her back – that's why he only took the front part of her body. Vic Two had scars on one leg and one arm, also she had piercings and, well, Vic Three was pretty clean so—'

'—That's why the most was taken from her,' Tina finished the sentence, catching on to his theory.

'What, you mean our guy is seeking out women for body parts? To do what?' McCall's patience was thin, and this guy was stretching it to the limit.

'Look, you said you could help,' she continued. 'But, frankly, if all your ideas are as half-assed as this, we are better off without you. I'm sorry.' And with that she stormed out, not because the idea was wrong, no. It was more maddening than that.

What *really* annoyed her was the possibility that he could be right and she had failed to see what he had.

The tall man walked up to Tina and took her right hand. 'I'm very sorry for the intrusion, Madam,' and, so saying, he gently raised her knuckles close to his lips. He delicately kissed the air just above her hand, so that she barely felt the touch of his warm breath. And then he left. Tina grabbed for the side of the table as her knees wobbled. All she could say to herself was *Wow*!

As he got out of the elevator, he was struck by the chaos of the office at work for the first time. Phones were ringing, computers flashed with information, and detectives were running here and there with documents grasped tightly in their hands. He stepped off and looked around to find Sam

McCall attacking a vending machine. Tooms and Tony were going through paperwork and arguing about what should go in a filing system, while the captain was at McCall's desk, yelling down the phone at some poor son-of-a-bitch about press at the crime scene. A smile crept over his face, as he nodded to himself reassuringly, approving the decision he had made. If he wanted Sam McCall to work with him, she would need some guarantee that he was a pair of safe hands. He just hoped the information he could provide would be assurance enough.

The stranger walked determinedly up to the captain and whispered into his ear, and the other man snapped to attention. He murmured something in return and beckoned the others to follow him into a small briefing room. The tall Englishman was already waiting there, and as they came in, he beckoned to them to sit down. Shutting the door, he moved to the centre of a wall on which there was a large map of the city.

He paused to take stock of the situation and held his two pressed-together index fingers against his lips, as if planning what he was about to say. 'My name is John Steel,' he began. 'And for the present, I have been assigned to your department to assist with these homicides. Much as I might wish to, I cannot disclose any more information than that at this time, neither my own position nor who assigned me. I understand that my presence may cause some issues with everyone's working relationships, however, details regarding my assignment are classified information. Thank you for your time.'

He waited for some comeback, perhaps even a snide comment or remark, but there was nothing. Everyone just left the room as though nothing had happened, they just nodded in acknowledgement, leaving behind a somewhat puzzled Englishman.

Steel walked over to McCall's desk with a sheepish look on his face that turned into a smile.

'Look, I'm sorry. We got off on the wrong foot, but—'

She cut him off in mid-sentence by raising a hand. She shuffled through some paperwork, searching for something, then stood and walked towards the information boards.

'He isn't done yet, is he?' She looked at him with saddened eyes.

John Steel shook his head, 'No, he's not finished. But we will catch this guy,' he said, turning back to the board. 'We have to.'

This left her with an even more puzzled look on her face. This time it was over the mystery man Steel. Who was he and what was his connection with the killer?

FOURTEEN

D r Colby Davidson sat in his black leather office chair, jotting down notes as his patient rambled on about how life was meaningless without her little Candy. The elderly woman was clutching a photo of her dearly departed Chihuahua in one hand and a pink, diamond-studded collar in the other. The doctor, sitting across the desk, was in his early forties, and really didn't get toy dogs. He listened patiently to what she was saying, appearing to be interested, touching her hand to comfort her, while being astounded that the dog's grand funeral had cost more than he had paid for his Mercedes. He was a tall, thin man with black, greased-back hair, and he peered over small half-moon glasses that obscured his large dark eyes. He did not need those spectacles, no, they were plain glass and he wore them to give himself an air of wisdom. His face was long, and a large Roman nose supported the unnecessary spectacles.

'Please go on, Mrs Burnett.' His voice was soft and sickly, like honey. He crossed one leg over the other, resting a three-thousand-dollar shoe on the knee of an eight-thousand-dollar trouser leg.

He smelt of money and so he should. For he was, in fact,

one of the best-paid psychiatrists in New York, if not the whole country, and his clothes and the furnishings in his office spoke volumes about the man. How had it come to this, he thought? How had years of training and hard work led him to a life of putting up with listening to the ramblings of tired old women? He looked towards his 'wall of fame', where trophies and diplomas filled shelves, photos of him shaking hands with famous people, even a President of the United States himself, while further trophies filled a glass-fronted cabinet.

An antique gold-and-black clock chimed in the background, signalling the end of the lady's session. She slowly rose from the leather chaise longue and dried her eyes with the corner of a white embroidered handkerchief.

'Now, Mrs Burnett, we are making progress.' He clasped her gloved hands. 'Don't worry, these things take time, dear lady, so if you speak to Beatrice on your way out, she will make you another appointment.' Mrs Burnett thanked him and left. Shutting the door, he rested his back against the cool oak timber, as he let his head drop back and his weary eyes close, thanking God that the session was over.

With a heavy sigh he moved to the drinks trolley next to a large dark wood cabinet, and could not help but think: *Is this it? Is it all over? Is there nothing left to challenge this brilliant mind?* Shaking his head, he poured himself a large Islay malt whisky and downed it in one. He refilled the glass.

The doctor sank into his heavy-looking office chair and turned to look out of the huge windows, which revealed a magnificent view of the park. He took a sip this time, sighing as he watched the people walking carelessly in the midday sun, then he smiled just for a moment until the intercom broke his concentration.

'Sorry to disturb you, Doctor. But you have the police on line one.' 'Thank you, put them through, Miss Kindle.' He was confused. Police? What on earth could they want? He had done nothing wrong.

He picked up the receiver gingerly and placed it slowly to his ear. 'Hello, this is Doctor Davidson, how may I be of assistance?' His voice was slow and tentative, but still ringing with his usual treacle tones.

'Yes, hello, Doctor. This is Captain Alan Brant of the New York Police Department. I wondered if you would be so kind as to come down to the station, sir. We could really use someone of your expertise to help with a case we're working on.'

Davidson's face cracked an eerie smile. 'I would be delighted to help you with your little case, officer.' He preened himself, arrogantly wallowing in this sudden recognition.

'Um yes, thank you, and that's captain, not officer,' was the brusque reply.

Davidson was suddenly taken aback by the policeman's correction. *He must think a lot of himself*, thought the doctor, admiring himself in the reflection from the window. *Almost as much as I do.* 'Yes, yes, whatever you say.' They agreed on a time. 'Till then,' he said, and put down the receiver before the captain could reply.

He sprang up, out of his chair and strode to the door. Swinging open the heavy panel, he stuck his head around the corner to see his secretary, a pretty young thing dressed in a short black skirt, topped with a frilly white blouse, an outfit that left little to the imagination. 'Oh, Beatrice?' She looked up with a start, as the fringe of her long red hair fell over her blue eyes. 'Yes, Doctor?' Her voice was slightly immature, still betraying the tone of the teenager she had been till recently. 'Listen, I will not be available as of tomorrow. The police have asked for my help with a case, I'm afraid, so could you cancel my appointments for the rest of the week? Thank you.' He studied her from head to toe. *Yes*, he thought, *very easy on the eye*, and as an added bonus, she could type accurately and fast. She was worth every penny he was paying her.

'We're not in trouble, I hope, Doc,' she joked, the gum in her mouth clinging between the upper and lower molars.

'No, no, nothing like that, don't worry your little head about it. Sometimes they need the assistance of a great psychiatrist, and this is one such occasion.'

He was back in his office. *At last*, he thought, newspapers, press; he would be back up there again.

The caretaker, a friendly, plump woman with large brown-rimmed glasses, had let Tooms and Tony into Karen's apartment. The place was large and airy with windows everywhere. The white-painted walls enhanced the natural light in the sitting area, and as they looked around, they noted the open-plan arrangement, with a kitchen next to the living space, with only a breakfast bar to separate the two. As they went through Karen's belongings, it became apparent to them that she had little social life: pretty much everything she owned appeared to be work-orientated.

Tony went through her fridge while Tooms checked her mail; they both came up empty.

'This girl was super clean, I mean the fridge is laid out in some sort of order, even her cupboards are labelled to show where stuff should go. Nah, this is freaky, bro,' said Tooms, shutting the fridge and joining Tony in the sitting area.

'Why is it whenever we come to a victim's home we try and find some dirty secrets in their life or something to try to make sense and explain the bad things that happened to them?' Tony said, going through her sock drawer. He found nothing.

'Human nature, bro,' Tooms replied. 'We can't accept bad things happen to good people; there is no justice in it. But if bad things happen to bad people, well that's fair. Unfortunately, we know that ain't always the way it works and it sucks.'

'Yeah, I guess you're right. I got nothing, just her diary and planner, let's get back.'

The two friends left for the precinct, leaving CSU to check for any more evidence about the woman. Charlene Walters had had a long day at the club, where the wives' meeting had gone on forever. The society ladies' meeting only convened once a month and it was a welcome chance for her to get out of the house for a bit. She had mingled, but it was time to go, so she said her farewells and made for the door.

The grey suit she wore clung to her body. Even though she was in her late fifties, she still maintained the body of a hot forty-year-old, so everyone told her.

A young twenty-something guy brought her car around; she observed him approvingly as he got out and held the door of the Mercedes SLK for her, then she slid into the driver's seat of the sports car, pressed a hundred into his hand, and winked. He shut the door, and she sped off into the distance. As he opened the folded note, her business card fell out, and he picked it up and stuck it into his vest pocket with a grin.

It was a long drive in traffic from the Hamptons to Manhattan; however, that could not be helped, it was either the drive to the club or stay home all day. And it was a beautiful night; the stars shone like diamonds in the dark of the heavens, shards of light smudged across the windshield as she sped past the streetlights guiding her path towards the city. As she crossed the bridge into Manhattan, she was aware it was not as late as she had thought, and decided to make a little stop-off.

The park house was almost empty, but she still decided to park as she always did, near to an exit or elevator and close to another expensive car, if at all possible; she found the perfect spot next to a black 911. The new Porsche's paintwork glinted in the light as she turned off the ignition and checked her image in the rear-view mirror. Fluffing her short brown hair, she exited the vehicle.

Looking around she saw a couple of people here and there, either parking or getting ready to depart. Pressing the small transmitter on her key, the lights flashed, and the horn emitted a *meep, meep* noise to confirm the operation of securing her car. Charlene opened her brown leather bag and dropped the keys in it then, reaching inside, she pulled out a compact and a stick of lipstick. She removed the cover and twisted the lower part of the stick, exposing the deep red lipstick's business end. With her other hand, she flicked open the compact and stared into the mirror. Charlene stopped for a brief moment, staring at her own reflection, but all she saw was a sad, middle-aged woman. A car sped past, shocking her back to reality. She regarded her face once more, then shrugged at the reflection and muttered 'liar.' After freshening up her makeup, she popped the lipstick and compact back into the bag, and closed the flap using the gold-coloured crossed CC buckle. Approaching the elevator and pressing the call button, Charlene watched impatiently as the small round disks above the sliding doors illuminated, showing which floor the elevator was on. The light held a position on the floor below, as her foot tapped restlessly on the hard concrete.

She smiled as the light went out and she could hear the faint rumble of the heavy metal box that was heading upwards through the shaft towards her. While the elevator approached, her bag gave off a faint tune as her phone played the theme from the musical Cats. As she looked down to answer it, the elevator's door slid open, and a bright stream of light shone out. She looked up, shielding her eyes from the blinding torchlight. A mighty hand reached out and dragged her in. As the doors closed and the elevator made its way upwards, a terrified scream filled the shaft, then abruptly it stopped.

'What's up, guys?' McCall asked, distractedly squinting around to see where John Steel had got to.

'Well, as usual, nobody knew her apart from some guy in

4c who said, and I quote: "She was really smoking",' Tooms replied, putting down the notepad he was reading from, his flat tone conveying the lack of surprise brought by years of experience. 'Nobody saw her, despite the fact she lived in a block with over thirty people in it. Apart from that, she was clean living, quiet, and always paid her rent on time.' He put the pad into the pocket of his thick, unyielding brown leather jacket.

'We didn't find pictures of family, kids, or boyfriends, in fact no pictures of anyone, period, not even herself,' Tony added, sitting at his desk as he started to dial a number on the desk's phone.

McCall worked on the whiteboard, which was now covered with photos and notes. She spun the whole thing around, revealing there were now three long black strips, one above the other. Each strip had several vertical lines coming off at the top of the baselines: this was her timeline board for each of the victims.

'McCall, you may need another stripe.' A call came from the door to the captain's office. 'I think we've got us another one.' The captain had a worn tone in his voice; he was tired of not having a single clue or anything to work on. This guy was good, and the knowledge of it was getting to him.

McCall didn't try and find Steel – in fact, she didn't want him around her; yes, fine, he had saved her from Jabba and his gang but she felt that something about him was wrong, and it wasn't just because he was so damn hot. There was something that was not quite right: she couldn't put her finger on it, but he made her nervous.

The detectives made their way to a dirty alleyway near the meat- packing district; the press was all over the area like a rash. Reporters and paparazzi were tripping over each other to get a glimpse or an interview. As she pushed forwards, microphones were thrust into her face as requests were yelled from the press for any information, along with inquiries such as 'was this one connected to the other killings?' She sighed with incredulity at how quickly the media people had got there.

Moving through the hordes of police, she found herself with the ME, Tina, who was kneeling while clutching a clipboard and looking over the remains of what appeared to have been a woman.

'Is it the same guy?' McCall asked her friend, afraid of the answer. 'Well, hi to you too!' Tina snapped at her without turning around. 'Uh, sorry, Tina. Hi. But is it the same guy?' Sam apologised, her expression that of a naughty puppy.

'Well, our vic has had both arms removed, and she has no blood present in her body. Until I get her back to the lab I can't say for sure, although it has all the hallmarks of our boy, but till then…' Tina suddenly looked worried as she noticed something. 'Tell you something, this one's real fresh.'

McCall looked puzzled. 'What do you mean, fresh?'

The ME stood up and called for the waiting orderlies to take the body away. 'The others were at least a couple of days old, but this one still had rigor mortis in the legs.'

A chill went down McCall's spine. 'You figure that he's stepping it up?' Tina nodded.

McCall waited for CSU to do their sweep of the area, taking photos and searching for fibres and prints. Once they were finished, the female detective and her team went in. Tony stopped at the entrance and looked around.

'Where's Steel?' he asked.

The others stopped and looked up and down the street to find no trace of the most recent addition to their team.

'I don't know, and I don't care.' McCall's look was stern; she didn't have time to babysit. If Steel wanted to be there, he would have made an effort.

Tooms stood behind them. 'Screw him, that brother smells like trouble if you ask me,' he voiced his opinion. He was unconcerned about John Steel; the case was his priority. The team made their way into the alleyway, examining it inch by inch, searching for pieces to the puzzle.

Each of them had spent at least an hour scouring through drains, under boxes, anywhere a clue might be hiding. Tony was now doing door-to-door interviews to try and find someone who may have seen anything unusual in the last few hours, but he turned up nothing.

'God, there are times when I really hate this city,' Tony grumbled. 'I can't believe nobody saw anything.'

'Hey, that's New York, man, if it don't concern nobody, no one's interested.' Tooms had had enough, they all had. The case was burning them out, and the sooner it was finished with, the better, but McCall had a bad feeling about this one. This was going to be trouble.

'OK,' she told them. 'We can't do any more here, so let's head back to the precinct and pick it up from there.' The others nodded, and they moved off. *It's going to be a long night*, she thought: great, that was all she needed.

High above them, a figure knelt on the edge of a rooftop, his gaze following them to their vehicles as they made their exit. He stood up, and his coat caught the breeze like some mythical bird, his shape silhouetted by the moon that shone brightly, creating a long shadow on the rooftop. A cloud crept across the sky, briefly blacking out the moon, plunging everything into shadow. In those seconds he was gone as if he'd been carried off by the darkness.

FIFTEEN

The next morning at the station, there was an air of panic as the news of yet another killing spread through the precinct. It wouldn't be long before the newspapers and TV stations had the grim information plastered all over the place: after all, the press had beaten McCall to the scene the night before. There would be hysteria throughout the city, precisely what the captain had been desperate to avoid.

The team searched through missing persons records and took calls from possible witnesses, while also doing their best to fend off the press.

McCall spied Steel heading towards her as he got out of the elevator. She braced herself for the inevitable question of 'Why did you not tell me about the latest one?' He arrived at her desk and sat down without a word. She spoke first, as she saw he was taking a breath in order to start.

'OK,' she said. 'I'm sorry we didn't come and find you, but when it all kicked off, we had to leave quickly, and no one knew where you were.'

'No problem,' he replied, evenly. 'In your position, I would have done exactly the same thing. If I want to be included in every development of this case, I have to be here all the time, and not just when it suits me.'

She stared at him with a look of utter disbelief. Had he just read her mind? Confusion knocked her off balance, as she stumbled through a quick briefing on what little they had found. He just smiled and handed her a coffee he had just bought from a coffee shop nearby.

'Thanks.' Shocked by his kind gesture, she took a sip of the coffee, and a burst of aromatic goodness flushed through her system. *Oh my God, that's heavenly*, she thought, while hoping her expression did not let on.

'So, what have you been up to—?' she stopped herself in mid-sentence, not wanting to go on.

'Do you really want to know or are you just saying that?' he asked.

'Not really.' Her eyes shot back to the paperwork as he smiled to himself.

'Well, you may want to know someone has just filed a missing person's report which may fit your vic's description.'

Her gaze shot up to his face. 'Where? When?' He pointed to Tony, who was approaching quickly with a slip of paper.

'You won't believe what I just got,' the other detective said smugly. 'Oh, I don't know about that,' she said, looking at Steel, who was busy sipping his cappuccino.

The Walters' residence was a penthouse in a massive complex of old stone, wrought-iron railings and plaster mouldings, a monument to bygone days. The view of Central Park was breath-taking, through the large windows of the lounge area. Throughout the place, marble floors glistened with the touch of the mid-morning sun. McCall gazed in awe at the fine furniture everywhere, most of which was probably the same age as the building, if not older. A pretty girl who appeared to be in her late twenties had let them in; her maid's uniform was a short black-and-white dress, the lacy white collar fluffed up around her neck. Her long blonde hair was styled into a bun then crowned with a small white maid's cap.

'Mr Walters, the police are here to see you,' she said, as she ushered them into the large sitting area. Benjamin Walters was seated in an old, heavy-looking Chesterfield armchair, its dark leather encrusted with shining brass studs.

'Please, come in and sit down,' he said, half-rising from his own chair, his pale hands gesturing to the long sofa of the same design. They all sat, and he waved at the girl, asking her to bring them some coffee.

'I'm Detective McCall, and this is Detective Steel,' she began. 'We are here because you reported your wife missing.' Her concern was genuine, fuelled by the very real possibility that the woman could be the next victim.

'Yes, she left for a damned wives' meeting in the Hamptons yesterday and has not been seen since,' Benjamin Walters muttered in a strained voice.

'I phoned the club to see if she could have stayed over, she does sometimes, but they said she left early evening.'

Ignoring him, Steel got up and walked to a marble mantelpiece, which surrounded a spectacular fireplace. He lifted up a silver-framed photograph that showed Mr Walters and a woman looking into each other's eyes. 'This her?' he asked, tersely.

Walters looked confused at first at the question; then he realised why Steel had asked it.

'Oh my God, do you think she's another victim of this killer that's been all over the papers? What will I do now? She was my whole life!' He broke down, sobbing into his hands.

Steel passed the picture to McCall. She looked at it for a moment and then put it down on the glass table in front of her.

The coffee had arrived, and the girl placed the tray on the table between Walters and the detectives. She carefully poured coffee into the antique bone-china cups. It was the kind of valuable chinaware that most people would keep in a glass cabinet, hardly something to be actually used. But what was money to this guy?

'We can't be sure of anything, sir,' McCall said tactfully, 'but we'd be grateful if you could come downtown and identify a body…'

He nodded, with his head in his hands.

'I'm sorry to ask, Mr Walters,' she said gently, 'but where were you around the time your wife went missing?' This was the question she always hated to ask a loved one, but sometimes it hit the right chord.

Walters composed himself and picked up the cup and saucer from the dark wood antique table.

'I was out at my club last night. I was there until midnight. We had a port tasting, so our driver had to bring me back. Is that the sort of time you mean?' He sipped the steaming coffee. The old boy was still sharp. They hadn't told him what time she had disappeared, so if he gave any indication he knew, it was highly suggestive that he had some knowledge as to what had happened.

'And which club would that be, sir?' She took her notebook out, ready to write down any new information.

'The Harvard Club, it's on West 44th.' His hands shook slightly. 'When did you see your wife last?'

'Around midday, just before she set off for her club.'

'And when were you expecting her back?' asked McCall, watching as Steel circled the room, peering at photographs on the walls and shelves. She wondered if he was even paying attention to her questioning, or if he cared whether he was here or not.

'It's hard to say, I never really expect her back when she

has been to the club.' He placed the cup and saucer back on the table. 'You see, it depends on what sort of day she has had.'

McCall looked puzzled, and Steel turned slightly, clearly intrigued by his response.

'How do you mean?' Steel exclaimed, turning back to study a rather colourful Rembrandt on the wall, trying to work out if it was an original or just a really good copy.

'If she has had a good day she will stay until late, sometimes she even stays over. They have rooms there, she tells me, especially for members who live in Manhattan or have had too much to drink to drive back safely. And if she has had a bad day, well, she gives herself some retail therapy and goes shopping on the way home.' A lonely look fell upon his weary face. He was not actually as old as he looked, McCall realised, but it seemed as if something had worn him down, making his features careworn and weary.

'Did she drive herself or was she taken to the club?'

'No, she took her car, a black Mercedes SLK.' His mind shifted, a far away look came into his eyes, and then, with a start, he was back again. 'I bought it for her birthday last year, and I can't get her out of the damn thing. Still, it's better than having an affair with the tennis coach, I suppose.' Bitterness swept over his face, causing the wrinkles in his skin to crease further. 'I will get you a copy of the registration and the other details,' he said, standing slowly. 'Please wait here, I won't be a moment.'

He left the room to go across the long hallway. From what the two detectives could see, he entered a dimly lit room with some sort of maroon velvet wallpaper and heavy-looking oak furnishings. Steel continued to contemplate the paintings and other artworks that were dotted around the large, luxurious room, which felt more as if it was part of a stately pile than a lived-in home.

Walters returned holding a piece of paper in his hand, his

suit shining in the sunlight as he headed towards them. 'I hope this helps.' His words were almost sincere as he spoke them, but Steel picked up on something in his demeanour that suggested he was hiding something. McCall looked at the piece of heavy office paper the older man had handed her and scanned the contents. The paper contained the licence plate and GPS number of the car. Also, her mobile phone number was amongst the details on the list.

'Perfect, Mr Walters, thank you.'

As McCall spoke, Steel turned and gave her a look of disbelief. Was she really buttering him up? He knew that the phone and car would probably be at the bottom of the Hudson. Unless the man was unimaginably naïve, he was being too thorough.

'Just one thing, sir,' asked Steel as they were making for the door. 'If something should... befall your wife, what happens to her money?'

McCall's face dropped in shock, not because Steel had asked such a question, but because he had thought of it, and she had not. And that stung. She flashed him a quick glance of annoyance, which merely seemed to amuse him.

'Sorry, but you do understand, Mr Walters, we have to ask certain questions for the report, it's so we can eliminate you as a suspect.' Her words were sympathetic, which reassured the older man.

'Well, I suppose I do, I... hadn't really thought about it.' His eyes glazed over but he said nothing more.

'Well, if that will be all, Detectives, it seems I have arrangements to make.' He raised his arm as if to beckon them to the front door.

'There needs to be a formal identification, sir,' McCall said.

'Of course, but you've just seen her picture, so there's little doubt, presumably?' he asked them.

'We still need you to come to identify her as soon as you can, sir,' she replied.

He nodded, apparently barely registering her words.

'We will do everything in our power to catch these people, I promise you.' McCall looked him in the eyes as she spoke, her face deadly serious. Steel thought it made her seem even more attractive.

Mr Walters thanked them as they left, closing the heavy door behind them; McCall took out her phone and pressed the contact number for Tooms.

'Well, we just left the husband, he seems genuine enough, where are we at on the car?' she said to him.

'Nothing yet but her credit cards haven't been used, so it's not robbery unless they're waiting until things cool down.' Tooms was sitting at his desk, hitting keys on the computer keypad, bringing lists of information onto his screen.

'This may help,' McCall told him. 'We are looking for a black Mercedes SLK, plate number is Yankee, November, one, four, two, one, and her cell is 555 12 412.'

Tooms read it back to her, so they both knew the information had been passed on correctly.

'So where are you guys are heading now?' Tooms asked, his phone tucked between his broad shoulder and large head while feeding the information into the computer.

'Well, Sherlock, where to next?' McCall asked the Englishman beside her, purposely trying to insult him.

'I would say a trip to the Hamptons, to this mysterious club, wouldn't you agree, Watson?' he threw right back at her, wiping the wide grin off her face.

'We are off to the Hamptons, let us know if you find anything, will you?' She hung up and scowled at Steel, making him chuckle to himself.

'You know, you were quite rude in there just then,' she told him. 'I mean, the guy just lost his wife.'

'Are you annoyed with me because I asked the question, or are you annoyed at me because I thought of it?'

She couldn't stand his smug grin. Not because his amusement was irritating, no. It was because he was right.

'Do you know you can be a real asshole?' she said, stomping past him like a grounded teenager. When he was out of view, she gave a little satisfied smile.

SIXTEEN

McCall and Steel spent most of the afternoon at the Hamptons club talking to over-privileged, under-stimulated, middle-aged women. The club itself was a large building of sandstone and glass, a testimony to nineteenth-century architecture. The place was swarming with brashly dressed women whose only lot in life appeared to be to drink and talk trash about one another. The interviews were endless and pointless, due to the fact that nobody actually knew anything, though the self-satisfied matrons all thought they knew everything.

McCall rolled her eyes as the last of the egotistical women got up and left, and she spotted Steel outside, leaning on a stone balcony, surveying the view of lush green fields spread out before them. He was lounging against the worn sandstone wall, his black suit and sunglasses blending in well with their surroundings.

'Well, that was the last of them,' he muttered. 'God, what a waste of a day.' He turned and looked at her as she joined him, propping herself against the wall, smiled, and turned back to admire the view.

'It's so beautiful here, so quiet,' she commented.

He nodded in agreement. 'Pity it's wasted on them, though.' He looked back at the gaggle of women parading themselves like flocks of flamingos. She laughed and, as they took a final look at the tranquil sight, McCall sighed deeply. 'OK, let's go back.' He clearly didn't want to, but there was a case to solve, and it would not solve itself.

McCall had received a text that the Mercedes SLK had been discovered in the garage and that CSU were all over it, searching for prints and fibres. Tony was checking the security cameras for any shots of that evening. McCall and Steel pulled up in her Mustang, running the gauntlet of the press, who were out snapping photos and virtually trampling each other every time a person they considered worth interviewing came close.

McCall headed for the tape at the far side, hoping to make it without the hordes of media noticing, but she failed. One of the press hounds spotted her and dashed in her direction, causing the others to follow like sheep in pursuit. She glanced behind her, but Steel was nowhere to be seen until she got to the vic's car. She stopped, startled for a moment, as he miraculously reappeared next to one of the CSU team members who was busy dusting the passenger side.

'Seriously, how did you get here?' McCall stood there, her arms stretched out in a sign of wonderment and disbelief, but she wasn't as surprised as the guard next to the vehicle.

'Hey, how the fu—' the officer demanded, pushing his chest out to make himself look more intimidating as he headed for Steel, only to be greeted by the detective's badge held up in his face.

'Oh, sorry, sir, I didn't recognise you,' he stuttered, apologetically. Steel put the badge away. His attention had not deviated one iota from the CSU tech, who was now lifting the powdery cast, using a special clear tape. The technician folded the two halves of tape, sealed the evidence in a bag, then labelled it.

'Nice catch,' Steel murmured to the man, and the CSU nodded in reply. 'Just hope we get something from them.' Steel said, patting the tech on the back.

Tony and Tooms were supervising the examination of the car, so McCall dropped Steel at the precinct because she had someone to see. She walked the length of the well-lit corridor of the morgue; the white-tiled walls throughout enhanced the brightness of the 'cutting room' as some of the MEs liked to call it. She could make out soft music in the background, and the smell of fresh coffee tingled at her nose.

On entering the room, McCall was taken aback to find John Steel already handing Tina a paper cup of coffee. 'What the hell is going on?' McCall was mad, so mad that she felt the veins at the side of her head throb.

'He brought me a Starbucks. You never bring me coffee, girl, it's not like it would kill you once in a while.' Tina gave her friend a stern look, then broke into a smile to lighten the mood.

'No, what I mean is,' McCall stumbled on. 'Oh, never mind.' She had lost momentum and her chance to give him another friendly scolding. 'Steel, you told me you had to check something.' McCall took the coffee that Steel offered up in his other hand. 'You never said it was here… or - with her…'

'What? Oh, yes, right, I had to see Tina - if I may be so bold…?' he said politely, turning to the ME with a small bow. Tina blushed and slapped him playfully on the shoulder.

'Well, if everyone has finished flirting…?' Sam McCall was now losing patience with him.

'Oh, well, yes, OK,' Steel looked almost contrite. 'Tina, did you establish yet what blood type Mrs Walters was?' He braced himself for bad news.

'Yes, she was AB negative. Why?'

The English detective looked at McCall, longing for her to make a connection.

'Yes, so what?' McCall was tired of his games.

He sat down at the workspace by the window. 'You don't see? She is a different blood type; the hair is all wrong – our guy prefers blondes. This is a cover-up killing, I'd bet my badge on it.'

McCall thought for a brief second and looked at Tina, who was nodding at her with a sympathetic look on her face.

'OK,' McCall mused. 'So, the husband can't divorce his wife because he'd lose everything, so he kills her.'

'Or he gets someone else to do it,' Steel said, jumping in.

'So now everyone thinks it's the serial killer's doing, and he is home free.' McCall's face lit up with excitement.

They were now facing each other and finishing each other's sentences. 'Oh, that's just so sweet.' They turned to see Tina giving them both a strange, dreamy look.

McCall swivelled around towards the door to see Tooms and Tony standing there.

'Hey, are we interrupting something here?' said Tooms, with the same expression as the doc had used.

'No!' said McCall, emphatically.

'Yes!' Steel said, almost at the same moment, with a big grin on his face.

'Find Mr Walters and bring him in.' McCall said, as she left the room as angrily as she had entered.

McCall and Steel scrutinised Mr Walters as he paced up and down the interrogation room like a caged animal waiting to be put down. They were sitting on the other side of the one-way mirror, watching him sweat. The captain entered the small room to join them.

'You had better be right about this,' he told the female detective. McCall just nodded.

'Alright then, break the son of a bitch. But make it fast, he's probably got a whole quarrel of lawyers headed this way.'

The pair of detectives got up and moved towards the interview room, deciding that if they were to do this, they had to do it as a team.

'Mr Walters, please sit down,' said McCall, as they entered the room.

'Do you know why you are here, sir?'

As Walters took a seat facing them across the table, a confused expression clouded his face, but behind it hid another look: fear.

'Your detectives said something about me killing my wife. But I would never—'

'Why didn't you ask us how your wife died?' Steel spoke from the far corner of the room, behind Mr Walters.

'What?' The older man's face twisted with anger at the absurdity of the question.

'Answer the question please, sir,' McCall jumped in, inwardly impressed at the way the Englishman had knocked Walters off balance.

'I – er – I don't know. I was upset. I had just found out my wife had been—'

'You see, an interesting - a universal - feature of the human psyche is that people desire closure,' Steel continued relentlessly. 'They want to know: did their loved one suffer? Was it quick? You know the sort of thing I mean. And the only people who aren't desperate to know are those who already *do* know all about it.'

Walters turned to where Steel's voice was coming from and was shocked to find him directly behind him, almost breathing down his neck. McCall jumped in, ruthlessly.

'Mr Walters, we know that you have had some gambling problems and we're aware of how much you owed the wrong people, and we believe you thought, if you could get rid of your wife, you could pay your debt and have enough to start over again. How am I doing so far?' She spoke harshly, as she sat down opposite him and leant forwards over the table.

'No, no, it wasn't like that, you have to believe me! Yes, I had a small problem. But I didn't kill my wife.' His hands clenched together so tightly that the knuckles were white.

'OK, so who did kill your wife - and why?' She leant back in her chair, awaiting his next lie.

'Look, the thing is Mr Walters, we've got you. If you tell us who the man you hired is, I can speak to the DA and let him know you cooperated.' Her voice had lost its aggressive edge and had become soft and sympathetic.

'I didn't hire anyone, for God's sakes, I loved my wife! Is she dead because of me? Yes! But I didn't kill her!' He was angry and upset. Steel had the feeling that there was more to this story but only Walters could tell it.

Sam McCall continued applying the pressure. 'We have a statement from your bank showing a withdrawal of two-hundred-and-fifty thousand dollars the other day, so don't tell me you didn't hire anyone.'

Walters glared up at her. His eyes were tired, but they burned with righteous indignation. How could she think such a thing of him?

'It wasn't enough, was it?' Steel chipped in. 'They wanted more, didn't they?' Steel came closer, his voice soft and sooth-ing, like a calming breeze.

Walters nodded, looking down at the table on which he'd unthinkingly laid his open wallet, displaying a photo of the couple.

'You don't understand - you see, I have more family and friends. If I talk - they said… they would kill them all. And I'm sorry, for that reason I would rather go to jail than talk.' Walters had pulled himself together and was now sitting upright in the chair.

'Then don't talk.' Steel moved his hand forward over the table and slid a business card out from the wallet in Walters's hand. Steel held up the card in front of Walters's face, and the other man nodded.

'See - you didn't tell us anything,' said Steel, tossing the card at McCall.

Oh great, she thought looking at the card, *the fucking Russians.* They slipped out of the interrogation room, leaving a sobbing Mr

Walters. Tooms and Tony joined them.

'What's our next move?' asked Tony, putting on his jacket.

'We go and catch a show.' McCall passed the card to the two detectives.

'I'll bring the quarters,' said Steel, following McCall to her desk. 'Russians? Are you friggin' kidding me?' barked Tooms. This was all he needed, a stakeout at a Russian strip club. Oh well, he figured it could be worse. He thought: *I mean, what could possibly go wrong?*

SEVENTEEN

The surveillance van was kitted out with a panel of monitors, in addition to a state-of-the-art array of listening and recording devices. Tooms and Tony occupied their usual seats while McCall had the final touches added to her disguise. Bugs and cameras were being hidden- improbably- in the little black number she was almost wearing.

'OK, you're good to go,' said Tony. 'Your transmitter is in the purse so don't lose it.' McCall nodded tightly in response.

'OK where the hell is Super cop?' Tony enquired. 'I thought he engineered this whole thing? Was the thought of coming face-to-face with the big bad Russians too much for him?' They all laughed nervously. But if that really was the reason, Tooms figured, it probably meant Steel was the smart one.

'Shit! Who needs the guy, he would just get in the way anyway,' said McCall, hopefully checking the rooftops as she got out of the van. 'You need us, we are there, got it?' Tooms's face was full of concern, and she knew he had a right to be worried. All of them were wary of this situation.

'Sure, man, wish me luck,' she said into her mic, using it as a communications check.

'You are good to go, girl, we gotcha,' the voice boomed from her ear. She slid a small bottle of whisky from a bag and doused her dress with the cheap booze. She approached the club with a cheap, fake animal skin coat over the top of her little black dress that now reeked of booze. As she got to the doormen, she put on a drunk act. The two large men, dressed all in black, stepped in front of her, barring her way.

'Where do you think you are going?' asked the door attendant, holding her arm.

'I'm going for a little party, party yeah party,' she sang. He held her at arm's length and moved his head away, in case her breath smelled as bad as the rest of her.

'You're not going in like that. You've had too much already,' he said, revolted by the alcohol smell. She moved closer and made as if she was trying to kiss him.

'If you lemme in we can arrange a private party later. Later, mm- hmm later!' She slurred and stumbled slightly. She worried she might have overdone it but the guy seemed to buy it.

'Get the fuck away from me,' he said, pushing her through the doors.

The other men laughed at him as he wiped the stinking saliva from his lips.

'I see you have a date later tonight, Vladimir,' one of them joked.

He just spat and gave them the bird.

'OK boys, I'm in. Let's do this.' McCall muttered under her breath as she wove towards the bar, which ran across the right side of the room. In the centre lay a long stage with mirrored sides, where girls far more scantily clad and much younger than McCall were performing erotic acrobatics on long shiny poles, while others danced in cages, which hung around the dimly lit room. The walls were covered in red patterned wallpaper and the floor covering was made of scuffed wooden tiles. She made a performance of grabbing hold of the backs of chairs to steady herself as she went, squinting in the bright club lights which reflected off the mirrored walls and brass fittings.

McCall sat unsteadily on a bar stool nearest to a wall at one end of the counter. The seat rocked as she perched on it and she pretended to have lost her balance – the bartender quickly grabbed her arm to steady her. She drunkenly thanked him, and he smiled.

'What can I get you, honey?' said the handsome young man in the black silk shirt. He had dark, greased-back hair, and his bulging muscles tried to push their way through his shirt every time he bent his elbow.

'Get a beer,' she slurred. The barman quickly looked away, but not before taking a peek at the cleavage she'd offered over the bar top.

'Sorry, lady, I think that you've had too many already.' He carried on polishing the glasses. 'I tell you what, kid. I get you coffee?' he said, picking up a cup and filling it from the machine behind him.

She thanked him and tried to drink the coffee without gagging. This stuff was so strong you could stand a spoon up in it, no sugar, just the caffeinated equivalent of tarmac. One cup of this, she thought, and any drunk would be sober in no time. McCall put down the cup and spun around so that the camera could get a view of the room, which was dotted with what looked to be businessmen and old army vets. A squirrelly-looking guy sat at a table in one corner, eating peanuts from a bowl and angrily arguing with himself.

'We got anything yet?' she murmured into her purse furtively as she pretended to riffle through it, looking for change.

'No, nothing,' Tooms replied. 'Wait. The guy at the far side of the room, just came in.'

She glanced up to see a group of men in suits gathered

around a heavy, dark man, all shaking hands and greeting one another.

'Is that him, is that the owner?' she said softly, but before she could get an answer, a man strode over to her displaying the squared shoulders and set jaw of a mean drunk.

'Who you talking to, bitch? Who sent you? My fucking wife?' The short, stocky man yanked her arm hard enough to spin her seat right around.

'Whoa, buddy, don't touch what you can't afford,' snapped Mc- Call. 'I don't know your goddamn wife.' She turned back to the bartender with what she hoped was a winning wink. 'Me and wives ain't usually the best of friends, ya know what I mean?'

'I saw you talking into something.' The man persisted. 'You wearing a wire? You some kinda PI? Are you?'

'I don't know what you're talking about, buddy. You're full of it,' McCall snarled at him, trying not to throw nervous looks at the guys in the corner, who had stopped their handshakes and backslaps and were outright staring at the little scene playing out before them. McCall turned away from the man and shakily reached for her coffee cup. A hand grabbed her by the shoulder and tried to pull her from her chair but succeeded only in ripping the tatty fur coat from her back, exposing a length of trailing wire.

'I knew it!' he yelled triumphantly, grasping at the wire and holding it up like a prize. 'You're a goddamn PI. You tell that bitch she can—' Those were the last words the stocky man uttered, just before three bullets passed straight through him into the bartender, sending them both flying backwards behind the bar.

Chaos erupted as bullets flew and flashes from weapons lit up the dimness. McCall spotted the group of men disappear through a door in the back wall. She grabbed the mic and yelled into it, past caring who saw, hoping it was still operational.

'Suspects are moving into a back room, request backup and medical, multiple civilian casualties, I'm in pursuit.' She didn't pause for an answer, which she knew would be to stay put and hold on for the cavalry. Every second she waited, the further the bad guys ran.

Keeping low and fast, McCall made it to the door and, weapon ready, cracked it open just enough to see the coast was clear. In one quick movement she slid through the opening and found herself in a narrow passageway. It was dark and silent, the worst possible combination for her, but unless she went back the way she'd come, there was little choice but to push on. Holding her weapon up at her shoulder, her arms ached, every muscle in them tensed, ready for action. Despite the adrenaline coursing through her veins, McCall crept forwards slowly and deliberately, keeping her back to the wall, both for protection and in order to present a narrower target as she went. The passage seemed to run between two build- ings, though she could see no sign doors or a way out until she found herself bathed in a green light, terrifying her. Looking up, expecting a sniper's laser sight, McCall exhaled silently as she saw instead a sign reading 'Exit'.

A deafening crash gave her a split-second's warning as a black- haired man suddenly burst through the door beneath the sign, his weapon blazing. McCall dived for cover behind a stack of old crates until she heard the repeated *click, click, click* which she knew signified an empty magazine. Reaching around the edge of the crates while trying to maintain cover, she pointed her weapon at the goon, yelling, 'Drop it!' Instead, the dumb-ass reached for his back up weapon and, without hesitation, McCall put two rounds into him. With a small thud, he dropped to his knees, then his face smashed against the hard floor.

McCall crept out from behind the crates and inched past the heap on the ground, keeping as much distance between them as possible. As she stepped towards the exit, her ankle turned over as the ridiculously high heels she was wearing as part of her undercover outfit, slipped. Barely pausing, she kicked the stupid things off. They might have been appropriate for posing as a drunken club floozie, but they were definitely surplus to requirement in this scenario.

Bracing herself, she inched the door open, keeping as low as possible. Shots rang out and the wood above her head splintered, as automatic fire peppered the door. Blindly returning fire, McCall heard someone cry out, then there was silence. Ducking back behind the door, she peered around the edge and saw what looked like several large, wooden packing boxes; if she could just get across to them that would be a start.

Searching for something she could use to prop open the door, she spied a mop lying on the floor of the passageway. She grabbed it and jammed it across the doorway. Another round of bullets rang through the alleyway, but now that the door was propped open, she had a chance. She sprinted through into the space beyond, skidding behind the wall of boxes like a batter sliding into base as the hail of bullets followed her. But she was safe – for now.

Drawing a breath, McCall assessed her situation. She knew that staying here was not an option. The gangsters were getting away or worse, they were setting her up. *Where's my fucking backup?* She thought, panicked at the idea of facing this danger alone.

McCall took three deep breaths, then decided she was ready. She didn't know what she was ready for, but she was ready for it anyway. Rolling out, she was expecting a rain of red-hot, copper-coated death, but there was nothing: the loading-yard she found herself in was empty. The detective got to her stockinged feet slowly and moved from shadow to shadow, towards where she had noticed a door swing slowly shut. Giving a wide berth to a dead goon who lay slumped on the ground, she realised that some of her shots had hit home and she felt a little easier.

'OK, Sam, you got this,' She assured herself. She eased the door open slowly and edged her way through. Inside was dark with only faint shards of light to help her eyes adjust, and as she moved around she brushed against several objects that seemed to run from floor to ceiling. Running a hand over one, it felt coarse, reminding her of the climbing ropes they had in the gym in high school. Where the hell was she? Moving softly and slowly, her path was crossed by what felt like fabric: heavy, dusty fabric. Using her fingertips, she followed it along until she found a gap in the material and chanced a look. The sight froze her with fear. She was in an old theatre, and she had the sense she was probably massively outnumbered, the auditorium, wings and rigs offering multiple vantage points for an ambush. She decided that the best course of action was to retreat and regroup, if that were possible for one person to do on their own.

Silently retracing her steps to the door, she tugged at the fire handle, only to discover it was now somehow jammed or locked.

You have got to be kidding me, she thought.

Her heart sank. The only way out was through the stage door and, due to the large, tiered auditorium, it looked to be a perfect shooting gallery. Reluctantly admitting to herself she had little choice, McCall moved slowly, avoiding every shaft of light that could give away her position. Out of the gloom, before her loomed a guard. He was of average height and build, and, more importantly, his back was towards her. Creeping up behind him, she held her pistol by the top slide and used the butt of the weapon to knock him out. As he fell, she caught him in her arms so as to avoid any noise, which almost certainly would draw attention to her. Dragging him off into the dark, she smiled.

One down, lots more to go.

Her purse was gone, dropped unnoticed somewhere along the way, meaning she had two ammunition magazines fewer, leaving only the one in the magazine housing. *Find somewhere to try and get a view-point,* she thought, calculating that her best chance was to find these bastards and take them out, one by one.

Creeping along the side of the curtain, she found herself in the wings, where some large prop barrels and crates had been left, with a few stage trees made from cut-out wooden boarding. There were not many but just enough to provide cover. Sliding behind a load of old barrels and heavy-looking, false turn-of-the-century chests, she sat for a moment gathering her thoughts, concocting a plan. *Damn it, where the hell is Steel?* was the thought that came unexpectedly into her head. Of all the times he just popped up when he wasn't wanted, why in hell couldn't the bastard ever be there when he's actually needed?

In the blackness, he stood alone. Stan was a new boy on the circuit, there was no denying that fact, but he had potential and was very keen, that's why they had taken him on. If they hadn't, his crew would have kicked him to the curb a long time ago. Sure, he didn't really have a Russian background as such, just some long-lost grandparent who was later sent to Siberia after the revolt, but that was enough to get him in. After all, family is family. He was tall and athletic looking, his physique that of a wrestler. To fit in with his comrades he wore his brown hair greased back, and a new blue nylon tracksuit, which made an annoying rustling sound whenever he moved but the others all wore such outfits, so he guessed he'd learn to live with it.

He gripped the MP5 tightly, the touch of the metal and plastic felt good in his hands. He felt the power emanating from it, and he felt invincible. His orders were simple: don't let the cop leave but don't kill her. No, Samuel was going to have that honour himself, and he would make her bleed first. His grin turned sour at the thought of that lady they had brought in days before. Her screams still rang in his ears; he could not believe what they had done to her. But that was the way it was; you had to do such things so people would respect you. His grip tightened, and he felt the gun's power once again.

Nothing would get past him. He was invisible, indestructible. Swaggering, he began to act out a scene, jabbing his weapon as if approaching some invisible target.

'Oh, you think you can get past me do you, ay?' He stabbed the air with the machine gun, to simulate firing at some imaginary foe. Yes, he was the man.

Behind him, a dark shape slithered down a rope that had been tied off at the base. The Shadow's descent was slow and easy, taking its time, until it silently stood directly behind the gunman Stan, who was now daringly fighting off whole hordes of cops in his imagination. Unseen, a pair of outstretched arms reached closer until, abruptly, one cupped his nose and mouth while the other applied pressure to his neck. Stan fell silent, and with immense control, the Shadow brought him down and dragged his unconscious body into a dim corner. Looking around for a brief moment, his attention was drawn upwards and he faded back into the darkness.

Ed looked down from the lighting walkway. The large wooden gantry was old but still held his weight. He contemplated how brilliant he had been to think of coming up here; from his lookout post he had a full view of every part of the stage and seating area; nobody would get past him, certainly not that woman cop. He was a short man, but stocky, with tattoos that covered his arms, and a shaven head that reflected the small specs of light that had dared to creep into the hall.

He had tried to join the army but had failed his psychological examination. 'Too fond of killing, a danger to all around him', was their conclusion. *Damn doctors, what did they know?* scowled Ed. So he got in with the Russians, they seemed to like his lust for the job. Even at twenty-five years old, he had done some questionable things for them, but he regarded his actions as thrilling.

Peering down, he saw nothing. Wherever the woman cop was hiding, they would find her eventually. He'd been there when Samuel made the phone call to Vik, telling him to lock the doors from outside so the cop would be trapped and easy to hunt down. He smiled at the thought of what he would be able to do to her; maybe he would film his actions and send the recording to the cops. He chuckled to himself, feeling that this job was too easy. A faint sound in the far corner attracted his attention, and he squinted over to where the creak of wood had come from, but saw nothing. Staring closer into the darkness, hoping to see something he could shoot at, turned out to be Ed's final act, before he felt a pinch on his neck and the sensation of falling, and then nothing.

Down below, 'Boris the Bruiser' walked his patrol, shotgun in hand as he paced the small space at the far end of the backstage area. He was a massive hulk of a man who, on first impression, seemed to have no neck, just a head balanced on his shoulders, yet for all his enormous size, he moved quietly. The automatic 12-gauge weapon looked like a child's toy in his grasp, but he knew how to use it. The other guys had been stationed here and there throughout the theatre, but his was a strategic post, he figured. Being right next to the exit, if someone was to try to get in or out, they would have to contend with him.

Something in the corner caught his eye. Was someone there? It was not possible; the area was covered top to bottom. He moved in slowly, shotgun at the ready.

Sam McCall hid herself behind the barricade, her back pressed up against the cold wood for comfort.

From the right side of her position, she heard a slight noise: not much of one, but sufficient to attract her attention.

Her hands tightened on the pistol grip; her trigger-finger dug into the cold porcelain of the top slide. She felt her heart start to race as the noise came closer, knowing that she had to be ready and focused.

Boris moved gingerly towards where he thought he had seen something. It may be nothing, he thought, reasoning that this place had not been used in decades. Rats! What if it was rats, he wondered? A shiver ran down his spine at the thought of the beady-eyed rodents, *please don't be rats*, he thought, *I hate rats*. His weapon was now beginning to shake in his hand, as he closed in.

McCall heard another sound to the left of her, and she cautiously dared to sneak a glance. Edging around, she saw nothing. She exhaled and shifted back to her position, her back resting against the security of her hiding place, when she sensed rather than saw someone standing to her right. McCall turned her head slowly; part of her did not want to confront what was there. As her eyes travelled upwards from an enormous pair of feet, her mouth dropped open on finding herself faced with a massive, bald-headed man. Her breath left her body as he reached down and picked her up as though she was a rag doll, pulling her close to his face. He breathed in her fear, and she glimpsed badly fitting teeth as he gave her a wicked grin.

'I'm a police officer, and you need to let me go!' she yelled.

He found her mixture of fear and attempt at intimidating him very attractive.

'Hello, little kitten,' he said, in a deep voice that echoed round the large space, and licked his lips. 'The boss has a surprise for you, I hope you like surprises?'

She shuddered at the thought of what he meant, but then her eyes widened. Her captor frowned in confusion, registering that his little toy was no longer looking at him but behind him. Was someone there? He turned to look, and a wave of fear washed over him.

Samuel went to great lengths to ensure he looked the part as the boss. Tall, muscular, and well-dressed, his long, white hair rested on his shoulders. He was Russian through and through, and after the Berlin wall came down at the end of the 80s, he knew that it was time for change, so he came to America to exploit the enemy, and business had boomed. He brushed off his blue Italian suit, removing a few tendrils of cobweb that were clinging to it from the stairwell he had come up; his vantage point in the presidential booth created a satisfying feeling of safety and superiority. *Who knows, maybe this was the very booth where Lincoln was killed, how appropriate that would be*, he thought.

From where he stood, he could see everything. A crash from the stage made him grasp his AKM in readiness. Had she been captured? Given up and surrendered? Craning forward over the edge of the stall, he witnessed the bizarre scene below as a massive bulk covered in rats blundered towards the exit, in its grasp the scantily clad woman in black who no longer appeared intoxicated in the slightest. In his despair, the immense form threw his captive aside as he fought to claw the clinging rats from his back and neck. Crashing into a stack of chairs, she rolled and made for cover.

Samuel had little patience for games. Somehow this bitch had evaded or taken out all of his men, and surely the place would be full of cops any minute. No, he decided, he would end her here, and then he would disappear. As he raised the weapon to take aim, some sixth sense made McCall look up directly at him. Staring up at the box, she felt as though time slowed for her to assess the situation. She observed the barrel drifting in her direction. She noted her own weapon at the other side of the gantries – when she was thrown, it must have been knocked from her grasp. She evaluated relative speed and distance. The question was, could she move fast enough to reach the gun and present an impractical target? She had to try, reasoning that, whatever she decided, he was going to shoot her, and if she could take him down as well, it would be some consolation. Samuel took aim, held his breath and began to squeeze the trigger as he saw McCall dive across the stage for her gun. He felt joy, he felt exhilaration, and then he felt something hit him on the back of the head. As he turned, he glimpsed a dark figure spring from the shadows behind him, leap forward and rugby-tackle him, propelling them both over the balcony. As they fell, John Steel ensured that the Russian man was underneath, and would absorb the impact. A cloud of ancient dust rose up as they crashed onto cardboard boxes full of crockery and props. The English detective rolled off his companion, winded from the impact of the fall, even though Samuel had taken the brunt of the damage. 'Cheers, big fella,' Steel said, patting the Russian on the head.

'What the hell was that? Did you use me as bait, you sick son-of-a- bitch?' McCall shouted up from the stage pointing her pistol at Steel, venting both her terror and fury.

'No, no, you don't have to thank me for saving your life, you're welcome, it's fine, and I am not hurt, thanks for asking.'

She stared hard at him, not knowing whether to shoot him or kiss him. Well, she knew what she really wanted to do.

Suddenly the exit door exploded, and a mass of armed police stormed in. Tooms and Tony almost tripped over the bulk of Boris, who had run into the locked door and knocked himself out. John Steel looked across at the broken body of Samuel. 'Just in time, eh, fellas,' he said, still winded from the fall, and then collapsed back on to the floor.

EIGHTEEN

On the blackest of nights, a figure sat in a small room watching a newsflash. The room's diminutive size amplified the TV's volume, and flashes of reflected colour painted the dirty brick walls. The room was empty apart from an old armchair and twelve TV sets stacked in a cube on top of one another as if to make one large one. In the chair, the figure swivelled the remote in his long bony fingers as though it was a baton.

The TV report showed the Russians being led away by police and Samuel Sokolov on a gurney being taken to hospital, while the reporter recounted the torture and murder of the millionaire's wife. With ill-disguised relish in the drama, he further mentioned that the latest slaying had employed the same modus operandi as that of the serial killer of three other women, a killer who currently, the young man emphasised, remained at large.

The crunch of breaking plastic echoed through the room as the viewer crushed the remote in one hand and tossed it into a pile of other broken zappers that lay in the corner.

'So, Mr. Sokolov, you wish to blame me for your sins, do you? Naughty, naughty,' the man cackled, his voice scraping through the air like nails on a chalkboard. 'We shall see, we shall see... Oh, I think the doctor has a patient to examine.' His laughter was low at first, then as it echoed through the building, it escalated into an eerie, nightmarish howl.

Steel returned to his apartment, sore but satisfied. He kept the lights off, preferring to enjoy just the illumination from the city streetlights, seeping through the windows, to break up the darkness. He removed the battered jacket he had used to help create the persona of the twitchy guy in the corner of the bar while he watched over Sam McCall, and hung it on the old-style hat and coat stand which stood at the doorway, then crossed the spacious room to where a well-filled book cabinet stood, and poured himself a drink from the desk next to the large piece of furniture. The desk was a heavy, vintage item with a large, leather writing top, catching the orange glow from the lights of the night landscape through the window.

He wandered over to the window and, raising his left arm as a support, leant upon the glass. Looking down, he spied cars and people going on their merry way - were they happy and contented? Who knew? John smiled and took a sip from the tumbler in his hand. Next to the window stood a small table with a group of pictures of family members. He reached down and selected a silver-framed photo of a beautiful young woman in her early twenties; her long, chestnut hair tumbled over her shoulders, and her clear, blue eyes caught the light and shone like sapphires.

'Good night, my love.' He kissed the photo then put it back in its special place; turning his gaze back to the city through the window, he sighed. Moving to a large couch, he stretched himself out and fell into a restless sleep. As John Steel dozed, his nightmares visited him as always: screaming voices that seemed familiar to him but that he could not place; laughter, deep and menacing, possibly from a big man, then the sound of six gunshots. The laughter, the screams, and the gunshots all blurred into one cacophonous hell. There was a crash, and he woke with a start. A crash? That was a new addition to his nightmares. And then he looked down and found the glass shattered on the wooden floor.

'Marvellous, don't tell me I will need to drink from plastic glasses from now on,' he muttered to himself. He rose and stepped over the glass, drawn back to the window and, gazing pensively down, to the photo of the woman. 'One day the dreams will become normal, and the nightmares will end,' he breathed, 'but until then, they're my strength.' He stared out across the galaxy of lights.

NINETEEN

The morning brought rain. Not a heavy downpour but the sort of drizzle that soaked you in seconds. However, the sky was blue with just a few patches of the rain-bearing clouds. The English detective walked into the police precinct, where he was met with the sort of stares that burn straight through you.

'Morning,' he greeted the desk sergeant, though he did not expect a response. 'Friendly bunch,' he muttered under his breath.

As he left the elevator, the mood was chilling. Everyone stared at Steel as though he had just murdered a cop, not saved one. He made his way to the coffee room, where two female officers stood talking.

'Morning,' he said, raising his hand as a greeting wave. But the officers just gave him a dirty look and left by the other door. *OK, I can see this is going to be a fun-packed day,* he thought to himself. Making McCall and himself a coffee, he brought the cups to her desk, but she wasn't there. Checking the squad room, he spotted her in the captain's office, obviously giving a de-briefing on last night.

As he watched, the office door swung open and McCall,

Tooms and Tony skulked out looking flustered and red-faced. But when they saw Steel, they gave him a collective scowl.

'Has Mr Steel decided to grace us with his presence yet?' The captain poked his head out of his doorway to see Steel standing there with a coffee mug in each hand.

'Steel, your ass in my office, now.' Steel put down the mugs on McCall's desk and headed for the captain's room and its angry-looking occupant. As they passed, Tooms made a point of bumping shoulders with the English guy and glaring him in the eye.

Steel followed the captain into his office and shut the door, standing at ease in front of the large desk, instinctively adopting an army stance, with his hands behind his back and his feet shoulder-width apart, as he prepared himself for the ripping of his life.

'Steel, I have no idea what the powers that be see in you,' the captain began. 'I was told that you were this hot-shot detective, that you'd be an asset to the team, but so far all I've seen is a loose cannon. And now I hear you were part of a half-assed scheme to let one of my detectives enter a building without proper backup to face half of New York's Russian mob.'

The captain leant forward, his knuckles resting on the desktop, his face scarlet with rage. 'Son, I've got no idea who you are and I've got no reason to trust you. And if there's one thing this job has taught me, it's that things you don't know or trust ought to make you nervous. Now, if you fuck up one more time, I don't care who you know, you are out of here. Do I make myself clear?'

'Crystal, sir.' Steel stood motionless.

'Now get the hell out of my office and do some proper police work without trying to get my people killed.'

Steel left the room and made straight for the elevator. On seeing this, the captain shot out of his office.

'Now where the hell do you think you are going?' the senior officer demanded.

'To give you a reason to trust me.' Steel tossed back over his shoulder, and with that John Steel departed, leaving the captain seething with rage, and everyone else shaking their heads.

Later that night, Captain Alan Brant sat down to a wonderful, home-cooked meal with his wife and kids, which they devoured amid the happy sounds of laughter and joking. The captain was a good man and a fine cop and he contentedly leaned back in his seat to watch his good-hearted family with a sudden swelling of pride and love. With the meal finished and the dishes done, he retired to his study to catch up on some paperwork. The room was dark, but he knew it like the back of his hand. Sitting down at his desk, he reached over and pulled the chain switch on his old-style desk lamp. With a click, the desk was illuminated. And so was the figure seated in the chair opposite.

Though he felt his heart skip a beat to find Steel sitting there as though there was nothing amiss with the situation, the captain reflexively reached for the revolver in his desk drawer, which he pointed at his visitor.

'Mr Steel, if you would care to explain what the hell you are doing in my house, before I repaint my walls with you, I would grateful.' The captain seemed both furious and nervous.

'I'm sorry to drop in like this, but I felt it was prudent to avoid anyone seeing me enter, and as for shooting at me with that pistol, I'm afraid it wouldn't do you much good,' he said, leaning forwards and placing the bullets from Brant's revolver on to the table.

'What do you want, Steel? Who the hell are you really?' Brant regarded his revolver for a moment, reloaded it and, after a pause, he put it back into the drawer and shut it. When he looked back at Steel, he was holding a bottle of vintage Scotch whisky distilled in the 1800s. 'I think you may need this,' said Steel, as Brant accepted the bottle.

His eyes opened wide when he saw the brand and the date on the label.

'What's the occasion? Are you finally leaving us?'

'I'm afraid not. What you are about to see can't be disclosed to anyone under any circumstances. Do I have your word?' Steel was insistent. 'I must have your word on this, captain. If I don't, I'm taking back the whisky.' He grinned.

'Yes, yes, whatever.' Brant just wanted him out of his house now and out of his precinct very soon.

Steel passed him a folder that was at least two inches thick. 'Goddamn, that's heavy,' said the captain.

'So is my past.' Steel said, with crooked smile. The captain looked up at Steel and, for the first time, met his eyes unguarded by the ubiquitous dark glasses. He shuddered.

The next morning the entire homicide department was summoned to a briefing from the captain. 'As you know, for the past week some sick puppy has been leaving us jigsaw puzzle pieces of females around the neighbourhood,' Brant began. 'It's imperative we find this guy before he strikes again.' He nodded to McCall, who rose to her feet and addressed the audience of cops.

'We know he has a fondness for blondes and he's familiar with their blood group, so we are looking for someone who has studied these women. What worries me is that his exploits have already generated one copycat, though we've taken him off the street. Going back to our original killer, we know that, although they are found naked, there is no sexual abuse. He has a comprehensive knowledge of surgical techniques so we may be looking for a trained surgeon. He doesn't choose them at random; he researches them. So far, we have not established identities for all these women, so we can't make a connection, though we're sure there is one. There are tens of thousands of attractive blondes in Manhattan with their blood group. So what else links them? We need to go through every database and find past crimes that have a similar MO,' McCall concluded, sitting down.

'Now, we have brought in an expert in psychological profiling. Some of you will already have met Dr Davidson.' The captain introduced the doctor, gesturing for him to stand. 'He is the best in his field, so with his help, we are going to catch this guy.'

Davidson stood up and gave a slight bow, then quickly sat down again.

'OK, people, we've got a job to do,' the captain said, finally. 'So, let's get to it.'

The crowd dispersed, and detectives started making phone calls and keying searches into their computers. McCall spotted the doctor looking lost and out of place, and she moved over to him.

'Doctor, hi, I'm Detective McCall,' she introduced herself, noticing how he looked up with a start as if she'd broken into his thoughts. 'Would you like a coffee or anything?'

He shook his head and gazed around him as if he were a child encountering the school playground for the first time.

'Sir, if you would follow me, we have set aside a room for you to work in,' she explained.

McCall escorted him to a spacious but windowless office, the sight of which seemed to bring him to life.

'I hope this is OK, it's all we have spare at the moment,' she apologised, though it seemed unnecessary, judging by his awed expression. 'On the contrary, this is perfect,' he murmured, taking in the facilities that had been provided for him. His gleeful face resembled that of a child in a candy store.

A large work desk was packed with files on the case, crime scene photos neatly stacked next to them, and by the far wall stood a large whiteboard that he could use to construct his own personal murder-board. He virtually floated around the room, eyes wide with excitement.

'So, Doctor, I will leave you to it then. If you need anything, Officer Thompson here has been assigned to you.' She waved at a slender, young redhead in uniform by the door.

'What? Oh, thank you, Detective,' Davidson replied, still apparently overwhelmed.

'You know, this is a very interesting case,' he said, flicking through the notes and photos in front of him.

McCall was already on her way out, but she stopped and turned. 'How do you mean?' she asked, cautiously.

'Well, most of those we call 'collectors' take a finger or locks of hair. I remember one man kept eyes in a pickle jar—' He smiled softly to himself as he remembered the grisly details. The expression on his face made her skin crawl.

'— But this man,' he continued, standing up and placing pictures of the victims on his board in the order they were found, 'he picks different parts of each body. I've no experience of anyone like that before. I find that odd: intriguing, but nevertheless odd.'

As McCall left the room, she glanced back over her shoulder to find him staring at the photos on the board, and shivered.

She made her way towards Tooms, whom she found at his desk. McCall perched on the edge of it and peered around to make sure nobody was watching.

'Did you find anything about Steel?' she asked, staring pointedly at one of the whiteboards rather than directly at her colleague.

'Well, our boy doesn't exist,' Tooms replied. 'I spoke to just about everyone for information about Mr John Steel but came up blank. Someone don't want us knowing his shoe size and mother's maiden name, whether that's the man himself or he's off the reservation and the men in black have deleted his info.'

McCall, caught off guard, shot him a surprised look. 'Oh great, so you're telling me our assistant is a ghost?'

'Don't worry, I've got more contacts off the radar, maybe they'll know who he is. But here's a question: do you really *want* to find out?'

She looked blankly at him.

'What do you mean by that?' she asked. 'I mean, somebody who goes to this much trouble not to be found, I guess they just don't want to be found. We already know he's one of the good guys after all.'

'I want to know everything there is to be known about this guy. I want to know what makes him tick, and particularly what makes him go cuckoo and how often, so we know when we can depend on him, and when we can't. Make your calls.' She stood up and walked towards the coffee area: she needed caffeine – badly.

McCall poured the coffee and sat at the table sipping the hot, dark brew. The pungent aroma filled her nostrils as she inhaled, taking a long-drawn-out breath, that was like pure heaven to her. Suddenly, Tony's head appeared around the corner of the door. He was waving a piece of paper, and his urgency made her sit up and take notice.

'What's up?' she inquired, watching him enter.

'I think we got something from the CCTV footage on the pier.' She leapt up, and they both hurried to the monitor room.

'OK,' she said immediately they'd closed the door. 'What am I looking at?'

The frame had been paused at 0200hrs.

'Just watch,' said Tony, as he pressed play. The footage rolled on, and at first, nothing happened. Then what appeared to be two homeless guys came into frame, pushing a large object in a shopping cart and carrying what looked like some rope. They disappeared around the corner and she noticed the counter clock jumped forward fifteen minutes when they returned.

'Stop it there,' she told him. 'Can you enhance the faces?'

Tony used the mouse to create a digital square around the men's heads, and with another click, the image was magnified.

'OK, make copies,' she said. 'I want that picture circulated to every shelter, church and hostel because we have got to find these men.'

At last, it looked as if they'd got a break. She just hoped that it would lead somewhere.

Hustling back to the main office, they were delayed from sharing the good news as Tooms's phone burst to life and, reaching over, he grabbed the receiver. 'Detective Tooms, homicide, how can I help you?' A voice announced they were calling from the medical examiner, telling him that they too had something.

'That was the ME's office,' he told McCall and Tony as he hung up the phone. 'They got a hit on the last victim. She was a Miss Marie-Ann Talbot from Manhattan.'

Walking over to the board, he rubbed out the name Jane Doe and wrote in its place, Marie-Ann Talbot.

'We got an address yet?' McCall asked, as she slid into place at her desk, pleased that things were starting to come together, even if it was a slow process. Tony was busy checking on his computer for any data on Marie-Ann. With a bleep, her picture came up on his screen, along with all her personal information, including her date of birth and address.

'We got her,' said Tony, positively giddy with excitement.

'OK,' McCall told him 'I'll meet you guys downstairs. I'm just going to phone CSU and get them down there to check the place.'

They both took off as she snatched up the receiver, ready to dial. McCall made the call quick, then jumped up and grabbed her coat. As she hurried to the elevator, she made a quick detour to knock at the room allocated to Doctor Davidson, sticking her head around the door when he did not reply.

'Hey, Doc, we have a name and address for the last victim,' she said. 'I wonder if you wanted to come with us to look over the place?' Deep down she prayed he would say no.

'What? Oh, I'm sorry, no, no, you go ahead I'm still catching up,' he said, delving through the photos.

'Sure, I'll leave you to it then.' And with an inward sigh of relief, she quietly shut the door and ran off before he could change his mind.

TWENTY

Samuel lay in his hospital bed. Almost every part of his body was enclosed in a plaster cast. However, even if he'd been fighting fit, he wouldn't have been able to go anywhere: the two large, uniformed police officers on the other side of the door would make sure he stayed put.

The man was conscious but completely immobilised. The TV in front of him was there merely for background noise; he had no interest in actually watching it. As the celebrity chef prattled on, he heard a different sound of the door opening, followed by soft footsteps padding across the floor as somebody came into the room.

'Hey, Doc, is that you?' Samuel groaned but got no answer. 'Nurse? Who is there? Answer me!'

Still, there was no reply. But there was some kind of noise. *What was it?* he wondered, breathing faster. He strained his ears, trying to make out what the sound reminded him of. A ringtone? There it was again! Was it music? Yes, it was music, from somewhere in the room. He could just make out a faint chime as if from a musical box or maybe a pocket watch. 'Please, who is this?' he called out, plaintively. Despite being unable to turn his head, he felt the presence of someone in the room, and if it had not been for the sedative medication he was on, a shiver would have danced up and down his spine. 'Interesting,' observed a sinister voice.

Samuel's head strained against the neck brace. 'Who is there? *Show yourself, you bastard!*'

'You do realise that, because of you, I have to reschedule my plans?' the disembodied voice mused. 'And that will not do, I'm afraid.'

Samuel could feel the man's breath in his ear, as he spoke, his tone eerily soft and calm. That was the most disquieting thing: the man's words were full of fury, yet his intonation was deadly calm.

'Oh, goodie.' The position of the voice had shifted to somewhere above him. He managed to make out a brief silhouette on the ceiling: it was thin, and the arms seemed too long, out of proportion to his body somehow, and then the image was gone.

'They've got you on a morphine drip,' the man reflected. 'Well, you don't mind if I put up the dosage, do you?' Samuel seemed puzzled. Why would he increase the dosage? 'What for?' the petrified Russian asked.

'So that you don't pass out from the pain, of course, you silly boy.'

'Who the fuck are you?' Samuel asked, his voice trembled with fear. He opened his mouth to call out for help, only for something soft and woolly - a sock? - to be shoved into his mouth. What was this madman doing? He struggled but in vain as his casts held him rigid.

And all the while he could hear this soft maddening laughter.

A blur shot from the dark as the increased dose of morphine kicked in. His heart froze as a face came into view, but all he could make out were massive blue eyes that held the look of a madman, and large, shining, white teeth within a grotesquely grinning mouth.

'Oh, I hope you stay awake for this,' said his tormentor. 'I wouldn't want you to miss it for the world.'

As Samuel's trapped face stared helplessly up, he caught a glimpse of something in the maniac's hand, something that shone in the light reflected from the TV screen. To his horror, he thought he could recognise a bone saw. And then the madman was gone from view.

A terrifying silence filled his ears. Could it be a joke, he wondered? Maybe it was a trick? No matter what, he vowed, he would eventually find this man and make him pay for this. He felt a twinge in his shoulder and then a strange dampness on his back. The musical chimes were the last thing he heard before the darkness took him.

The apartment belonging to Marie-Ann Talbot was pretty spacious for Chelsea. It was decorated with wooden floor tiles and white walls, designed to make the rooms seem bigger than they really were. The three detectives walked in and found themselves directly in the sitting area. The view from the large picture windows overlooked the High Line. It was obvious that Marie-Ann had a successful career, considering the apartment's fashionable location and her hip taste in furnishings. They had been let in by the caretaker, an elderly gentleman in his late sixties but apparently quite active for his age. The team split up, inspecting the residence room by room, but turned up nothing obviously relevant to the case. Their primary objective was to uncover any clue as to what sort of person the lady was, and to establish any contact she had with others, but they found nothing to help them.

'OK, people keeping things private I can understand,' said Tooms, coming out of the bedroom with a disgruntled expression. 'But this ain't right. People don't keep secrets from themselves like these ladies did. There are no pictures of family, or of friends, there's nothing. I mean she doesn't even have a naughty drawer.'

McCall looked up. 'So? Your point is?'

'Nah, nothing, just blowing off steam I guess, but in both these victims' apartments things seem the same. It's more than just being super clean and not putting personal stuff on display. If you ask me, it just seems weird.' He trudged back into the bedroom to continue his search.

McCall shook her head and smiled. She felt his confusion, they all did, but she had faith something would come up. It had to: nobody was a blank page.

The phone in her pocket buzzed and vibrated, and as she pulled it out, the blue screen lit up the words 'number with-held'. She looked at it for a moment then pressed the accept button.

'Hi, it's Steel,' stated the caller.

She took the phone away from her head quickly and looked at it in surprise.

'McCall, are you there?' The voice sounded bewildered.

'Where the hell are you? Never mind, I don't think I want to know.

What's up?' she said, adjusting to the shock of hearing his voice.

'I got a name and address for victim number two.'

'Really?' She sounded surprised that he was capable of doing some actual police work.

'Don't sound so amazed. Anyway, the second victim was a Miss Susan Black, and she had an apartment in Queens; I just texted you the address.'

She tried not to sound too excited about the new lead, not wanting to give him the satisfaction, but a lead was a lead no matter where it came from.

'OK, I will meet you outside the block, you hear me? *Outside the block.* Don't you dare go in by yourself. Oh, and by the way, do something about that phone. If it ever tells me 'number withheld' again, I won't answer it.' She deliberately kept her tone blunt.

'Yes, mummy,' he chirped, and hung up. She scowled to herself at his childishness.

TWENTY-ONE

S am McCall drove up to the main entrance of the apartment block and parked. Climbing out of her car, she caught sight of Steel, leaning against the white plaster wall of the massive tower block. He wore black jeans, a strange black shirt that had only three or four buttons and what appeared to be a clerical collar, which looked stiff against his neck apart from at the front, where there was a small gap. Over that, he wore his long, black, three-quarter-length suit jacket. It looked smart but casual, and his costume was topped off as always by those dammed sunglasses. At least at the moment he was outside.

'Detective,' he greeted her with a smile.

'Detective,' she returned the greeting, but not the smile.

'Shall we?' he said, opening the door for her. McCall used the other door just out of spite, a trace of a smirk passing over her face, smug in her small victory. Steel held the door a moment longer to allow a curvaceous brunette to sashay through. The woman thanked him and went on her way, throwing him a smile over her shoulder that he wouldn't forget in a hurry. McCall shot him a disapproving look, but he just raised his hands, palm sides up.

'What?' he said, innocently.

The lobby they stepped into was covered in gleaming tiles and dominated by an immaculate marbled front desk that ran the width of the space, behind which stood a large, well-built Hispanic man. His dark suit and white shirt suggested that he held a position of authority, and as they neared the desk, they noticed that the tie he wore bore the name of the tower.

'Good afternoon, can I help you?' he said, his voice deep and with a definite Latino accent – McCall guessed at Columbian. She reached for the badge clip on her belt and held the shiny piece of tin up for him to inspect.

'I'm Detective McCall, and this is Detective Steel. I believe you have a Miss Susan Black living here, is that correct?'

'Miss Susan, yes. A very nice lady, she always says hello whenever she sees one of us on duty. Why are you asking? Has something happened to her?' His smile was replaced by a real look of concern.

'Yes,' McCall tried to break the news gently. 'I'm sorry to say that she has had an accident, and we are trying to establish what she was doing in the hours before it happened.'

'Whatever we can do to help, please ask,' he said, realising that, at the very least, Miss Susan was unable to tell the *Federales* anything herself. The shock of this revelation registered on his face.

'Would it be possible to take a look at her apartment?'

He nodded and called to one of the cleaning girls who was just passing. 'Melanie, can you take these people to 121 please?'

She nodded and asked them to follow her to the elevator. The cleaner was maybe twenty years old, if that, with short dark hair and a light-blue uniform with short sleeves and buttons all the way down the front.

'Did you know Miss Black at all, Melanie?' asked Steel softly.

'Not really. We spoke now and then, but just in passing.

She was friendly like that. She was a nice person. She doesn't deserve to be dead, if that is what you're saying.'

'Nobody does,' said McCall, with a strange look in her eyes that Steel took note of.

The girl let them inside the spacious apartment. Like the other victims, she lived alone, and her home had no photos of family or friends on display or even tucked away privately, nothing that could lead them to her personal contacts, if indeed she had any. McCall and Steel searched high and low for something revealing but, just as before, they kept coming up empty. Eventually, Steel walked into the living area, carrying a pink notebook with a miniature padlock on its corner, apparently Susan's diary.

'Look what I found,' he said, waving the small book.

'Not really your colour,' said McCall, sarcastically. He smiled.

'I'm betting it's her diary, and I guess if we want to know something about a person, it could be right here…' He was right, and she knew it. And boy, how she hated that.

'OK, bag it, and we will take it back with us.'

McCall's search of the kitchen achieved nothing, except to make her feel hungry after inspecting the contents of Susan's refrigerator. Steel trudged back out of the bedroom and peered around, his brow wrinkled with confusion and concern.

'What's up?' McCall asked. Even knowing him for just a short time, she'd picked up on his *I'm on to something* expression.

'Did the other victims have computers?' he asked, still looking around the room.

'I think so, why?' Now she was intrigued.

'If you were a successful businesswoman, you would have your life planned out. So far, have all the apartments been like this? I don't mean size, just as organised as this place is?'

He poked his head into a small space that had probably been designed as a child's room or a guest room. Instead, it was arranged as a home office, with piles of business-related papers and a laptop.

'McCall,' he called for her, as he leafed through a large stack of papers. neatly arranged on a pine-topped desk. McCall entered and looked around the small office. The walls were painted lilac, and many pin boards hung from them, covered with flow charts and diagrams.

'OK, I'll get CSU in here, looks like there may be something relevant here,' she said, punching in the number as she spoke, and waited for the crime scene team to take over.

Following his return from lunch, the psychiatrist was engrossed in his office at the department. Dr Davidson had created his own 'murder board', though his assembly of information was based on personality analysis rather than physical facts. It included pictures of the victims, and handwritten notes in Sharpie here and there, aiming to highlight similarities in the victims, in the hope of analysing what made the killer tick.

On another board he had collated what was known about the killer himself; for Davidson, the presence- or absence- of even the smallest, most obscure detail spoke volumes to him. For instance, he judged that the perpetrator demonstrated highly complex attitudes towards women in general, and to these women in particular.

The doctor was perched at his desk scanning through some medical reports that had come up from downstairs, while taking fastidious little sips from the water glass at his elbow.

Now that he was banned from the ME's lab (because Tina had thrown out 'the freaky bastard'), all reports had to be brought to him by Officer Jenny Thompson. The young woman, little more than a girl really, was a promising uniformed officer, eager to be a detective, who regarded any experience she could gain from working with the homicide department with enthusiasm.

Thompson knocked on the door, but he gave no reply. Again, she knocked but heard nothing. One of the detectives noticed her dilemma and waved to her, indicating that she should go straight in. She nodded and obeyed, and as she entered, she caught sight of Dr Davidson staring at some of the photos from the crime scenes. And she could have sworn that he was actually stroking them.

Shocked by the sight, she didn't notice the chair in front of her, colliding into it and jolting the table. The doctor scowled up at her with maddened, red-rimmed eyes and pupils so dilated they seemed almost black.

She stared, horrified at his gaze, and froze, unable to move or speak. It was as if his glare had trapped her in some kind of stasis. A long strand of thick saliva slid from his mouth, reminding her of a rabid dog. Abruptly, Thompson broke free from his gaze, squealed and fled from the room, white-faced, attracting the attention of those nearby. One big detective who had witnessed this scene burst in to confront the doctor, but on catching his gaze, the seasoned cop turned pale and backed out hastily, unable to hide the tremor in his hands. The detective had seen evil before but never felt it, not like that.

Not like that.

McCall and Steel stopped at a street corner vendor and ordered a couple of hotdogs.

'So, Mr Steel, why don't you tell me something about yourself?' McCall grinned as she shot the question at him.

'Such as what?' Steel smiled. He had been wondering how long it would take for her to ask him something personal.

'Such as *anything*,' she said, taking the steaming dog off the man and covering it in ketchup, to Steel's disgust.

'Would you like a hotdog with your ketchup?' John Steel said, transfixed by the sauce running off the paper napkin.

She gave him a quick *mind your own business* stare and bit into it. Steel took his hotdog and paid for both of them. The air was fresh with a slight breeze, and they wandered over to a bench where they both sat down to eat. Steel squinted upwards as if he was trying to gather some of the rays of sunlight from above.

'So, what do you want to know?' he asked.

'I don't know: where you were born? What you did before you came here? Why did you join the US police and not the British force? You know, little things like why you don't seem to exist.' She gave him a grim look, and he just smiled.

'Wow,' he said, biting into the hotdog that was mostly bread. 'No wonder you put so much ketchup on it.'

She could see he was evading her questions.

'Look, I know, Detective, that I seem … How can I put it—'

'—An asshole?' she butted in, with her mouth full.

'I was going to say secretive, but if you prefer, I guess that could work. Thing is, right at this moment I've got a couple of trust issues, but I promise I will tell you everything once I know where I stand, OK?'

It wasn't OK, but she could sense there was definitely more to this story. The question was, did she want to know about his life, or to be a part of it?

Her phone buzzed, and she slid it out of her pocket and pressed the receive button.

'We got a body at 42 and Lex.' The voice on the phone was Tooms, and he did not seem happy.

'OK, Mystery Boy,' McCall told the Englishman, after finishing the call. 'Let's go, but we will pick this up later, believe me.'

'Perhaps over dinner?' Steel suggested in a hopeful voice.

'Yeh, we just tried that, and believe me that's the only

dinner we will ever be sharing.' She gave him a scornful look that made him grin, maddeningly.

'See, you're warming to me. Before, you would have thrown the food at me, not let me eat it.' He looked up as a sudden thought struck him.

McCall picked up on it immediately. 'What is it?'

'I was just wondering which would have been worse, eating the hotdog, or wearing it.'

She pretended to throw her phone, but he jumped into the car quickly to dodge her. She smiled before getting in, but once inside the car the good humour had vanished from her face.

Dr Davidson rose from his seat after reading the ME's report on the latest victim, lifted the jacket of his thousand-dollar camel suit from the back of an empty chair and shrugged it on, stroking his hands down the sleeves as if to smooth out the wrinkles. Heading towards the door, he grabbed a worn, black briefcase with brass catches then, as he stepped through to the outer office, he halted, put down the case, and slipped his long, bony hands into a pair of black leather gloves that had lain upon the case while he worked. He surveyed the officers and staff going about their business and smiled.

While he waited for the elevator, a voice called out, 'Leaving so soon, Doc?'

'I have work elsewhere,' Davidson replied, without slowing down his pace.

'Thank fuck for that,' spat another voice from somewhere in the room; this did make him hesitate for a brief second, and then the elevator doors shut behind him and he was gone.

TWENTY-TWO

McCall and Steel arrived at the address they'd been given, a shabby hotel on the East Side with wallpaper that looked like it had been hung in the 1930s when the place was built. Despite the dim wall lights, it was dark and gloomy, the minimal illumination utterly inadequate.

Outside the victim's room, two patrol officers were stationed either side of the door, securing the scene. McCall flashed her badge, and they both nodded. As the detectives entered, they each snapped on a pair of blue latex gloves before walking through to the sitting area. There they found a man with a shaved head and tattoos that covered his arms and most of his neck, slouched in an armchair. He wore blue jeans, a white shirt and black army-style boots, and his tanned complexion minimised the colours of an array of gang-related tattoos, the style of which suggested they had been collected in jail. A greying goatee beard sprouted from his long, thin face. As they approached from either side, Steel sensed that something was not right. The man remained entirely motionless, his eyes wide open and unblinking. He hadn't responded in any way to the detectives' arrival. Was he dead? On immediate impression there was no apparent cause. Steel halted where he was and started to scan the room. McCall was about to reach out to the man in the chair when he yelled at her abruptly.

'Stop! Don't touch him,' he commanded. 'In fact, do me a favour and get against that wall.' He pointed at the wall behind her, which had no view to or from the only window.

'God, you are so paranoid! Look, anyone can see the man is dead: we need to find out at the very least who he is, and I can't do that cowering against the wall.' She was rapidly losing patience with him again. Nobody had developed this skill of rubbing her up the wrong way as quickly as he had over the last couple of days. McCall didn't know or care why he wanted her to quit but she was damned if she was letting him interfere with her job.

'Don't you find it strange that he is just sitting there dead, facing a window, with no clear cause of death?' he asked.

'Maybe it was a heart attack or some other medical explanation.

But I won't find out standing here,' she said.

'Look, take it from me, I have seen a setup like this before, and to me it smells like a trap, that's all.'

She threw him a weird look and took a step towards the body. Steel immediately lunged at McCall, knocking her to the floor in a football tackle. Just as he did so the window shattered and there was a popping sound as the dead man's head exploded over the back wall behind him. Blood and skull fragments peppered its surface.

Catching their breaths, Steel looked at McCall, who lay underneath him.

'You OK?' he asked as they lay there, his legs astride her.

She looked up at him, their eyes met, and she felt a momentary attraction that she soon managed to shake off.

'Are you hurt?' he repeated, sounding concerned.

'What? No, but you are squashing me.' He realised the position they were in and rolled off her.

'Sorry,' he said, and they both clambered to their feet and surveyed the now headless corpse.

For a moment she wished he had kissed her. She owed him that at least. 'Well, I guess you were right - how did you know?' She gave him a wary look as he examined the wall.

'I can tell you one thing,' Steel muttered drily, still panting from the adrenaline rush.

'And that is?' she asked, hopefully anticipating some illuminating insight.

'Well, if he wasn't dead before, he sure as hell is now.' Steel said, contemplating the pattern of blood and brains on the wall and giving a shrug.

She just gave him a *sick bastard* look and called the incident in to the precinct. Within minutes, a flurry of police and members of a SWAT unit were swarming all over the building opposite in an attempt to find the shooter or at least some clues. Once the area had been decreed safe, the CSU teams had split in half and began the task of processing the two scenes. McCall was slouched in the back of an ambulance with a blanket draped around her shoulders, getting checked out by a medic, when Steel walked up to her with a cup of hot chocolate.

'Here, drink this,' he said, passing her the beverage. Sniffing it, she peered up at him quizzically.

'Hot chocolate? Really?' She looked sceptical.

'Yes, the sugar will help compensate for the adrenaline loss so you won't feel faint,' he said, sipping his own.

'Oh really? And where did you learn that?' she said, dubiously.

'Discovery Channel. It's brilliant – you'd be amazed how much you can learn from that.' She knew it was an evasive answer, but she decided to let it pass, for now.

'Thanks.' She smiled up at him.

'Any time.' Steel returned the smile.

McCall was given a quick all clear by the medics and they

were preparing to head across the street to the building the shots had been fired from, when the captain blocked their path.

'Where the hell do you think you are going, Detectives?' He stopped them both.

'I was...We were just going to—' McCall started to stammer.

'—Go home and get some rest, is how I hope you were going to complete that sentence, Detective.' His look was severe.

'Hey, don't look at me, Captain, I was just following her,' Steel said, innocently sipping his drink.

'But sir,' she protested, 'we were just shot at from over —'

'—Yes, you two were just shot at,' he interrupted, 'so that makes it someone else's case. You're too close to it, so go home. Do it now!'

TWENTY-THREE

The evening drew in, and the sun began to disappear below the horizon, leaving in its wake a sky that looked as if it was on fire, with the dark oranges and reds that bled across the heavens. Streaks of dark cloud cut across the view as if the canvas it had been painted upon had been slashed, hiding the last remnants of the sun. The bar was quiet, just how he liked it. It was a spot he could come and gather his thoughts. The place was old, dating back to probably before Prohibition; the booths were heavy oak with dark green leather padding, the tables supported by shining brass pillars, and the floor was tiled. The bar ran the breadth of the room with tall stools lining its counter, ready to house the next happy customer. Tooms loved this place, it was his retreat, and that was why he had suggested this venue for a meeting. As he walked in, he was greeted with friendly hellos from the staff, which he returned with equal warmth. He scanned the long room, until he spied a huge figure of a man with a short buzz cut, sipping a long, cold one.

'Hey, Sergeant Biggs, you know, you get uglier every day,' Tooms said, standing in front of the table, fists clenched, ready for anything.

'Well, Tooms, your wife don't seem to mind.' The two men laughed and embraced.

'How long has it been, man?' said Biggs.

'Too long,' Tooms replied, delighted to see his old friend.

'So, what's up, what do you need, man?'

'Information, information on a guy,' Tooms answered.

'OK, tell me what you know, and I'll see what I can do for you.' The two men had served together many years ago in the Marines, but Biggs had ended up in the SEALS and Tooms had become a cop. 'What's this dude's name, to start with?' said Biggs, tucking into the massive burger that had just arrived.

'He's, well, a new guy at the precinct. Problem is he doesn't seem to exist, at least on paper. I can't find any record of the man anywhere.'

Tooms reached for his phone and pulled up a picture which he showed to his friend.

'He said his name is—' That was as far as he got.

'—Sergeant fucking Steel!' Tom Biggs completed the sentence for him, more or less. 'You've got Sergeant fucking Steel working with you? That must be acres of fun.'

Tooms's face dropped. He did not know whether to be thrilled or terrified by his pal's reaction.

'You know him then?' Tooms asked, realising as he spoke it was somewhat redundant to enquire when the answer was obvious.

'Know the man? I'd say I sure do. That bastard owes me twenty bucks.'

'So where did you come across him?' Tooms was intrigued.

'They used to call him The Phoenix, 'cause every time the man went down, the fucker would get back up again.'

Tooms now had a lost look on his face, which his friend couldn't help but notice.

'He used to be attached to special mission groups,' Biggs elaborated. 'Now, SEALS are mainly about teamwork, but this guy was special.'

'Special? Special how?' Tooms asked, stealing a French fry from the other man's plate.

'You stealin' a brother's food?' he laughed. 'Solo stuff, this cat could go in and clear a hotspot by himself. They used to send him on hostage retrieval, not the negotiating kind.'

Tooms stared at his friend like he was a child listening to a grandfather's stories.

'See, if we were worried about entering a hotspot, they would just send this crazy British bastard in. You wouldn't hear a thing unless he wanted you to. I remember one story from Afghanistan in the early days, when about fifteen of our brothers were being held for ransom on TV; you know: 'free our brothers-in-arms, or we will kill your men'– that sort of thing.'

Tooms nodded. He knew that scenario all too well since a friend of his had been captured, but he had been rescued by an extraction team. 'Anyway, Steel decides to take a walk and gets himself captured. I don't know what happened in the camp, and God knows I don't want to, but they said he got every man out and took down the whole cell of terrorists, and that's when they made him a 'lone wolf' operative. The man's a ghost.'

'So, what happened? Why did he leave?'

'Can't really say. But we did one job together, and it almost went south. He reckoned it was a set-up, and he said he had to leave so the teams would be safe. Later I heard agencies were interested in him for recruitment. I don't know.' Briggs shrugged. 'What I do know is, if you're in the shit, this is the man to have at your back.'

'And if you're not on his side?'

'Don't bother to run, buddy, just end it yourself 'cause he will find you.'

Tooms swallowed hard, almost choking on the latest fry he had stolen.

'See? That's what you get for stealing a brother's fries.'

They both laughed and went on to catch up on shared old times.

A shot, laughter, a scream, a scent, caused Steel to wake up suddenly. A scent that was new to his dreams. He stumbled to the bathroom and ran some cool water into the basin, splashing it onto his face. What could it mean? He struggled to remember it before he fully woke up and forgot the aroma. Then he wandered to the kitchen, grabbed a juice carton from the fridge and padded over to the sofa where he collapsed. Opening the carton, he filled a glass and swallowed the whole lot at once. The juice was refreshing, and the suede leather felt soft on his bare skin as he looked out of the window into the night.

Closing his eyes, he tried to place the smell from his dream, but it was no use for now, he was fully awake. But it didn't matter: if he had dreamt of it once the same thing would happen again, and when it did, he would be ready. His dream seemed to progress, a little bit at a time. John Steel glanced over at the antique clock on the fireplace. The lights of the city shone directly onto its face, showing him, it was half past eight. *Great*, he thought, he had enough time to shower and change.

The water felt good; the droplets followed the curves of his muscular body. Fully dressed, he appeared to be of average build, but his nakedness told a different story. His muscles were almost like a tightened cable that protruded though his skin; his body was firm and tanned, with scars from a lifetime of narrow escapes etched into the skin, each one a reminder of the motive for the path he now followed. As the creamy lather of the soap washed away under the flow of warm water, his fingers touched the six-round exit-wound scars marking his body. Six mementoes to show how lucky he had been. Six promises that someone had to pay, and that it was his job to extract that payment. He wished he could stay under the water forever, soothed by its therapeutic caress. However, he had to be somewhere; there was someone he had to meet.

A few hours later a blacked-out limousine pulled up to the entrance of the gala. As the vehicle came to a stop, the valet opened the door and the mayor, who was busy talking to a rather plump gentleman with a balding head and a neatly trimmed beard, peered over the man's shoulder and grinned at the sight of the car. The mayor excused himself and bustled over to greet the passenger as the car door opened, and he leaned forwards.

'It's OK, come on, you will have fun, I promise,' he said, laughing to his new guest.

Steel exited the vehicle and straightened his tux, saying: 'You know I hate these things, right?'

'Relax. Besides, everyone thinks you are here on behalf of the department. Nobody knows you.'

Steel didn't feel reassured but what the hell, he was here now. And besides, who would find out?

TWENTY-FOUR

Morning came, blessed by a warm sun and a cool breeze as the city went about its business. Steel had installed himself in the chair next to McCall's desk, waiting for her to come in. While he waited, his gaze was morbidly drawn to a tall, thin man, who was in one of the briefing rooms that he seemed to have taken over to use as his own personal office.

A young uniformed officer passed by. 'Hey, Rachael, who's the spooky guy?' John Steel asked her.

She gave him a friendly but mystified look.

'I'm asking, who's the strange, spooky guy over there?' He pointed to the room across from where he was sitting.

'That is our local expert, Dr Davidson,' the woman replied. 'He's a guy the cap calls in when he thinks we're in trouble. I'm not sure what he's an expert on – apart from freaking people out.' And with that, she left him staring at the precinct's new addition.

Sam McCall strolled in and sat opposite him. 'Morning,' she said, spearing Detective Steel with one of her special grins.

'Morning. Satisfy my curiosity,' he asked bluntly, jerking a thumb at Davidson. 'Who is that guy from the freakshow?'

'Well, if you showed up for briefings now and then, you would know that Dr Davidson is helping with the investigation,' she said, sipping the coffee she found on her desk.

'What do we know about him?' he said, watching as the man in the room opposite began leafing desperately through paperwork, obviously searching for something.

'What do we know about anyone? Especially you,' she added, drily.

'What? Ha ha, OK, I take your point. But really, something about that guy…'

McCall could tell Steel was unsettled by the psychiatrist, that something did not sit right, but she had no idea what it was, and she was not sure that Steel knew either.

'Well, it appears your hunch about the 'date' books being on their computers was right,' she said, reluctant to admit it to him. 'We are just waiting for a copy so we can run through them together and check for any matches.'

As McCall sifted through her emails, she too found herself distracted by the doctor; he was peering at the board and muttering to himself, wringing his hands, and then going back to the papers on his desk.

'Do we have anything on Susan Black yet?' Steel asked, bringing her back into the here and now.

'Not much, we know she worked on Wall Street. She was one of the top female sellers there and oh yes, we've finally got a photo of her.' McCall opened the file in front of her, and pulling out the picture, she passed it across the desk. Steel's face suddenly dropped. He snatched the picture from her and strode across to the board.

'Hey, watch it will you!' said McCall in protest. 'What's the matter with you?' she asked, looking at the fingers he'd just pulled the photo from.

'It's not what's wrong with me, the real question is, what's wrong with this picture, or should I say, all these pictures?' As he placed the picture of Susan Black in the blank space under her name, McCall saw what he meant.

'See? They could be sisters, they're so similar.' He turned and looked at her.

'Really similar,' she agreed. 'I would have said almost identical myself, but that's just me.'

Tooms and Tony appeared at McCall's desk and she could tell they were about to start filling her in on what they had found downtown, when they too were struck by the pictures.

'Hey, is it me or do they look alike?' asked Tony, with a dumb expression on his face.

'Do they? I hadn't noticed,' McCall said with a grin. 'OK, what did you guys get?'

'Well, we got all three diaries and date planners from CSU, and we were just about to run them to see if anything breaks,' said Tooms, waving a CD case in his hand.

'OK, let me know if anything comes up,' said McCall, frustrated because they already had far too much evidence that led nowhere. Steel stared at the photos for a moment and then shot over to where McCall sat.

'May I?' he asked, pointing to the computer on her desk, as she stared up at him with a baffled look on her face.

'What are you thinking?' she asked, leaning on the corner of the desktop as he sat in her place.

'Well, we found no pictures of family,' he said, typing something on the PC.

'So, maybe they fell out or something.' McCall was up for ideas, sure, but she could not see where this was going.

'All of them? Let's say for the moment that Ms Black didn't have any?'

'She's adopted?' asked Tooms.

'No, there would still be pictures,' Steel replied. 'Now what I'm thinking is—'

'—Orphanage!' interrupted McCall, with a *penny dropped* look upon her face.

The computer spat out some facts on Susan Black, including her old addresses.

'All Saints' orphanage?' McCall wrote the address down, and Tooms snatched it up.

'Come on, fancy a road trip?' Tooms waved the piece of paper at Tony, who needed no second bidding, and grabbed his jacket.

'What are you thinking, Steel?' McCall asked, noticing the longing look on the English detective's face.

'If I am right, she won't be the only one who went there.' The words slipped into a whisper as he looked up at her with a strange look, she had not seen him use before: he looked lost.

Dr Davidson was frantic. Somebody had been messing with his notes and photos, and this did not sit well with him. He appreciated the fact that the department had called him because they realised his greatness in the field of psychology, but his charity had limits, and he was horrified to see what some moron had done to his board.

He slumped into a seat and gulped some water. His head was killing him – ever since childhood, he had suffered from terrible headaches. He had consulted a number of colleagues, but nobody had ever found out what caused them. He swallowed some more water and took an aspirin.

As he sat, he surveyed the chaos that his system had become. Why would someone do this? Why? For goodness sake, they invited me here to help! Yes, sure, the publicity would boost his medical practice no end, but did he really need this kind of hassle?

'Must calm down, must calm down,' he kept repeating to himself, checking his pulse. Then he noticed the ME's file: it was empty. That was it, he had had enough. As he jumped up, the wheeled chair slid backwards, pushed by the back of his knees, and careered into the wall behind him. 'Ladies and gentlemen, I acknowledge that my presence here is apparently a cause of resentment for most of you, however, if we could be a bit more professional about this, that would be much appreciated. Thank you!' he shouted, as he walked across the main office, only to return seconds later. 'And where is Officer Thingamabob who is meant to be working with me? Or did someone get rid of her as well?' He grabbed his blue blazer and stormed off towards the elevator. 'I can't work like this,' he growled to himself, stalking into the elevator as the doors swung open, leaving everyone leaning over their desks gawping at the scene in bewilderment. With a soft *clunk*, the doors closed, and he was gone.

'Wow, what was all that about?' asked Steel.

'Beats the hell out of me,' said McCall, and they went back to their search of the diaries.

Tooms and Tony arrived at the old building. Its white walls, that once shone as a beacon of hope for the children in the home, now showed the passage of time. But the place still retained a homely feeling. Kids played in the front yard, and music could be heard booming through the windows, probably from a home-grown amateur band.

The two detectives walked through the green painted gate and approached the front door. The sun was high, and the reflection glared off the door's glazing. Tooms leaned over and rang the bell, producing a friendly chime within. As they peered through the glass, Tooms and Tony saw kids playing tag in a large room to their left; to their right was what appeared to be a sitting room of some kind, with a group of children practising on stringed instruments.

At that moment a face appeared on the other side of the glass, belonging to a cheerful woman who appeared to be in her late seventies. She opened the door, and they took in the black-and-white of her nun's habit which clung to her ample figure, and the small black-rimmed glasses that perched on the end of her button nose. In spite of her years, she possessed the vigour and spring in her step of someone half her age.

'Can I help you?' she asked, with a smile.

'Yes, ma'am, we hope so. I'm Detective Tooms, and this is Detective Marinelli of the NYPD, and we would like to speak to you, if we may, about a girl we think may have lived here some time ago.' He waved his tin badge at her.

She beckoned them into a small office down a long corridor, passing another nun along the way, who looked to be in her late twenties and quite attractive, Tony thought. The elderly nun, perhaps she was even the Mother Superior, spoke to the younger sister and asked her to bring some refreshment to the office. The office was large, with a bay window that let an amazing ray of light into the middle of the room; old pictures in dark wooden frames adorned the white wall- paper patterned with a gold fleur-de-lis design. A red shag-pile car- pet was laid widthways across the long room and at its centre stood an antique-looking coffee table, with four matching chairs arranged around it.

She raised a hand to indicate that they should sit down, and as they did so, the young sister came in with a silver tray, on which was balanced an old, mismatched crockery tea set. She placed it on the coffee table and left promptly, closing the door behind her. Tooms noticed a huge, heavy-looking dark timber desk at the end of the room, behind which hung a large golden-framed painting of The Last Supper, which almost filled the wall.

'So, Detectives, how can I help?' she asked expectantly.

'Was there ever a girl called Susan Black living here? It must have been twenty-five years ago at a guess,' asked Tooms.

At that, her smile dimmed, and her face shone less brightly. 'Yes, poor child.'

'What do you mean by that, ma'am?' Tooms enquired, his curiosity piqued.

'Well, gentlemen, there was a child by that name brought to us in… 1972, I think it was. A sad tale,' she said, getting up as if drawn towards a group of black-and-white photographs on the left-hand wall. She took one down and stroked it with affection.

'So, what happened?' asked Tony, the abruptness of his question making her shudder slightly, as though someone had walked over her grave.

'She was brought in by a sweet young thing, far too young to be a mother herself, you see. Anyway, she gave the baby up for adoption, hoping the child would find a good home and a better start in life than she could give her herself, you understand.'

Tooms and Tony, transfixed by the story, asked her to continue. 'Oh, Susan was a brilliant, talented young thing, a catch for any parent.'

'But she was never taken on?' guessed Tony, surprised.

'Everyone thought that the girls were sisters and didn't want to break them apart. She and the other girls were inseparable, you see.'

Tony and Tooms glanced at each other with a puzzled expression and then turned their attention back to the Mother Superior.

'What other girls?' asked Tooms.

The nun passed him the photo, and the two detectives' jaws dropped at the sight of three girls, standing side by side. The three children each wore identical long, dark-coloured dresses and boasted the same long, blonde hair.

'Good as gold they were, always helping out, and the other kids loved them like big sisters, especially one boy, oh, I can't remember his name. A real pleasure to have with us, they were, and then finally they left for different colleges and universities. But they always sent Christmas cards every year.' Her smile widened. 'Yes, the other two were called—'

'—Marie-Ann and Karen,' the two detectives said in unison, twin shocked expressions on their faces.

'Yes, those were their names. Oddly enough they were all brought in at roughly the same time and under similar circumstances.'

Then a look of realisation dawned on her face. 'What has happened to them?' asked the nun, predicting that she was about to get some very bad news.

The detectives helped her back to the chair by the table and poured her some water from a carafe on the desk. She thanked Tony as she took a sip from the glass.

'What has happened to our girls? Please tell me.' She began to cry and, grabbing a handkerchief from her sleeve, she patted her eyes, absorbing the cascade of tears that flowed down her rose-red cheeks.

'I'm sorry to tell you, ma'am, but they have all been murdered,' Tooms spoke gently, compassion evident in his words.

'Was it you two who you killed her?' asked the nun, coldly.

Her mood had changed. Now they were seeing a different side of the old lady, and it was harsh.

'No, ma'am.' They both looked shocked at the question.

'Then why are you sorry?' Her eyes seemed to glow with fury, and the two detectives felt as if the room was closing in around them.

'I meant we are sorry for your loss, ma'am, sorry to have to bring you bad news.' Perhaps what he really meant was that he was sorry he had drawn the short straw to come here. She seemed to calm down, but there was still a lingering anger in her eyes.

'Do you know who this did?' she asked, pulling herself together. However, her smile had not returned, nor was it likely to while they were there, they guessed.

'Not yet, ma'am, but we promise to keep you informed as and when we get something. Do you mind if we borrow this picture?'

She nodded and thanked them. The two detectives, shaken by the encounter, said their goodbyes and headed back to the safety of the station.

TWENTY-FIVE

It was just after nine o'clock in the evening, and a light breeze flowed through the maze of tall buildings. The night sky was clear but there was no moon visible, just the twinkling of millions of stars that sparkled in the heavens. Steel decided to go for a stroll, just to clear his head, since the streets were not particularly busy, which he found preferable to the daytime waves of pedestrians. As he ambled by Grand Central Station, he noticed a grubby white boy with a shoeshine box. The lad looked around twelve years old with unkempt brown hair, falling into his big blue eyes, matched by an even bigger smile. His face and clothes were grimy, and a pair of grey woollen fingerless gloves covered his hands.

'Interest you in a shine, Mister?' called the kid in a loud, positive tone.

Steel slowed his steps, the grubby, young face dredging up images from the past. Grief flooded his heart at the thought of the little brother he had lost at the same age, so long ago.

'Hey, Mister, you OK?'

Steel's thoughts returned to the present, his reverie interrupted by the squeak of the boy's still unbroken voice.

'What? I'm sorry,' he said. 'Yes, of course, I'd like a shine, why not?' 'You from England, sir?' the kid asked, eagerly. He had shone plenty of shoes, but he could not remember polishing an English gent before. 'Yes, but I haven't been home for quite a while.' Steel's tone was friendly, and he smiled at the boy.

'Wow, have you been to London? What is it like? I've heard it's great there. All those castles and stuff must be so cool. Hey, do you know Harry Potter?' The boy was so full of enthusiasm, and his innocent exuberance touched the English detective. They sat and chatted for a while about England, and the kid spoke of his ambitions of visiting exotic places, exploring the world. Steel smiled with genuine encouragement as the boy enthusiastically laid out his hopes and dreams, but all the while, Steel was only too aware of the distance between the fantasies and the reality of the child shining shoes on the street.

Steel stood up and looked at his boots: they gleamed like new. He grinned at the kid.

'What's your name, kid?' asked Steel. 'Luke, sir, Luke Johnson,' he said proudly.

'Well, Luke Johnson, it's been a pleasure to meet you. I'm John Steel. So what do I owe you, young sir?' he said, reaching into his pocket.

'That's two dollars please, sir.' The boy stood up and whipped his buffing rag over his shoulder.

'Well that's a shame, I've only got a fifty. Tell you what, you keep the change for the time being, and get yourself some new clothes, OK? When I need another shine, I'll have already paid for it.'

The boy looked shaken at the offer.

'Sorry, sir, I can't take that, it's only two dollars.' The smile had gone from his little face and Steel sensed something was amiss.

'OK, tell you what,' John said, putting the money back in

his pocket. 'Here is your two dollars plus another twenty as a tip.'

The boy still looked unsure until he glimpsed the detective's badge clipped on to Steel's belt. Once he had seen that, the smile returned.

'Thank you, sir, hope to see you again soon,' chirped the lad.

Steel ruffled the boy's hair and strolled on, a big smile on his face fading as his memories returned.

The next morning brought a cold wind, even though the sun was shining, and the skies were cloudless. Steel stepped out into the bustle of the early morning chaos and, hoping that the crowd would act as a windbreak, he ventured out towards the precinct.

As he reached the corner where the boy had been last night, he peered through the mass of people to see if he could spot him again. The kid was at his workstation, but Steel noticed something different about him. He was holding his right ribcage as if he was in pain. Steel moved closer and called out to him.

'Morning, Luke.' Steel called out. But his face dropped as the boy turned around and Steel saw that his left eye was almost completely closed by an angry-looking bruise.

'Morning, Mister Steel.' He remembered. The boy tried to affect his casual banter, but his words ended as he winced in pain.

Steel bent down and laid a gentle hand on his shoulder, but the boy flinched at the touch. Steel's blood began to boil.

'What happened?' Steel demanded, his fists clenched ready to take action, if only the boy would give him the information he needed.

'Fell down the stairs, sir, that's all.'

Steel was disappointed that the lad was lying to him, well

aware that unless the boy said something, nothing would change. Clearly the boy was scared, he could see that, but not of him. No, there was something else he was scared of, *someone* else.

'You need to go to the hospital, young man,' said Steel, standing up. 'Get yourself checked over.'

The boy grabbed his trouser leg and pierced him with a pleading look. 'No sir, please don't interfere, everything is fine, honest.'

The Englishman knew that the boy was lying but what could he do, call child services? Unless the kid cooperated, that would not fix his problem and would likely make it worse. There was no alternative; he had to respect the boy's wishes, no matter what his personal feelings were.

'Here is your usual fee.' Steel gave the boy the same amount as yesterday, but the boy gave him back the twenty.

'It really is too much, sir.'

Steel could see that the boy had been beaten, probably for having taken the extra money.

'See you tomorrow then, kid.' Steel forced a smile as he stood in front of the suffering boy.

'Sure thing, sir, see you tomorrow, sir,' replied the boy, trying to return a grin.

'Steel, the name's John Steel.'

The boy nodded. 'I know, Mr. Steel,' he said

As Steel walked off, his guts moved. He had a bad feeling about the boy, and he had to do something fast.

At the station, Steel stepped off the elevator and headed for McCall's desk, where he found her checking her emails from the previous day. 'Morning,' she greeted him, but her words fell flat when she saw the expression on his face.

'Morning,' he replied, the thought of the bruised boy still upper-most in his thoughts.

'What's up?' she said, appearing to be actually concerned. 'Yesterday I got my shoes shined by this brilliant young lad –

we spoke for ages about this and that. He had so much life; it was inspiring.'

McCall was now waiting for the punch line.

'This morning he looked like he had gone twelve rounds with Mike Tyson.'

'Did he say anything about it?' she asked, now feeling actual concern.

'No, he said he fell down the stairs, but it's so frustrating when I know he's covering up for someone.' Steel looked as though he could hardly contain his anger.

McCall tried to reason with him. 'You know that unless he, or someone else, gives us something to work with, we can't do anything.'

He knew she was right, but what could he do?

'Look, do you want me to call child services?' she asked, picking up her phone.

He gave her a puppy-dog look and put his hand on top of hers, and she put down the receiver.

'I get the feeling that if we did that, things would get even worse for him.'

She could see he suspected the situation was bigger than they knew, and that he felt powerless to stop the inevitable, whatever that may be.

'Coffee?' he asked abruptly, grabbing her cup.

'Yes, please.' She was surprised at this sudden change in mood.

The English detective marched resolutely over to the coffee room to make a couple of cups of the foul-smelling brew. On his return, he placed the cup of steaming coffee in front of McCall on the desk. She thanked him and smiled. This was a new type of behaviour that she had not expected from him, and she had to admit, it fitted him admirably.

Steel sipped the coffee, trying not to inhale the fumes that arose from the cup. As the vile-tasting liquid pierced the back of his throat, he screwed up his face and the burnt, acrid taste filled his mouth.

'Really, you actually drink this stuff?' he said in incredulity.

She smiled airily and gulped down a big mouthful of the brew, looking him straight in the eye as if it were some macho test. All the while, she was concealing the need to retch because this batch honestly tasted like battery acid.

Steel shuddered at her expression.

'Don't feel bad, Steel,' she giggled. 'If the coffee's too strong for you, you could put in a request for milk and cookies.'

The two of them spent the next few hours browsing through the diaries and date planners, not coming up with anything of interest. McCall leant back in her chair, her arms stretching wide, which had the effect of stretching her tight-fitting, V-neck jumper across her ample breasts. A young, male, uniformed cop passing by caught this display and, transfixed, bumped straight into the captain.

'What are you doing, boy, were you bottle-fed or something?' the senior officer bellowed at the flustered young cop. 'Now it was god-damn lucky one of us wasn't carrying a cup of that puke we call coffee!' The young man looked like he didn't know which way to run.

Spotting the opening elevator, he made for it gratefully, leaving the captain chuckling to himself, before turning to McCall. 'And as for you, McCall, keep those things under control, will you? Someone could get hurt.'

They both laughed.

'You hear that, girls?' McCall addressed her bosom.

'Behave yourselves- we don't want to give Mr Steel here a heart attack, do we?'

Steel looked up at the mention of his name. 'Those things I can handle,' he replied confidently, adding ruefully, 'The coffee, however, not so much!'

He stood up and made for the elevator.

'Where the hell are you going?' asked the captain, still chuckling to himself.

'To get a bit of heaven,' he replied, 'Just to get a bit of heaven.'

TWENTY-SIX

Having composed himself, Dr Davidson had returned to his room at the precinct and was absorbed with sifting through the new data on the victims. Installed behind his desk, which was now brimming over with paperwork, he made notes from this page and that. *'Fascinating, oh, intriguing,'* he muttered to himself, as he went through the transcripts. He was utterly possessed by the case; this killer was, for him, the ultimate psychopath.

As McCall and Steel entered the room he was preoccupied and didn't seem to hear, even though McCall had knocked loudly. She threw Steel a *can you believe him* look, then tried coughing, but still he didn't answer.

'Morning, Doc,' she announced. This finally had an effect. The doctor glared at her, and she stared right back at him. He seemed discomfited by her assertive presence. After all, he was usually the one in charge, but she had somehow turned the tables. It was an interesting new experience for him.

'Can I help you, Detective?' he said slowly, his voice grating, ranging in pitch from high to low.

'Well, yes, I thought that was the point of your being here?'

Steel tried to hide a smirk as she took the doc down a couple of pegs.

'Forgive me,' Dr Davidson apologised. 'You see, I'm used to working alone, you understand, and, er…'

He only then seemed to notice Steel and stared at him in surprise. 'Who's this?' He pointed to the second detective, who was studying the doctor's information board.

'That is Detective Steel, don't mind him, he always wears his shades indoors, he's British. I don't think they have artificial light over there.'

Steel turned around and adjusted his sunglasses with his middle finger.

'Pleased to meet you, sir.' Steel stepped towards the strange doctor and extended a hand so they could shake, but the doctor ignored it and looked straight through him.

'So, what have you got so far?' Sam McCall asked, snickering to herself at the Englishman's rebuff.

'Well, your man is calculated, brilliant, methodical, and cunning, which may make him the most dangerous character you've ever tracked.'

They all moved forwards towards the information boards. There were pictures of the victims with any defining characteristics noted down under their names.

'He is a master with the scalpel and other surgical tools and he is well-versed in their methods of employment,' continued the arrogant medical man.

'And you know this how?' asked Steel, somewhat uncomfortable with the respectful tone Davidson used in describing the killer's attributes.

'Well, let's look at the evidence. All the cuts are precise – whereas most lay-people, when they cut someone up, would create saw marks all over the bone.' He pointed to a close-up picture of the severed stump where an arm had been removed.

'As you can see, it's properly separated at the joint. The synovial capsule has a straight incision, no jagged edges, no nicks on the bone. Our killer took his time and he knew exactly what he was doing.'

Steel peered closer at the photos and shook his head.

'What's wrong, Detective, not got the stomach for this?' The doctor tittered. 'Doesn't surprise me, though.' He was clearly on a mission to undermine the Englishman.

'Really?' Steel replied, keeping his cool. 'Please elaborate?' Steel stepped back from the board to face the doctor, who had a very strange grin on his face.

'Well now, let us see. You consider yourself a man of action, but something tells me the only fighting you've ever seen is on television. You wish to project an image that is intimidating to others, so that's why you wear those sunglasses indoors. I suspect you wear them all the time, don't you?'

McCall stood listening, engrossed, wondering if the psychiatrist's vicious analysis had any basis in reality. Oh, she hoped so, she really hoped so.

'Anything else?' Steel asked in a detached tone, his arms clasped loosely behind his back.

'Well, if you insist.'

A small crowd had gathered outside the room, with Tooms and the captain in the front, ready to jump in to support the man who was being insulted, on the off chance he decided to rip the doctor apart.

'I imagine your mother brought up the family in a slum residence, your father no doubt took off when you were just a child. This explains why you seem to be in awe of people with wealth, and also your need to try to present yourself as a man of means because you are desperate to be one of them.'

Steel remained stock still, arms behind his back, unflinching as the doctor tried to make a fool of him, ripped apart his reputation and his family. By this time the expression of bloodlust on the doctor's face as he proceeded with his assault was evident to all.

'You are a nobody, Detective,' said the doctor with a vicious grin, 'which raises the question, how did an insignificant Englishman worm his way into the NYPD?'

This immediately touched a nerve with everyone in the room. Steel noticed the crowd in the adjacent main office suddenly start to mutter amongst themselves. *The doc was right*, they all thought. The doubt on their faces was clear.

'I applaud you, Doctor, on your talent for creating such an entertaining piece of fiction. Sadly, as the finest cop I have ever had the good fortune of knowing would remind us, we work with facts, not hunches or feelings. But, to follow your example, I would suggest that you are a man who takes pleasure in dumping on people that you consider a threat, using your pseudo-scientific gibberish. You reached the top of your field, and now you probably spend all your days treating sad, old women who have lost their pets, or are miserable that the gardener doesn't want to sleep with them anymore.' By now the smug face of the doctor had turned sour, and his teeth began to show.

John Steel wasn't finished with him. 'You've tried to malign my family, which leads me to speculate that you yourself are an orphan. You probably weren't ever selected for adoption. No, I suspect that, even as a child, you were so odious that you scared people, for which reason the adoption services never put you in enough limelight to be picked up by adoptive parents. I have also observed that you that have issues of power and rejection with women, which is why you bully the pretty ones.'

Davidson's expression could have curdled milk.

'Added to that, you have a strange fascination with death, *an overwhelming fascination* perhaps. Cops are forced to deal with the ghastly aspects of death, but someone with your qualifications?'

The doctor's face was almost purple at this point, but McCall noticed that throughout the confrontation Steel was almost eerily calm. He looked like he was about to slam another nail in the man's coffin when they were interrupted by the *ding* of the elevator, and a uniformed officer from downstairs emerged from it with the small shoeshine boy, Luke. Steel immediately turned his back on the shrink, and strode over to the boy, apparently forgetting immediately about the doctor, much to the captain's relief. 'It's OK, Colin, he's with me,' he said to the uniform, who lifted his hands from the boy's shoulder and left.

'So, did you get it?' Steel asked his young friend.

The boy nodded conspiratorially and handed over a large duffel bag to Steel, who unzipped the bag, peeked inside and sniffed eagerly.

'Oh yes, that's the stuff,' he sighed. Everyone one looked puzzled.

'You see?' piped up the doctor, believing he had found a new weapon to use against Steel, after witnessing the little scene unfolding. 'He has brought drugs into the precinct. And he has used a small boy as his courier.'

Davidson pointed accusingly at the boy and Steel. The detective turned towards him and held up his hands.

'Wow, OK, Doc, you got me. The bag is stacked with bricks of drugs. How much would you say?'

Steel turned to the boy, who was sharp enough to know that Steel was messing with the doc.

'I couldn't say, sir, but I do know you owe me a tip,' the boy replied with a grin.

The detective cracked a smile, 'Hundred bucks suit you, including the cost of the gear?' he asked, tossing a green note to the kid, who deftly caught it and pushed it into his pocket.

'Now you get back to your shoe stand, and pencil me in for the same deal every fortnight if that's okay with you.' He glanced around the room. 'Tell you what, I'll let you know if there are any changes in my order when I next see you.'

The boy shot off, using the side stairs.

'Steel, what the hell is in the bag?' Sam McCall demanded.

Steel grinned and headed for the coffee room, trailed by the squad of detectives who'd been watching the incident, leaving the doctor standing alone, unwilling to follow, still contemplating how to prove his point. As soon as he reached the refreshment area, Steel grabbed the jugs from the machines and emptied their vile contents down the sink. He prepared the three machines then reached into the bag and took out a small black-and-blue vacuum-wrapped packet.

'Steel, what the hell is that?' asked the captain. 'Is that what I think it is? Now, don't you mess with me.'

Steel slowly nodded as he raised the brick up.

'Ladies and gentlemen,' he declared theatrically. 'Prepare for paradise.' He filled the machines with water and packed the hopper with aromatic black powder from the package, then neatly folded over the top of the package and stored it in the fridge. Before saying another word, he listened for the distinctive *burrrr* of the hot water filtering through the coffee grounds.

'I would like to offer you a little taste of heaven,' he announced as the machines stopped, and the detectives poured into the room like some zombie horde. Steel sought refuge beside the doctor, who scowled at Steel's approach.

'And what do you want now, Detective?'

Steel bit his lip at the doctor's unfriendly tone.

'Look, Doctor, we are both professionals, and we're both here to perform a service. I'm here because I have to be, you are here because you need to be, so let's just forget our differences and be civil.' And with a flourish, he produced two cups of coffee from behind his back and giving one to the doctor he raised his as a sign they should toast the agreement. The doctor hesitated, shrugged, and tapped his cup against Steel's. McCall stood behind them, watching the display between the two rivals and shook her head. Every time she thought she had gotten a read on Steel he threw a curve ball. She took a preliminary sip of her coffee.

Oh, it is good, she thought as her eyes rolled back.

TWENTY-SEVEN

The hour was late, and Steel bid his colleagues goodnight. The sun had sunk below the horizon and washes of colour painted the skyline with purples, reds, and oranges. He decided that he would go and check on his young friend. As he approached the spot where the boy's shoeshine box normally stood, he saw only an empty space, and a sickening feeling crawled over him like a heavy blanket. He kept walking, hoping to catch a sign of Luke, but he saw nothing. The streets were oddly silent as he ventured home, hoping and praying the boy was OK.

Steel slid his key slid into the door and let himself into the apartment, hanging up his jacket before moving to the drinks cabinet and picking out the bottle of Glendronach malt whisky. He poured a little of the golden-coloured liquid into a tumbler and tossed it back like a Schnapps. Putting down the glass, he poured a second, more substantial measure. This time he was going to savour the aromas and not just light his fire. Lost in thought, he drifted across the room and settled himself on the chaise longue that faced the window. Gazing out across the expanse of the city, he feared for the boy's safety.

. . .

As the dawn broke, the city appeared to be covered with a blue-grey tint. The air was fresh and moist, as a figure in a black hooded tracksuit pounded towards Battery Park. The streets were almost empty. The only noise to be heard was from the hydraulics of the garbage trucks echoing through the maze of buildings. Intermittently, the peace was pierced by the wail of sirens, as cop cars, fire trucks, and ambulances raced across town, carrying heroes with lives to save.

Steel liked to jog at this time of day; the cool, fresh air cleared his airways from the filth of the previous day's traffic. He slowed and came to rest by the railings that overlooked the bay, where the dull brown water lapped up the sides of posts that were sunk down into the murky depths.

Taking the bottle from the pouch on his belt, he popped the stopper top and took a mouthful of clean water, swilling it round his mouth before swallowing. Finding a bench, he sat and looked out across the bay and regarded the blood red of the sunrise. He reflected that, in ancient times, a blood-red sky meant blood had been spilt the night before. He hoped to God that was not the case, thinking back to the boy, Luke. Jumping up, he set off once more.

Sundays held a special place in McCall's week. It was the one time she could go and see her mom in Boston. She would go every weekend if work allowed. Her mother had a small place in a quiet part of the city; it was a modest, residential area with white picket fences, where the kids could play safely in the street. The sun shone brightly, a breeze rustled through the trees and, as she stood at the front porch of her mom's house, she closed her eyes and listened to the nothingness, and it was great.

Reaching forwards, she pressed the bell. Its loud chime

echoed through the house, and moments later a cheerful voice called from somewhere deep within. 'I'll be with you in a minute,' McCall heard, then she saw through the small slits of glass embedded in the door a figure moving quickly towards her. Her mother threw open the door, a diminutive, older lady in a long white dress covered in faded, flowery patterns, reminiscent of the 1970s. Her hair was obviously dyed brown and showed signs of a recent perm.

The two women embraced at the sight of one another.

'I don't understand why you never use the key I gave to you,' her mother said, a big grin on her round face.

'You know why, Mom? It's because I love the look on your face when you open the door to me. Like you, just got a happy surprise. It's great to be here.' Her mother pulled her inside.

'Drop your bag there and come into the kitchen,' McCall's mother chattered over her shoulder as she bustled them along the hallway. 'I made some coffee and an apple pie.'

McCall didn't need to be asked twice; as she entered the spacious kitchen a waft of freshly percolated coffee and cinnamon filled her nostrils and tickled her taste buds, prompting her to pause a moment to inhale the rich smell of home. She took a seat on one of the wooden chairs around the pine table in the middle of the room. The kitchen was quite large with old-style fittings, and McCall had always loved it here. The house had a welcoming, homely feel, fitted with a lot of stained-wood-and-brass doors and cosy furniture.

McCall's mother passed over some cups, saucers and side plates, and McCall helped set the table. The older woman brought over a great bone-china pot filled with fresh coffee and a huge pie on a plate that matched the tea set. The daughter poured the coffee, while her mother cut slices of the hot, steaming pie and put them on plates. Spooning mounds of freshly whipped cream onto the side of her plate, McCall dug into the pie with a small fork, the sugar-crusted pastry pressing down upon the fruit, causing chunks of apple and filling to ooze from the sides before the top broke with a mouth-watering crunch.

The two women talked about this and that, who was going out with whom, and all the regular local gossip, which McCall so enjoyed catching up on. Sometimes she thought, why didn't she just quit the force and get a normal life like this? And then she recalled the reason she became a cop in the first place. It was a difficult memory, and her happy expression faded. Her mother took her hand, sensing her daughter's distress. McCall snapped back to reality at her touch.

'It's OK to remember him, dear, just don't let his death take control,'

McCall looked puzzled for a second. 'What? Oh no, Mom, it's not that I'm thinking about, it's something else completely.'

Her mother had one rule: don't bring your work home with you, and McCall liked it like that.

TWENTY-EIGHT

M onday morning brought a new sunrise heralding a new day, and McCall was back in the precinct, hoping for a fresh lead on the killer. She was at her desk, reading through some reports, when Steel walked in. Even she had to admit he looked good in the black suit, with its strange three-quarter length jacket that almost hid the black, silk shirt, the top three buttons undone.

She tried to pretend she hadn't seen him and hoped she had not been gawping noticeably. From behind him came a wolf whistle and he just raised his hand to thank his unknown admirer.

'Morning,' she said, still burying her head in the paper-work, 'Good morning. And how was your weekend?' he asked, clearly happy with himself.

'It was good thanks; I went to see my mom,' she replied, somewhat surprised at his interest. 'And yours? Did you do anything for fun or were you just chasing bad guys?' she giggled at her joke.

'No, I had a quiet time. I tracked down some old friends, got tied up with them for a while but then they had to go – I guess they had a pressing engagement,' McCall flashed him a concerned look, not wanting to know what he was actually talking about, though she had a gut feeling that it hadn't been good for somebody.

Tony and Tooms plodded in, their expressions spoke volumes, suggesting that their weekend had not been so successful.

'Hi guys, what's up?' she asked, not really wanting to hear of any problems until at least midday.

'While you two were off for the weekend, we got a nasty one.' Tooms grimaced at the recollection. He held the file close to his chest as McCall reached for it, a perplexed look crossing her face.

'Why didn't anybody tell me we got a case?' she asked.

''Cause we got assigned this one. Sorry, the boss said you two would be too close to it.'

Now she really was puzzled and annoyed. 'What do you mean, close to it?' she asked, clearly put out.

'It was your boy from the theatre that Tarzan here put into hospital after using him for a crash mat.'

'Yes, what about him?' asked McCall, a terrible feeling creeping over her as she glanced at Steel.

'Someone went to pay him a visit,' Tony said, sounding troubled. 'Cool. So, who was it? Did we get a name on them?' asked Steel, enthusiastically.

'No, we did not. Whoever it was crept in like a ghost and cut him up pretty good.' Tony said, looking as if the memory made him nauseous.

'OK, not so cool. But how did it happen? There were cops on the door, right?' Steel said, taken aback.

'Like a ghost, you said?' McCall commented acidly. 'So, what was it you said you did this weekend, Steel?' Her eyes were burning with distrust.

'Come on,' Steel replied, resenting the implication. 'You can't be serious. You don't honestly think I snuck in and knifed the silly bastard, do you? If I'd wanted him dead, I'd have killed him while ,he was still underneath me.' He realised everybody was watching him closely. 'Look, on Friday I was playing poker with some friends.' Steel said at last.

'I bet you're good at that because you don't give anything away, do you?' she taunted him. Her voice was cold and hard. Ever since the theatre incident, she'd begun to get good vibes from him, but now, well, once again, she had no idea what to think.

McCall grabbed her cup and made for the coffee room, Tooms and Tony following, pointedly leaving Steel behind.

'So, what did you find out about him?' she asked Tooms surreptitiously. He perched on the edge of the table while the others gathered around.

'Well, I spoke to my buddy from the SEALs, and he said that our boy there was attached to whatever team was going out. They classed him as a 'lone wolf', but he was real good at making everyone's job easier. He mainly specialised in hostage rescue. Also, he would go in before a building was going to be stormed, and even the odds or just get intelligence. They used to call him 'The Phoenix', 'cause nothing could put him down.'

The room fell quiet as they absorbed the revelation.

'OK, so he was in the military,' McCall said. 'It's cool we have a lead. What else did he say?'

'If he is on your side you can walk away from pretty much any- thing.'

'And if you're on the other side?' asked Tony. Tooms just gave him a *don't go there* look. 'And before that?' McCall asked, keenly.

'Nothing. Officially the man didn't exist till he got to the TEAMS, then after an incident, he fell off the radar again until now.' They regarded Steel studying the information board and flicking through notes.

'Oh yeah, one thing; you'll never guess who he's really

friendly with?' Tooms said, producing a paper wallet of pictures.

McCall shrugged. 'Who?'

He passed the photos across for McCall and Tony to inspect. 'The mayor. Steel's big buddy here's the mayor.'

'OK, we keep that to ourselves but if it becomes a problem, we'll share it with the captain,' she advised them.

They all nodded in agreement.

Tooms then pulled out a slip of paper and passed it across to McCall. She looked at him warily, unprepared for any more surprises.

'What's this now?' she queried, the strain of recent days starting to show in her voice.

'It's an address,' said Tooms, with a smug smile. 'What sort of address? Is it a witness?' McCall asked. Tooms shook his head.

'So, whose address is it? Not Steel's?' Tony was torn at the prospect of discovering his mysterious colleague's personal territory. Tony had conjured many images in his head of where a man like John Steel might reside, but he was also starting to feel a bit treacherous to be investigating another cop, even one as strange as Steel.

'Well, I guess we all have somewhere to live, but most of us don't have an apartment on Central Park West on a detective's pay check.'

The other two cops' mouths dropped open.

'He lives on Central Park West?' repeated McCall.

Tooms nodded. 'So it appears.'

'How the hell can he afford a place there?' Now she was mad, really mad. Was he a mob boss or something? All sorts of weird ideas filled her head.

She turned furiously towards the information board, where she'd last seen Steel, but he'd vanished. Had he caught on to the fact they were investigating his life, she wondered?

She shot out of the room and caught Officer Brenda Grant walking past.

'Have you seen Detective Steel?' she asked, urgently.

'He got a call from downstairs and shot off. He looked quite upset,' she replied.

McCall waved the others to follow and ran to the lower floor. 'Had somewhere to go, did he?' she muttered to herself. She had got the address, which was in Harlem so, taking both cars, they raced there to confront Steel about what the hell was going on.

As they approached, they were confronted by a barricade of police cars, ambulances, and two coroner's trucks. They pulled up and parked, ready to leap into action. Then McCall caught sight of Tina and was struck by the realisation that she had never seen the ME looking so sad before.

Then she saw him. Steel was slumped on a step, staring vacantly at his blood-soaked hands as though they did not belong to him.

McCall strode towards him, passing Tina as she went, unaware in her fury of her friend trying to stop her. Suddenly all those days of John Steel wearing down her defences had made her angry enough to tell him how she felt.

'What's the matter?' she yelled at Detective Steel. 'Did one of your gangsters piss you off? Is that it? God, you come to Manhattan thinking you can stop every little crime, well you can't! This time you have gone too far, Mr Steel!'

He gazed at her and rose to his feet slowly; his clothes sodden with blood. What the hell had he done, she thought?

'You're right, Detective, I can't,' he answered. 'Maybe I should stop trying.' And with that he walked off, leaving her still boiling.

'We are not done yet, Steel,' she shouted after him, but he just raised a hand as if to wave her away.

She made her way back to Tina, who had just processed the last body and closed the body bag.

'So, what has Dirty Harry done this time?' she joked, hoping to lighten her mood with her friend, but instead Tina just gave her a frown of anger and disappointment.

'What?' McCall asked in surprise. 'What did I do?' Tina opened the bags, saying, 'Look.'

As Detective McCall peered inside, she saw what appeared to be a small boy's corpse. The other body bag contained the corpse of a grown woman, of similar colouring to the kid, with similar injuries to her body. Were they related? She noticed that the boy was wearing a jacket similar to the one worn by Luke, who had brought the bags of coffee into the precinct that day. All at once, the full horror of the situation hit her. A lump filled her throat and she felt hot tears rolling down her face. She was not just weeping for the boy and his mother, but for what Steel must be feeling too.

The captain ordered McCall to go home, and Steel had already disappeared, so Tooms and Tony had to pick up the slack. The murderous Steve Johnson was now the DA's problem, and his lawyers would have a hell of a job defending him, considering the fact that when the cops had busted his door in, he was in the process of putting a hammer through his wife's skull. That, and his comment, when asked why he did it, that she would not give him money for booze and she just got in the way, after which he laughed. A slam-dunk for an insanity plea, Tooms thought, but the bastard deserves the chair.

McCall did not go home. Instead, she went to the station gym and rode a million miles on the bike, followed by several rounds with the punch bag. Her black all-in-one gym suit clung to her sweating body, accentuating every curve; she could feel the hungry eyes of the men nearby on her, her resentment at their uninvited attention fuelling her to kick the hell out of the black, worn bag. That, and the uncomfortable feeling she might feel differently if it were Steel there, gaping at her. The punch bag swung with every hit as she gave it everything she had. Sam McCall showered, changed, and bought two coffees from the coffee shop around the corner from the morgue.

Approaching tentatively, she hoped to find Tina in a forgiving mood. Not so much, Tina's eyes were still red with rage and grief. McCall gingerly stepped forward, a steaming coffee cup in her out- stretched hand as a peace offering. Tina took the cup, almost snatching it from her friend's hand, while still fixing her with the evil eye.

'Look, I'm sorry I lost my temper back there and—'

'—Uh uh, girl, you do not apologise to me.' Tina raised a hand to stop her. 'You know who you have to say sorry to.' She nodded at the sad little corpse on the table in front of her.

Father Gabriel O'Donnell was naturally cheerful and good-spirited. He rarely had reason to be otherwise, for he had originally been a military chaplain and now he had a decent parish in New York so, all in all, life was good and less complicated than before. He wore his thick, dark hair short and, though he could be mistaken for a thin man at a superficial glance, under his clerical garments, his muscles and physique were still those of a trained athlete.

Beneath the graceful, vaulted stone ceiling of the church, he paced steadily up the centre aisle to the red-carpeted transept, where he knelt and bent his head in prayer for a few moments, then raised his eyes and crossed himself before the crucifix that hung above the altar. Rising, he made his way to a discreet door set in the far corner that led to the back rooms and his office. As he did so, he noticed that the confessional box was occupied. He quietly slipped into his side of the cubicle, sat and slid across the small shutter that separated the two cells. He made the sign of the cross and kissed the rosary in his hand.

'Forgive me, Father, for I could not sin,' breathed a shallow voice. The priest thought for a moment and then responded, 'Do you wish to discuss something with me that is outside the purview of the confessional?'

'I expect so,' the voice replied, 'whatever that means.'

The priest stood and opened the communicating door to find John Steel sitting in the dark box, covered in blood. The priest, shocked at the sight, glanced around before hurriedly ushering him to the back of the church and into his private office. Quickly Father O'Donnell worked out that none of the blood was Steel's, which raised the question, whose was it? Which generated further questions. He strode over to a large wooden globe that stood in a dark corner of the room and lifted the lid, revealing several bottles of whiskies, brandies, and scotches. Taking two heavy, beaded glasses, he poured them each a drink from a well-aged Irish whiskey. Passing Steel a glass, O'Donnell brought his chair forward slightly and settled himself facing the morose-looking detective.

'Do you want to talk about it?' asked the priest, leaning back in the creaking leather chair. Steel stared into his glass, swirling the contents around, watching the liquid rise near the top and fall again to the bottom.

'A couple of days ago I was walking past Grand Central when this kid pops up out of nowhere and asks can if he can shine my shoes.' Steel took a sip as the priest leant forward slightly.

'I swear, when I saw him, I thought it was Thomas, you know, the kid was the spitting image of him.' Steel smiled slightly but was lost in his thoughts again.

'OK, go on Jonny,' the priest prompted, unsure if he actually wanted to hear this story.

'Anyway, this kid and I got chatting, and it turns out that he was getting together the money to go to school, trying to make something of himself, but his dad is a drunk and a bully, so I figured that the guy was swiping the few dollars the boy earned.'

The priest was confused for a moment. 'How did you know about the father? Did this just come up in conversation or did you follow the boy?'

'No, but I could tell. Every time I saw him, he had fresh bruises, and he got this panicked look on his face when I mentioned family.'

The priest nodded. He too had seen what Steel described, far too often.

Steel swallowed the complete contents of his glass in a single movement. and the priest just swapped their glasses. He felt that if he got up to pour a fresh one, the moment would be lost.

'At the station today, my work colleagues were having a private chat, and I can only imagine what that was about.' Steel took a swig from the glass. 'That's when I got the call from the uniforms downstairs, a disturbance at the kid's address.' The priest got up. He knew he was about to need a drink, his stomach sinking as he imagined what was coming next. Crossing to the cabinet, he just grabbed the bottle and returned to his seat.

'We got to the address, and there were more uniforms there waiting to go in.' Steel looked up at his old friend, but his pained expression was lost behind his dark glasses. 'We bust the door in to see the guy with a hammer beating in the heads of the kid and his mother. There was blood every-where.' He downed the contents of his glass and the priest refilled it, his hands shaking, as Steel noticed immediately.

'Are you OK, Gabriel?' asked Steel, now concerned about his friend. The priest nodded heavily and begged him to continue.

'As we got in, Officer Pike, just a young kid but a good cop from what I saw, goes in to disarm this scumbag and gets himself slammed against the wall. The guy has Pike pinned there and a hammer raised, ready to smash the cop's head in.' Steel shook his head and frowned up at his friend, who was pre-empting the narrative in his head.

'So, what did you do?' Fearing he'd guessed the answer before he said it, the priest asked anyway.

'This lunatic has a freaking hammer over his head, dripping blood, and he looks at the cop for a second, then he looks at me, then he fucking smiles and pulls the weapon further back to get a better goddamn swing.'

'So, you shoot him?' Knowing Steel for so long, the question seemed redundant.

'No,' he replied.

His friend froze with astonishment. Father Gabriel O'Donnell knew Steel well from their days in the TEAMS. John Steel was a man who scared most of the toughest SEALs, not just because when he exploded he was nothing short of an animal, but because the man could move like a ghost: one member of the team called him 'unnatural' and another, who was of Native American descent, called him a 'wraith'. But what he had just described went against the nature of the beast. Steel saw the look on his friend's face and smiled, ruefully.

'Don't get me wrong, Gabriel, I wanted to blow this guy away so badly, but in that split second I had to make a choice.'

'Between what exactly?' The priest was incredulous, and excited at the progress Steel had made.

'Between going back to what I was and losing everything I had worked for, and being a decent cop and not failing the incredible people I work with and, incidentally, failing you, my old friend.'

The priest smiled and rested a reassuring hand on Steel's shoulder. 'Well, one thing hasn't changed, my friend,' Gabriel said, still grinning.

'What's that?' Steel looked worried. 'You're still full of crap, buddy.' They both laughed.

'Anyway, go on, now you have my full attention,' said the priest, sliding back in the seat and getting more comfortable.

'So, this guy is smiling at me, the other cops have their pistols raised, and what do I do? I rugby tackle the bastard, and while he is on the floor, *that's* when I draw my piece. I put it against his temple and look him right in the eyes.' Steel took another hit from the glass.

'At first this guy was taunting me – daring me to shoot him. But that death was too quick for him and too much paperwork for me. No, this bastard was going to jail and going to trial.' At that point, the priest knew that the old Steel was still there, it was just that now he used brainpower instead of brute force to get things done. The question was, which was deadlier?

'I had him. I could feel the anger swelling up inside of him when I told him he was going to live and when I said that I would visit him every day if I had to, to remind him of what he had done, that put the fear of God into him.'

'Did you enjoy it?' asked O'Donnell, now getting worried.

'At first yes, but then I got my shit together and cuffed him. Picked up the cop who'd been attacked and got him back on his feet while the uniforms booked him.'

'Are you OK, Jonny?'

'Yes, I'm fine, and that's the problem, after everything that happened. Well, you know?'

The priest nodded.

'I'll get you a coffee,' Gabriel said, taking the empty glass. Steel smiled and nodded.

TWENTY-NINE

B ack at her desk, McCall flicked through the mountains of files cluttering her desk concerning the three murders, including all the forensic and ME reports, but she still drew a blank. Slamming shut the file she was reading, she stood up and turned to the set of information boards set up in front of her desk. One board was entirely taken up with a street map of the city, laminated so it could be written or drawn on repeatedly.

Standing back, she considered the pins that had been placed to denote the sites at which each victim was found. She perched on the back edge of her desk and peered closely at each pin, each connecting line, each street name. What was she missing, she wondered? Tony and Tooms wandered up to her, each clutching a mug of coffee and a hot dog, and smiled at her.

'What are you thinking?' asked Tooms, as he slurped his coffee by her ear.

'Don't know yet. It must be there, I just can't see it.' she said slowly, as though some idea was stirring at the back of her mind.

'Did you get anything?' she asked.

Tony shook his head as he polished off the rest of the hot dog. 'The homeless guys struck out; these guys are either in the wind or dead,' he remarked.

She had to agree, but she wasn't about to give up yet. She stood up and grabbed a handful of different coloured marker pins.

'What are you up to?' asked Tooms, puzzled. Taking a yellow pin, she stuck it into the map, then used a felt marker to draw lines from one victim to the other. Wherever the lines crossed, she put a pin.

'You are working on the basis that all serial killers have a comfort zone?' said a voice from behind them. They all turned to see the doctor standing there.

'What if this guy doesn't have a comfort zone?' asked Tony.

They looked nervously at each other, hoping someone would say something to shatter that horrifying thought. 'Well, Doc?'

Doctor Davidson scanned the map for a moment. 'You suggested he used homeless people to move the bodies?' he asked, still staring at the board.

'Yes, why do you ask?' queried McCall. If the doctor were a genius, now were the time to prove it.

'Well, it could mean he felt close to the victims, he couldn't bear to see them in their end state, that would shatter the illusion he had built of them.'

All three detectives gaped at one another, mouths open in surprise. 'What do you mean? That this killer feels he has a relationship with the victims, so he cuts them up and keeps the parts he wants but can't bear to get rid of the rest of their bodies?' Tooms speculated, confused by this line of thought.

'This man you are after,' the doctor continued, 'from what I can tell, does not identify with the entire victim, just specific parts that catch his attention or excite him, in the same way that a man with a foot fetish cares little about the appearance of the whole person, he's only interested in their feet.'

'Ok, Doc,' Tooms replied. 'Given this information, where do we start looking?'

The strange medical man turned to them. McCall could sense that an idea was blooming inside that narrow skull of his.

'Check men who work at beauty salons, spas, anywhere that guys might have had contact with our victims in situations where he could see them partially dressed.' The doctor moved closer to the board, and a strange expression crossed his pale face that was almost sadness, or perhaps remorse.

'You're looking for someone who has been fixated on the victims for a long time, maybe even years. Look at co-workers who may have played sports with them on occasions. Anyone who has seen them in the flesh. Judging by our victims' lifestyles, that list should be quite short.'

Tony raised a hand once he had jotted the information down. 'What about the kid the nun told us about?'

The doctor's eyes remained transfixed by the photos of the women as they had been in life.

'It may be a lead, OK, go for it,' McCall instructed him, and turned to Davidson. 'Nice job, Doc,' she said with a smile, the first proper smile she had given him. He returned the smile, but she wished he hadn't. It sent a shiver shooting through her spine.

The midday sun burned brightly, but down in the homeless shelter it was cooler. The empty, old school building was now home to the lost, the destitute or those who didn't want to be found. Raggedy people shuffled in to find a hot meal, a bed for the night or both.

The queue for food was long, and empty seats in the

dining hall were getting fewer but, for the raggedy people, even a safe spot on a clean floor could be considered a relief.

Eric and George were buddies, they had seen many cold winters and blazing summers together, and in this world, they lived in, a friend to watch your back was never a bad thing. The pair had endured much but still managed to keep cheerful.

'So, have we got another job coming up, Eric?' asked stickily built George, as he moved along the queue. George was smaller than Eric, but his build was that of a steel worker: his many years in the navy had given him some bulk. He had seen many wonderful places in far off lands, but after his life in the services, he'd fallen on hard times, and now he drifted on the city's tides with his pal. There were too many veterans who had served their country well, and yet over time their country had forgotten them.

'No. It's somewhat queer that we haven't heard from him, don't you think?' replied Eric. He spoke and carried himself well. In his former life, he'd been a distinguished surgeon, but he had succumbed to the grip of drug addiction and lost everything: his job, his wife and kids, everything. Eric was a tall, skinny man with brushed back, receding hair, and his long, thin face was notable for its elongated Roman nose and large mouth, whose broad smile could crack his face apart.

'Shame, we sure could have used the money. Oh well,' George sighed.

Eric straightened his filthy red tie. He may have been down-and-out, but he still insisted on wearing a suit. George might have once found this strange, but Eric had never done him wrong, and he no longer noticed his friend's eccentricity.

'Work, did I hear you say work?' They both turned to find a bearded hunchback leaning towards them, wearing an expression of eager inquiry.

'What of it?' Eric addressed the stranger. 'And may I point out, it is most impolite of you to eavesdrop, sir, now hence and away with you.' Eric turned back to his friend, and the bulky hunchback, who was almost the same height as George, moved a little closer, cupping his hands together as if begging for forgiveness.

'Please, sir, I meant no disrespect to you or your friend, it's just hearing the talk of work that excited me so much, please accept my apologies,' the newcomer wheedled.

Eric turned and gazed at the man whose eloquence had touched something within him.

'You look upon me, sir,' continued the man, 'as though you wonder what a man in my condition can possibly do for work, but I assure you, sir, I am as strong as an ox.'

Eric considered for a moment, patting his bottom lip with a raised index finger. 'If we want you to help us, where might we find you?'

'Under the Williamsburg Bridge, it's nice and dry there.' The queue moved forwards.

'Again, I'm sorry,' said the hunchback offering a grimy hand to shake. 'They call me Pat.'

Eric shook his hand, noting the firmness of his grip.

'This is my colleague and friend, George, and I am Eric,' he said.

The ex-surgeon gave Pat a smile that chilled him to the bone.

They had reached the food serving area at last and held out their trays to receive whatever delights were on offer.

'OK, Pat, welcome aboard,' announced Eric. This time his grin held something undeniably sinister.

McCall's phone started to ring. Still concentrating on the monitor, she picked up the receiver and hooked it between her head and right shoulder. 'McCall, Homicide, how can I help you?' She spoke as she typed something into the database about one of the victims. 'Sam, it's Steel.'

The phone almost dropped from her grip at the sound of his voice. 'Steel! Where the—?'

'—Look, I got a tip,' he interrupted her. 'Something is going down under the Williamsburg Bridge tonight, something to do with the killings. So I would suggest you come heavy and silent.' And with that he was gone, leaving her staring down at the receiver.

Her heart was racing. Was she falling for this guy, she wondered?

No, she thought to herself. *Don't even think about it.*

She waved to her two colleagues to follow her, and they trooped off to consult the captain. Brant waved them in as McCall knocked on the door, and they hovered in the office, waiting for him to finish his phone call.

'What's up, Detectives?' he asked, putting down the receiver. 'Steel just contacted me with a heads-up that something is planned to go down under the Williamsburg Bridge tonight. Something connected with the murders,' she explained, shifting her posture.

'Did he say what it was?' the captain asked, leaning back in his chair.

'Not a cheep, he just hung up and was gone. I hate to admit it, sir, but he has come up with the goods a few times, so yes, I think we ought to follow it up.'

Captain Brant nodded to himself, agreeing she had made the right call.

'One more thing, sir,' she mentioned, as she was about to leave. 'Yes, Detective?'

'He suggested we go in heavy and silent.' The captain looked worried.

'Do what you got to, McCall.' He frowned. Knowing what he did about Steel's past, his advice probably meant that the shit really was about to hit the fan.

The night air was still and cloudless, and the sky was a dark blanket of twinkling beauty. Under the vast metal construction of the bridge, a hunchbacked man crouched in front of a small fire. As he sang to himself, he poked the fire, causing the flames to rise, and embers to spew up and be carried on the slight breeze, like fireflies.

McCall and the SWAT team moved in, with Tooms and Tony following. Suddenly the team leader dropped down on one knee and raised his left fist. The others went to ground, disappearing into cover. 'What's wrong?' asked McCall softly. The point man indicated a package resting on a section of broken brick wall next to him.

'Bring it,' ordered the team leader, and the lead scout picked it up and tossed it. Catching the package, the sergeant glanced at it and passed it to McCall.

'It's addressed to you, Sam. Merry Christmas,' he joked. Opening the package, McCall found four earpieces and a recorder, which was connected, possibly by Bluetooth. She took one and passed the rest of the equipment to Tooms, Tony and the team leader.

'I guess someone wants to be heard,' the sergeant joked. They each fitted an earpiece, and the sergeant gave the signal to proceed. Creeping past abandoned, wrecked vehicles and the bridge's vast, iron supporting struts, the cops reached a safe position which offered a good observation point. Hearing a voice, they all took cover. The sergeant asked for a situation report from the lead scout.

'Just some homeless guy, all clear – wait.' He saw several figures approach the homeless man, conspicuously dressed in some sort of black tactical gear.

'Hey, old man, have you seen a cop around here?' The new arrival was tall and broad shouldered, his blond hair cut short.

'Nah, sorry son, just me, what you want him for anyway?' asked the hunchback.

McCall had a bad feeling about the situation.

'We were sent to clear up a loose end. Our employer don't

like loose ends, see.' As the blond man spoke, they caught sight of a form standing behind him screwing a silencer onto a pistol. The hunchbacked guy spotted this and raced off towards the river. McCall watched in horror as the shooter let him think he was home free, then fired three rounds into his back. The hunchback was thrown forward from the impact of the bullets, right into the river.

'Stop, police! Put down your weapons and put your hands up,' cried McCall, her weapon trained on the obvious leader of the team.

'Sorry, officer, afraid I can't do that.'

And with that, a blaze of automatic gunfire rang through the night air. Both sides opened up as bullets shattered brick-work and caused sparks to fly off the steel bridge. McCall dived for cover as a stream of brass and lead flew her way. She noted the SWAT team take down two of the assailants then lost one of their own.

'Damn it, Steel, where the hell are you?' swore McCall, making pot shots as she and Tooms tried to get around the side of their opponents. As they edged around the foot of the bridge into the open, her earpiece activated.

'McCall! Above you!' Instantly she leapt for cover, at the very moment the ground exploded where she had been stand-ing. Tooms and Tony swung their weapons up and took down the sniper, who plunged from his hiding place just under the span of the bridge. The support harness stopped him from falling all the way, but he was unquestionably dead. The fire-fight dwindled out, with most of the gang lying injured or dead on the ground.

'OK, you two, on your feet, hands on your heads,' snarled McCall at a pair spread-eagled on the ground. The team of cops stepped forward, weapons trained on the crew.

'McCall, get the hell out of there,' a voice screamed, as one of the uninjured men staggered to his feet. There was a clank which she recognised as the distinct noise of a grenade safety being released, and seconds later a deafening spray of gunfire as the SWAT team took the man down before he was able to throw it. A thunderous explosion echoed off the metal beams, and the ground shook as the activated grenade detonated, showering deadly shards of metal in every direction.

'Is everyone OK?' inquired an anxious voice in their earpieces. 'Yeah, we are fine, thanks,' replied McCall. There was a pause. 'Uhm, can you give me a thumbs up because this thing is only one way? Sorry.'

'Asshole,' she said, raising a fist with the middle finger sticking straight up.

'Yeah, that will do,' said the voice with a chuckle.

The area had been sealed up tightly, and CSU were having a field day, marking all the bullet strikes and collecting evidence, while the SWAT sergeant, McCall, Tooms, and Tony were debriefing the captain on the events that had taken place.

'Steel never showed up, he led us into a war zone instead,' spat McCall, angry that she had trusted him.

'Well, your boy was right, something was going down. And I want to know, who's the cop they were after? You?' wondered the SWAT leader, looking at McCall.

'What cop?' demanded the captain. He looked troubled, disturbed by the idea that Steel had possibly lied to everyone.

'One of the gunmen asked the homeless guy where 'the cop' was, I don't know any more than that.' McCall snapped, tired and annoyed. 'Could Steel have led us into a trap?' queried Tooms. 'I mean, the boy's not here, is he?'

'Couldn't be him, he was telling us where the sniper was, and he alerted us to the guy with the grenade,' interjected the sergeant. 'No, he saved your butts. All of our butts actually.'

'I want to know where Steel is, Captain.' Detective McCall was really mad. 'The guy brought us all out here but he's a no-show. He's just a voice hiding behind this thing?' She ripped out her earpiece and crushed it in her fist. 'I don't buy it.' The thought of John Steel being dirty was ripping her up, after the way he had been leading her on.

There was a rustle of undergrowth and they recognised the hunchback staggering slowly towards them, his arm outstretched, his mouth stretched in a silent cry for help, just before he collapsed. Tony and Tooms rushed forward, the medical teams not far behind them. Tony put two fingers on the man's neck: there was no pulse.

'He's gone,' said Tony, standing up. 'What did they have to kill the bum for? He was no harm to anyone.' Tony kicked an empty can that lay by his foot, sending it sailing away.

'I will get him back and see if he's got any evidence on him,' said Tina with a sympathetic smile.

THIRTY

Normally Tina would have music playing while she worked but today felt different, there was a melancholy atmosphere, but she didn't know what to ascribe it to. McCall had followed the coroner's transport and was now spinning distractedly on the swivel chair, waiting for the body of the homeless guy to be brought in.

'So, what happened out there?' asked Tina as she stirred her coffee. 'Really don't know,' McCall shrugged. 'I got a call from Steel, who said that something was going down, next thing we know we are at the OK Corral.'

'And where was Steel in all this?' asked the puzzled ME.

McCall shook her head, 'Don't know, but he was talking to us. God, it was weird, it was as if he set us up for something and then couldn't go through with it.'

Tina frowned. 'I can't believe he set you up.'

'I know, you're right, after everything that has happened.'

'No, I mean I *can't* believe he set you up, there has to be more to it.' Tina hadn't spent much time with the mysterious Englishman, but she was good at reading people. And what she read in him was goodness. He was a little messed up maybe, but nevertheless a man of honour.

The doors of the morgue banged open, and two orderlies arrived, pushing a gurney carrying Homeless Pat's body. They lifted it on to the wash table.

'Thanks, guys,' Tina said. She took a deep breath and snapped a fresh pair of gloves on, ready to search for any evidence that could help them make sense of what had happened that night. She studied his large, round face, observing that, even in death, he appeared to be wearing a smile.

Tina's thoughts were interrupted by the sound of the door bursting open in the next room, followed by the clump of several pairs of heavy footsteps. Tina and McCall glanced at each other, raised their eyebrows and headed through, where they were confronted by the captain, Tooms, and Tony, each clasping their phones in their hands.

'So, what's up, Doc? We got your invite,' the captain greeted them, surprised to have been summoned, and cracking the same joke at Tina he had cracked ever since she joined the department.

Tina looked at McCall and shrugged in surprise

'We didn't send for you – for any of you,' Tina frowned, as con- fused as the others.

'No, I did,' a muffled voice spoke from behind them and, rising from the shadows came the figure of the homeless man, Pat, previously witnessed lying dead on a gurney. Tina and McCall shot to the other side of the room, taking refuge behind their open-mouthed colleagues. Pat strolled over to where Tina had been standing, reached for his left ear and pulled it off. They all looked away in disgust.

Daring to take a peek, McCall saw Pat shaking with laughter, pieces of latex still dripping from his face.

'You asshole!' she shouted, partly in anger as she recognised him, at the same time almost laughing with relief.

'But I checked your pulse,' said Tony, completely baffled by what had happened. 'You were dead.'

'Don't be hard on yourself, Tony. It's special latex, feel it if you like,' said Steel, still grinning. Tooms grabbed his hand and as he shook it, pulled him close and hugged him,

'Cool move, bro,' he nodded.

The captain, however, was not in a brother-hugging mood. 'Steel, do you want to explain what the hell is going on?'

Steel's smile vanished. 'Sir, if I may get out of this clobber and grab a shower, I'll meet everyone in the briefing room in ten.'

The captain nodded. 'You got ten minutes, no more.'

Steel entered the briefing room to find everyone sitting around the large table, and he felt a touch of déjà vu, remembering the previous such meeting.

'OK, Steel, what the hell is going on?' asked the captain. 'You disappear, you get my people into a fire fight, people are dead for Christ's sake, I mean just what the fuck are you taking, boy?'

Steel looked lost for a moment, as if a thought had just occurred to him.

'Well?' prompted the captain, who was by now at breaking point. 'They asked for a cop,' said Steel, with a long, distant gaze above everyone's heads, as he slid into his seat.

'At the bridge, they asked where was the cop. At first, I thought he meant me but of course—'

'—You were in disguise.' McCall finished his sentence. Was that going to become a habit? she wondered, sharing a conspiratorial look with him.

'Steel, what the hell are you talking about?' demanded the captain. Steel turned to answer the captain. 'I'm not sure. It's still puzzling me, who they were and how they are mixed up in the case, unless these are now two completely separate affairs, but my gut says they are tied together somehow.' His expres-

203

sion was distracted, as if he wasn't concentrating on his own words.

With a sudden shudder, he seemed to come back to earth. 'Yesterday I got to thinking about the homeless guys we have been looking for.' He took a sip from the coffee, and his eyes rolled back with pleasure at the smooth, rich taste. *Thanks, Luke*, he said to himself, sadly.

'It occurred to me that the occasion when they moved Marie-Ann was perhaps not the only time our killer used these guys.' Steel put his cup down for a second. 'We have been mapping out routes for vehicles, figuring how long it takes to drive from a to b. Well, just suppose we were looking for, say, a shopping cart or something similar?'

McCall's face came alive as Steel started to make some sort of sense. 'Of course! Everyone would remember a van or a car, but they wouldn't think twice about seeing a vagrant pushing a shopping cart,' she said.

'Anyway,' Detective Steel continued. 'I got to thinking that the only way to find them was to become one of them.'

'And did you find them?' asked the captain

Steel nodded as he took another sip of coffee. 'It took some time, but I think I know who they are. They were talking about doing another job for "The Man". My idea was to stir up their interest and, well, get noticed.'

'OK, what went wrong?' Tony jumped in, leaning forwards with interest.

'At the most, I thought "The Man" would pay me a visit, not send a team of goons from The Expendables. I was just trying to get a reaction.'

Tooms laughed, 'Well, you got that, my man, big time.'

'Yeah, well, I was expecting a few homeless guys on a pay check, not a squad of mercenaries with a death wish.' This struck a chord with everyone around the table, and the mood turned dark.

'How do you know they were mercenaries?' asked Tooms, a curious expression on his face.

'Tooms, man, you were in the forces, you'd recognise a professional soldier, right?'

Tooms nodded in agreement, 'I guess.'

'That's how they appeared to me, professional soldiers, bought and paid for.'

'Well, for a start these were not some last-minute bargain types, they were organised and kitted out,' Tooms added, nodding in agreement.

'What are you thinking, Detective?' asked Dr Davidson, who had been hunched silently through all the revelations, watching not the room but Steel: his gaze focused on him alone.

'Actually, I'm wondering how a squad of highly-trained soldiers, a couple of homeless guys, and a psycho killer all come together in the mix.'

The captain stood up and put his hands on his hips. 'So, how do they? Any ideas? Anybody?' he asked, reluctantly acknowledging he might be a little afraid of the answer.

'They don't,' said Steel, taking a sip from the cooling coffee. 'What do you mean they don't?' yelled Tooms.

'Let's go over it again. The lead merc asked for a *cop*, not a bum, a *cop*.'

McCall suddenly looked alarmed, and glanced up at Steel, who must have read her mind because he nodded in confirmation; he had been struck by the same thought.

'The hotel room,' she murmured, her mood one of mixed emotions. 'Did we get the rifle from the sniper you lads so brilliantly found under the bridge?'

Tony and Tooms looked at each other, and simultaneously made for the door.

'Ballistics should match the hotel room,' said Tony, as they left. 'You know, it's so cute the way they do that, are they a couple?' Steel asked, succeeding in making the captain and McCall smile.

Steel glimpsed Dr Davidson out of the corner of his eye as he felt himself being scrutinised. He shuddered.

'So what now, Steel?' McCall challenged him.

The captain was facing them from the other side of the table and crossed his arms, watching the pair plan their next moves together. *Don't they realise that they're behaving like a couple too?*

'We carry on,' John Steel replied. 'We carry on as though last night never happened. If we go off chasing mercs, we lose sight of what we are really after.' Steel sank back into the chair and finished the now-cold coffee.

'And what about the mercs?' the captain asked.

Steel thought for a moment. 'We have no idea who sent them or why.' He paused. 'But I can tell you that someone knew about the operation and was planning to take out either myself or Sam. Bottom line, you got a snitch in the department.'

The captain looked around the room and shook his head in disbelief.

'Our best bet is to forget about them, carry on, and solve this investigation.' Steel stood up.

'And if they try again?' urged McCall, a lump in her throat.

'Then we make sure we catch one alive. Either way, our attitude should be if we don't bother them, they don't bother us.' Steel shrugged. 'We'll catch them later'

They left the briefing area, and Steel headed for the coffee room. He badly needed a refill. Hours of drinking bad coffee and worse booze had numbed his taste buds.

The afternoon had grown late by the time the workforce had cross-checked known whereabouts for the two homeless guys, possible sightings, anything to find a pattern. Earlier, McCall had told everyone to focus on the two drop-off guys, as they were the link. Find them, she explained, and they were one step closer. Steel staggered in to the office under the weight of a large, heavy-looking box, which he cradled in his arms.

'Hey, man, what's with the box?' asked Tooms, as he peered over the top of his monitor. 'Do I smell dim sum?' The team dropped everything to see what the English detective had brought.

'Wow, Chinese, is this for us?' McCall asked, assuming it was and helping to lay out paper takeout cartons on desks.

She sauntered over to Steel who had just bitten off half a red-hot spring roll. She grinned as he tried fanning cool air into his open mouth to cool it down.

'Can I have a quick word with you, please?' she asked, hovering over him and extending an arm towards the coffee room.

'Yeah, sure, after you,' he said, dabbing his mouth with the napkin.

He followed her in, and she shut the doors.

'What's up?' he asked, his voice calm but inquisitive.

'Look, about the other night,' she began, remorsefully. 'I never gave you a chance to explain that it was your friend who got killed. I'm sorry.' She peered into his sunglasses and hoped he was staring back at her with the kind of emotion she was feeling.

'It's fine,' he reassured her. 'It's my fault for being so – well – secretive. I'm the one who should be sorry. Like I said before, I have some trust issues and after the bridge affair, I think I was right to —' She shot him a sharp look of anger and disappointment, which he picked up on straight away.

'I don't mean you guys,' he assured her. 'It's someone else here. I would trust you and your team with my life.'

He held out a hand, amiably. 'Friends?' he asked.

She considered his offer and smiled. As she took his hand,

he pulled her close and hugged her to his chest. 'I'm so happy,' he whispered into her ear.

She pushed him off quickly. 'You are such an ass,' she said. But as he strolled off, she felt herself go weak at the memory of the hard, muscular body that had impressed its lingering sweet smell all over her: a mixture of male pheromones and sweet-smelling deodorant and aftershave. She glanced around self-consciously and straightened herself up. *Nothing just happened*, she told herself forcefully.

They returned separately to the group and delved into the scant remains of the meal, once the guys had picked it over like ravenous hyenas.

'OK, people, it's getting late, we have all had an eventful day, so let's get home, shake out and come in fresh tomorrow,' the captain called from the doorway, his coat already over one arm. And with that, the gathered personnel started to thin out, rapidly shutting down their computers and tidying their desks.

Steel, lolling in the chair next to McCall's, shouted after the captain:

'Hey, Captain, when do I get a desk?'

The captain chuckled as he stepped into the elevator, yelling back, 'If you can find one, it's yours!' And with that, the door shut.

Brant blew a sigh of relief at the thought of another day over. He had come to realise that, once this case was done, Steel was gone. It wasn't that he didn't want him there, it was simply the nature of the man.

Steel stood, stretched and shrugged on his long coat. 'Did you want to get a drink or something?' he asked McCall nonchalantly. 'It's not a date or anything, just two people getting a drink,' he mumbled, tripping over his words.

She stared up at him and thought for a moment. Once again, a voice said a brusque *no* in her head. 'Sorry, I have plans, but you go ahead.'

He returned her smile, sadly.

'Hey, fellas, you up for a drink or something?' he shouted to the other two, who were heading to the lift.

'Cool,' said Tooms, putting on his jacket.

'Where we going?' asked Tony, logging off on his computer. 'Oh, I don't know, there is a little place I go to sometimes.'

McCall watched the three detectives walk off towards the elevator and shook her head with a beaming grin on her face.

The dimly lit bathroom was aglow with the tiny flames of a dozen candles, and the steam from the running shower created a haze that hung in the room. A fog of condensation blanketed the mirror over the sink, and the screen around the shower unit was full of mist that billowed from its open top.

Sam McCall took a sip from her large glass, the red wine appearing almost black in the muted light. Placing it on a small side cupboard, she moved to the shower and slipped off her robe, the silk of the gown caressing her firm body as it fell to the floor. She dipped the toes of her left foot gently under the running water to test the warmth; *just right*, she thought, and stepped into the small, glass compartment.

The water cascaded down the contours of her slender, athletic body, washing away the troubles of the day. She lathered up a sponge with jasmine-scented soap and thoroughly massaged the soapy foam into her skin. Soft music played in the background, and the strong scent of candles and soap filled the air.

Placing both palms against the tiled wall of the booth she stood under the shower head and let the water pour over her. McCall was lost in the moment when she felt a pair of strong hands start to stroke her skin from her shoulders to her hips. She shuddered as she felt small, delicate kisses caress her back, moving tantalisingly slowly downwards to her buttocks. Her nails pressed against the wall, making scratching motions as her body tingled with pleasure.

Teasingly, the hands swept back up to cup her firm breasts and pulled her back, as the intruder began to nibble at her neck and ears.

She reached back and felt the firm, sinewy male body that was pressed against hers. Provocatively, she leant forwards, steadying herself against the wall as they melted into one in a passionate embrace. His hard body grinding against her drew groans of pleasure from her lips, her fluttering hands reaching backwards, digging her nails into his muscular buttocks, urging him to increase the speed and depth of his thrusts inside her. Water splashed against the glass, and bottles of soap and conditioner were cast aside in all directions as they moved in synchrony.

Her knees began to buckle as she felt him lunge against her, her arm reaching back and weaving her fingers into his hair, pulling him closer as he began to bite hard into the side of her neck, his hands running up and down the front of her body, tracing the shape of her breasts. She began to gasp as she felt every rigid, muscular inch of him, driving into her ever deeper. Her moans of pleasure were drowned out by her hands banging against the safety glass.

Together, they crescendoed to an earth-moving climax. She turned, her eyes, unable to focus as they kissed, and she fell back against the hard, tiled wall, her arms braced against the walls of the shower as her legs felt weak, and what felt like small electrical shocks buzzed through her body. Her eyes fluttered open to absorb the view of his firm, naked body, his erection still standing proud. She gazed at his firm chest muscles and noticed what appeared to be a tattoo of a strange, aquiline bird on his right shoulder. Her eyes dropped closed again. Perfect, she thought, just perfect.

With a start, she bolted upright and gaped around in a panic. Where the hell was she? She leant over and found the light switch. She blew out a sigh of relief. She was in bed, her own bed, alone. She was dry, but naked. She looked around the room; there was nobody there. She let her head fall back into the pillows.

What the hell just happened here, she thought? She grabbed a pillow from the other side of the bed and put it over her face to hide behind. Was that all a dream? If it was, she knew who she had just dreamed about.

THIRTY-ONE

The next morning, McCall sat in the ME's office with Tina, and described the recent goings on over a cup of coffee bought from the store around the corner. McCall often came down before the day officially started to shoot the breeze if they had the chance, unless somebody inconsiderately died early and ruined the whole 'ease into the day' thing. Their careers had put them through a lot together over the years, and a powerful bond of friendship and respect had developed. They had fallen into a natural routine of getting together in the morning or maybe sometimes after work, just to talk about nothing in particular, as long as it wasn't work. The nature of the job demanded that they depressurise with a few moments of trivial chitchat.

But this morning talk did turn to work, with Tina pressing to know the ins and outs of what she had heard about the other day; she found that the drawback with being closeted down in the ME's office was that she missed all the chatter and gossip.

'God, Steel really pisses me off sometimes,' McCall growled as she spoke his name. 'I mean, he just breezes in out of nowhere, messes up the crime scene and wafts away again.'

'Saved your cute little ass two or three times,' Tina butted in, then hid behind her coffee cup as McCall shot her a disapproving look.

'Comes and goes like he owns the place, sits at my desk and bothers me,' McCall went on, trying to work up some genuine anger. 'The sneaky son-of-a-bitch even gate-crashed my dreams the other night.'

Tina spat out her coffee and stared at her friend with a *do tell* look on her face. McCall immediately realised her blunder and glanced away with an expression of exaggerated innocence. 'What sort of dream?' Tina asked in a slow, meaningful tone.

'Um, nothing, forget it – it's not important.' McCall blushed, cursing herself for letting slip any mention of her erotic dream.

'Come on, what sort of dream?' Tina pressed her until she caught a glimpse of McCall's flustered expression and the penny dropped. 'Oh my God! You had a wet dream about him? Okay, now I want details.'

Tina made a big display of getting herself comfortable and prepared to hear the rest. 'Was he any good?'

McCall nodded, 'The best.' As Tina's eyebrows shot up, she added, 'They're always the best in that sort of dream. It's doing the deed in real life that's so disappointing.' Tina's expression of expectation made her feel obliged to reveal some of the explicit details, as her friend's eyes widened. 'What does it mean?' McCall asked, hoping for some deep insight into dream analysis.

'I know what *I* think it means,' Tina chuckled, 'but what do *you*

think it means?'

McCall shot her a look of reproach. 'It was probably just the adrenaline of the shoot-out. Or, it's been pretty intense, like we have been through a lot together in such a short time, so maybe…' she fumbled her words, trying to find some other explanation for the experience.

'Really? So you're going for PTSD?' Tina fixed her with another long stare.

McCall paused for a moment before replying, as she ran the thought through her head. 'Yeah, that sounds good to me.'

She grinned, while Tina snorted at the idea and drank her coffee.

Steel had got in to work early. The night before had been a good one, probably one of the best he had had in a long time. He switched the coffee machines on in anticipation of a couple of sore heads, and after making himself a coffee, he moved to the white board to review the evidence. As he perched himself on the edge of McCall's desk and sipped the fresh coffee, his gaze was drawn to the map board. The loud chime from the elevator disturbed his concentration and he smirked as Tooms and Tony crept in, looking a bit worse for wear.

'Morning, guys' he shouted, laughing as they flinched at the assault on their tender senses.

'The coffee is ready.' They replied by raising their hands and made their way to get some refreshment. After filling their cups to the brim, they joined him at McCall's desk.

'You guys okay?' he asked, amused, nonchalantly sipping his coffee.

'Us? Never better, man, and you?' replied Tooms, shifting his sunglasses around to screen out as much light as possible. 'Fine, fine,' Steel said as he stared at the two boards.

'What you looking at?' asked Tooms, as he took a sip from the coffee, his glasses steaming up as he did so. Steel smiled as his colleagues struggled to disguise their hungover condition.

'Something's bugging me, but I cannot put my finger on it,' replied Steel, with a look of intense concentration as he stared. 'Supposing all the bodies were moved by the homeless guys, but…'

Tony scratched his head as he tried to follow John Steel's train of thought, finding it hard to concentrate.

'Wow,' Tony said at last, 'so you figure the fellas on the street may have moved more than one body. Pushing those trollies must have been a right bitch.'

Detective Steel suddenly snapped bolt upright. Narrowing his eyes, he studied the map board, taking note of the pins that showed the locations of the bodies. Using his two index fingers he appeared to measure something on the map, then spinning round, he strode over to Tony, saying, 'You little dancer,' kissed Tony on the forehead, then made for the elevator, leaving Tony to wipe his forehead, and try to make sense of it all.

Tina and McCall were cracking each other up with revelations of their most unlikely celebrity crushes, and McCall felt more at ease with her friend than ever, having opened up about her secret erotic dream. She didn't have to be back upstairs for a while, and if somebody had been unable to find her, she could easily claim she was checking something out. Their dirty sniggers were cut short as the door swung open and in rushed Steel.

'Well, speak of the devil,' said Tina with a suggestive grin. Steel hesitated for a second, puzzled by the welcome.

'Well, Mr Steel, do you have a special mark on your right shoulder?' Tina asked, still smiling. Beneath the confusion, McCall also detected something new in his expression: a fear of being emotionally hurt.

'You know, a tattoo?' Tina clarified, noticing his distracted expression.

'Um, what? No. No tattoos, sorry. Why do you ask?'

McCall gave Tina a slap on the arm and shot her an evil

look. 'We were having a bet,' she said pointedly, then turning her attention back to Steel, she pulled herself together, 'Never mind. Okay, Steel, you found me, guilty as charged, what do you want?'

'Well, actually, I was after the good doctor.' He smiled at Tina, who could feel her cheeks warming to a charming shade of red.

'Oh, okay,' McCall said, feeling slightly disappointed.

'Okay honey, what's on your mind?' Tina asked, sipping her coffee. 'You remember Miss Talbot? I want to know how much she weighed.'

Tina and McCall gave him a curious look. Tina searched through her notes.

'She was fifty-four point four kilos. Why?' Both women drew in closer, intrigued by the question.

'Oh, just a little experiment I had in mind,' he tossed over his shoulder, already striding out of the door.

The ME and the detective stared at each other for a moment and then took off after him. They burst out of the elevator and onto the homicide office floor. Tooms and Tony looked up from their desks with a start, to be faced with two women racing towards them like a couple of kids at Christmas, heading for the tree.

'Have any of you seen Steel?' asked McCall, slightly out of breath. 'He was here a moment ago,' replied Tooms. 'He was going over the board, then he took off after Tony here mentioned something about shopping carts.'

McCall and Tina rushed to examine the murder board, when suddenly Tina yelped in excitement. McCall's head snapped round as Tina pointed to a post-it that had been attached to the map, using the pin which marked the location of where Marie-Ann's body was located.

It was a simple note saying: *Meet me here and bring Tina. J. S.*

McCall and Tina's eyes met as they yelled 'road trip' in unison and rushed off, leaving Tooms and Tony still hungover, and now completely baffled.

'Never again, man, never again,' said Tooms, slurping his coffee and rubbing his temples to try and ease his throbbing headache.

The sun was high in the cloudless sky, flocks of birds darted acrobatically over the water in formation, and boats of all shapes and sizes cruised tranquilly up and down. Tina and McCall leaned back on a bench and enjoyed the chill of their ice creams, pondering how invigorating it was to be outside in the fresh air, rather than cooped up in an office, or staring at a corpse.

'Okay, where the hell is he?' asked Tina. She was enjoying herself, but she did have other things to do. She peered at her watch for what seemed to be the tenth time.

'I don't know; he's probably sitting up on top of that building, watching us.'

'Which building?' Tina scanning the rooftops for a lurking figure. 'Any building that we're not looking at,' she replied, and they both laughed. McCall gazed across the bay and filled her lungs with salty air as the fresh breeze rippled across the water. As they contemplated the view, a vagrant flopped down on the bench next to Tina. She stared at him for a moment whilst surreptitiously edging away. He smiled, but she did not. Tina studied him closely and suddenly shot backwards. Casting an angry glare towards him, she yelled: 'And where the hell have you been, Mister? You know we've been waiting, right?' Her voice was bitter. The man startled with the shock of her attack, and searched behind him on the off chance someone else was standing there.

There was no one.

'Come on then, where have you been? Look, it was you who invited us down here.'

The homeless guy regarded her warily, as if she was some sort of crazy person.

'Well, missy, I's sorry I's late, not that time means anything to me, but as you's upset, I's real sorry again.'

There was a light cough behind them, and they turned around to see Steel leaning his elbows on a shopping cart full of heavy-looking items. Tina's jaw dropped, and McCall tried to swallow her laughter.

Tina and McCall hopped up to join Steel, and the homeless guy lay down on the bench to enjoy the warmth of the sun.

'So, Detective, what's the big experiment?' McCall asked, still choking back giggles. 'Push the cart till we get tired?'

'Sort of, but he will be pushing it.' He pointed to the bench, from which they were greeted by an up-stretched arm and a dirty hand waving to them.

'I take it you have met Jerry.' He smiled, broadly as Tina brushed imaginary dust from her clothes. They considered the bulging cart he'd brought along. It was covered with flies and other insects swarming around.

'So, what have you got there?' asked McCall. She frowned in distaste as if she'd really rather not know but couldn't resist asking.

'Oh, this? Well, of course I had to slit some poor bugger's throat and wrap him up like this, for the experiment. I mean, if you're going to carry out a scientific procedure you have to do it right.' He smiled, watching their faces.

'Yeah, really.' Tina muttered, still flicking at herself as she spoke. 'Yes, really,' he replied, trying to sound sincere, amused that for a split second maybe they believed his joke.

'Seriously, you thought I had actually done that? Oh, please!' he said, pretending to sound disappointed in them.

'You're a real bastard, you know that?' said Tina,

smacking him on the shoulder. He bowed slightly as if to thank her for her comment.

Steel had come across the homeless guy, Jerry, in an alleyway, while he was sifting through the garbage, hoping to score some 'disposable items' as he put it. And now Jerry was about to help break the case, or so Steel hoped.

'So, why him?' Tina scrutinised Jerry, wondering how she had ever mistaken him for Steel. They'd laugh about it one day. Jerry leant forward from his resting place and shot her an evil look.

'Now, I didn't mean it like that,' she responded, returning the look, waiting for Jerry to lie down again. 'What I meant was, why go for the small guy and not the thin one that you mentioned?'

Steel shook his head. He had already rehearsed the scenario carefully in his head, and after the brief encounter with the men, he knew who to match with each role.

'No, George was the muscle, Eric was the brains,' Steel explained. On the mention of George and Eric by name, Jerry sat bolt upright.

'What do you want with them?' Jerry sounded confused, but McCall detected an element of fear in his words.

'You know them?' asked Steel, surprised at his luck. The man nodded as he noticed McCall returning from the small coffee stall carrying a fresh doughnut. His eyes widened at the pastry she held.

'Jerry, how do you know these men?' McCall waved the doughnut, clicking her fingers to snap the man from his trance.

'What? Oh, we did some moving jobs together.' Jerry smiled and edged closer to McCall, eyes fixed on the doughnut. Steel looked down at the pastry and realised that this was the key to getting him to talk.

'Moving what?' asked Tina, sliding closer to the man, making him feel a little edgy.

'Oh, I don't know. Packages. Big ones, long ones – all sorts.' McCall passed him the sticky prize, which he bit into slowly, savouring every sugary mouthful.

'Did you pick up from the same place each time?' Steel's interest was growing. He couldn't believe his luck in finding this guy, and it set alarm bells ringing in the back of his head. Yes, a remarkably lucky find, he thought. Jerry had devoured the doughnut and was dabbing his lips as though he was royalty.

'Sure. We would pick up from this old warehouse in the meatpacking district, a real spooky place, lots of dark rooms, but we got our stuff from the big store room at the back,' Jerry recounted as Steel passed him another doughnut, which he snatched from the detective's hand. 'Jerry, can you take us there?' McCall's kept her voice soft and reassuring. He nodded and attempted to cram as much of the doughnut into his mouth in one bite as possible. Steel watched Jerry turn an interesting colour as breathing became an issue, but eventually Jerry swallowed hard, and his large mouth was free to gulp in air.

'Jerry, take us to the place, and I swear I'll buy you as many doughnuts as you like,' he promised.

The man nodded hard, conjuring up a vision of a pile of doughnuts that made his mouth water. Tina decided that, as no dramatic experiment was about to take place, she would head back to the desk full of paperwork she ought to be attending to. She left them to play detective and, chuckling quietly to herself, added *and whatever else might take their fancy*.

It was a day of celebration for Jenny Thompson. She had worked alongside the homicide detectives for a few years hoping to join their ranks, and now her dream had come true – her beaming smile and civilian clothes said it all. Jenny proudly approached Tooms and Tony, who hunched over their work, oblivious.

'Well?' She hovered by their desks, hands clenched

together, bouncing on her heels, waiting for some recognition from them.

'Well, what?' asked Tooms, straining to keep a straight face.

'I made Detective.' She showed off her badge like a six-year-old that just came in first at a school race.

'Cool,' replied Tooms, lifting his cup to her. 'You can get the coffees then, rookie.'

She scowled at them as they burst out laughing, before jumping up to shake her hand and hug her, offering sincere congratulations. The captain walked out of his office and headed for her.

'Thompson? Your desk is a mess – sort it out.'

She looked puzzled. 'I've got a desk?' she asked, and followed the captain's gaze to the far corner, where she spotted a desk on which stood a name plaque engraved with 'Detective J. Thompson' etched in white with a shiny black background. She rushed over and seized the plaque in shaking hands, feeling the lump in her throat growing larger. 'Thanks, Captain.' She felt like she wanted to throw her arms around him, but you don't hug the Cap, not ever.

'Oh, don't thank me for anything, you're still working with the doc.' Her face fell. 'Is there a problem, Detective?'

She stiffened up and put the plaque back down on her *own* desk. 'No sir, no problem.' She faked a smile and walked into the doctor's office.

The captain smiled fondly. She'd be a good detective, he thought, in time. Thinking of another attractive woman who was already a seriously good cop, he asked, 'Where are McCall and Steel?' He peered at the fresh scribbles on the white board and the pins on the map.

'They went uptown to check out an old warehouse in the meat- packing district, but they had to pick up some dough-nuts or some- thing first,' replied Tony, shrugging. The captain nodded in acknowledgement, and Tony and Tooms got up and joined him at the boards. 'Steel had a theory that homeless people were used to move all the bodies in shopping carts,' continued Tony.

The captain turned to them. 'Makes sense. Well, as much as anything the Brit does. Let me know if his theory holds water.' there was a loud ringing sound from the captain's office, and he headed off to answer the phone. Tony watched as the captain lifted the receiver, listened for a moment and then proceeded to bawl out the unfortunate on the other end.

'I don't get it, Tooms.' Tony flicked through the files, searching for something.

'You don't get what?' Tooms could see his partner getting agitated. 'These women. They grew up together, we hear they were BFFs up until high school, then after they left to go to college, I don't think they had any further contact with one another whatsoever. I bet they didn't even know they were all living in the same city.'

Tooms balanced his bulk on the edge of his desk as he pondered the question.

'So what's on your mind, man?' Tony slammed down the files and leant back, swiping his hand over his face in frustration. 'There has to be something that ties our three women together, other than sharing their early upbringing and looking like sisters. I mean, who waits twenty years to kill a person? Why?' Tooms had to agree but he had nothing further to offer.

THIRTY-TWO

Normally there would have been witnesses, people of interest, someone stewing in the interrogation room by now, but this was different, and it weighed heavily on Tooms. He turned to the board nearest where he was sitting, stirred by a sudden sadness for the victims, not so much because of their violent deaths, but more because they seemed to lack any intimacy or affection in their private lives.

Tooms's gaze turned to the framed set of photos on his desk. A plain, silver frame held a collage of snapshots of himself and his family. He fondly picked it up and smiled, then looked up at the pictures of the women victims, and his melancholy returned. Tony saw the expression on his partner's face and walked up to him.

'What's up, man?' Tony could clearly recognise the signs of Tooms's dismay on his face.

'What do you figure would make these very attractive women give up any kind of a personal life and just live for work?'

Tony studied the photos on the boards. 'Don't know, man, but some people do, and they seem happy.'

Tooms's computer made a *ding* noise to signal the arrival

of an email, and Tony returned to his desk, reminding himself that he hadn't checked his inbox that day.

Detective Tooms sifted through the dozens of junk mail messages on his screen, deleting each of them, noticing that one stood out. He glanced around, making sure nobody was paying him any attention before he opened it. The address was from a friend of his in financials, and the message read:

HI JOSHUA.

GOT YOUR E-MAIL. REF: JOHN STEEL.

NATIONAL BANK ...... $ 56,457.99.

OFF SHORE ACCOUNT DIFFERENT NAME: $443, 867, 897.95 WATCH YOUR BACK BUDDY.

Tooms's jaw dropped. Over four hundred million dollars? Who was this guy and how did he come to have so much cash in an offshore account?

For him, there were too many questions about Detective John Steel and not enough answers.

Quickly, he printed off the email and headed for the captain's office. He needed to know the truth, regardless of the sanctions he might face for delving into another cop's private affairs, a violation he had considered necessary.

As he approached the closed door, he stopped for a moment and contemplated the piece of paper, wondering if he was doing the right thing. Before he could turn around, the door opened, and he stood face to face with the captain.

After cruising up and down the colourful streets of the Meat-packing District for several weary hours, McCall and Steel pulled up at a large, disused building. On first impression, it looked like an old delivery or storage place. Its red brick walls showed their age, and the wooden framed windows held thick glass that appeared to be encrusted with the dust and dirt of forty years.

McCall parked some distance from the building, just in case someone was watching: the last thing they needed was a welcoming committee.

'You're sure this is the place, Jerry?' she asked jadedly, staring at the homeless man in the car's back seat through the rear-view mirror.

'Are you really sure, Jerry? Because this is the fifth place you have brought us to,' Steel added, turning around in his seat to regard him sternly.

Jerry could feel Steel's eyes burning into his own, even though the sunglasses.

'Yes, that's the place. Can we go now?' McCall now also turned around to face the nervous man.

'What's your rush, Jerry? We only just got here.' Steel had a bad feeling, the *you've just been set up* feeling, and that was one experience he didn't need. All three of them got out of the car and moved towards the building.

An eerie silence filled the air, and as they ventured closer Steel couldn't help but notice Jerry was lagging behind.

'What's the matter, Jerry? You've gone a little pale.' McCall was gradually gripped by the same unease as Steel and drew her weapon. Clutching the pistol grip tightly with both hands she let her arm hang down in front of her, keeping alert and ready for whatever was to come.

'OK, Jerry, when we get inside, I want you to show me exactly where the parcels were when you collected them, OK?' McCall told him.

Jerry's expression twisted with fear, the sort of fear you would expect to see from someone facing a ravenous lion that had you in its sights. Or someone who knew exactly what lurked inside the building. 'No!' Jerry yelled suddenly. 'You can't make me go in there! I won't go in there. Fuck you, lady!'

Jerry turned to make his escape, but Mc- Call grabbed him by the arm.

'What about that free meal we promised you, Jerry?' Her appeal wasn't working.

'Fuck your meal! Fuck them! Fuck you all! You're all fucking crazy,' he yelled.

Steel grabbed him by his coat lapels and dragged him to the nearest dumpster. 'You don't want to go in, fine, but you are not leaving either,' and with that, he seized the back of the man's belt, heaved him up and tipped him into the rubbish container. A large 'thung' echoed through the empty steel box as Jerry hit the bottom, and, whipping out his handcuffs, Steel secured the handles that closed the container, locking Jerry inside.

'Shall we?' Steel raised an open palm in a courteous *ladies first* gesture. Proceeding cautiously, they slunk close to the walls, McCall in the lead. As they neared the doorway, she turned and noticed Steel's empty hands. Shooting him a disappointed frown, she grabbed her back-up Glock pistol and passed it to him.

'I can't believe you don't carry a gun,' she said, 'Jesus!'

He shrugged, 'You flatter me. I assure you, I'm not Jesus,' he said, and cocked the weapon.

Entering a long, dim corridor, the musty smell of a decaying building filled their nostrils, and they quickly covered their noses and mouths until they adjusted to the stagnant air. Moving wordlessly, they covered each other's backs, weapons held firmly in their out-stretched arms, as they came to the first set of rooms which faced each other in the long walls. They stopped, backs against the brickwork and counted together.

'Three, Two, One, Now!'

Swinging around, weapons ready, they each charged through a door, but they encountered nothing but an empty room. Edging down the corridor, they did the same for the next four rooms until they arrived at a chipped, blue door at the end of the long hallway.

'This one?' Steel asked, surprising McCall by consulting her. 'We go in on three, keep low, find cover, and we check it out,'

He nodded. 'Did you call for back up or something before we came in?'

She smiled at him with a cocky sort of grin. 'Why? Don't you think that we can handle this on our own?'

He registered the grin and realised she was teasing him. He grasped the handle and turned it slowly, as McCall crouched in front of the door, ready to move in as soon as it opened.

'Okay,' he whispered. 'Three, Two, One!' He shoved the door open, and she rolled in, while Steel stared into the room, still holding the handle.

'Houston, we have a problem.' His words were more for himself than for McCall, but she jumped to her feet and turned towards her colleague.

'New plan?' she asked, shrugging.

The room was vast, and its high glass roof had been painted or boarded over, allowing only a few shards of light to creep in. Stacked around the room, there was a vast number of huge wooden container boxes, each around six-foot square, arranged as if to form some kind of maze.

The labyrinth was too high to be clambered over, meaning that the only way to investigate was to move in amongst the boxes. Slowly they crept in, towards the first bend, a couple of feet away. Inching along slowly, they stopped at a T-junction. 'Left or right?' Steel asked. McCall peeped to either side, concluding that both directions looked exactly alike and equally dangerous.

'Right, we go right,' McCall decided.

The maze of passageways they found themselves in was evenly spaced, and the only light came from the stray chinks of daylight falling from the ceiling. As they approached one of the rays of sunshine, Steel noticed that the beam was wide enough to cover the space between the two opposing walls. He raised a hand, signalling *halt*..

'Do you like movies?' His question puzzled her: this was an extremely peculiar time to invite her for a date, not that she would ever agree to one.

'Steel, this is not the time or place,' she snapped.

He turned to her, crouched as he was with his back against one of the containers. One side of his face was in a pool of light, and she could see he was smiling.

'One of my favourite films was "Raiders of the Lost Ark",' he told her.

A grin spread over her face as McCall understood where he was going with this.

'Stay out of the light,' he said, scraping up some dust from the floor and throwing it into the ray of light.

'Stay out of the light,' he repeated. As the dust fell, tiny red beams were revealed, criss-crossing the way before them.

Steel turned to McCall. His expression said it all. 'I think we have to leave, right now.'

Tooms walked heavily into the captain's office. The decision to talk to his boss about John Steel had been taken out of his hands, but it didn't make him feel any better. The captain closed the door behind them, manoeuvring himself awkwardly between the bulky cop and the wall to his desk, where he sat, leaving Tooms standing uncomfortably in front of him.

'So, what's on your mind, Detective?' Captain Brant sat back in his chair, causing it to tilt against the hinge mechanism.

'I got some information back from financials and they came up with something disturbing,' Tooms admitted, passing the copy of the email to the captain. Brant leant forwards, propping his elbows on his desk. After reading it, he frowned up at Tooms, his face filled with regret and also a trace of anger, which didn't, Tooms thought, seem to be directed towards him. 'What's this, Detective Tooms? Are we checking up on our own guys now?' His voice tried to mask his disappointment.

'Sir, something felt off about the guy, so I —' Tooms didn't know which way to look.

'— Had him checked out,' completed the captain. 'Well, I guess I probably would have done the same in your position.'

Tooms's mood lifted for a second.

'However, you need to stop conducting any further investigations on Mr Steel, is that understood?'

Tooms's stomach turned.

'OK, Detective Tooms, if that's all, I believe we still have a killer to find.' He not unkindly ushered Tooms out of the room.

'Um, yes sir.' The detective was filled with confusion and dismay at the implications of what he'd just heard. Was the captain in on something shady, he wondered, as he returned to his desk and slumped in his chair.

As he watched, the captain picked up his phone and rapidly dialled a number from memory, waited for a beat, then began to speak animatedly. As he spoke, he noticed Tooms monitoring him and turned in his chair, as if to conceal the conversation.

Tony strolled up to his partner and noted his hardened expression. 'What's up, man?' he asked his stony-faced partner.

'What's up is we have a problem, man, and I think the captain is in on it.' He showed Tony the sheet of printout.

Tony absorbed the information, his eyes widening in astonishment.

'What does it mean?' he puzzled, passing it back to Tooms.

'I don't know, man, but what I *do* know is things have gotten pretty dicey since this guy showed up. And right now, he is out there somewhere, and he's got Sam McCall with him.' A sense of foreboding settled over them like a cloud.

Right then, Tooms's phone rang, making them jump. He grabbed the receiver quickly as though expecting the worst, and as he listened, he scribbled down an address in the Meatpacking District.

'Yeah, OK, we'll get there quick as we can, see you soon.' He put down the receiver and ripped the piece of paper from the pad he'd used.

'Trouble?' Tony asked, grabbing his coat and following his partner to the captain's office.

'Not sure yet but we got to go.' Tooms knocked on the captain's door and stuck his head inside the room as the captain waved him in. 'What's up now, Tooms?' he asked, replacing his phone's receiver into its cradle.

'McCall and Steel need back-up, of the special weapons type.' The captain stood up and grabbed the slip of paper from him.

'OK, you two get down there and I'll meet you at this address with the teams. And no heroics from anyone.'

Tooms nodded grimly and left.

Brant picked up the phone and dialled the extension for SWAT and the bomb squad. He couldn't help but think, *what the hell have they gotten into over there now?*

Within the hour, the building was surrounded, streets were blocked off, and helicopter units hovered above. The captain pulled up, closely followed by Tooms and Tony.

'So, you two clowns, what sort of hell have you got for me today?' They had gathered around their vehicles, the captain clearly annoyed, though they realised his anger wasn't directed at them. A banging sound emanated from a nearby dumpster.

'What the..?' spluttered Tooms, as he and Tony both drew their weapons. Steel swiftly materialised out of nowhere and darted between the detectives and the dumpster.

'As much as I would love you to shoot the bastard, he may be our only witness.' Steel removed his handcuffs from the container's handles and lifted the dumpster's lid. All four men peered at the raggedy man inside. He looked up sadly at them but didn't move. 'Dumpster guy may have some answers,' McCall's voice came from behind them. 'Get him out of there,' yelled Brant, and two officers hauled the homeless man out of the container, cuffed him, and led him away.

The group assembled next to a patrol car. In addition to Brant's team were two sergeants, one from the bomb squad, the other a SWAT commander.

'Captain. I'm Sergeant Matt Carter of E.O.D, and this is Sergeant Jack North of SWAT,' the bomb squad man introduced them. The captain shook their hands in turn.

'Gentlemen, I'm Alan Brant of Homicide, and this unlucky pair of sons-of-bitches are Detectives McCall and Steel.' After performing the usual courtesy handshakes, they leaned over the car where, laid out on the hood, was a blueprint of the building.

'OK, so, what we got?' asked the tall, ageing Sergeant Carter. Carter had been in the force a long time, but he knew everything there was to know about explosives. A bald, African American man, he sported a small goatee. He had the build of a prize-fighter rather than that of a technical type. The other man, Jack North, was much younger and had an arrogant presence about him: McCall noticed his body language towards Steel, almost as if he viewed Detective Steel as a potential threat to his masculinity. He was shorter than those around him, even Sam McCall, and his large-jawed head terminated in a blond, flat-top hair- style. The man was keen and looked as if he might have a complex where authority was concerned.

Sam stepped forwards and inspected the plan. Using her finger, she described their entry into the building and what they had found in each of the rooms up until she reached one specific door marked on the plan.

'This room here is where the problem is.' She glanced around to check she had the full attention of her audience, scowling as she noticed that Steel had found a squad car's flat, wide hood to lie on while she gave the briefing.

'Inside, we observed that the place had been set up like some kind of maze.'

The two sergeants looked up, suddenly curious.

'A maze?' Sergeant North stepped back and crossed his arms as if to demonstrate his scepticism.

'Yes, a maze. Large cargo boxes stacked up to a height of, I don't know, five, six feet, maybe more.'

Sergeant Carter gestured for her to continue. 'Go on,' he said. 'That wasn't the problem, however. As we progressed further in, we noticed shafts of light created by holes in the ceiling. Steel threw some dust at the one of these sunbeams, and that's when we saw the lasers.'

This got everyone's attention. Steel smirked to himself as he felt the mood change.

'What sort of lasers?' asked Sergeant North, his arms falling from their scornful pose.

'Beams of light, pretty much like on a laser sight,' she shrugged.

These were the experts, she thought.

'Any ideas, Jack?' asked Sergeant Carter. The two men faced each other, almost as if they were in a private conference.

'Well, it could be some kind of alarm system,' replied the SWAT commander.

'Claymores,' called Steel from his resting place, making everyone turn to look at him.

'Excuse me?' Sergeant North looked at Steel with an air of con- tempt. 'And what makes you think Claymore?'

Sergeant North turned away from the recumbent Steel as if dismissing the idea.

'New type Claymores have laser trip wires, not conventional cord ones,' Steel pointed out, still lying prone, getting some sun. Sergeant Carter nodded to concur, 'He's right, of course,' he said, studying the floor plan once again.

'So, what are your thoughts, Mr Steel?' Carter asked, adding, 'Why don't you come and join us?'

Rolling off his comfortable perch, Steel strolled over and considered the floor plan. 'Our best bet is to get a bird's-eye view up there, and then plug the holes.' He stood back slightly and let them figure it out.

'OK, you lost me,' said Sergeant Carter.

'The glass roof,' McCall spoke up, her face suddenly animated. 'The building has a glass roof, that's where the rays of light are coming from. We can look through the roof then plug the holes where the light comes through.'

The captain smiled as he noticed how his pair of detectives sparked ideas off each other. *My children*, he thought to himself.

'To what end?' Carter asked, then went on, 'Ah, I get you, ok, I got it, good idea. Plug the holes, then we have a better chance of seeing the lasers.'

'But just in case, when we send the teams in, they will have infrared attached,' added North.

'So, what do you think?' Steel said, turning to Tooms.

The detective was caught off guard. His guilty mind was working overtime. Had the captain been on the phone to Steel after their recent conversation about the mysterious Englishman's bank accounts?

'Why you asking me?' Tooms huffed nervously, crossing his arms in front of his chest to try and show some sort of defiance.

'You were Special Forces, weren't you, Joshua?' Steel asked. Tooms suddenly found himself muddling his words. 'Yes, why?'

He could hear the defensive tone in his response.

'Hey, look man, I was just asking for your opinion.'

McCall gave Tooms a strange look; she had never seen him behaving like this.

'Oh, OK,' Tooms answered, and cleared his throat as if he were going to deliver a lecture. 'Well, the thing about those mothers is knowing which is the business end. It's not like the cable ones, where you can just snip it in the middle, no, these are real bastards.' He looked at Steel, who flashed him a friendly smile.

'Plus, we may face another small problem,' announced Steel. Until now, McCall hadn't fully realised how bad the situation was. With Steel's next words she learnt the worst.

'The other problem being secondary devices. If they are mad enough to put Claymores out, they are sick enough to back them up. That's the bad news.'

Everyone stared at him in surprise.

'And the good news is?' asked Tony, whose head was still spinning from hearing about the possible devices inside the building.

'My guess is there must be something inside worth getting rid of, don't you think?'

The captain had to agree: there had to be something really important inside, something worth booby trapping the building and blowing it up rather than letting it be found.

'Sir, how long could a laser light last for?' McCall asked Sergeant North.

The sergeant looked puzzled. 'Couldn't say, really. Why?' He leant forwards onto the hood of the car and studied the plan, trying to look busy.

'Well, how long would it last, unless it was plugged into the mains, which I doubt very much. The fact they're still working suggests to me that someone had to have recently turned them on.' The captain now had a bad feeling where this was going.

'And your point, Detective?' North didn't have time for games.

'It means we've been set up. Again.' McCall's words were bitter. Steel had always maintained his fear of revealing too much on the off-chance of having a mole within the department. Now his uneasiness was hers; she hated the thought that someone in the station could set them up like this. And, try as she might, she couldn't work out what this had to do with the dismembered women.

THIRTY-THREE

Not wanting to risk anyone seeing them through the weathered skylight, they sent up an tactical drone. The small, nimble craft was propelled by quad rotors and had a built-in camera that could transmit data back, so that the room could be mapped out. Before anything else was done, the holes in the roof had to be covered to ensure complete darkness: one lucky volunteer made his way onto the roof and sprayed paint over the exposed glass.

'OK, sir, roof secure. Teams Alpha and Bravo report ready,' declared the radio op to Sergeant North.

'OK, move them in, but first sign of trouble, get them out,' North replied.

The man nodded and relayed the instructions.

The two teams moved in slowly. While their pistols were drawn, the men's Heckler and Koch UMP machine guns were slung on their backs and ready to go. Creeping down the long corridor, they reached the target room. Both point men stopped and regarded the mass in front them. Through their night vision goggles, the scene looked immense and somewhat terrifying.

'Fuck me,' said the Alpha team man.

'Report teams, what do you see?' asked the HQ party. The operations room for the SWAT team was located inside a large, blacked-out van down the street. Monitors flickered, and voices crackled over the loudspeaker.

'Sir put it like this: what we see don't look good,' the reply squawked.

Moving in further, the units split apart, each taking one side of the junction, when they suddenly stopped and went to ground.

'Sir, we have a big problem.' The two-point men switched on small helmet cameras so that HQ could see what was happening.

'What in the name of everything holy is that?' Sergeant Carter eased forwards to get a better look. On the small monitor they saw a long corridor of boxes, and down the centre danced the lasers, hundreds of thin beams of light, some running vertically, others travelling horizontally, creating a deadly, red net.

'Get your teams out now!' yelled the captain, but North didn't require prompting, he was already nudging the radio operator to retrieve the teams.

All units confirmed their position when they were at a safe distance, returning as ordered. Sergeant North grabbed the communications set from his head and hurled it on to the makeshift operations desk. They stepped outside the enclosed space, which suddenly seemed unbearable.

'What now?' asked Brant. He could see the frustration on North's face, and he felt the same.

'I think we should blow the building and make it safe.' Carter stepped forward, calm and confident in his solution.

'We can't do that, there could be evidence inside,' said Captain Brant.

'Yes, there could be, but we don't know that for sure, do we?' North was still mad, his face was red, and beads of sweat rolled down his tanned skin.

'We have to check first.' McCall lined up beside her captain.

'Oh, really, and who is going in? You?' North replied sarcastically. 'What about the whirlybird?' asked Steel. Everyone turned to look at him. Steel was back lying on top of the squad car, grabbing some rays.

'He's got a point. What about it, would that work?' Carter stepped towards Steel, considering this strange man, wondering who he was and where he came from.

'Well, fly the drone in, have a snoop around and if there is something we can get to, we just drop in from above.' Steel didn't move, just casually lay there gazing up, admiring the beauty of the day.

'We go in from above?' North looked puzzled.

'The roof has a skylight, remember?' McCall agreed, smiling at the idea, knowing it would infuriate Sergeant North if it worked.

'Sounds good to me,' announced the captain, confidently.

'OK then, so who is the lucky bastard who is going in the harness?' Sergeant Carter asked, rubbing his hands together. The group turned, and Steel could feel all their eyes burning into him.

'It was his idea.' North jabbed a thumb at him with a wide grin. 'Thought so.' Steel stretched, sat up and strolled over to McCall's car that they had arrived in so many hours earlier, where he popped open the boot, removing a large, black canvas bag. Heaving it over his shoulder, he set off for one of the other disused buildings.

'Where the hell are you going?' asked Sergeant North, thinking Steel was making off.

Steel turned and smiled. 'Just slipping into something more comfortable,' and so saying, he headed into the building.

'Captain Brant?' Sergeant Carter asked the commanding officer, as he watched Steel disappear into the building.

'Yes?' Alan Brant observed the others as they watched their colleague prepare for this dumb-ass mission.

'Captain, where the hell did you find this guy?'

The two men regarded each other, and eventually Brant smiled. 'He found us, man, he found us.'

The captain turned and headed back to check on the drone operator. It had taken some time for the metal construction to be put together, and now it resembled the skeletal structure of a medium-sized marquee tent or the roof frame to a house. This framework would be put over the skylight and would support Steel as he was lowered into the room below. The detective walked out of the building and made his way towards the command centre. His kit caused quite the commotion, being some state-of-the-art tech and, as far as McCall could see, fitting pretty snugly. The all-in-one outfit resembled a diver's wetsuit apart from having carbon woven patches on the knees, elbows and shoulders. The gloves and boots were attached to the strange-looking suit, so it was entirely one unit, with only John Steel's head remaining uncovered. McCall sidled over to the English detective.

'You don't have to do this, you know,' she whispered, urgently.

He just smiled.

'Are you are volunteering then?'

'Sorry, not my style, but it's a cute outfit.'

He shrugged and continued to smile at her, as she stared into the strange new glasses he had on. 'Look, someone has to go in, I know he has left something, it's part of his game.'

McCall admitted that he was right, but on the other hand she really didn't want to lose what they might be about to have. She turned and saw the drone take off and make its way to the entrance. All doors had been locked open, thus facilitating easy access for the helicopter.

'He's right,' said a sickly-sweet voice from behind them. As soon as she heard him, she knew that it was the creepy Doctor

Davidson. Mc Call observed the way he kept brushing his trousers. He didn't want to be here, and frankly, most of the rest of them would have preferred him to stay away.

'Any thoughts, Doc?' Steel didn't really need any psychobabble pontifications to know that this was one big trap, but he felt kind of sorry for the guy.

'It's clear that the person we are looking for has a flair for the dramatic, he is meticulous and brutal,' Davidson responded in his usual heart-warming manner, though he still seemed more concerned about the dirt on his suit.

'In other words, watch your ass,' Tooms added. He didn't like the idea of the coming operation either, but like Steel said, someone had to do it. Steel continued on his way to the command centre, where the chiefs were waiting for him.

'Steel, what the hell are you wearing, son?' The captain's face betrayed his wonder and amusement as he studied the tactical suit.

'You know it's not underwater, right?'

Steel flashed him a patient smile. 'This suit blocks any heat signatures normally given off, so if there are any sort of heat-sensor traps, I shouldn't trigger them.'

The captain looked puzzled as he studied the suit more closely.

'I don't know, I find it kind of fetching,' declared Tina as she sauntered up to the party, her eyes trained on John Steel.

'The doctor is here on the off chance that there are casualties.' The captain announced quickly, then changed the subject.

'Christ,' muttered Steel. 'In case of casualties they bring a Trick Cyclist and a Pathologist. Don't they have an honest to God repair man?' McCall heard, and gave a little smile.

The man at the flight controls yelled for the others as his drone had moved to the middle of the room.

'Hey guys, I think we have something here,' he said. The screen showed the centre of the maze, and the clear image of a man seated in a chair. Steel straightened up, looking troubled. McCall turned to him, concerned at his dark expression.

'What's the matter?' she asked.

'Is it just me or does this guy have a nasty thing about placing people in chairs in the middle of really bad situations?'

McCall had not thought of it like that, but she had to agree.

'OK, so we have one male in the centre of a room, any theories?' The captain asked, arching his back, which ached after leaning in on the monitor. He looked searchingly at the others.

'We go with the plan,' Steel said firmly and shrugged as if to say *no other options.*

'OK, you go in from the roof, grab him, and then get the hell out of there, understood?' the captain ordered. Steel had no objections. The thought of going in didn't appeal anyway, but the idea of staying in there was worse.

Steel broke away from the group and was halfway to the warehouse before McCall caught up to him and grabbed him.

'You know this has 'trap' written all over it?' she told him urgently. 'So why are you going?'

'We need this evidence – you need this evidence. Besides, it's a piece of cake: like the captain said, I go in, get him out, we go home. Simple.'

She knew he was playing it down for her and wished that she could see behind his shades, directly into his eyes, to know what he was really thinking. 'You better get your ass back here in one piece, or I'll kill you.' She hoped that a display of anger would mask her concern.

A tactical officer ran up to Steel and tapped him on the shoulder. 'Sir, we have to go,' he said. Steel nodded and they hurried off.

'He is too much of a pain in the ass to die,' Brant

murmured to her quietly. 'Hell wouldn't have him, he's too much trouble and you know he ain't ever going upstairs.'

She smiled uncertainly and looked up at the captain who had appeared at her side just as Steel had left. He had noticed the tears gathering in the corners of her eyes and placed a massive hand on her shoulder.

'It's like Dad all over again.' She had lost the smile.

Brant shook his head.

'This is nothing like your father's murder. You know Steel will get in and out of there, you hear me, Detective?'

She nodded and they turned back to watch as Steel was lowered steadily into the building. An ominous feeling crept over the two of them.

'I have to go.' She dabbed at her eyes and turned to face her captain. Somehow, the concern on his face made her feel a little better.

The roof had been made secure, and a hole cut above the target. Steel stood open-armed as the team fitted the harness, finally latching the cable onto him via the clip; the team leader gave it a sharp tug to check that it was securely attached.

'OK, central, we are good to go here.' The leader gave a thumbs up to Steel, who stepped off the roof into the open frame of the window. As he fell into the open air the gears of the mechanical pulley locked in, leaving him suspended in mid-air a few feet from the roof's entrance.

Back at the command centre, they watched a second monitor, which held live feed from Steel's head cam. They saw the rocky motion as he was lowered into the depths. Suddenly, with only a few feet to go, Steel yelled for them to stop.

'What's up? You changed your mind?' North spoke into the headset.

'How did you check this part of the room?' Steel asked. North seemed confused at the question.

'What do you mean? We used every sort of sensor and view the bot has, you're safe to proceed.' North shook his head as though to comment how unbelievable this man was.

'Did you use X-ray?'

North's back stiffened. 'And why would we use x-ray? So far he has used every high-tech gadget we know.'

'Because this guy is smart, and at the moment I'm looking down to a large area that could have anything in it. Listen, if I know this guy he will start with technology and revert back to old-school, just to throw us off.'

North glanced at Doctor Davidson who gave a tight nod, signifying he believed Steel was right.

'Listen, Sergeant North, all your scans, can they pick up old-fashioned trip wires?'

North's face abruptly changed, and he dashed over to the techs.

Steel knew from the silence that the answer was no.

'OK, bring back the bot and set it up for X-ray, even though we know it will be a waste of time.' North was mad, smarting with the feeling that he had just been shown up as incompetent. After some readjustment and new equipment, the drone was good to go. Dipping through the gap in the ceiling it made a sweep and found all to be clear, also establishing the bound man was alive. Using the x-ray, they scanned the man for any internal sign of movement, which was slight but definitely discernible.

Viewing the scene through Steel's cam, the captain and the rest watched Steel untie the captive and carry him forwards towards the cable. Locking him off onto the winch, the rescued man disappeared slowly into the haze of light above. Everyone cheered as the man was retrieved through the skylight.

Immediately, alarms blared inside the complex, and a loudspeaker activated. McCall and the others listened in horror as they made out a countdown being hailed from within:

'30, 29, 28, 27…' the voice continued.

North ordered his men off the roof, at which McCall turned and howled abuse at him, demanding how he could leave Steel behind. Then everyone fell silent as they heard: '5, 4, 3, 2, 1.'

Steel listened intently, as Sinatra's silken tones crooning *My Way* crackled over the speakers. *Nice touch*, he thought, rapidly surveying the area for cover. He spied the perfect spot: a metal plate, like a man-hole cover, protruded slightly from the ground, and he dived for it.

Using all his strength, he ripped up the metal cover and scrambled in, yanking the cover back over his head. A clang of metal echoed in the small crawl space as it crashed into place above him.

A blinding white flash radiated from the building, then the area where the extraction team had stood moments before, was covered in debris as the roof structure collapsed, swallowed up by a dazzling blaze. Four simultaneous explosions could be heard, the building immediately consumed by a fireball. Detective McCall and the two SWAT team members were flung across the street, where smouldering bricks and timber rained down on them.

North and Carter stumbled forward, their faces stamped with the shock of the carnage they had just witnessed, while McCall crawled to her knees and screamed Steel's name over and over again, frantically hoping that this phantom of a man would rise up, desperate that this annoying magician would be perched on a building somewhere, laughing at them for being so foolish as to think he had ever been in the building in the first place. But all that met her eyes was fire, smoke and death.

She tried to throw off the two SWAT guys who were struggling to restrain her from racing into the inferno.

'Ma'am, there's nothing you can do, sorry about your guy but he's gone,' one of them yelled.

Her eyes blazed as she snarled at the two men, who released her, raised their arms in surrender and backed off.

'They are right, McCall, as much as I hate to agree,' the captain's voice murmured in her ear, as he folded her shaking frame in his powerful arms. 'Steel gave his life for this sorry son-of-a-bitch. Let's just hope it was worth it.' Brant surveyed his crew and was struck by how upset everyone was. He brusquely ordered them all off the scene, even if 'off scene' was just around the corner.

The CSU had set up a field post, and because the area was large, they were forced to examine it a section at a time and hope that the weather would hold. The press had wasted no time in sending out their crews, and cameras and vultures with microphones circled the scene, hoping for an exclusive to broadcast. The response crew stared at the press, sickened, and shook their heads.

'Look at them, building burns down, couple of press guys arrive,' growled Tooms. 'Put a cop in it, whole fucking press corps turns out.' There was nothing that the homicide department could do, not here. As small consolation, they had two people to question; unfortunately, one of them had to go to hospital, but the other was all theirs.

THIRTY-FOUR

T he next morning the press was giving maximum coverage to the story about an unnamed cop who gave his life to save a homeless vet in a booby-trapped building. McCall smiled sadly to herself, grateful that at least the press had made a hero out of Steel. She had arrived at work early, not wanting to waste any time. They had someone to talk to, Jerry the homeless guy, and she reckoned he had better have some answers, for all their sakes.

As she sat at her desk, sipping her coffee, her gaze transfixed by the empty chair opposite, she felt the presence of someone standing behind her and turned quickly, hoping to find Detective Steel loitering there in his black suit and Chesterfield jacket. Her face fell when she saw that it was only the captain.

'Hoping it was him?' Brant smiled, reading her mind. 'Yeah, the bastard really knew how to get into your head.' He settled himself awkwardly on the edge of her desk as she gazed up at him.

'Why, Captain?'

'What do you mean "why"? Why did he turn up here? Why did he request you as a partner? Or why did he go into that building?' He shrugged. 'Thing is, Sam, I really don't know. But I do know he cared about this team, and you can be sure he cared about you.'

She looked puzzled.

'What, you think he needed to sit here all the time?' he said, pointing to the vacant seat beside her. 'The man had an office of his own.' He levered himself to his feet and laid a paternal hand on her shoulder. 'What we need to do is catch the bastard who did this.'

McCall stared at him thoughtfully, a thunderous expression sweeping over her face, transforming her sombre smile to a stone- cold scowl. At that moment Brant pitied whoever was responsible for Steel's murder.

Tony was on the phone to the CSU department, speaking to Cindy Childs, a one-time girlfriend from his college days, now a professional colleague. They chatted for a while about this and that, but mostly she was anxious to let him know that she sympathised with his loss. She had spent some time down at the scene, and her heart had gone out to the department, and not just because Marinelli was part of it.

'Hey, are you guys OK?' Cindy asked. 'I mean, it's all over the TV and everything, and I even saw you on the box. All I can say is I'm real sorry.'

Tony was touched at her words. 'Yeah, I guess, to lose someone like that is just – well, you understand how I feel.'

She gently steered the subject to the reason she called in the first place. 'Well, you'll be glad to know Mike from ballistics came up trumps for you.'

He was bewildered for a moment.

'You know that sniper rifle you sent down from the shooting at the bridge?'

He tasted his coffee, reflecting soberly that none of the people responsible for it being there were with them anymore.

'Yeah, don't tell me it was used at the hotel shooting as well.' He dismissed the idea as ludicrous.

'Not that one, no. But it was used in another shooting we've got on record.' She described some details of the weapon's history, which came as a shock to Tony, while he jotted down the salient points on a pad in front of him. He thanked her and slowly put down the receiver. McCall was with the rest of the team in the briefing room. The captain was giving a breakdown on the incident as it had unfolded and bringing them up to date with new information as it emerged, trying to create a clear chain of events. Tony knocked and slowly walked in, drawing the captain's attention, who trailed off from what he was saying and eyed him warily.

'What's up, Detective?' he asked, reading trouble in Tony's pensive expression.

'Uhm, I've just got the report back from ballistics, about the bridge shooting.' He waved the piece of paper he had taken notes on, which he was grasping tightly.

'And what did they come up with?' asked the captain, unable to figure out what was wrong.

Tony ignored him and caught McCall's eye. 'Sam, can I speak to you alone for a moment first, please?' he said, quietly.

McCall wasn't in the mood for messing around. 'Tony, if you have something to say, spit it out right now, will you? I can't be bothered with cloak-and-dagger drama right now.' She leant back in her chair and rubbed her eyes, feeling as if she hadn't slept for a month.

'Okay. That weapon was used in several recent shootings. Recently at the bridge, as we know, but its first recorded use was just over eight years ago.'

McCall's eyes snapped back into focus. At last, they had a lead. 'Who was the target then?' she asked, eagerly.

'A detective called Samuel Robson.' Anxiously, he watched her stagger slightly as if she had been shot herself. She looked across at him, feeling as if her legs wouldn't support her.

'Are they sure?' she mumbled.

He nodded. 'That's what they're saying.'

She stumbled out, white-faced, making for the ladies' room. Meanwhile, Doctor Davidson and Detective Thompson looked baffled.

'Who the hell was he?' the doctor asked.

Captain Brant sank down and composed himself before he spoke: 'About ten years ago I got partnered with that hot-head; he wanted to save the world – a good guy, a good cop.'

His audience listened respectfully.

'We kicked some serious ass back in the day, breaking up all sorts of shit. So, one day, we busted a big weapons cache. There was heaps of money too, serious shit. Now, one detective made it his mission to find who was shipping the stuff. He wanted to shut them all down himself.' Pausing only to take a gulp from his coffee mug, the captain continued.

'Around eight years ago he tells me he is close, he needs one final piece of the puzzle, and he's got everything. But he warned me it was bigger than we thought.' He coughed and loosened his tie. 'One day we were called to a hotel room in the Bronx, something trivial we thought, you know, distur-bance and possible use of weapons, so we go in nice and quiet, not wanting to spook anyone so they run, you know?

Anyway, we get to the room, the door is open, we could see a body on the floor from the door, so Samuel goes in to check his vitals.'

The captain stood up and walked around, finding the recollection of painful events difficult.

'What happened, Captain?' prompted Doctor Davidson, gently. He could see the anguish in Brant's face and sympa-thised with him.

'A bullet, from God knows where, smashed straight through my partner's chest, throwing him across the room. I tried to do CPR but it was useless, he was gone.' He wiped his eyes, weeping openly at the memory.

'So he was your partner. But McCall can't have worked

with him, so who was he?' Jenny, the new detective piped up, still confused.

Everyone fell silent as McCall came back into the room. 'He was my father,' she stated simply.

Jerry, the homeless man who'd led them to the booby-trapped building, was settled cosily in Interrogation Room One. On the table in front of him sat a large plate of hamburger and fries. For a moment, McCall watched the man through the other side of the two-way mirror. She was consumed with loathing for the man who sat calmly eating, while her partner had been vaporised in the blast. The captain, who was standing next to her, also wore a grim expression. Yes, she now definitely considered Steel to have been her partner.

'You okay going in there?' Brant's words were intended to be a comfort, but she knew she had to do it. Pausing outside the door of the interrogation room she blew out a lungful of air, preparing herself for the ordeal.

As she entered, Jerry glanced up at her, and then over her shoulder, expecting to see Detective Steel.

'Where's the big guy?' he asked through a mouthful of ground beef. She sat down slowly, not saying a word, not even looking at him.

She shuffled some paperwork before meeting his eyes and offering him a wide smile.

'Hello, Jerry, how is the food?'

He began to chew slowly, sensing that something was wrong.

'It's real good. Thanks.' His nervousness grew as, his feast forgotten, he cast anxious glances at the door, hoping that Steel would come striding in. The realisation began to dawn on him that something was terribly amiss, and he began to twitch with tension.

'Where's the British detective? Whatcha call him, Steel?' he asked again, with a note of alarm in his voice.

She shot him a look of fury so intense he almost wet himself. 'Don't you even speak his name, you do not have the right ever to speak his name, you piece of—' A bang on the glass behind her shook her back to reality.

After a lengthy period of questioning, all McCall could get out of Jerry was that he denied all knowledge about any bombs or of his friend George being roped to a chair in the middle of the scenario. George was in hospital, guarded by four men; the captain was not prepared to risk losing another witness.

'So, Jerry, tell me again about the deliveries?' The man she was questioning was tired and just wanted to sleep, but she figured that put her at an advantage.

'We would pick up the parcels and take them wherever we were told to go.' He drained the coffee she had put in front of him. 'We would get word through Eric when to meet, and we would just deliver the goods.'

'What sort of goods?' She leant back in the chair, so it rocked backwards.

'I don't know. Some big, some small – just packages, we never opened them,' he said, tipping the dregs of coffee down his throat.

'Where to?' She could see he was breaking. *Just a little further*, she thought.

'All over the place. Parks, disused lots – all sorts.' He was so exhausted that his hands were shaking. His eyes widened as she opened a file and laid out the crime scene photos of the women. Tears ran down his face as he realised the locations.

'I had nothing to do with any of this,' he vowed wretch-edly. 'Really, you've got me all wrong. As God is my witness, I never knew what was in those parcels.' He began to sob. 'I was just told to take the parcels to places and leave them. I didn't even give them to anyone; I just left them where I was told. That's all. Please, you have to believe me.' He collapsed forwards on the table, the horrific images seared into his brain.

'Okay, Jerry, I believe you,' she said, thinking, *for the time being*. She put the photos away.

'So, these parcels. How long was that going on for?'

He gazed up at her, surprised at the question.

'Months? Years? I really don't know. I don't have much to do with time, you know.' He had stopped sobbing and peered dejectedly into his empty coffee cup.

McCall stretched and went to the door, where she spoke with another officer outside the room. Returning to her seat, she regarded Jerry, silently. She had so many mixed emotions about this poor soul. Because he had led them into a trap, she would have liked to put a bullet into his brain. But on the other hand, this poor bastard had just been used by one organisation or another his whole life.

A knock on the door roused her from her reverie, and a hand appeared, clutching a map and coloured marker pens. McCall accepted them and brought them over to the table.

'Jerry, can you put a mark on this map any places where you delivered things to?' she asked, laying the map on the table in front of him.

Jerry checked around nervously, then nodded. 'But, see, if I help you, I'll have to disappear completely afterwards.'

McCall leant back in her chair, and her phone buzzed. Picking it up to read, she saw a text from the captain, saying: *get the locations, I will speak to witness protection*. She nodded to herself and put the phone back on the table.

'Okay Jerry, you show me where you delivered the packages, and then I'll help you disappear. The captain's arranging that as we speak.' He looked back at her, suspiciously. She held up her phone and showed him the screen displaying the text from the captain. She saw the beginnings of a smile of relief touch the corners of his lips. A moment later there was a knock on the window, and she knew the deal was done. His head shot up, eyes darting around desperately.

'Are you expecting someone to come here, Jerry?' His fingers drummed on the tabletop, beads of sweat pouring down his dirty brow. He grabbed the pens and started to mark spots on the map. She instructed him to put a red dot to signify where he'd delivered a large package and a blue mark for a small one.

'You never know, he could be here, couldn't he?' Jerry's nervous scribblings on the map continued frantically.

'Who could be here?' McCall asked, intrigued. Who was it that was terrifying him?

'The Man, of course! That's who! He is everywhere and everyone.' As he picked up his empty coffee mug, she noticed that his hands were trembling.

'Who is he? Have you ever met "The Man"?'

He shook his head, still looking around, anxiously.

'Listen, Jerry,' she tried to reassure him. 'You know you are safe now. Nobody can get to you in here. Have you met this "Man"?'

He peered up at her, his eyes full of fear and remorse, before lowering his gaze back to the map.

'No,' Jerry muttered at last. 'I never met him. Nobody has. All we know is Eric gets a call, he still has a phone that works. Eric finds whoever he needs and we go to wherever and move whatever.' He shrugged, and McCall could see her assurances had him calmed slightly.

McCall studied the map he had filled out, then she stood up and reached for it. 'I think that should be more than enough, thank you, Jerry.' She headed for the door and knocked to be let out. The door clicked open slightly, where it was held until the officer was satisfied that it was her leaving and not the prisoner, then he let her through.

'Well, did we get anything?' asked the captain. 'Sure,' she said, holding up the map.

'Wow, we are going to need some more people,' reflected Tooms. The map was covered with red and blue dots, bunched around particular areas.

'What about Jerry?' She sounded genuinely concerned about his welfare, to the surprise of her colleagues.

'Witness protection will be here in the morning,' the captain assured her. 'Until then he will be kept in a cell, with a guard.'

'Good,' she nodded.

'So, what now?' asked Tony.

McCall started for the computer room. 'Now we try to narrow our search down.'

Inside the IT centre, she hunted out the computer tech, a man in his late twenties with spiky black hair and large black-rimmed glasses. His clothes were more street than NYPD, but he was there for his brains not for his fashion sense.

'Hi, Louie, how are you today?' she greeted him with a smile.

He squinted up at her from his monitor and returned the smile.

'How you doing, Detective Sam?'

She shrugged. 'Guess I can't complain.' 'So, what you got for me?'

She spread the map out in front of him. 'I need to know about all of these marked areas. Are there any warehouses or disused properties nearby?'

He looked at the groups of multi-coloured dots and flashed a confident smile, which gave her faith in him.

'Sure, I can do that, but it may take a little time, even for me.' he grinned brightly, jumped up, and pinned the map onto a board so that he could get a better view.

Satisfied, McCall strode back to the interview room where

Jerry sat, nervously fidgeting. She had brought him a fresh coffee, which she set in front of him as she sat down.

'Jerry,' she began. 'My captain has spoken with some people, and by tomorrow you will have a new life and a new identity.'

He looked up, and she could see the relief in his eyes. 'So, Jerry, let's talk more about "The Man". How do you know he exists at all?'

He leant forwards, and she bent towards him to hear, as he was now talking in whispers.

'I have seen Eric on the phone with someone, and he always called the guy 'Sir', then he would turn to the other dude and say something like, "The Man said we are still go." '

McCall looked thoughtful for a moment. 'This other dude, what did he look like?'

'I don't know. Tall, blond, always wore black.'

McCall shot a glance backwards towards the mirror. Pieces were falling into place.

She excused herself and hurried to the outer room where the others were waiting for her. 'The asshole at the bridge that got away,' growled Tooms. She nodded, but her thoughts were elsewhere.

The captain narrowed his eyes as he looked through the two-way mirror at Jerry. 'What the hell is going on here?' he muttered, as puzzled as ever, then he turned and faced the others. 'OK, there's nothing more we can do here until tomorrow.' He checked his watch, realising that the hours had just melted away. It was now nine o'clock in the evening, and he needed to go home to his family. 'Go home, get some rest, and hopefully we'll have some doors to kick in tomorrow. All of you get out of here.'

McCall watched as Jerry was taken to a quiet cell for the night and she smiled with relief. They'd got through the day, and no one else had died. That was something to be grateful for.

. . .

A breeze blew across the remnants of the warehouse, taking with it small shreds of debris, sighing off the scorched walls that lay broken and scattered. Loose timbers where windows once stood now smouldered and released wisps of ash into the night wind. Metal beams lay bent and deformed where the blast had twisted them into angry-looking shapes. What had once been the large storage facility that held the maze was now a scene of devastation, its appearance more like a scene from a war movie than a crime scene. Burnt, shattered fragments lay strewn across the blackened floor. The wind howled through the carnage like a wounded beast, bringing a chill to the bones of the two officers sent to watch over the crime scene.

Rats scurried across the pieces of broken timber and brick, hoping to sniff out a meal, but the officers knew that if anything edible had been inside, it would have been turned into ash instantly.

The beams of the officers' flashlights cut through the night, causing long, haunting shadows as they swept past the gnarly looking ruins. The two men stepped carefully through the rubble-strewn areas they had been ordered to patrol.

'This place gives me the creeps,' announced Officer Timmins, a tall, skinny young man with mousy-coloured hair. At twenty-five, he had already spent the last five years working with his current partner.

'Yeah, I hear ya, man,' replied Officer Doyle. 'But still, it beats the hell out of hanging around in that alleyway they gave us to guard.' Memories still lingered about the ghostly figure they had seen, and Doyle shuddered at the thought of the place.

Doyle was a good cop and, while he was not the brightest officer on the force, he was honest and hardworking, and he kept everyone happy; he was shorter than his partner, but stocky and well built, with a bushy moustache that compensated for his receding, greying hair.

Their route was specific, because much of the scene was covered by large plastic sheeting to preserve whatever evidence there was for CSU. As they paced, they detected a strange mist starting to creep over the scene. Though it was low on the ground, it still blanketed the floor, giving the place an even eerier feel.

'Oh boy, you have got to be kidding me,' Doyle said as he watched the fog build up. He did not want to be here, and this extra weirdness did not help. The moustachioed officer stopped and turned his head slightly. Timmins stared at him, worried something was wrong.

'What's up?' Timmins asked, only to have Doyle clap a large hand over his partner's mouth.

'Do you hear that?' the shorter man asked, forgetting to remove his hand. He peered up as Timmins made a muffled sound, and withdrew his palm. 'Tell me you heard that?'

Timmins listened carefully, and then he heard it. A scraping sound, distant, but definitely a metallic scraping noise. It was too loud to be rats. They eased forwards in the direction the sound was coming from and found themselves at the entrance to what had once been the main storage area. Beams from their flashlights scanned the space like anti-aircraft searchlights.

They froze. There it was again! It sounded as though something underground was clawing its way to the surface. The two officers drew their weapons and held flashlights aloft, ready to lock on to whatever it was.

Moving slowly towards the sound, they noticed the mist was getting thicker as they got closer, a great white shroud of fog clinging to the ground, obscuring it completely.

As they watched from one corner, a figure emerged from the cover of the fog, rising up slowly, as if he was surfacing from below. The two police officers crouched, mesmerised, as this phantom straightened itself out.

'Uh – hey, you! You're not supposed to be in here!' yelled Doyle, nervously.

The form stood motionless for a second, silhouetted in profile.

Doyle nudged his partner, urging, 'You go ahead, I'll cover you.' Timmins stepped backwards. 'Fuck that! You go, I got *your* back.' Both men were bathed in cold sweat, their quivering fingers poised on their triggers.

The shape turned and faced them. Nonchalantly reaching down, it plucked something from the mist that resembled a blanket or was it a long coat? It saluted them, and as Doyle and Timmins looked on in dread, the figure swung the long coat over its shoulders, and suddenly they realised they had seen this phantom before.

Shakily, the two cops shone their flashlights on him, when a loud crash made them spin around. A startled rat scurried away after knocking over a mangled ceiling light that had been balanced on top of a ruined piece of wall. The pair turned back seconds later, only to find that the figure had disappeared into the fog.

With trembling hands, the two frightened officers re-holstered their weapons; walking unsteadily backwards, as if afraid to be snuck up on, they made their way back to the entrance of the crime scene. Doyle mumbled quietly but loud enough for Timmins to hear, 'You know what, this is the last time we guard a goddamn crime scene.' Timmins nodded in agreement, unable to speak. As they broke out of view of the ruined room, the two men spontaneously sprinted all the way back to the main entrance.

THIRTY-FIVE

T he hour was late, and Eric and the blond mercenary sat side by side in a dimly lit room. The sparse furnishings were a mixture of modern and antique. They were seated facing a large, dark wood desk decorated with curious carvings on its panels. The chairs on which they sat had tall backs upholstered in thick, red velvet, and the ornately carved wood was gilded with gold leaf. The room itself was large but offered very little in the way of furnishings from what they could see, apart from the chairs underneath them and the desk the mercenary rested his elbows on. The only light illuminating the room was emitted from the monitor screen on top of the desk.

'So, gentlemen, what news?' The voice from the monitor was soft, with gravel notes that suggested a forty-a-day habit, beneath which chimed a note of authority. Eric was mesmerised by the swirling patterns that swept across the screen of the monitor. Each time the voice spoke, the smoke-like images eddied according to the strength of each beat of the voice's words.

'The one called Steel is no more, sir.' Eric held himself ramrod straight as he spoke. Something about this whole faceless charade made him uneasy, but on the other hand, the money was good. His words came out as a squeak, making the mercenary next to him squirm uneasily. 'The operation is safe, so we can proceed as planned,' Eric concluded, nudging the mercenary beside him to speak.

'Well, sir, everything is in place, and the police are still chasing their tails. And we have left them several tails to chase.' The blond man added, betraying a hint of a German accent. His tone was hard and confident.

There was a brief silence that made them both uneasy. Beads of sweat started to form on Eric's forehead, but he dared not move to wipe the running droplets away.

'And you know this how?' inquired the voice. As Eric listened, he could make out an accent, a mixture of English and American, though he couldn't quite put his finger on which was the most prevalent. Their boss was well-spoken and employed an inflection one might associate with an American who had spent a long time at Oxford or one of the other British blue brick universities.

'We know it from our source, sir.' The blond man replied, succinctly. The patterns on the screen resolved into soft waves as if the news had pleased whoever was on the other side of the feed.

'So, we still have someone on the inside of the department, this is good news,' the voice from the monitor said. 'And as for Mr Steel, how do we know he has joined his family?'

Eric looked at the other man, who shot him an exasperated look in return. It was Eric's turn to continue. 'We dropped a building onto him by setting off several hundred pounds of explosives inside it, sir. There was nothing left but ash.'

The blond man's skin crawled as he heard sickly laughter from the monitor. As he watched, the screen became a mass of violent nightmarish shapes that seemed to claw at the glass.

'Then let us proceed with the operation, gentlemen.'

And with that, the monitor went dark, and the room lights snapped on. The two men stood, still a bit shaken from the briefing, and faced each other.

'And now?' asked Eric.

'We do as The Man has instructed.'

Eric shrugged and smiled, the blond man shivering at the sight of his ghastly grin, as they parted ways.

The morning was grey and dull; each detective had been assigned a location to check out and a uniformed officer to assist them. Their task was simple: check out the sites at the addresses Jerry had given them. The captain disliked the fact that he didn't have the manpower to send detectives in pairs, but the department had been hit hard by cuts, and now the loss of Steel made things even harder. However, special units were on standby just in case they were needed. Brant certainly couldn't afford any more losses.

McCall had arrived at an old power station. The tall, derelict building was shadowed by its twin that stood around a car length's distance away. She parked and peered up at the two foreboding old constructions. Built in the early 1900s, they still held a presence of awe about them. The red brick showed signs of decades of wear and weather, and the structures' gloomy aspect gave her an uneasy feeling. She sat where she was for a moment and scanned the area, her grip tightening on the wheel, causing the leather to creak under the pressure. McCall leant forwards and assessed how to approach their task.

Officer Paris, a keen young recruit, sat beside her, in awe of the moment. He had heard stories of Sam McCall; her courage and tenacity were the politically correct parts of what was said about her. He had been unprepared for what a knockout she was to look at, or the enthusiasm that oozed from every pore.

'So, what's our first move, Detective?' Paris asked, a childish grin on his face.

She turned slowly and fixed him with a look which soon melted the grin. He swallowed hard and sat back in his seat.

'We check the perimeter,' she instructed him, grimly. 'When I'm happy it's safe, we move inside.'

She glanced at the poor little bugger, and began to regret her severity, but reasoned that this was not playtime, and if he was going to survive as a cop, he had to learn to keep his wits about him. He nodded solemnly, very much aware of the fate of Detective Steel, and understood that she would be doing all she could to prevent anything happening to him. He had never met Steel, but from what he had heard, the man was something of a legend, and everyone was shocked by his death.

Quietly, they climbed out of the car and moved towards the buildings. A breeze wafted down the street at their backs, almost as if they were being ushered towards the twin buildings. They took the one on the left first. A quick glance yielded nothing, so that developed into a thorough search. During her years of service, McCall had learnt that it paid to have thoroughness as her watchword.

It had taken them a good two hours to go methodically through every room, closet, and cubbyhole in the building on the left, but having established to their satisfaction that it was clear, they proceeded across the walkway to the one on the right. Both their weapons were drawn as they approached the entrance. The entrance mirrored that of the other building: large, metal doors that were sparsely covered with the last remnants of flaky, green paint.

They advanced cautiously and took position either side of the doors. Detective McCall stretched the muscles in her hands, compressed muscles that had held her weapon too tightly for too long, causing a clicking sound. Paris looked up at her, observing the concentration on her face, and felt safe under her command.

She looked over and smiled at him. 'You ready, Mister Paris?' she asked.

He raised his weapon, so it sat in his double-handed grip at head level, blew out a massive puff of air, then nodded.

The door creaked with age as she heaved it open, the screech echoing along the seemingly endless corridor. Stepping inside, they could make out the dark walkway bathed in large squares of light that beamed from the doorless rooms on either side of the hallway. They counted six rooms, each of which was no bigger than a small office but knew that all of them had to be checked.

Creeping forwards to the first two rooms, McCall and Paris stood to the side of the two entrances; they would take a room each and would follow this routine until they reached the door at the end of the long corridor. Establishing that the hallway was clear, they found themselves by a big, metal sliding door. McCall noted it was grey and rusty and looked heavy, and that it somehow did not match the rest of the building. Judging by Paris's expression, she could see that he was pumped up, full of adrenaline, which could lead him to react in one of a number of ways, depending on his personality. He could either be the bravest son-of-a-bitch on the planet, or he might freeze on the spot. She breathed a slight sigh. *Time to find out*, she thought to herself.

The younger officer grasped the door and waited for McCall's signal. Together they counted down from five. When they got to zero, he swung the door open, allowing her to roll in and aim for cover. No sooner was she in than the door slid shut and a loud 'clang' echoed behind her, indicating that locks had engaged, and she was locked in. Snapping her head around, she banged it on the crate behind her. Swearing under her breath, she checked her situation. Her hiding place was four huge moving crates piled up to form an upside down 'T' shape. She cursed herself for not keeping Paris closer, a regret that intensified as she heard screams from the other side of the door, dying away in the distance. Peeking over the barricade, she was met with the sight of around twenty men dressed in black tactical gear, training weapons on her position. Laser dots danced on the wood of the crates, just awaiting the word to lock on to her and bring her to a bloody end. 'Good morning, Detective,' called out a voice from the floor above.

The room was vast, with a walkway that ran around the upper floor, creating access to the upstairs offices.

This was obviously a huge storage area, into which could be packed hundreds of small items, or a smaller quantity of large ones. She caught a glimpse of the man who had been speaking, he had fair hair and spoke with a slight but unmistakable Central European accent. She scowled inwardly at the sight of him.

'Now, Detective,' he went on. 'Drop your weapon and come out if you please.'

There was silence for a few moments. 'I promise no harm will come to you if you surrender now,' he went on. 'You have my word.'

McCall felt as if she had no choice but to comply and hope that the cavalry would come racing to her aid in time. With that thought, she froze in place, and her heart sank, realising that her white knight in black armour could no longer come to rip her from the clutches of destruction, and a single tear trickled down her cheek.

She straightened up and held out her weapon, dangling it from her right index finger. Immediately, men rushed forwards and surrounded her, one of them snatching the pistol from its perch.

'Have you missed me?' She spoke ironically, which he seemed to like.

He strode up to her, keeping his face a polite distance from hers and smiled softly. 'Welcome,' he said, then suddenly swung about and stalked off as a trio of his associates seized her wrists, bound her hands and led her towards a wooden chair that had been placed in the middle of the dusty floor. She struggled and fought, flooring two of the men, causing the other to trip as they fell. Though her arms were restricted, her legs were free, so she raced for cover. She almost got there too, but not quite. McCall felt a sharp pain in the back of her left thigh, and as she crashed to ground, she saw a dart with multi-coloured strands sticking out of her upper leg.

'You bastard — you said, "no harm",' she grunted.

The blond man walked forwards and looked down at her, smiling patronisingly. 'What a silly girl,' he tutted, 'only if you behave yourself. I would have thought that was obvious.' He clicked his fingers at the chair and watched his men carry her back to it.

The mid-Manhattan library was bustling with crowds of people. Students rushed silently here and there in search of project information, others sat alone and read. A figure passed unnoticed, books and folders in hand it made its way to the archive vault, then sought out a dimly lit alcove housing a vacant computer. Sliding into the seat, the stranger began to type, feeding names into the database, seeking out any information on the orphanage where the murdered women had lived.

The computer monitor flashed up photographs and extracts from newspaper articles. There were stories of a mass rapist in the area, and a tragic tale of a mother forced to give up one of her twins after a house fire killed her husband, leaving her unable to cope with the quarrelsome pair on her own. The shadowy figure stood up and moved to the printer, which was busily spurting out page after page of information.

Having collected all the sheets, the individual moved back to the computer and discreetly closed the pc down. Melting back into the crowds outside the library, the figure vanished.

McCall forced her eyes open, but they felt heavy. She was disorientated and giddy from the poison that had infected her system after the dart had entered her leg. A splash of cold water abruptly brought her fully awake, gasping for air from the shock of the quick shower. She gazed around and identified the chair to which she was now tied as the same one she was being propelled towards as she losing consciousness. McCall narrowed her eyes to a squint before slowly widening them again, letting them adjust to the light and the effects of the drugs that were still affecting her. She looked around slowly, absorbing as much detail as possible. She established that she was secured in the middle of the large empty floor space, and that the only objects it appeared to contain were the chair she occupied and a desk, which had been placed neatly under the long walkway she had noticed earlier. Turning her gaze up, she saw that this structure wrapped right around the walls, terminating in a large area in which was set another door.

The blond man, who had been in charge of her capture, was seated casually on the desk. Realising that he had her attention, he filled a tall glass with water, which he carried towards her. He offered the glass to her lips, but she turned her head quickly. Stepping back slightly he smiled, ironically, saying: 'My dear detective, if we were going to kill you. I would not have bothered to tranquilize you, we would have simply shot you on sight.'

McCall saw his point and took a sip of the water. She glanced up to the balcony, where a procession of armed men had taken up position above her, then turned her gaze back to her blond captor.

'Welcome, Detective,' announced a strange voice. She tried to wriggle round to get a look at this new foe.

'What do you want with me?' she asked. 'I warn you, the cops outside will come in looking for me if I don't show up soon. They know I'm in here.' Her thoughts suddenly turned to Officer Paris, who had entered the building with her, ashamed that up until now she had forgotten about him. Sam fervently hoped the eager young officer was still alive, but she feared the worst.

'Really, my dear, I thought you were braver and more intelligent than that,' her captor tutted.

'Well, can't blame a girl for trying.' Her words brought a smile to the blond man's face.

'Firstly, nobody will be looking for you for some time,' continued the blond man. 'And secondly, we are very keen to find out what information the police have uncovered regarding our activities.' McCall was distracted from this speech by odd sounds that seemed to come from all directions as she struggled to locate the sound.

'Who are you?' she asked, as her head weaved from left to right to catch a glimpse of the other person.

'My name is of no importance. However, *what* I am is critical. You see, I'm a fixer; I fix things for people who require plans to be put into action. I arrange introductions, meetings, whether it be for business or death.' The blond man smiled and shook his head. 'Sometimes, it's both at the same time.' She heard footsteps from somewhere but, again, couldn't pinpoint them.

'We are all just parts in a grand machine, you understand, and you and I are cogs in the same wheel, so we come back to the question, what do the police know? If you help me, I promise I will kill you quickly. If you don't answer me, well, let's just say the boys haven't had a date for a while.'

McCall struggled with her bonds to no avail.

'My darling little detective just tell us what we want to

know and it will be all over, nice and easy. If you don't, it will be nasty and rough, but it will still all be over.'

She was afraid, knowing that whether she talked or not, either way, she was dead. This time there was no Steel to come bursting in to save her, she was alone. From the left corner of the room, she made out a shape coming towards her. Turning her head, McCall was faced with a tall, thin man, his clothes in tatters, his hair tousled and unkempt, as though he'd just woken up, possibly awakened by things living in it.

As he drew nearer, he took off his jacket and threw it to one side, then removed his ragged tie and shirt.

'We all have our parts to play, Detective.' He walked past her and disappeared into a room opposite.

She strained to catch sight of him, as his words echoed through the building:

'Even you, and of course, the late Detective Steel.'

Her head dropped at the mention of his name, as a flood of emotions swept through her: anger, hatred, sorrow, guilt. Then, from behind her, there came the tapping of patent leather shoes stepping across the dusty floor, and as she raised her head towards the sound, her mouth fell open. There before her stood Doctor Davidson.

'You?' she yelled. 'How the hell are you messed up in this?' Her fear was rapidly replaced by an overwhelming desire to break free and kick his ass. Steel had said all along that there was someone on the inside, but the doctor?

'Now, Detective, tell me what you know?' the doctor demanded again, and she had the chilling feeling that he wouldn't repeat it another time. As the tense atmosphere stretched on, a phone chimed loudly, and they both watched the blond man take the call. 'Yes, yes, I understand, yes, but…. what time?' He tapped the off button and put it into his jacket pocket, waving for the doctor to come over. He excused himself, politely, and stalked towards his waiting colleague.

The two men stood for a moment, discussing something in a whisper. From what she could gather, the discussion was heated, because their arms flew erratically in all directions. Eventually, they calmed down, and the blond man laid a hand on his companion's shoulder and waved for the other men to follow him.

'Eric, are you sure you don't want…?' The doctor raised a hand and flipped it in a *go on* motion, as he waited for the last of them to leave before returning to slowly circle the incapacitated McCall as the heavy door shut with a loud clang.

'What now, Davidson?' Anger had boiled up and made her oblivious to her fear, but in answer, he only smiled widely at her and, reaching into the vest pocket of his suit, he withdrew a pocket watch. As he flicked the antique open, it played a tinkling chime of music. He glanced at the time, nodded, and replaced the watch.

'As it happens, I have a very important meeting to attend,' said Davidson. 'So, if you will excuse me, I'll be off. But never fear, I'll be back to continue our little chat.' He was maddeningly polite and composed. 'Tell me what this is all about, Davidson!' she screamed at him as he turned to leave.

He stopped and turned to face her, his menacing grin sending a shiver down her sweat-soaked spine.

'You really don't know, do you?'

And in that moment, he knew everything was back on schedule. He crossed the floor towards her, slowly drawing a huge revolver, whose barrel was a good eight inches long, from its holster under his left arm. She gazed in horror at the massive polished steel pistol he now wielded.

'What? Couldn't you find anything bigger than that?' she asked, in a resolute attempt to mask her fear.

He raised the firearm so that it was level with her eyes, a glint of light reflected balefully down the spine of the barrel. She stared directly at him, as she watched him take aim at her head down the sights of the weapon. Why he needed to take aim from that short a distance, she had no idea. A malevolent smirk crept across his pale, sweat beaded face, while he performed a bizarre routine, twisting the barrel and changing stance as if he was trying to pose for the perfect picture. All of a sudden, the sadistic grin vanished as his hand dropped and the shining revolver came to rest alongside his leg. 'Bang,' he said. 'You know, my only real regret is that the dreaded Steel could not be here to watch me kill you.'

McCall was repelled by the genuine look of sadness on the face of the tall, thin man as he walked right up to her and knelt at her feet. She was choked by the potent waft of cologne, body odour and deodorant, making her nauseous.

'You must understand, Detective, for me it's not about the act of killing, it's all about how the deed is performed. Yes, sure, anybody can pick up a weapon and take a life, but in my hands, it's an art.'

She looked at him, slightly puzzled.

'With skill and finesse, the act of creating something wondrous is the reward.'

McCall saw a spark of passion in his eyes as he eulogised, as if he were a painter or sculptor creating a masterpiece, rather than a psychopathic butcher.

'That's all very pretty, Doc, but why don't you explain to me why you chose to kill those women?'

Her question seemed to amuse him. He unfolded his lanky frame from his position at her knee and stood upright with a grin on his face. 'You really don't understand anything, do you, Detective?' he said condescendingly, crossing his long arms in front of his body and shaking his head in disbelief. He strolled over to the desk and sat upon it, allowing his legs to dangle, swinging idly, like those of a child at ease. 'You thought we were on to you?' she guessed. 'You thought when we arrived there would be more of us?' She had questions, too many questions.

'The only one who came close to figuring everything out

was Steel!' he chuckled. 'But he couldn't say anything because he didn't know who to trust, even you, who delighted him so much. Yes, poor old Steel, I will miss him.' He affected a false look of sadness that made her truly furious. McCall fought and struggled with the ropes binding her, prompting him to get to his feet and raise his weapon once more. 'Oh, my dear detective, you really do want me to kill you right now, don't you?'

She glared at him with a burning desire to see his head separated from his shoulders. With a deep breath, she forced herself to stop struggling and compose herself; then she smiled coyly and looked up at him.

'So, Doc, since you're going to kill me anyway, why not just tell me what this is all about?'

He smiled arrogantly back and shook his pale head, then he raised his arm and targeted McCall down the sights of the gun again.

'My dear, this is not some film where the villain clarifies the plot, makes a full confession and is then foiled by the dashing hero just in the nick of time. No, I'm afraid you need to figure this one out for yourself. Especially as the dashing hero is already dead.' He glanced up into the air as if considering for a moment, then just as quickly his gaze and his weapon returned to McCall once again. 'Well, with whatever time you have left anyway.' He smiled odiously and drew closer, his movements slow and deliberate, almost as if he was dancing towards her.

'No? No ideas? Nothing?' His voice was filled with disappointment. 'Well, tell you what, let's see if Detective Steel had any more luck shall we?'

Her face was filled with confusion until a familiar voice floated from the shadows.

'Sam, are you OK?' She nodded.

'Of course, she is. She's waiting for you to ride to the rescue, you fool.' The tall man sounded almost insulted by the very question. 'Anyway, Mister Steel, satisfy us with your theory, if you please.'

As he pulled back the hammer McCall saw the gun's chamber revolve, lining up one of the huge rounds along its polished barrel. The welcome voice echoed around the large room. McCall tried to detect its source, but the acoustics made it difficult - that and trying to follow events with a colossal pistol pointing directly at her head.

'Well, to start with, you are not Doctor Davidson, as much as I would have liked that to be the case, but no.' The voice had all the attributes to be that of John Steel.

McCall could do nothing but stare up at the tall man incredulously; he shrugged and smiled in an almost apologetic manner.

'Actually, your companion's name isn't Eric either,' Steel continued, remaining shrouded in the shadows.

'Go on.' The tall man, no longer smiling, still held his gun at Mc- Call's head, poised to end her life at a single wrong word or movement from the darkness.

'You see, Sam,' Steel recited, 'long ago, let's say about thirty years, shall we?'

The nameless man gave a half shrug to acknowledge the assumption.

'There were two brothers, twins to be exact,' Steel went on. 'Anyway, these boys grew up in wealthy surroundings, without a care in the world.'

McCall could hear the voice move around them, as if Steel was somehow circling them.

'Yet, as the children grew up, the mother started to notice certain differences in her boys. Even though they were identical in appearance they were very different in personality. One was as good as gold, the other mischievous and mean. Years passed and life continued to treat them well until one day, when the boys were around seven or eight, there was a terrible accident and part of the family home burnt down.'

McCall noticed the tall man's grip tighten on the pistol's handle. 'Everyone called it an accident, but the mother knew that little Steven had somehow caused the fire that killed her husband. Of course, she couldn't prove anything, but she knew - she knew -who was responsible. So, she sent Steven to an orphanage, where he would be safely looked after, allowing her to attend to her good son without fear.'

McCall regarded the man before her with apprehension. In turn, he could see her evaluating Steel's words.

'Go on, Mr. Steel, I'm all ears.' The tall man spoke as if he was almost amused.

'Life was tough for a rich kid at the orphanage, right from the start. The boy was bullied and beaten by the other kids at first. But there were three girls, who could have been sisters, they looked so alike, who took pity on the boy and cared for him, and how he learned to love those girls. But life remained hard, harder than any boy should have to endure, although over time the other kids came to accept him and he was received as a member of the large, happy family. However, because of his past, the nuns made sure he was not available to be put up for adoption, so that no other family would suffer. As for his twin brother, he had an excellent education and lavish lifestyle, he was doted on and groomed for greatness.'

McCall's face registered her comprehension and she almost felt pity for the man who stood before her, but for one thing that still puzzled her.

'If you loved those girls so much, why did you kill them?' she asked him. 'It doesn't make sense.'

The man they had called Dr Davidson never flinched, merely staring indifferently down the gun's barrel, cold and devoid of emotion. After everything Steel had explained, McCall felt as if things were finally making sense. If this man had been a troubled little boy and then subjected to such hardship, it was reasonable to suppose he'd evolved into some kind of sociopath, certainly. But to deliberately kill the only people who cared for him? That was something else altogether.

'Unfortunately, this story is even more messed up than you think,' Steel went on. 'At first, I considered the brilliance of the murders: no clues left behind, nothing to link the women socially, only their past history, yes, brilliant. But then I began thinking that something didn't sit right.'

These words were followed only by silence, compelling Steven Brooks, aka Dr Davidson, to look warily up and around, his weapon following his gaze.

He hurried across to McCall and, as he stood behind her, he pressed the cold steel against her temple.

'No more games, Steel,' he yelled, nervously.

McCall could almost feel the fear pulsing through the man behind her, and she wondered what it was about Steel that frightened him so much.

'Come on, Mr Steel, you haven't finished. You come out now, or I paint this room with the inside of her head.'

Then from a corner of one of the empty lower rooms something fell. McCall flinched in shock as the huge handgun fired in the direction of the noise, her ears ringing from the loud explosion. From a different corner came another clatter, like a bottle rolling on the ground. He fired again.

'What's wrong, Mr Steel?' called Brooks. 'Are you afraid to face me?' He was yelling upwards, hoping the acoustics would travel. As he placed the gun's barrel against McCall's ear, she felt the metal's heat against her skin, 'Enough of these games, Steel. If you will not come out willingly, I know how to bring you out.'

A clatter to his left drew his attention but he did not fire in the direction of the noise, he merely gave an evil grin and eased back the pistol's hammer.

'Last chance!' he yelled at the disused room. 'Look at this face. You like this face, don't you? Now imagine this face splashed all over the room.' There was no response. McCall's eyes widened as she felt the minute alteration of pressure against her head as the trigger was being pulled. The maniac laughed as he stared intently ahead. The hammer fell.

Sam McCall could never figure out why she had shut her eyes as she felt the sudden pressure being released as the hammer fell. It was as though not seeing the events would protect her in some way. Those brief milliseconds seemed to stretch into hours, during which so much passed through her mind.

She opened one eye and looked up to find the confused killer still checking around the room while also peering in mystification at his gun.

He had been keenly anticipating the spectacle of a fountain of blood and brain, splashing vibrant colour across the dusty floor. But instead of the loud crack of a gunshot and the sweet, metallic scent of blood, grey matter and gunpowder, he was rewarded only with a disappointing, dull crunch like the sound of a twig snapping underfoot. He glared down at his weapon in consternation to find a pencil jammed between the hammer and the breech. He was equally astonished to find Steel standing just behind him, smiling.

'Hi.' Steel said, before smashing his fist into Brooks' face. The man stumbled backwards but, before he could recover, Steel had sidekicked his left knee, bringing the man to the ground. Brooks raised the gun, only to be met by a kick to the hand, which sent the weapon skidding across the floor, still with the pencil jamming the firing mechanism.

With Brooks on his knees, Steel trained a .45 automatic on the man while, with his left hand, he cut McCall free, using a field knife. She got to her feet unsteadily, rubbing the marks the bonds had made.

'What kept you?' she said, trying to sound annoyed with him. 'Well, you know I like to make an entrance, plus the deli had a special deal on.'

She felt like punching his head.

'So, Mr. Steel, what happens now?' said Brooks from the floor. 'You know that when you tell that touching story they will put me into an asylum, and I will never even get to court. Who knows? I may even be out in five years with good behaviour.' The man grinned, watching McCall's face as she did the calculation.

'He is right, you know,' she admitted, panicked by the very thought of this madman ever being on the streets again.

'Fine, we could just kill him and say it was the blond guy. Less paperwork,' Steel said coldly as he raised his weapon.

Brooks' face dropped as he saw the massive automatic swing upwards towards his head. After studying Steel's life, he knew what the man was capable of and that was what frightened him; in many ways, Steel was more of a monster than he was. McCall shoved the weapon out of the way and gave him a scornful look, only to have him smile at her.

'There is one little problem with the story, though,' Steel said, as he pushed Brooks down into the chair and handcuffed him to it. McCall peered at Steel curiously.

'What's the problem?' McCall and Brooks asked, simultaneously. 'It was this asshole that had the good home. It was Davidson who got sent to the orphanage.'

Brooks smiled complacently. 'Shame you can't prove that, Detective,' he replied with a smirk. 'As far as everyone knows, it was I who suffered the tragic childhood.'

McCall looked confused. 'I just don't get it. All we have to do is get the doc to tell his side.' She trailed off as she noticed the look on both of their faces.

'The doc is next?' she asked. Steel nodded. 'But what if…?'

Steel raised a hand. 'I have left word for him to be kept safe.' She blew a sigh of relief, then she looked from one to the other and asked. 'So why kill the women?'

'Well, you know the first victim was a lawyer working on a big case?'

McCall nodded.

'That wasn't just any big case, that was my big case. It concerned arms smuggling, and if she were to disappear before she was able to make her argument to the partners. it could get swept under the carpet. But an assassination would set all sorts of alarm bells ringing. It had to look like an accident, or more imaginatively, the work of a serial killer, so naturally when Brooks learnt of the other women and his brother's connection, the pieces began to fit. I mean, what better way to hide a hit on an individual than make it part of a multiple homicide. If things went wrong, his brother would be investigated, as the women and he all went to the same orphanage. Also, he could 'become' his brother at the precinct to spy on what progress we were making. Brilliant, really.' McCall wandered over and leaned back against the desk, her head still buzzing from the mass of information. 'So why cut up the women?' Steel smiled and walked around the back of Brooks to ensure he didn't have any lock picks or tricks hidden away.

'The thing about most professional killers is, they enjoy what they do. That's bad enough, but when they are sociopathic that really tips the balance.'

McCall had to confess that this was the strangest case, and probably the deadliest one, she had encountered.

Somewhere outside, sirens could be heard wailing, heralding the arrival of the cavalry. Steel smiled tenderly at McCall, taking in her expression of relief. They could track the unit's progress drawing closer by the welcoming cries of 'Clear. Room Clear.' Suddenly the sliding door flew open and the team, in their distinctive urban camouflage uniforms, burst in, weapons held high at their shoulders.

As the captain hustled into the dimly lit room with the rest of his team in close pursuit, they were met by McCall and Steel, waiting by the entrance. Faces full of confusion glared at Steel, as though a ghost was standing before them.

'McCall, are you OK?' Brant asked, quickly scanning the room. She nodded and smiled gratefully.

'I'm fine. Shaken, not stirred.' She grinned.

'Detective Steel, where the hell have you been?' roared the captain, winking playfully at McCall. She raised her eyebrows and followed Steel as they led Brant towards a figure across the room, hunched defiantly in a chair. Doctor Davidson entered reticently, taking in the scene around him and then, as he made his way towards Steel, he froze, along with everyone else, as their gaze fell on a familiar face. The captain's jaw dropped open as his eyes flicked between the doctor at his shoulder and the man in the chair.

'Steel? McCall? What the hell is this?' Davidson's index finger pointed firmly at Brooks. As the astounded team members regarded the two men, the supposedly strange behaviour of the doctor started to make some sort of sense; shaking their heads dumbfoundedly, they dispersed throughout the building to try to glean any clues as to the identity of the gang who had abducted McCall.

With two officers assigned to watch Brooks, Steel chaperoned McCall to the waiting paramedics outside, where she was made to sit on a gurney while a softly spoken young man wrapped a blanket around her shoulders and proceeded to tend to her injuries. McCall stared up at Steel and smiled. Her eyes were red from the ordeal but seemed to glint with joy, in spite of it all.

'Are you OK?' he asked.

She shook her head in disbelief at the question, and said 'No,' but kept smiling.

'What's the matter? Is it something I said?' He seemed confused, but then that's what Steel liked about her: he never got her. She was the mystery he would someday try to solve, but not just yet.

'Never mind, Steel,' she replied, giggling to herself, thinking about the dream she had the night before.

Steel left her having her abrasions dressed and made his way back to ensure that Brooks was smoothly transferred when the transport arrived. He was about to enter the room, when he nearly bumped into the two guards coming from inside.

'Hey, why are you guys leaving? You haven't been replaced yet?' he demanded.

The officers seemed confused. 'Yes, sir, we have. Two plain-clothed detectives said they were here to pick the prisoner up and they also suggested the doctor travel with them as a precaution.'

Steel raced into the empty room then turned accusingly to the men. 'When did they leave?'

The older officer thought for a moment. 'A couple of minutes ago,' he said, apologetically as it dawned on him what had happened.

Steel sprinted out of the building to try and catch any vehicle that was leaving the site but was only greeted by a confused-looking Captain Brant.

'What's up?' The captain looked calm, but his serenity would be short-lived.

'Oh, your guards just handed the prisoner and the doc over to a pair of "detectives".'

Brant exploded with rage, heading for the door to read the riot act, until Steel stopped him.

'What's done is done, Captain, you can kill them later. First we've got to get those guys back.'

They walked silently, side by side, in the direction of the line of vehicles at the perimeter of the scene, Brant taking the time to pull himself together, though he made a mental note to put the men on traffic duty for the next twenty years.

Tooms strode up, while Tony was still keeping an eye on McCall. 'Steel, man, we thought you were toast!' his friendly handshake subsided as Tooms noticed the mood. 'Hey, what's up?'

The captain seemed unable to reply.

'Nothing major, our prisoner and the doc have just been abducted from under our noses,' Steel told him. Now Tooms understood the sombre atmosphere.

'So, we find them and bring them back,' Tooms suggested. Steel and the captain turned and glared at him.

'You don't get it,' Steel explained, flatly. 'Firstly, these men are identical twins, together, not helpful when one of them has made a dammed good job of impersonating the other.' Steel slumped down next to McCall and contemplated the group in front of him. 'Secondly, the killer will probably try to get his brother committed instead of himself if he can. That's my guess, anyway.'

Steel knew they would be long gone by now and chasing them would be futile, especially given they had no idea which direction they'd taken.

'I'll notify public transport and get his picture out just in case they skip town,' said the captain. 'Plus, I'll send word to the border control.'

It was something, but Steel just shook his head and scowled at the floor.

'What?' asked Brant, before Tony headed back to the station to put out an APB.

'I don't think he will leave,' Steel looked up at the captain. 'If anything, he will try and take over his brother's life as a cover.'

'But?' asked McCall, knowing all too well what the look on his face meant.

'We messed up. I still think he will go ahead and commit him, even take over his brother's life, but he won't do it in this city.'

Tony nodded and shot off, knowing how urgent it was to put both the doctor and his brother's names down as fugitives.

There was a buzz on Steel's phone. He reached into his short, biker-style jacket, and peered down at the display.

'Oh, that's not good,' he said, slipping it back into his pocket.

'What's wrong? Bad news?' McCall felt like making a joke, but it didn't seem to be the time.

Steel stood up and straightened his clothing. 'The big case that our first victim was working on, you know, the arms trafficking case, well, the reason she was working late was to put her case together to show it to the board. Apparently, it was huge and could hurt a lot of people– important people.'

'Sounds like a motive to me.' The captain popped a mint into his mouth, as realisation dawned over McCall's face.

'An arms deal?' she demanded. The detectives exchanged puzzled glances at her outburst.

'What now?' asked Tooms. He'd had a long week, and this case was the most confusing one he had ever worked. It was an experience he hoped never to repeat in the future.

'Brooks kept asking me how much the cops knew, and when he could see the answer was zilch, he told the blond mercenary from the bridge that they were good to go.' Sam McCall explained, her face brightening as the case, at last, was becoming clearer.

Tony's mind was swiftly processing the fresh data. 'But that doesn't give us any idea where they will be now.' He was a good cop, but he needed information, something to work with. Now the missing pieces of the puzzle were falling into place, he was happy.

'One of the addresses for the drop-offs was near where my dad was killed, did anyone check it?' McCall said. The captain looked at the map. 'We had two officers take that, but we haven't heard anything back from them yet. Do you think they might still be there?' he asked, unsure how McCall would handle seeing the place where her father had died.

'Yes. If not, they'll be somewhere nearby. At least it's a start.' The captain had to agree. Tony hurried around the corner, shoving his phone into his pocket.

'We are good to go on every route out of the city.' The captain nodded, issuing instructions. 'OK, you four, head up to that address, the teams will meet you there. You wait until they are ready, understood?' Brant didn't look directly at Steel, but he understood that last comment was intended for him, and he smiled inwardly.

'If it's OK, I have to stop off at home to get a couple of things first,' Steel said, as the four of them climbed into McCall's car.

'Where to?' McCall inquired, catching Steel's eye in the rear-view mirror.

'Head uptown; I have a place there.' Steel replied. She nodded and pressed her foot on the gas pedal. With a screech of tyres, they took off. Tooms didn't know what they were heading into, but he knew they need a little more firepower than the weapons they carried – they needed an army. Luckily, they had one, a private, one-man army. As he peered over his shoulder and noticed Steel nodding off in the back of McCall's car, his friend's words from days before drifted back to him:

'What I do know is, if you're in the shit, this is the dude to have at your back.'

Tooms felt warmed by the reassurance of that thought, but he knew tonight would get bloody.

THIRTY-SIX

As McCall steered through the wide, congested city streets, the head- lamps and streetlamps all seemed to blur into one, the sky above a strange mix of blue and purple watercolours. The sun was setting, but this evening was not blessed by its normal fiery display. McCall, however, was too preoccupied to notice the scenery, all her attention fixated on getting to that hotel and ending the crisis.

She glanced in the rear-view mirror and discovered that Steel, behind her, had fallen into a deep sleep. She smiled. Seeing Steel at peace like that made him seem just a little more normal. The man had been through so much lately, she was surprised that he could sleep so soundly.

Tooms, who was riding shotgun, peered into the backseat and saw that Steel had wedged himself into the corner while Tony was tapping at the screen on his phone. Tooms turned back to face the front and eased out his weapon. Sliding out the magazine, he pushed down on the top round to check the pressure of the spring inside, to be sure that there'd be no loading problems. Satisfied that his clip was full and working, he reinserted the magazine and returned the weapon to its holster under his arm. 'I radioed through,' Tooms told them.

'The doc is safe, they found a car on the freeway with him tied up in the trunk, but no sign of Brooks or the two goons.'

McCall was unsurprised by the news, though she wondered whether it was the doc they had rescued.

'Do we know what to expect when we get there?' asked Tony, who was now checking his own back-up weapon. The baby Glock was ready to go, and replacing it back into his leg holster, he felt a little reassured. She shook her head. 'No, not really, but I can guarantee one thing-' she paused.

Tooms turned slowly to look at her.

'—Somebody's day is going to get ruined.' And with that, she swerved around a slow-moving taxicab, put her foot on the gas and sped off with a purpose.

Steel screamed garbled noises that sounded like, 'Helen!' and 'NO!' then his eyes flew open. McCall pulled the car back under control, having been scared out of her wits by his yell.

'What the hell was that, Steel?' McCall barked.

'Sorry, bad dream,' Steel waved dismissively, making an effort to downplay it and soothe their nerves.

'Really, you think?' Tony was readjusting his seating position.

As Steel gazed out of the window, he felt a wave of clarity. He sensed that he was drawing closer to finishing the dream.

'Don't forget we have a stop to make before we meet the captain and the others,' Steel reminded McCall, leaning forwards.

'Yes, where are we going?' asked McCall, a little suspicious and a lot curious.

'A place I have,' he replied, vaguely. 'We need to pick up some stuff.' 'Oh yeah? You got a bat cave?' Tooms joked, but the smile faded when he saw the expression on Steel's face.

'Trust me, you will all thank me. Always assuming we live to tell the tale, that is.'

All three of them shot Steel a nervous look.

· · ·

The night air was warm, and menacing clouds covered the sky. In a multi-story parking complex men in dark uniforms hurried about, loading large, reinforced carrying boxes into several white vans. On the level above stood a tall man with blond slicked-back hair. He had overseen the labours of his men and now he just wanted to look down upon the city. Soon their business would be concluded and there was nothing to stand in their way. He had heard of the demise of Detective Steel and it saddened him slightly. Since the first time their paths had crossed, he had heard so many tales of the man's valour that he had assumed the status almost of a legend.

He wore a black suit, underneath which an elegant, high-necked collar fitted tightly around his throat. The outfit was similar to those the other men wore, but he'd had his designed to be more elegant. The breeze brushed his face, and he closed his eyes and breathed in the evening air. Life was good, he thought, opening his eyes just as, down below, a black Mercedes pulled into the parking lot.

Two men in long, stylish jackets could be glimpsed in the car as it drew up to the barrier. The window rolled down with a faint whining sound from its motors, and a gloved hand stretched out of the vehicle's window and flipped open a pass. The guard waved at his colleague to open the barrier and, as the large yellow-and-black metal gate was raised, the guard spoke into his radio. 'Sir, Mr Smith has just arrived.'

On the roof, the blond man smiled. 'Very good.'

The Mercedes travelled up the winding ramps, the driver dimming the headlights, until they reached the floor where the men were busy loading up the vans. The vehicle cruised to a stop alongside one of the armed guards, and the window lowered again.

'Where is he?' requested Mr Smith nervously. The guard pointed upwards, then continued with his patrol.

The black car reached the roof level and slid smoothly into a parking spot. Four men, including Smith, climbed out and walked in step towards the blond man. Smith noticed he hadn't even turned around, he just expected them to approach.

'Good evening, Mr Smith,' the blond man hailed his colleague. 'Good evening, Mr Jones,' the man from the car replied. He waved the others away. 'Your report, if you please.' The man they referred to as Smith stepped forward to stand beside the blond man, who was several inches smaller than the man he addressed as Jones. They stood shoulder to shoulder, contemplating the shimmering view before them.

'The cop is with Mr Williams, they're er... having a conversation.' Jones inclined his head with a smile. 'There will be no mistakes, Mr Smith.' His voice was stern and deep.

Smith nodded. 'Don't worry, Steel is dead, the other cop is... otherwise engaged, shall we say. I don't foresee any problems.' Smith was uneasy but didn't wish to show it.

'Then let us proceed.'

Jones turned to Smith and, solemnly placing his left hand onto Smith's right shoulder, gave a nod. Walking away, Smith took that as a sign for 'now'. With a screech of tyres, the convoy ventured through the maze of the garage until they reached the exit, then one by one, five cars and seven white vans journeyed out into the night.

McCall followed Steel's directions, which led them down back streets and darkened, empty blocks, until eventually they arrived at an old rundown building, with three roller door entrances set into the front wall.

'What is this place?' she asked, apprehensive at what they might find. Steel grinned mischievously and withdrew something from his jacket pocket. He held up what appeared to be a palm-sized remote-control device. Pointing it towards the building, he clicked a button and a small red LED light blinked three times, then with a loud metallic bang, the middle door started to roll up.

'Can you drive in, please?' His tone was assured and quietly amused, anticipating what he was about to reveal. The car rolled slowly forwards into the dark, where Steel got out and used the torch on his phone to light his way over to a small panel on the left-hand wall, which obviously operated as a control centre.

Inside the car the others glanced at each other, nervously. It was dark, apart from the blue glow from the vehicle's stereo system. Steel reached for a button that looked like a fire-alarm, lifted the fake cover and, holding the remote, pressed another switch. A hidden key extended out of the side of the small remote device. Inserting the key into the slot under the fire alarm, Steel turned to the others, nodded, then peered up. With a sharp turn of the key, the roller doors instantly descended. And the whole garage began to move downwards.

'Hey, where the hell are we going, man?' yelled Tooms in a sudden panic. 'Don't tell me you really *do* have a bat cave?'

McCall grinned sarcastically, but her mirth soon faded when she saw Steel's unnerving smirk. All the while, the elevator echoed with a clang of ancient gears.

The captain and the special weapons teams had arrived at the hotel. Black Humvees screeched into position, spitting out armed men in black tactical gear, who burst out and moved swiftly to the building, weapons held at the ready. The two teams divided: one would cover the back, the other would breach the front, but any action would have to be performed simultaneously. The captain peered down as the phone strapped to his belt buzzed, the screen displaying McCall's caller ID.

'McCall, where the hell are you people?' he demanded.

'We are all set up and ready to go!' Brant's voice was quiet but urgent.

'Hi, Captain we just had to grab a couple of things from Steel's place,' she replied. 'According to my satnav we are about fifteen minutes out from your location, sir, and we will be there as soon as we can.'

They terminated the conversation, as the team's commander indicated that they were ready for the signal from the teams. Captain Brant looked up at the old hotel, and tears suddenly pricked his eyes, his heart sinking as he realised where they were.

'Alpha in position,' the voice came over the speakers in the tactical truck. Inside the command vehicle, they were equipped to receive audio and video feed from all members of the team.

'Bravo in position,' the commander replied. 'Okay, we are good to go, on my mark… mark.' Each team used a large metal battering ram to demolish the two doors, then they moved quickly and loudly inside. Team Alpha stampeded straight upstairs while Bravo cleared the lower floors. 'Clear, clear,' both teams reported, certifying the building safe for the captain and the others to proceed to enter. Then an unwelcome message crackled over the comms: 'Sir, we have something on the second floor.' The captain froze in apprehension. 'In what room?' he asked, uneasily.

'Room 207,' came the reply.

The captain's eyes squeezed shut. *Not that room*, he thought. *Of all the rooms, not that one.*

A surge of panic swept through McCall and the others. Tooms leapt out of the car and was striding towards Steel to demand answers, when he stopped dead, his mouth falling open. The elevator settled with a gentle bump at the bottom of the shaft, opening up as lights began flickering on, starting at the entrance and illuminating in sequence to reveal a long, underground room.

'What in the name of everything that's holy..?' Tooms's voice trailed off and he simply stood and stared, as did the others. The basement was around twenty feet long and twelve wide, the walls were painted a glossy, sterile white and double-sided shelving ran down the centre. The place looked more like a grocery store than anything, but instead of tins of beans and corn, the shelving held weapons of every description. This was no hideout; this was an armoury. Each shelf held a different type of weapon, beside which a range of accessories were laid out, including scopes and suppressors. These were arranged so as to be accessible to the guns they were compatible with.

Tooms squealed like a child in a candy store as he slowly wandered around, then gave a low whistle as he caught a glimpse of the black Ford F-150 Atlas vehicle. 'Hey, Steel,' he called out. 'I thought this was just a concept vehicle?'

Steel just shrugged as he headed towards a metal locker, remarking: 'We can expect to be outnumbered but I don't believe in being outgunned.'

McCall stood, her mouth open, nodding her head in agreement. 'Steel, what the hell are you preparing for here, World War Three?'

Steel padded over to a locker from which he extracted four black canvas kitbags, taking one for himself and throwing the rest to the others.

'If you can carry one of these, you should take it,' he told them. 'What's in these bags might make the difference between us walking out or getting carried out.'

They all knew that the shit was going to hit the fan, and now they felt they had an edge.

'What's the plan?' asked Tony, shoving a pair of MP7 4.6mm machine pistols and a bundle of 5.56 mm assault rifles into his bag.

'We find them, and we bring them down, by any means necessary.' Steel exuded an air of calm as he spoke.

The others packed what they could and crammed several extras in the trunk of McCall's car. Steel hefted a long, heavy-looking canvas bag, which he carefully placed in the trunk of the Ford F150 Atlas along with his other equipment.

'What's in the bag, you planning on going fishing?' joked Tooms.

Steel smiled. 'No, but a spot of hunting may be in order.' And with that the trunk was slammed shut. They were ready.

McCall announced, 'I promised the captain we would be there as soon as we could, so may I suggest we skedaddle.'

Captain Brant trudged up the stairs. He felt as if events were unfolding in slow motion. He passed a group of team members in the corridor, and he seemed to see through them as if past and present were colliding. People's voices seemed muffled, as though they were speaking from a sealed container, then one voice became clearer, bringing him back to reality.

'Sir?' the voice said. 'Sir?'

Brant shook his head to clear it as a team member grabbed him. 'Are you okay, sir?' asked the man, clearly concerned.

'What?' muttered Brant. 'Yes, I'm okay, it's nothing.' Both the team leader and his officer eyed him, dubiously.

'Eight years ago, I watched my partner take a sniper's bullet in this room,' the captain explained.

'So, do you think I have a problem with this place? Damn right I do. Will it affect my judgment? No, it will not.'

His voice and stature shifted, becoming more assertive, more like his old self.

'So, what have we got?' he demanded, sliding his hands into his pockets.

'We found a note, sir, it's addressed to you.'

Brant frowned at the officer, then using a gloved hand, took the piece of paper. It simply read: *Captain Brant - sorry we missed you, hope to catch up with you next time.* The note was scrawled in red wax crayon, as if by a child. Brant handed the note to the officer, who immediately bagged it.

As Brant entered Room 207, a chill ran down his spine as if a ghost had passed straight through him. The place hadn't changed in all these years. Brant gazed around and sighed, then he distinctly felt a presence in the room. He closed his eyes, imagining the spectre of his old partner, then slowly turned, hoping, as he opened them, that he was wrong in guessing who the newcomer might be. He was not.

There, clutching the doorframe stood Detective Samantha McCall, looking pale and sickly. One of the team members rushed to her side, asking urgently,

'Are you okay, Detective?' The captain threw him a sorrowful look.

'Son, the man who died here was my partner, but he was also Detective McCall's father.' The team member uncomfortably studied his feet and tried to melt into the background.

'You okay, kid?' the captain asked, and she nodded, silently absorbing the atmosphere of the room. Steel and the others came up behind her. Sweeping his gaze around the scene, Steel understood immediately that McCall was suffering.

'God, this fucking place hasn't changed in eight years,' said the captain. 'I'm quite surprised the new tenant didn't spruce the place up.'

Steel looked up in bewilderment. 'What new tenant? This place has been empty for the last eight years.'

'Really?' The captain's words sounded hollow as Steel turned to face him.

'So who cleans the place? There's no dust, no cobwebs or roaches, nothing.'

There was a strained silence, in which Steel turned his attention to the window.

'So, this place looks exactly as it did eight years ago, yes?' Steel asked.

The captain nodded.

Steel's feeling of unease grew as he cautiously crossed to the window, then turned and faced the others. 'Sam was explaining you were looking for places where the packages were dropped off. If there was some sort of deal going down, this place is too cramped, and there are no escape routes.' Then he turned and pointed out of the window. 'But that place is perfect.'

Across the street stood a multi storey car park.

'But why preserve the room as it was?' Brant asked, puzzled.

'To mess with you,' Steel answered. 'Don't you see, this is what he does? He gets inside your head and plays with your mind.' The Englishman turned his focus back to the view from the window.

'That must have been where the shooter was who killed my dad?' McCall framed it as a question.

Captain Brant nodded. 'After the shooting, we did a canvass and found nothing.'

Steel squinted at the structure, realising that the closed walls of the car park gave it perfect cover. 'I don't know what, but my gut tells me something over there will dictate our next move.'

The SWAT commander corralled his teams and gave them new strike orders: if something was going down, his team had to be the first ones in.

'Tony, can you get the footage from those cameras? I want to know who came in and out,' requested McCall, peering up at the CCTV cameras covering the entrance to the lot.

'What are you thinking, McCall?' asked the captain.

'Well, we can get an idea of numbers and which direction they took if they left,' she reasoned.

Steel watched as Tony raced off down the street.

The teams had their orders and were ready to move in. But as far as John Steel was concerned, something did not sit right, and the captain could read the discomfort on his face.

'What's up, Steel? Man, you have that look, and I don't like that look.'

The SWAT commander was just preparing to give the order to go. 'Tell your teams to stand fast, something's not right about this,' Brant ordered.

The commander regarded him with a confused expression, complaining, 'Listen, if you have some information, we should know about it.'

'It's just that the bastard running this show is thorough and calculating,' Brant commented. 'He would anticipate we would come here, just like he knew we would be at the warehouse.'

The commander stood up from his chair.

'So, Mr Steel,' he snapped. 'What do you suggest we do, sit on our asses?'

Steel shook his head and considered the layout of the building. He faced the commander. 'We're going to need your drone again.'

The commander studied him for a moment. 'You think this place is rigged?'

Steel stiffened, as he drew himself more upright. 'Sir, I think this place is a loose end and this sick fuck doesn't do loose ends.'

The captain and McCall both nodded at the commander, who reflected for a moment, before turning to the man next to him at the desk. 'Get the copter ready and get me E.O.D, will you?' The young man gave the thumbs up and got onto it.

'Okay, people, what's your plan?'

THIRTY-SEVEN

I n a cargo dockyard stood a massive metal beast of a ship, its silhouette illuminated by the glow of the yellow security lights glinting from the black weathered hull. Down below at the dock, a convoy of vehicles rolled onto the concrete, as the seven vans and five cars raced to the rally point. The procession drew up, discharging a swarm of men who dismounted the vehicles and surrounded them. The sentries stiffly held their positions, watching the progress of a figure venturing down the gantries, while the lead car door swung open and Mr Jones stepped out, regarding the man who was approaching. He was shorter than Mr Jones but had broad shoulders and wore his long black hair tied back in a ponytail, a short beard disguising his massive lower jaw, while his eyes were so dark, they appeared almost black.

He advanced, and Jones moved forwards to meet him, the two men embracing like brothers. 'My friend, it has been too long,' the man with the ponytail remonstrated in a Middle Eastern accent.

'Mr Moses, I believe your absurd ponytail is getting even greasier,' said Jones.

Moses stepped back. 'Mr Jones, I do believe your unfortunate face is getting even uglier.'

The pair laughed and strolled along the dock a bit. 'We have the merchandise if you care to inspect it?' Jones gestured at a group of men, who swiftly started to unload the cargo.

'Has he sent word yet?' Mr Moses seemed uneasy discussing 'The Man'.

'No, we haven't heard anything for a while, so I presume it's business as usual.' Mr Moses was anxious to change the subject.

'So, I heard you had an interesting guest?'

Mr Jones smiled with pleasure, imagining what his employer might be doing to entertain himself with Sam McCall. 'Yes, her father was a nuisance and it seems to be a family trait, and on top of that, we had to deal with Steel as well. No matter, that business is resolved, it's just a pity I missed it.'

Moses whistled, impressed. 'How did you get Steel out of the way?' he demanded in astonishment.

Jones laughed. 'Mr Smith dropped a building on his head. Apparently, it made delicious viewing.' The two of them chuckled, realising that there was no longer anything to stand in their way.

Jones caught a glimpse of Mr Smith's approach, who waited at a respectful distance until the pair's conversation came to an end.

Mr Jones turned towards Smith, who made his way forwards and passed over his phone for Mr Jones to speak with the caller.

'You are sure of this?' Jones said, raising an eyebrow at Smith while he considered the information. With a soft grunt, he ended the call.

Jones tossed the phone back to Smith. 'Well, Mr Smith, it appears we will be having guests; they have found the garage so it's only a matter of time. Tell the men to prepare for intruders.'

Smith squared his shoulders and marched across to the men at the convoy.

'Problem, Mr Jones?' asked Moses.

Mr Jones just grinned and shook his head.

The bomb squad had made a search of the lower levels and, sure enough, they had found enough explosives to reduce the building to rubble.

'We were lucky, Captain,' the young sergeant explained. 'We found shaped charges in strategic places, controlled by a remote, so once activated, kaboom!' He used his hands to drive home the point.

Sergeant North thanked the bomb squad commander and gave Steel a gracious nod, which was reciprocated.

'The thing I don't get is,' McCall addressed Steel, 'how come we are always one step behind on this?' The captain fixed Steel with a penetrating glare, but Steel did not flinch.

McCall had noticed the exchange of expressions. 'What? What am I missing? What the hell are you not telling us, Steel?' She was angry. It was true enough that she was exhausted, and these past couple of weeks had been an ordeal. However, she had not had a building collapse on top of her as Steel had – the English detective still hadn't offered an explanation for his escape. She felt they all deserved an answer to her question.

'The reason Steel kept everything hushed up was because he thought someone in the department was, shall we say, less than trust-worthy.' Captain Brant admitted.

McCall shot Steel a furious glare. 'Oh, you don't trust me?' she spat. Steel didn't react for a moment, then replied,

'It's not you guys I don't trust.'

She bit back a retort, her eyes blazing with rage.

'Who then?'

'I don't know yet. Listen, I trust you guys: in fact, right now you're the only people in the world I do trust.' His words were evidently sincere.

Sam McCall knew little of his past, but she understood that something unimaginable must have taken place to give the man this kind of paranoia.

'Captain, we are ready to go up,' a man from the SWAT team announced, as he strode up to the group.

'Okay, let's get these bastards!' Brant's tone was harsh and filled with determination, as the band fastened on their body armour and prepared to go in. The captain remained at the operations van while he watched his people join their units, the plan being that each detective would accompany a team. The SWAT commander didn't like this idea, but he knew that every officer was more than capable of taking care of himself.

Four teams would advance into the building, taking and clearing a floor each.

'How are we looking, people?' asked the teams' commander. 'Alpha clear, Bravo clear, Charlie clear, Delta we may have something on the top floor, over.'

The captain and Sergeant North looked at one another apprehensively, as North commanded, 'Sit rep Delta'.

The speaker crackled for a moment before the report came through. 'We have a white van, no visible movement from within. Over.'

North deliberated for a moment. 'Okay, all teams converge on Delta's location, close the net from all sides. Out.'

He leant back in the chair, running his fingers through his hair in frustration. 'What now?' he groaned.

Brant peered at the head cam feed from Delta, and, sure enough, a light-coloured van was visible, the windshield facing the camera.

The Delta team members were crouched behind the curved wall of the rampart; a sniper had his weapon trained on the vehicle and the leader stood watch, while the others kept low and ready. Steel came jogging up the rampart towards the team, calling, 'Hi guys, car trouble?'

The leader threw Steel a *very funny* look, as Steel crept forwards and took out a strange set of binoculars. 'What you got, Steel?' asked the leader, quietly.

Steel sprinted back to the rampart. 'North, pull your teams back!

Right now!'

All the teams froze, taking cover as they waited. 'What's the matter now, Mr Steel?'

Steel's back slammed against the wall of the concrete as he slid down. 'Sergeant,' he began. 'How hard were the building explosives to find and remove?'

The E.O.D sergeant leant forwards and picked up the microphone. 'Well, quite difficult, we had to use—'

Steel butted in: '—Given what we know of these people's expertise, how difficult was it?'

There was a pause.

'Given that,' the sergeant replied, 'I would say relatively easy.'

North tapped on the desk with his pen. He knew that Steel was making sense but was reluctant to admit to it. 'All teams return and cover the exits, Steel come to me, if you please.'

All the teams confirmed the orders with a 'Roger that,' while Steel and the other detectives raced back to the command vehicle where the three chiefs were waiting.

'Okay, Steel, what have you come up with now?' The SWAT commander did not like Steel much, and made little effort to hide the fact. In McCall's judgement, he was engaged in a massive testosterone battle, only Steel was unaware of it, which in her view made it funnier. North was greener than green, regarding this operation like his personal toy train set, and Steel was not a welcome player. North could see that Steel had had some type of training but didn't know what.

Admittedly, the advice Steel had given in the past was spot on, but now he was making him look bad.

'The van,' Steel said intently.

'The van, yes, it's a van, in a car park, what about it?' North snapped. Steel was starting to lose patience with the sergeant; his ego was overriding his judgment, as far as Steel was concerned. 'Sergeant, everything for this guy is about tying up loose ends, so I strongly suspect something of significance has been left either in the van, as it was in the warehouse, or in the building itself. And hey, if a few cops get caught in the crossfire, so much the better. Look, these people, whoever they are, like to leave breadcrumbs for us to find, then lead us into a trap. Well, as I see it, this is an entire loaf.'

'Okay, what do you suggest?' North put on his sunglasses, in an effort to look superior.

'Send in the bot, get the drone to scan it with everything we've got.

My gut says something is wrong.'

North nodded, reluctantly. 'Fine, we'll try it your way.'

With a cloud of dust, the mini helicopter swooped off towards the car park building. The open walls allowed a perfect view for the cameras as it hovered past, making sweep after sweep. Using infrared, and X-ray, they scanned the van with everything.

'Okay, what we got, son?' asked North, coming up behind the technician who was flying the four-rotor beast.

'Problem, sir,' the pilot answered. 'First, we have this.' He pointed to a scan on the screen, which showed what appeared to be boxes underneath each wheel.

'What the hell is that?' asked McCall, peering closely at the picture on the monitor.

'They are anti-tank mines, TMA-2s.' Steel's voice was soft and full of alarm.

'So, no problem, we get EOD to blow it and we move on.' Tooms declared, getting tired of the games.

'Tell that to the guy in the back,' Steel said, pointing to another cam that displayed a human-shaped heat signature.

'Who is that in there, do you think?' McCall wondered, stepping back from the table.

Steel shrugged. 'I've no idea, but if these guys are clearing house it's someone who can talk, and probably has a lot to say.'

It seemed like forever since Tony had arrived at the precinct, having spent ages chatting up the cute woman at traffic. He had got the footage they needed and her phone number, so he was now a happy man. He stretched in his seat. After viewing hours of footage on the screen in front of him he thought he had to be close. He needed coffee, but, just as he was getting up, he caught a glimpse of the back end of a van leaving the complex. He cursed himself and rewound the disk. There, processing down the road was a convoy of cars and vans.

'Got ya,' he said, thinking out loud. Now that he knew he had to plot a route of where the vehicles might be heading, he could get himself a mug of coffee. As he turned, he jumped, startled to find himself face to face with the newly-minted Detective Jenny Thompson, standing close behind him.

'God, you scared me,' he said, laughing. She smiled and moved even closer.

'What you doing?' she asked, sounding intrigued, as she leant forwards to check the screen.

'We – that is, I – found the vehicles they used to transport the shipment from the garage.'

She turned her head slowly, her face just inches away from his. He closed his eyes, inhaling her perfume, all manner of exciting possibilities running through his head. He opened them and gazed directly into her freckled face, lost in the moment. The fresh prettiness of youth shone from her young face, her curves were slender, and her azure eyes were friendly and eager. He couldn't help wondering how the doctor had missed all that. A run of sleepless nights and all the extra work combined to lead him to imagine forgetting convention, grabbing her and making love on the spot, forget the coffee. Moreover, her expression told him that she wouldn't object, as she licked her lips provocatively. She wore a swipe of red lipstick that glistened as the lights from the monitor's screen flickered. He was feeling hot.

'Isn't it warm in here?' she murmured, smiling, popping open a couple of buttons on her blouse. His eyes felt drawn more deeply into hers, then something inside of him crashed him back to reality.

'Sorry, Jenny, I have work, and so do you.'

Her mood soured as she refastened her buttons.

'Sorry, Detective,' he tried to apologise. 'But we have to find where these trucks are going. Now is not the time, can we take a rain check till this is over?'

Steel had found himself a nice, comfortable car hood to lie upon as the bickering commenced about how to get the man out of the truck without blowing the rescuers to bits.

'Can't we just go up to it, open the door, he steps out? Simple,' asked McCall, recognising that wouldn't work, but wanting to understand why.

Tooms shook his head. 'We can't. The mines are probably set in place so any change in weight would trigger them. Why don't we just hook up the van to a tow-truck and drag it?'

Detective Steel smiled as he lay there with his arms crossed.

'No, we can't do that either, we don't know how secure the structure is,' grimaced North. 'We have to do something, we are losing time, people. We may have a clue or evidence in that vehicle, and we definitely have a living human being in there, so we need to get our butts in gear.'

The captain, too, was out of patience.

'We do like Tooms suggested,' Steel offered, good-humouredly. Tooms gave him the thumbs up for backing him. 'However, we use a helicopter not a tow-truck. We attach the van to cables, then float it out through the central opening.'

Everyone stared at him as though he was nuts.

'Really?' North had his arms crossed in defiant dismissal of the idea. 'And who will go and rig it up?'

'Well, I appear to be the only one dumb enough, so I guess that would be me.' Steel replied, drily.

This time, North smiled at the idea.

At the precinct, Tony had determined the destination of the convoy, which was identified as a cargo docks to the north. A few minutes of computer checks had revealed that the vehicles were rented to the captain of a container ship out of the free port of Gdansk, the *Eisen Wolff*. After getting in touch with the port authorities, he was waiting to discover the destination and place of origin.

Tony was pondering the manner in which Jenny Thompson had suddenly come on to him. He wasn't object-ing, it was only a few moments ago that he realised that the pretty, young redhead was even aware of his existence. He concluded that it might just be the effects of the stress of the situation. After all, he reminded himself, everyone had been working around the clock since this whole business started, and Jenny's new post as detective had brought her new responsibilities with which she was as yet unfamiliar. He smiled to himself, flattered at the notion she might be inter-ested in him. Suddenly the phone on his desk uttered its shrill ring, shocking him back to reality.

'Detective Marinelli.' He concentrated on the voice at the other end, scribbling down names and an address, then thanked the caller for the information and hung up. Jumping to his feet, he grabbed his coat.

'Hey, Jenny, I'm going back, can you stay here and man the phones, just in case something else comes up?' he called out to her.

She peered at him, puzzled, and said: 'Don't you want me to come with you?'

She seemed genuinely keen, but Tony knew deep down that such keenness was often quoted as part of a eulogy for someone lost in this kind of operation. 'No, we need someone to stay here. If we call for feet on the ground somewhere else, you'll need to contact one of the teams that are on standby and get them to where they're needed.'

She offered a disappointed fake smile and nodded, and Tony returned a regretful but genuine one. 'Till later then,' he added, but deep down he knew that what had just not-quite-happened might never happen again with her.

THIRTY-EIGHT

As they waited for the helicopter on the roof of a nearby high-rise, Captain Brant had a bad feeling. He knew that Steel could handle himself, he had read the man's service file and it scared the hell out of him, knowing what this man had been through and what he was capable of. However, the rest of the team was not so indestructible, and he had perceived that the crazy stunts Steel managed to pull off made them all a little more reckless.

He reached down and pulled out his vibrating phone. The screen displayed Tony's caller ID.

'What's up, Detective?' Brant's attention drifted upwards, caught by the flashing lights from the CH-47 Chinook.

'Captain,' came Tony's voice on the phone. 'We have a report that an unregistered convoy has arrived at a shipyard in Brooklyn, they are off-loading unidentified cargo into shipping containers. Are those the weapons?'

Steel noticed the expression on Brant's face and realised that something was wrong. 'What's the matter, Captain?' Steel asked as a crew of men were strapping him into the harness.

'We got a location for the convoy, they are off-loading cargo onto a ship at the Brooklyn shipyard,' Brant told him.

The SWAT commander smiled grimly. 'What are we waiting for?

Let's go.'

Brant and Steel stared at the commander, a little thrown by his sudden gung-ho attitude. 'Really, let's go!' he repeated.

Steel was still standing there, arms outstretched like some weird mannequin.

'Sergeant, aren't you forgetting something?' Brant asked the SWAT commander.

Steel interrupted, shaking his head. 'Look, he's right, you all go. All I need with me is EOD and CSU.' Brant slapped him on the shoulder. 'You really are a crazy son-of-a-bitch, you know that?'

Steel just nodded and got ready for his ride. 'Got me in one,' he replied.

'One question,' asked McCall. 'Where are they going to land?'

Detective Steel just laughed and ran over to a man kneeling in the middle of the roof.

The captain watched Steel run over to the winch cable and strap himself in, then with a pulsing *thwack* from the rotor blades the helicopter took off with Steel hanging underneath. Brant watched, with his heart in his mouth, as the craft neared the parking structure. The bad feeling he'd had was not bad enough, he thought to himself.

Steel spun in the air, watching the fleet of police vehicles leave, heading out to their next location. *Good*, he thought, at least they will all be safe from any blast we might create here. But then he considered the dockyard and the possibilities there.

He rotated to face the oncoming building, aware that he had more pressing things to worry about. The helicopter turned and was manoeuvred neatly towards the opening that ran from roof to ground level, around which the ramps wrapped, and Steel lowered himself through the aperture to the second floor where the van stood. As soon as his feet touched the ground, he unhitched himself and attached the hook onto the middle of a long lashing strap. He put down the rucksack and withdrew two large magnets, which he placed onto each the side of the van. With great care he then attached the lashing strap to them. When all was in place he knocked softly on the side of the van. 'Hi, we are going to get you out of here. Now listen carefully, you need to hold onto something if that's possible. You may feel a bit of a tug but don't worry about that, it will be fine.'

Steel looked up and pressed his palms together in a sign of prayer. 'Who are you?' yelled a voice from inside the van.

'Oh, no one special,' answered Steel. 'Just hold on. Okay?' And with that Steel ran like he had never run before.

'Echo One, this is Phoenix,' he yelled breathlessly into the radio mic, 'proceed in figures ten, over. Copy that.'

Steel realised that he had not really calculated how long it would take to sprint the distance from the second floor to the exit, but it was too late to worry about things like that now, so he raced like a scared jackrabbit and hoped for the best. He heard the noise of the chopper pull away but he still had some way to go, having only reached the first floor. There was nothing for it, so he headed for the nearest alcove he could see.

A massive explosion shook the building, concrete falling in slabs the size of sedans. As the pilots observed, the building crumbled from the centre, leaving a cloud of thick, grey mist. Below them hung the white van. They had made it, but they could detect no sign of Steel.

'Hello, Charlie One, this is Echo One, we have the package, over' crackled over the radio. The captain held his breath. 'Echo One, any sign of Phoenix, over?'

There was a moment of silence. 'Negative, we do not have eyes on Phoenix, sorry, over.'

McCall and the rest sat open-mouthed with desolation as

the captain concluded the conversation. 'Roger, deliver package to CSU and return home. Good job, boys. Out'

Brant put the handset back onto the dash. 'He will be okay, the son-of-a-bitch has more lives than a roomful of cats, he will be at the meeting place, you'll see.' Everyone recognised that he needed Steel to be there, to show that there was still hope for them to get out of this mess alive.

Around a mile from the port, the police convoy halted and made plans. Tony had joined up with the captain, having first obtained the plans of the ship and the ground plans for the shipyard.

Laying the designs for the vessel onto the hood of his car, Tony explained that Blackheart Industries from England currently owned the *Eisen Wolff*, and the captain was an Egyptian known as Moses.

Sergeant North scrutinised the map for a moment. 'Okay, here's the plan,' he said. 'Alpha will clear these buildings to the left here, and here, then move to this location.' He jabbed his finger on the ground plans, showing several large buildings with a view of the ship.

'Bravo, you will take the one on the right, clearing here and here, then stand fast here.' Sergeant North pointed out a small workshop to the rear of the ship. 'Charlie, once Alpha and Bravo have cleared these buildings you then become top cover for when Delta team goes aboard.' The team leaders nodded.

'Delta, you will move up as soon as they both reach this position.' North indicated the two entrances to the lower decks under the bridge house. 'Your objective, to secure the bridge.' Their team leader analysed the blueprints quickly and gave the thumbs up.

Since everyone knew what they had to do, all teams replied, 'Roger that.'

McCall glanced around. 'So, what do we do?'

North looked coldly at her. 'Stay here. You and your people aren't SWAT, so you keep out of the way.'

McCall was livid. Damn it, this was her case, and now she was being pushed out by a jumped-up squaddie. Captain Brant sensed her frustration but knew that North was right.

'Sorry, Sam, this is his ball game,' Brant muttered softly in her ear.

She felt the swell of the sergeant's ego as he caught the captain's words.

'What about Steel?' McCall asked.

North looked puzzled. 'What about him? We don't even know if he made it, but even if he is still in one piece, he isn't SWAT so he is out as well.'

McCall was consumed by the desire to punch the smile off his arrogant face.

'Now if you people don't mind, we have work to do.' North made a shooing gesture, as Brant turned to join them.

'Thank you, Captain,' North added, unable to suppress a grin. 'What are you thanking me for? Don't get ahead of yourself, North.

You wanted it; you got it. Thing is, if you fuck this up, it's all on you. We are only Homicide, remember, it's not our ballgame.'

So saying, Brant turned and left a stunned Sergeant North to watch his departure.

The SWAT teams had made it to the fence line, just beyond which lay their first objectives. Working on the assumption there would be a guard watching the main gates, their only option was to go through the fence. Alpha team sat ready, waiting for Bravo to give the thumbs up, and on the signal a member sprayed a circle on the fence using a can of dry ice. There was a hissing noise followed by a crunching, like the sound made by stepping on eggshells, as the solution ate through the metal. The spot in the fence was then easily kicked in, opening up a breach. As both teams crept towards their first targets, North monitored their progress with anticipation.

'Alpha Phase One complete, Bravo Phase One complete.' North gave a satisfied smiled and looked at his second-in-command. It was time to move. 'Let's go, Charlie.' He was unquestionably a brave man but was now oozing with over-confidence as he and his men sped towards the large building that overlooked the container ship.

On entering the building, North and his comrade found the stairwell to what they had designated as the operations room. Creeping in cautiously, the senior man looked around. All the power was off in the building, the only faint illumination provided by the silver moonlight. He pointed to a table near to the right-hand wall. The other man nodded and unloaded his backpack. As he laid out laptops and microphones, he began to set up the mini command centre. There was a flicker of light as the screens came online.

'We are go, sir,' the second-in-command said in a low voice.

North smiled, as he stared through his tactical binoculars. 'All teams sound off,' he ordered.

There was a crackle of static on the line, followed by: 'Alpha ready, Bravo ready, Charlie ready, Delta ready.'

North took a deep breath before giving the command. 'All teams go.'

As he watched, Alpha and Bravo teams took the ship from both ends and converged on to the bridge house, moving fast and professionally, until finally all three teams were at their target point.

'All teams breach when ready,' he ordered, and with that the teams disappeared from view.

A rasp of metal-against-metal echoed through the Operations Room, which North recognised as the top slide of a pistol being re- leased. He closed his eyes in anticipation of the inevitable shot. But instead of a bullet, pain, and death, he merely heard two loud thuds of bodies hitting the ground.

The two SWAT officers turned, warily, to be faced with the sight of two men in a heap on the ground, each with a knife buried in the back of his head. North glared at the empty doorway and screamed, 'Steel!'

McCall and the others were loitering restlessly by the cars, Tooms cleaning his pistol, while Sam McCall paced back and forth. Captain Brant looked up as she came up to him.

'Captain,' she began, 'couldn't we just…?'

He frowned at her. 'Just *what*, Detective? We are Homicide not Special Weapons. Besides, we don't have the firepower, we have just a couple of hand guns and whatever we have in the trunk.'

Tooms grinned slyly. 'He doesn't know?' His voice was full of glee, as the captain glared at them.

'I don't know what?' He followed McCall to her car's trunk with trepidation, and as she opened it, his eyes widened. 'Holy Mother of… You've got to be kidding me. I take it this was what you had to stop off for?'

In the car's trunk, their armoury lay before him. 'Okay,' he conceded. 'We've got the tools, but it's still SWAT's show. We must wait till North fucks it up.'

The captain put down the AR-14 rifle he had been examining to answer his phone. 'Brant,' he snapped, his mouth dry. He listened to a brief statement, then put the phone away.

'Detective, be careful what you wish for,' he remarked to McCall. She looked puzzled.

'That was Steel. The son-of-a-bitch made it out, and he needs us to go in.'

They leapt into their cars and made for the entrance.

. . .

High above the dockyard, a lone sniper perched in the *Eisen Wolff's* crow's nest, observing the entrance to the dock, ensuring that no unwanted guests could sneak in to back up the SWAT teams. For him the boredom had set in long ago, since all he had to do was look through his scope from time to time.

Then, from one of the buildings, a flash of light and movement caught his eye. Using his scope, he homed in to find a TV set had been left on, playing a porno film. He contemplated shooting it, just to prove he could, and then didn't. He pointlessly glanced around his crow's nest as if someone might be hiding there, watching him, then turned his attention back out of the window.

As he zoomed in to watch, he was startled to discover another sniper aiming his weapon straight at him. Before he could react, a .338 round had penetrated the glass of his scope.

Having observed the puff of red where the man's head used to be, Steel packed away the powerful MSR sniper rifle and moved off.

One down, lots more to go, he thought to himself.

Pulling up by the SWAT vehicles, McCall and the others slid out of the car and crept around to gather the weapons from the trunk. Slinging the canvas bags over their shoulders, they prepared themselves for what was ahead. The captain had ditched his Remington pump-action, and swapped it for an automatic shotgun, thinking to himself, *don't mind if I do*.

Finding the entrance that Alpha team had created, the group moved quickly from building to building. With Tooms in the lead, taking point position, he kept them to the shadows and as close to cover as he could, until they reached the building where the SWAT leader had set up. Alert and silent, they inched on up the stairwell, McCall noticing how everything appeared to loom larger as the light diminished. Beads of nervous sweat collected on her brow.

Tooms edged upwards checking the corners, and all his military training came flooding back to him.

'God, I miss this, bro.' he muttered to no one in particular.

Tony smiled, recognising that his friend and partner was in his element. Finally, they reached the top floor. Beyond the door ahead of them lay the corridor to the Operations Room. Tooms's heart was beating hard in his chest, and the rush of adrenaline was intoxicating. Easing the door open, he glimpsed flashes of brightness from the monitors lighting the hallway. Creeping forwards they reached the room. Tooms froze and raised his fist to signal stop, and everyone crouched down as he edged forwards. McCall saw him kneel before he stood up and waved them in. On the bare concrete. lay two men in black, knives embedded in the backs of both their heads.

'Is it them?' Brant asked, using his boot to roll one of the blood- soaked bodies over onto his back.

'Unfortunately, no. Looks like someone bagged the bad guys.'

Tony squinted outside, and whistled 'Yeah, I wonder who?' He pointed up to the corpse hanging out of the crow's nest.

'Ouch.' McCall said, and turned her gaze away from her scope and the headless man to concentrate on the main deck of the massive ship below them. 'I found Steel, he's on the main deck,' she declared excitedly, and re-slung the rifle. 'Okay, people, let's go and help the man. Tooms, you still happy taking point?'

The big man grinned and took off.

Deep in the belly of the ship, Alpha Team entered a massive, iron hold, the only light the glare from their weapon lamps.

'Oh my God,' gasped the team leader, held motionless as he realised, they had stumbled into a room full of missiles.

'All teams converge on my location; we have a problem.'

Bravo and Delta confirmed the request, arriving moments later. 'Jack, what the hell is going on here?' someone asked.

The team leader shook his head. 'I don't know, man, but what I do know is—' His speech was cut short as the door clanged shut. The three team leaders rushed forwards. '— What the hell, who the hell was on guard?'

Delta team leader peered down through the tiny glass panel set in the door. He could dimly discern a man lying unconscious as two men in black lifted him up and threw him into another room. The trapped team only hope was that the captain and his crew had defied North and made it down to the shipyard.

Brant and the others were currently poised behind a stack of crates, next to the gantry, two armed men standing between them and the hostages. McCall and Tooms moved forwards, their silenced Beretta ARX160 rifles raised, ready for contact.

'Police! Put down your weapons,' McCall shouted, while Tooms covered her. The two guards turned and hoisted their weapons, preparing to fire. There was a dull popping sound, as Tooms shot one and McCall the other, dropping the pair to the ground. Creeping over to the two bodies, McCall checked but found no pulses.

'Damn, girl,' remarked Tooms, 'You can shoot. Respect.'

'Hey you!'

The voice came from behind them. Two armed guards knelt ready, and McCall and Tooms realised, with dread, that the guards had a bead on both of them, so they put down their weapons and raised their hands. McCall heard no sound; she just saw each man lunge forwards as something ripped away their faces and their lifeless bodies fell into the water below. The two detectives exhaled the litre of air they had taken on board anticipating their execution.

Shakily snatching up their weapons, Tooms waved to the others, who followed them up the gantry to the main deck. There, the containers, stacked one upon another. provided good cover from the mass of mercenaries who were no doubt waiting for them.

Tooms once again took point and McCall followed, as the group moved tightly and stealthily. As Tooms darted across an exposed corner, a huge man grabbed him, raising his arm to plant a huge blade into his head. But instead came the sound of a dull thud and the man fell, blood oozing from the wound in the back of his head. The captain spun around as four mercenaries rushed towards them. Dropping to one knee he opened up with his shotgun, each of his targets spinning off their feet as hot metal pellets made contact, ripping through flesh and cloth.

The police unit moved as one through the maze of containers. Why McCall glanced up just at the moment she did, she would never know, but lifting her gaze, she saw three mercenaries perched on top of a container, weapons at the ready. With a burst of gunfire, she tore into them, spraying scarlet fountains into the night air, as the men's bodies went reeling over the other side. The others swung around, weapons trained on the targets, but it was too late. McCall grinned, remarking, 'Too slow, boys.'

Crouching behind a triple stack of metal containers, they spied their target. The entrance to the bridge and the lower decks was not far from their position. McCall's phone vibrated in her pocket. Sliding it out, the text on the screen simply read: *Found hostages, come to lower decks. Steel.*

McCall put the phone away, feeling puzzled. She looked up to find Tooms was wearing the same troubled expression.

'What's wrong with you two?' asked Brant.

Tooms looked around them. 'Why does Steel need our help?' he asked.

Tony seemed confused by the question, but the captain had a spark of realisation. 'He doesn't need our help,' Brant told them. 'Hell, the guy did this sort of thing for a living – ah.'

McCall and the others frowned at him in bewilderment. 'Did *what* for a living?' she asked.

Brant cursed and hastened to dismiss his gaffe. 'Ask me if we live, hell, we'll all ask him for the finer details if we get through this.'

This did nothing to reassure McCall and the others. 'Okay, my question is why does he want us down there?' she repeated.

Tooms was now feeling extremely uneasy.

'Well, my question is why you are getting texts from me when I didn't send any.'

They all looked around, stunned to discover Steel looming behind them, gripping the massive sniper rifle. 'Steel, what the hell is going on?' McCall demanded.

Steel stepped over to her. 'Hi, may I borrow your phone please?' She passed it to him with a puzzled look. 'They are tracking you through your phone. All of you get off this ship right now.'

Brant stood and faced Steel, asking gravely, 'Where is everybody?' Steel slipped McCall's phone into his pocket. 'The teams are downstairs, and the sergeant and his second are back at the van, so it's time for everyone to go, right now.' McCall shot him an angry look.

'Sorry, Sam, but no, you can't help, you'll slow me down.' Steel's words were cruel but accurate. He had to move quickly and someone alongside him would get in the way, she realised that. Steel swapped weapons with Tooms. 'Sure you can handle that?' he asked, grinning, as Tooms shot him a sarcastic look.

Reluctantly, they obeyed the Englishman and headed for the side. As they passed, Steel grabbed the captain's arm. 'Sir, this boat cannot leave these waters.' He shoved a manifest into the captain's hands, a list detailing an arsenal of weapons.

'This ship is heading for the Middle East,' Brant was so angry he was practically foaming at the mouth. 'So, was this whole thing was about delivering weapons to ISIS?'

'No,' replied Steel. 'It was all about money.'

Steel slunk down the metal stairs, the darkness suffused with a menacing glow from the dim, red lights. He had to find the teams and fast, but first, he had to even up the numbers. In the hull, he came across a compartment full of crates, and smiled at the irony of the situation. Creeping inside, he withdrew McCall's phone and hid it deep within the hold, before retreating to a spot in the shadows at the end of the corridor to wait.

He did not have to linger there long before several red beams of light cut through the dimness of the corridor. Steel counted twelve heavily-armed men, smiling as he watched them troop into the room one by one.

'Where are they?' one of them called.

A short man referred to an electronic tablet and watched the display bring up a map of the boat. With a tap on the screen, it zoomed in on the hold. 'They are in here,' he insisted. 'Or at least her phone is.'

'You dumbass,' yelled another man, stomping around the corner of the boxes, holding McCall's cell phone aloft. At that moment, the door slammed shut and they heard a creak of metal as the brace went on. The imprisoned men surged forwards, firing into the impenetrable door as they went, blind rage overcoming their ability to reason logically.

'Fucking great,' spat the man with the phone, hurling it into the corner, and hearing it disintegrate against the wall.

THIRTY-NINE

I nside the Operations Room, Brant and the others watched in desperation as the ship released a bellow of smoke in preparation to depart. Brant grabbed his phone, scowled at it for a brief moment and then shoved it back into his pocket.

'Find me a secure line,' he ordered.

Everyone searched for a landline phone that was still functioning and had not been ripped out.

'Will this do?' asked Sergeant North. They spun round to face him and his second-in-command. He was offering his phone in an out- stretched hand, looking guilty and ashamed.

Brant took the phone from him. 'This was nobody's fault but theirs, so let's have no guilt or recriminations, let's just get our people, and get these sons-of-bitches.'

The captain swiftly called the commissioner and appraised him of the situation, at the same time fulfilling his promise to Detective Steel, grimly explaining that it was vital to stop the ship by any means necessary. The group stared at Brant, fully understanding what that meant. 'He will get those men and himself off that ship before any action is taken,' Brant assured them. 'I know he will.'

They all nodded and perched restlessly on whatever seat

they could find. The situation was out of their hands now and there was not a damned thing they could do to help. They watched helplessly as the ship got underway. 'God speed, Steel,' the captain muttered under his breath.

Steel raced down corridor after corridor until he heard the sound of banging. At first, he thought he was close to the engine room but this wasn't a mechanical sound, this was a more disordered knocking. Drawing closer, he could hear the frantic yells of trapped men. Recognising it wasn't the room he had trapped the morons in earlier, he estimated it must be the captive SWAT teams. Steel wrenched open the door, causing the men to draw back, seeing only a silhouette, until one man flicked on his flashlight and shone it on Steel.

'Any one order room service?' Steel quipped.

The men rushed forwards to greet him. 'Daniels,' someone called urgently. 'They took him somewhere.'

Next to the hold was a broom closet with no handle. With a huge kick, the team leader of Alpha recovered his man, who was still unconscious.

'We have to go now,' Steel told them. He could feel the engines working harder, and Captain Brant being a man of his word, Steel knew that very soon all manner of hell would be raining down on this ship. Peering through his binoculars, Tooms spotted heads bobbing in the water. Adjusting the focus to zoom in, he identified them as belonging to the missing SWAT teams, struggling to tread water, weighed down in their tactical gear.

'Well I'll be damned, he got them off, the bastard did it,' Tooms declared.

Everyone cheered, before Brant turned to them imperatively. 'We've got to get them out of the water.'

Leaving their equipment, they raced down to the dock to assist the half-drowned men. Finding several small boats, they set off to rescue as many as they could, leaving McCall and Tony on the bank.

Steel was last to leave the cabin. He could see the city lights sparkling brightly ahead of him, and as he broke out of the doorway two powerful hands grabbed him and tossed him like a doll. Hitting the deck, he rolled and adopted a crouched, alert position. Towering above him, stood a large man with blond, greased-back hair.

'So, Mr Steel, it appears my men didn't kill you after all.'

Steel raised one eyebrow and tilted his head in a defiant gesture. 'No, it seems you're right, apparently I'm still alive.'

The two men sized one another up. 'You are full of surprises, Mr Steel,' began the blond man who answered to Jones, though his accent wasn't in the slightest bit Welsh. 'I must say, our employer finds you a most fascinating man. He would really like to offer you a job, if you're interested in making a little money.'

This was new information for Steel. It seemed that these were not just random mercenaries teaming up the one time for a quick buck, this was a coordinated organisation: the organisation his father died trying to root out. These were the people who had killed his family, all those years ago. He glared at his old enemy. Even with his eyes covered by the sunglasses, Mr Jones could sense the clear, cold hatred. 'That's a bit of a facer,' Steel replied, airily. 'What sort of figures are we talking about?'

'I daresay your specific skill set would be well rewarded. Would you really consider the offer, Mr Steel? As I say, you are always full of surprises'

'Oh, you'll never guess just how many surprises I've got lined up.' As he spoke, there was a rumble from down below. There followed a massive explosion that ripped a hole in the side of the ship. 'What?' said Jones in dismay. 'Have you been playing with explosives again, Jonny?'

The man who called himself Jones lunged for Steel, who

simply rolled out of the way. Another explosion rocked the ship, knocking both of them off their feet, but Jones was quick to recover, and he dived on top of Steel and smashed down with one punch to the face and then an uppercut to the stomach.

Detective Steel spat blood as the large man grabbed him by the collar and hauled him off the ground.

'Well, Mr Steel, let us see how un-killable you really are,' Jones snarled.

As he spoke, another explosion rocked the ship, once again knocking them both off balance. Steel head-butted his adversary and then, as Jones dropped, Steel brought his knee up to Jones's groin. The large man folded forwards in agony, only to be met by Steel's other knee to his jaw. Jones spat teeth and bloody saliva. Snatching a blade from behind his back, he swept forwards, slicing a nick into Steel's torso.

John Steel glanced down at the rip in his top and noted the faint line of red spreading across his muscular stomach.

'So, Mr Steel, to the test, which of us is really the better man?' Jones shouted. The Englishman regarded him in amazement: This guy was spoiling for a knife fight as the ship they were standing on was being ripped apart beneath them. The man was mad. Steel dashed for the gunwale, when a sudden instinct told him to drop down, just as a twelve-inch blade whizzed past his head.

'I knew you were a coward,' Jones said.

Steel stood up and faced the man. 'There is a difference between bravery and stupidity. At this moment, staying on board an exploding ship is in the realms of being friggin' nuts.'

Jones gave an evil grin. 'Don't you want to find out who is the better man?'

Steel shook his head. 'Not really. As far as I'm concerned, I know.' He moved towards the rail.

'Or to find out who killed your parents, your brother and sister?

You never did find that out, did you?'

Steel turned back slowly, his jaw clenched.

'Now we shall see.' Jones produced a boot knife. 'Come, your Lordship. Let's do battle.'

McCall, viewing through the binoculars, gaped at the two men exchanging blows. 'My God,' she called out. 'It's Steel, and some monster of a man. They're fighting.'

Tony stared at her, horrified, snatching the binoculars from her. 'Is he nuts? Don't he realise that ship's going to go blow up any minute?' Before them, the boats were quickly filling with members of the SWAT teams, while others clung to the sides.

Explosion after explosion shredded pieces off the ship, shards of metal sent hurtling into the harbour with each eruption, but the men on board battled on. Jones was surprised by the sheer power of the fury that drove this beast. Now he realised that what had left the mansion all those years ago was no longer a man. Jones recognised that, for the sake of the organisation, Steel had to be put down.

The two men faced each other. He had observed the scars covering Steel's body, but that was not fazing Jones. For the first time in his life, he felt fear. He now understood all the stories he had heard about the wrath of the man they called the Phoenix and properly grasped its significance.

'Come on, Steel,' he taunted. 'If you still have the strength.'

He gripped the knife tighter. After studying his strategy of attack, he knew Steel would rush in headlong, trying to dodge the knife and get in a couple of punches, but now he was ready for him. With keen anticipation, he watched Steel start his run up. Jones gripped the knife tightly and braced himself: this time he would leave the knife strike for last.

With a couple of feet between them, Steel hit the deck and slid, knocking Jones's feet from under him. As the blond man's back slammed against the floor, Steel rolled over and knelt on Jones's arms, delivering him six massive right hooks to the face. Blood flowed freely and the sound of crunching bone filled his ears.

Steel leapt up, panting for breath.

'Come on, you gutless wonder, come and get me if you're able. I'll make you bleed for my family, I'll make you bleed from everywhere.'

Then Steel was knocked backwards by a massive explosion. Once the smoke had cleared, he saw chunks of hot metal had pierced the deck, one of which had neatly decapitated his enemy. Steel smiled wryly at the irony of the man's own weapons being the cause of his death. Whirling away, he dived into the water, just as the ultimate, massively powerful explosion vaporised the ship.

A cheer went up from the dock. The remains of the ship turned turtle and began sinking fast: it was all over. McCall and her companions didn't cheer, they raced down towards the waterside, searching for Steel. McCall's heart pounded as she picked up speed, her arms pumping like some old locomotive, her eyes scanning the harbour, from the spot where he'd hit the water, to the shore.

A loud *crack* split the air, and she felt a blow to the head. At first, it did not register until she found herself falling down. The others hit the deck or dived for cover.

'Sam, are you okay?' hollered the captain, tears springing from his eyes. He kept his gaze fixed on her as she lay there motionless. Bits of ship were still being thrown back up from the stone of the harbourside.

A pair of burned and battered hands broke the surface of the water and seized the side of the harbour wall. Hauling himself out of the sea, Steel rolled onto his back and gasped for air. His head fell to one side, giving him an oblique view as the remains of the ship continued to erupt, reminding him of the Fourth of July celebrations.

He sat up and spotted a figure lying on the jetty. Staggering to his feet, he slowly moved towards it, his heart starting to pound frantically in his chest. As the woman on the jetty came into focus, memories of all the women he had ever loved merged together in his mind. Just a couple of feet away, his strength gave out and he dropped to his knees. Brant and the others lay prostrate and helpless, for fear of joining their fallen colleague. McCall was bait and Steel was the prize, and they couldn't do a damn thing to help either of them.

On hands and knees, the battle-scarred survivor crawled towards McCall's limp body, leaving a bloody trail on the ground.

The Englishman reached out to grasp her pale hand but the few feet between them seemed like a chasm. Tears cascaded down his face, stinging the wounds criss-crossing it, as he inched closer, his body numb, with memories of past conflicts flooding his mind. From here, he could smell the mix of sweet perfume and the metallic tang of fresh blood. Brant and the others gazed in trepidation as Steel tenderly slid his arms under her limp body and cradled it close, doing all he could to squeeze life back into her shattered form.

Steel kissed her forehead, and, rocking her back and forth he whispered softly in her ear. 'Helen. Helen, my darling. It's going to be okay, you will see.'

This was a broken man the police officers saw before them. Never could they have imagined that, after all this, he would crumble. Only the captain understood that he wasn't there with McCall. He was back in the attic of his ancestral home with his wife as she lay dying.

A scent wafted on the breeze, a scent of bad deodorant and body odour. And a laugh he had not heard for so long pierced his ears. Steel's head snapped up and, every sense alert, he heard the click of a revolver's hammer being drawn back. A blink of an eye was all it took. Brant and the others never even saw him toss the blade. But in that blink of an eye the large bald man was on the floor, clutching the gushing mess where his trigger finger used to be. The chromed weapon had tumbled from his grip. Steel didn't really know if something or someone had guided the knife or it had just been blind luck, but as an added bonus, the .50 calibre revolver spun towards the ground, firing as it landed, blowing off the man's left foot.

Steel staggered upright and stumbled towards the bleeding man. He was operating in a trance, unable to hear the others calling him. He reached down, grasped the man by the collar, and started to drag him towards a tool shed.

'Steel, what the hell are you doing?' yelled the captain. 'You're a cop, for God's sake!'

They watched him turn around, seeing him for the first time without his shades. Emerald green eyes stared back at them, soulless, remorseless, sending a chill down their spines.

The captain glimpsed something hit the ground at his feet and, in horror, recognised Steel's badge lying there.

'Not anymore,' he muttered.

They were rooted to the spot, unable to stop him, as he dragged the wailing man into the shed. The door shut with a loud bang, followed by a bone-chilling shriek.

As she lay in the hospital bed, listening to the sounds of people passing up and down the corridor, the squeak of safety shoes on non-slip floors, ringing phones answered by loud-voiced nurses, McCall felt safe but disappointed. All of her colleagues had been to visit and her room looked more like a flower store, while Get Well cards littered a small table by the door, a testimony to her colleagues' affection.

But there had been no sign of John Steel. Considering all the times he had appeared from the shadows, when they thought he couldn't possibly come back, why couldn't he turn up now? The one time she wanted him and he was nowhere to be found.

McCall turned her head as Tina knocked, holding a bowl of cherries and another card.

'Hi, honey, how you feelin?' the ME asked.

McCall struggled to sit up.

'Uh uh, you lay right where you are,' Tina told her, reading the pain in her friend's face. 'So, any word from *you know who?*'

Sam McCall shook her head, even though it hurt to do so.

'So, what's the last thing you remember?'

McCall closed her eyes for a moment.

'The captain told me he saw Steel dragging some guy into a shed. They say the guy killed Steel's family.'

Tina smiled. 'Well, he never really gave anything up. Now we know why.'

The pensive silence was broken by Tina's phone, vibrating in her bag. The screen displayed that she had a call from the precinct.

'Do you know what happened to Steel after that?' McCall asked.

Tina put the phone away. 'He threw the guy at the captain before he wandered off. Nobody gets why, hell if it had been me, I would have dismembered the bastard!'

They both laughed, a breeze blew the curtains and Tina crossed the room to close the window. 'You need anything, babe?'

McCall shook her head and smiled painfully. Tina kissed her on the forehead and left.

'I couldn't do it.'

The voice from the shadows at the other end of the room startled her.

'Steel?' she called out.

He stepped into the light and there he was, larger than life. Her expression ranged from pure joy to astonishment.

'What do you mean, you couldn't?'

He sat in the chair next to the bed. 'After years of searching for them, in the end I couldn't bring myself down to their level. You taught me that, Sam, thank you.'

She winced in pain as she tried to smile.

'Look on the bright side,' he said, encouragingly. 'Next time the guys are showing off their scars, you'll have a few of your own to boast of.' McCall tried not to laugh.

'What about you?' she asked.

He stood up. 'I've got some leave so I'm off back home. I have some loose ends to tie up.' McCall looked worried.

He hovered by the bed, staring into her sparkling blue eyes. She returned his gaze, wishing he would take off those damned glasses so she could look at him properly.

He bent over her and she could feel the warmth of his breath on her skin. Closing her eyes, she tilted her head forwards, her lips opened slightly to catch the kiss, but his mouth landed softly on her forehead. McCall's eyes opened, a solitary tear rolling down her cheek. Raising his hand to catch the tear she brushed her cheek against his hand. He smiled lopsidedly and straightened up.

Crossing to the window, he turned back to her. 'The ones we killed out there, they are just pawns, you know that. The chess masters have been chasing me for years.'

She managed to sit up. 'You don't have to run anymore,' she urged him.

'I was never running: just waiting. Now it's time to bring the fight to them.' He stepped forward and placed a white rose beside her on the pillow. Picking up the flower, she inhaled the perfume. A sudden waft of cold air made the curtains of the bed space opposite billow. She watched as he placed his right hand over his heart and took a small, dignified bow. As he did so, he moved back into the shadows. 'We will meet again,' he said. 'Promise.'

With a yelp of pain, she reached for the light switch, only to find the room empty. McCall grimaced as she forced herself up and shuffled to the window. Gazing out upon the night, the breeze was refreshing against her skin, and the moon was as full and bright as a winter's morning. Holding up the rose, she once more inhaled its sweet scent. He was gone for now, but she knew with absolute confidence that one day, he would be back.

In the darkness of his apartment, the priest observed as Steel packed a suitcase. Their mood was sombre.

'Where are you off to?' the clerical man's words rather disappointed Steel, he knew they would never discuss a mission in advance. Steel took a handful of black suits, still dangling on their hangers and care- fully placed them into the Samsonite case. 'I have to go to London to follow up a lead,' was all he would give him.

Gabriel stood up and walked towards the window. The orange glow of the city's lights was soothing, and he could see why Steel preferred to have the lights off.

'A lead? From whom?' he prodded. He saw Steel smile coldly and knew then he did not really want to know. Steel faced his friend.

'Santini. It's not a "he", it's a "they".' Gabriel nodded; it made sense that the organisation had a name.

'And what about your partner, did you tell her where you were going?' He glimpsed, in the reflection of the window, Steel pause while folding a shirt and nod slowly, a sorrowful look on his face.

'She will be fine, they all will.'

Gabriel turned and made his way towards his friend. 'And

you, John? Will you be okay?' The priest's voice was soft but held a stern tone. The other man looked up and smiled.

'You know me, I am always fine. Look, I am just going to find someone an old friend asked me to look for. There won't be any trouble. It's a simple quick there, quick back. No problem.'

Gabriel reached down and picked up the black-and-white photograph. The picture was of a woman in her late thirties with a cascade of shining hair. He turned it over to find the name *Tarrasa Benning* inscribed.

'Who is she?' Gabriel asked, putting the photograph back on the table. Steel picked up his glass of whisky and moved towards the dresser.

'I don't know who she is, but I know she has answers. And I have a lot of questions.'

He was holding his .45 automatic. Slipping out the magazine, he pulled back the long slide and checked that the chamber was empty. The light from the city cast a strange reflection on the weapon's grey steel, making it seem as though it was glowing hot.

The top slide had sideward angled recesses cut into it, revealing the polished barrel. Steel reinserted the magazine and tossed the weapon into a drawer. A shiver ran down the priest's back. He recognised that the soldier had returned.

Steel had stepped out from the shadows.

Dear reader,

We hope you enjoyed reading *Steel and Shadows*. Please take a moment to leave a review, even if it's a short one. Your opinion is important to us.

The story continues in *Hidden Steel*.
https://www.nextchapter.pub/books/hidden-steel

Discover more books by Stuart Field at https://www.nextchapter.pub/authors/stuart-field

Want to know when one of our books is free or discounted for Kindle?

Join the newsletter at http://eepurl.com/bqqB3H

Best regards,
Stuart Field and the Next Chapter Team

Steel And Shadows
ISBN: 978-4-82410-454-0

Published by
Next Chapter
1-60-20 Minami-Otsuka
170-0005 Toshima-Ku, Tokyo
+818035793528

7th September 2021

Lightning Source UK Ltd.
Milton Keynes UK
UKHW042315281022
411289UK00001B/35